"A timely story about the dangers of propaganda and the life-or-death fight for truth, *The Girls of the Glimmer Factory* exposes a little-known aspect of WWII that will enthrall readers. Coburn delivers a heartfelt story of courage where two women use their talents to take their destinies, and the lives of millions of innocents, into their own hands. Gripping!"

—Heather Webb, *USA Today* and international bestselling author of *Queens of London*

"A haunting page-turner of a story about friendship, bravery, and resistance, *The Girls of the Glimmer Factory* brilliantly illustrates the need to combat propaganda as it threatens to gloss over evils. Written in shimmering prose, this deeply researched, must-read historical novel is acutely relevant to our present day."

—Jennifer Rosner, author of *Once We Were Home* and *The Yellow Bird Sings*

"*The Girls of the Glimmer Factory,* set in Theresienstadt, the Nazis' supposedly 'model' ghetto, is a skillfully crafted, thought-provoking novel based on historical events. Coburn's multilayered characters demonstrate the full range of human contradictions—weakness versus strength, self-delusion versus self-sacrifice, cooperation with evil versus resistance to it—in a story that is powerful and sobering but also infused with hope."

—Marie Bostwick, *New York Times* bestselling author of *The Book Club for Troublesome Women*

"Powerful, brave, and an absolute must read! Coburn has penned a story that is compelling and immersive, informative and illustrative. *The Girls of the Glimmer Factory* opens a window into our history and humanity during one of the darkest chapters of the twentieth century, a time when evil and cruelty threatened, but failed to defeat, light, goodness, and the indomitable human spirit for sacrifice and love. Her research, while astounding, never overwhelms her narrative and gives her novel a firm footing that draws us close and invites us to never forget."

—Katherine Reay, bestselling author of *The London House* and *The Berlin Letters*

"*The Girls of the Glimmer Factory* is a powerful, gripping, captivating, page-turning novel about a little-known event in World War II. The Theresienstadt, a concentration camp, where thousands were murdered, was portrayed to the world as a work and art colony. Unfortunately, this propaganda proved to be effective, but Coburn superbly portrays the characters' struggles to keep their sanity and humanity while being forced to use their inborn talents to create art in the midst of the most horrific evil this world has ever known. As a Holocaust survivor, I feel that this book is a must read."
—Tova Friedman, author of *The Daughter of Auschwitz*

Cradles of the Reich

"*The Handmaid's Tale* meets WWII in *Cradles of the Reich*, which explores the little-known history of Hitler's Lebensborn program and its goal of mass-breeding racially fit babies for the master race. Three German women are destined to collide at a Bavarian breeding home: a blond beauty desperately concealing her unborn child's Jewish heritage, a Nazi official's fanatical young mistress, and a nurse determined to keep her head down in the home's increasingly sinister program of forced adoptions, queasy eugenics, and racial cleansing. Jennifer Coburn's debut historical novel is adept, unforgettable, and brilliantly unsettling!"
—Kate Quinn, *New York Times* bestselling author of *The Rose Code*

"I loved *Cradles of the Reich*, Jennifer Coburn's fascinating and incredibly well-researched look at this little-known Nazi breeding program and three women whose lives intersect there. Don't miss this wonderful historical fiction debut!"
—Martha Hall Kelly, *New York Times* bestselling author of *Lilac Girls*

Also by Jennifer Coburn

Cradles of the Reich
We'll Always Have Paris
Field of Schemes
Brownie Points
The Queen Gene
Tales from the Crib
Reinventing Mona
The Wife of Reilly

The
GIRLS
of the
GLIMMER
FACTORY

a novel

JENNIFER COBURN

sourcebooks
landmark

Published by Sourcebooks Landmark, an imprint of Sourcebooks
P.O. Box 4410, Naperville, Illinois 60567-4410
(630) 961-3900
sourcebooks.com

Cataloging-in-Publication Data is on file with the Library of Congress.

Printed and bound in the United States of America.
MA 10 9 8 7 6 5 4 3 2 1

For those who perished in the Shoah

This novel follows the *Chicago Manual of Style*, which capitalizes German nouns and italicizes foreign words. However, when the author uses German words and Czech words that are commonly used by English speakers, used frequently in the text, or found in the Merriam-Webster Dictionary, they are neither italicized nor capitalized unless they would be formatted as such in English.

A Note to Readers

Much of this novel takes place in the Theresienstadt ghetto, which the Nazis established for propaganda purposes. Opened in November 1941, the ghetto was set up in a former military fortress in the Czech village of Terezín, sixty kilometers north of Prague.

As they plotted their genocidal plan known as the Final Solution, SS operatives knew they would need a "model camp" where they could film documentaries and invite Red Cross inspectors. Two months before the Nazis codified the Final Solution, they began transporting Czech Jews to Theresienstadt, promising them it was a "paradise settlement" and "Hitler's gift to the Jews."

In reality, Theresienstadt was a ghetto where prisoners provided slave labor for the German war effort. They survived on starvation rations and lived in squalor. The ghetto also served as a way station to death camps in the east, primarily Auschwitz.

Despite these conditions, a vibrant cultural life emerged. This is a testament to the resilience of artists, musicians, and intellectuals imprisoned at Theresienstadt. They could not help but create, and audiences flocked to witness the thousands of shows, concerts, and lectures offered by world-renowned artists, performers, and academics. To many, embracing joy was an act of resistance. Since the Nazis needed to showcase talent in their propaganda campaigns, they permitted these activities.

In a time when anti-Semitism and Holocaust denial is rampant around the world, I want to be abundantly clear that Theresienstadt should never be regarded as *not that bad*. It was hell. Of the 155,000 prisoners who spent anywhere from a few days to several years at Theresienstadt, 88,000 were deported to death camps; 35,440 died of starvation and disease in the ghetto. The existence of beauty and art was a result of two things: the cynical needs of the Nazis and the sheer fortitude of the prisoners.

Prologue

Berlin
October 1944

F OUR FASHIONABLE YOUNG BRUNETTES HUDDLED AROUND A
table in an immaculate dormitory room playing bridge, chatting affably as a maid appeared with an enamel pot and refilled their coffee cups. The ladies' hair was neatly rolled, and the eldest of the group had tied a cloth into a flirty bow atop her head. Another twisted her pearl necklace as she contemplated her next move, then laid down a card. A new servant approached carrying a silver tray piled high with almond cookies, but the women declined with the lift of a palm or polite shake of the head. *No, no, I'm watching my figure*, their gestures said.

In another quarter of the Dresden Barracks at the Theresienstadt camp, a mother balanced a girl of about six or seven years old on her lap as the two shared a rocking chair and flipped through a storybook. The child smiled at the fairy tale as her mother's T-strap high heels tapped the floor planks. A record spun on the gramophone beside them.

A dozen men in yarmulkes gathered around a conference table, perusing papers in front of them, some squinting through their eyeglasses. At the head, a member of the Council of Jewish Elders lifted a finger. He paused to look at his dozen colleagues, then smiled broadly and moved his lips. Because this segment of the film was narrated, it was impossible to know what the old man said, but the others nodded in agreement, and one jotted notes with his fountain pen.

The film narrator's resonant voice told viewers, "While the Jews sit in the Theresienstadt settlement with coffee and cake, German soldiers bear all the burdens of a terrible war, want and deprivation, to defend the homeland."

—◇—

In a darkened screening room at the Ministry for Public Enlightenment and Propaganda, the steady hum and crackle of the film projector was interrupted by Reichsminister Joseph Goebbels clearing his throat. Yet he said nothing, his eyes focused ahead.

Sturmbannführer Hans Günther felt the muscles in his neck tighten as he willed himself not to turn to Goebbels to gauge his reaction to the footage. Discreet as the filmmaker might be, it would be impossible for Günther's move to go unnoticed, because he and the reichsminister were the only two people in the small theater. He had to muster faith that Goebbels would be impressed by the third attempt at making a documentary on the Theresienstadt camp in the Protectorate of Bohemia and Moravia. The failure of the first film two years earlier hadn't been Günther's fault. That had been shot by the prisoner Irena Dodalová, but it failed to present the settlement in the proper light. The blame for the second lay squarely at Günther's feet. Filmed in January, Günther's version caught nothing more than

Jews wandering about a bleak and icy town square. Günther had been promised performances of Verdi and Mozart at this privileged camp for artists, veterans, and the elderly, some great material for footage, but all these Jews seemed to care about was getting to the front of the soup line. The failed second attempt lasted less than one day, and Reichsminister Goebbels was losing patience with his subordinate.

The shoot in late summer for this third try had been different, though. Watching the screen, Günther hoped his efforts had paid off. His film crew had returned to a Theresienstadt that looked vibrant and lush after the ghetto had been "beautified" for an inspection by the International Committee of the Red Cross in June. In anticipation of the tour, the camp commandant, Karl Rahm, launched Operation Embellishment, in which he ordered residents to plaster crumbling foundations, build a music pavilion and playground, and paint facades. Rosebushes were planted beside freshly lacquered park benches and whimsically adorned signposts reading TO THE PARK and BATHS THIS WAY. Colorful flower boxes hung from every window of the tidy, *prominenten* homes. The old and sickly were hidden away and healthy prisoners placed in hospital beds. Fewer people all around as well, since seventy-five hundred people—nearly one-sixth of the population—had been deported to camps in the east so the ghetto wouldn't look as crowded when inspectors arrived. Günther was among the SS who joined the inspection and had to give Theresienstadt commandant Karl Rahm credit. The ghetto looked very *komfortabel*.

Emboldened by the successful Red Cross inspection in June, Günther decided to take another shot at a propaganda film about

Theresienstadt. This time, he would have two new assets: the upgraded setting and Jewish prisoner Kurt Gerron, the famous actor and director.

For the summer filming, Günther decided to play it safe and spotlight the same areas and scenes Commandant Rahm had selected for his earlier guided tour with the Red Cross, down to the staged soccer game, where a goal was scored just as inspectors arrived. It had been difficult to time that just so, but it was worth the effort. The Red Cross inspectors had been thrilled by the sight and sound of the cheering crowd, and Günther knew audiences would be too. His assistant suggested a few film scenes that hadn't been part of the Red Cross tour as well, and irritating as the girl had been, Günther had to admit her ideas were clever. The one where ten men prayed in the staged synagogue would be particularly appealing to audiences. *The Jews are living well. They play cards, enjoy sports, and are even allowed to perform their rituals.*

———◇———

The ninety-minute film came to an end. Günther folded his arms and leaned back to appear relaxed.

Goebbels rapped his knuckles on the wooden arm of his seat. "*Gut, gut.* You make Theresienstadt look like youth camp."

Günther gave a quiet, confident chuckle, as though he had been expecting the praise all along, though inside, he wept with relief. "A real family holiday at a KdF resort," he blustered. "The musical performances at Theresienstadt were particularly—"

Günther interrupted himself as Reichsminister Goebbels stood, placed his fedora on his head, and made his way toward the door, his left clubfoot dragging slightly. Nothing could deflate the filmmaker, though. His superior had approved. The hope was that this film would finally stop the global community from its increasingly pointed questions about death camps and gas chambers. Germany had to use its resources fortifying its military efforts, not appeasing the League of Nations, where they were discussing Germany's mistreatment of noncombatants. These countries could wag their fingers all they wanted, but the Fatherland could not afford the Americans sending even more soldiers. With the Allies making their way from the west and the Soviets closing in from the east, Germany was in a precarious position, though articulating this reality was an act of treason. In the privacy of his thoughts, Günther admitted to himself that if Germany should lose the war, his documentary film would help Nazi officers like himself claim they had no knowledge of harsh treatment of the Jews. *We thought all the camps were as lovely as our little Theresienstadt.*

And for now, as the war still raged throughout Europe, the film sent an unequivocal message to the world: Theresienstadt was a self-governed, free Jewish settlement, and death camps were mere Jewish sensationalism, rumors with no basis generated for political gain by the *Lügenpresse*, the lying news.

Günther nodded to himself, satisfied that the film would prove useful to the party. He turned his head toward the back of the room and held up his index finger, spiraling it at the projectionist to signal they had wrapped up. "*Gut, gut,*" he said, mimicking the reichsminister's earlier praise. The lights brightened the room, and Günther rose from his seat. As he passed the young man standing behind the spools, he said, "Be proud. We've done something great today."

PART I

1

Hannah

HANNAH KAUFMAN WATCHED HER MOTHER STRIKE A match and light two white candles, then circle her palms around the flames and cover her eyes. At first glance, the family dinner table looked the same as it did on any other Shabbat celebration, but Hannah could see the small differences: the way her mother's hands trembled, how her father jiggled his leg under the table. Hannah pretended not to notice. Her Opa Oskar had shared that Oma Minna's deepest hope was that their last meal together would be a joyous one with no talk of their uncertain future. Smiling through the throbbing pain in her head that had plagued her for days, Hannah looked at Oma Minna beside her and inhaled the fragrance of her rose perfume mingling with the sweet smell of freshly baked challah. Hannah's mother recited the prayer to welcome the Sabbath, then lowered her palms. Family was the best medicine.

Hannah absorbed the details of her life so she could replay them in her mind as the family waited for Oma and Opa to meet them in Palestine. The glow from the flames always made the

Kaufman family dining room look majestic, the way it illuminated the gold in the damask wallpaper, caught the reflection of
the silver candleholders, glinted from daggers on the small chan-
delier above. Rainy spring evenings like this brought the added
beauty of droplets trickling down the windowpanes. Hannah
usually found it soothing to watch veins of water descend the
glass, but tonight nothing could calm her.

Her thoughts drifted. How long would it be before her
grandparents could secure travel visas and join Hannah, her parents, and younger brother, Benjamin? *Three months? Maybe six?*
Then her greatest worry forced its way into her mind: *Maybe
they'll never be able to leave.* Legal migration papers were limited,
and plenty of Jewish families now had to rely on smugglers to get
them out of the country.

Hannah's father, Rolf, repeatedly reminded nineteen-year-
old Hannah that if every step of their escape didn't go perfectly
the following day, they might not get another chance to flee
Prague until they could afford new travel papers, and money
was already scarce. The community was abuzz with rumors of
upcoming deportations of Jews to work camps in the east, and
Hannah didn't want to stick around to see if they were true. But
she also couldn't bear the thought of her grandparents stranded
in Nazi-occupied Czechoslovakia—or what Hitler now called
the Protectorate of Bohemia and Moravia. Elders whispered that
their age would keep them low on any transport lists, and veterans of the Great War were favored by the Nazis, but these days,
no one could be certain what was true.

"Dinner smells delicious," Opa Oskar boomed.

They continued the charade of normalcy, and Hannah

followed her mother and grandmother to the kitchen to begin the shuttle of dinner plates to the table. From the back, Hannah took in their forms: Oma Minna with her curvy hips and plump waist could nearly eclipse her daughter-in-law, Hannah's mother, Ingrid, who was slender and tall. Hannah barely reached one hundred and fifty centimeters and looked nearly identical to her grandmother as a young woman. Hannah's days of growth spurts were behind her, but Oma Minna's plump body was a crystal ball into Hannah's future. As Hannah eyed her mother before her, she warmed at the sight of their similar features, thick brown curls that fell to their shoulders, and long musician fingers, though Hannah did not play an instrument. *A waste*, a piano teacher from the apartment building said nearly every time she glanced at Hannah's hands.

When her mother turned back to face her, Hannah noticed Ingrid's thin lips looked like a closed drawstring pouch.

"Are you all right, Mama?" Hannah asked.

Ingrid waved a hand. "Be strong, Hannah. It means a lot to them that we have a lovely last night together."

Hannah set down a plate in front of her younger brother, Ben. Napkin tucked into his collar, he leaned over the roast chicken and potatoes. "Mmm, the leg, my favorite," he said, lifting his fork.

Oskar patted his grandson on the back. "One for you and one for me."

Rolf lowered his brow, his message to his son clear: *We are leaving your grandparents in Nazi-occupied Prague. No one cares about your preference in chicken meat.*

"Rolf, please," Ingrid scolded her husband. "We're celebrating."

Hannah's father smiled tightly. "Let us thank God for making chickens with two legs."

Minna placed the last plate onto the place setting. "We should thank God for many things. Food on the table. Travel papers in your hands. And"—her voice caught in her throat—"one another."

The women took their seats, Minna straightening her back before picking up her cutlery. Hannah noticed her mother inhale deeply as she looked at Minna. She too seemed to be drinking in the small details of her mother-in-law: the way she sat like a queen and held her silverware as if every meal were a royal gala.

Ben swallowed his first bite. "Delicious."

"Know what else I hear is delicious?" Oskar asked, too loudly. "Avocados. They're fruit, but they taste like butter. They grow like weeds in Palestine. You remember Naftali from shul?" He cut his chicken, not waiting for a response. "He's in Palestine now, and Rabbi read me his postcard. Said you can't walk two meters without getting hit on the head with an avocado."

Hannah watched her father spear another slice of chicken, then closed her eyes and rubbed her temples. The stress had been giving Hannah a headache for days now, and no amount of aspirin seemed to cure it, nor did the chill that had settled in her body.

Minna dabbed the corners of her mouth with her napkin.

Ingrid offered an accommodating nod. "Avocados sound very nice, don't they, Rolf?"

"Yes, very nice," he replied dutifully. "We will tell you all about them in our letters. Avocados. Our new home. Everything that waits for you in Palestine." Rolf tried to hide the twitch of his lip as he smiled, but his neatly trimmed pencil mustache betrayed him.

Unable to bear the forced cheer any longer, Hannah blurted, "Why do we have to leave them?" Her throat thickened unexpectedly. "Can't we wait for travel papers for all of us and go together?"

Eyes darted back and forth, each person waiting for another to speak. Finally, Minna reached to place her fingers on Hannah's cheek. "*Shayna punim*, you know that's not how these things work. We are fortunate to get the four of you out. We won't be far behind, I promise."

Hannah's mother nodded. "We always manage," Ingrid reassured her, and Hannah understood what her mother did not say: *When it was time to leave Munich, we were able to get the family here piece by piece. We'll do the same this time.*

Oskar chortled. "We're Jews. We wander."

Hannah knew she was being ungenerous, but she couldn't play along, and she gave her grandfather a blank stare. She'd had enough wandering. Once the family was settled in Palestine, it was where she would remain for the rest of her days. Her family had moved from Munich in 1935 after Germany passed its anti-Jewish Nuremberg Laws. When Hitler marched into Czechoslovakia last spring, he brought Reich anti-Semitic restrictions with him. Like Germany, Nazi-controlled Czechoslovakia made it nearly impossible for Jews to hold employment or run businesses. Shopping hours for Jews were limited; it was verboten for Jews to visit most public spaces.

In the past weeks, while flipping through Oskar's old books about Palestine, Hannah's spirits soared at the photos of men laying the cornerstone of the Hebrew University that Chaim Weizmann and Albert Einstein founded not twenty years earlier. She squinted to study the faces of five nurses, eyes shaded by the brims of their straw boater hats. They looked as though they could be Hannah's friends. She envisioned herself digging through Megiddo and Beit She'arim with her fellow archaeology students, then walking home with her hands wide open to catch the avocados. She dreamed of summer dips in the Mediterranean Sea with friends. Hannah would meet Jews from across Europe who finally had a place to take root. She understood that there was tension, animosity even, between the Jews and Arabs, but she was hopeful that in time they could all live together in peace.

Ben reached for the pitcher of water and refilled his glass, proclaiming as he poured, "This Jew will be wandering straight back to Prague when the war is over. I love it here."

Hannah sniffed. "Too bad Prague doesn't love us back."

She regretted her words immediately. Hannah knew she should have long outgrown bickering with her brother, four years her junior, but she resented Ben for forgetting the strife that drove them from Munich and dismissing the current conditions in Prague. A year after the family relocated to Prague, Hannah asked Ben if he ever had nightmares about the time the Gestapo hurled an elderly rabbi onto the cobblestone street and forced him to clean it with a toothbrush, likely his. Ben didn't remember the incident. Even after Hannah tried to jostle his memory with details—it was a foggy afternoon in April on Dienerstrasse on their way home from the cinema—he couldn't recall a thing. He shrugged and asked, "You sure it was me who was with you?" Nor did he remember the time a pack of wild Hitlerjugend taunted them, calling them *Judenschweine*. Years before the pogroms the

Nazis coined Kristallnacht, the storefront window of Kaufman Apotheke was shattered, and every pill, tincture, and remedy was stuffed into the pockets of Germans drunk on hatred. But Ben appeared unscathed, the violence erased from his memory completely. How was that even possible? Hannah knew it was unfair, but on some level, she felt that Ben had left all the pain behind for her to absorb. He was ten years old when the family left Munich, not a baby. Meanwhile, Hannah startled awake at night every time she heard a mosquito buzz, mistaking it with the rumbling of an approaching mob.

"Prague likes me just fine," Ben said, though seeming somewhat deflated by his sister's barb.

Hannah felt a wave of shame. Her grandmother had made this final Shabbat dinner—*on a Sunday night because God loves a creative spirit*—and had asked Hannah to let the evening carry them through the next few months. When Minna shook her head, Hannah felt the silent reproach.

"I'm sorry, Ben. Prague likes you just fine. But Palestine is going to *love* you." She winked at him from across the table. Ben smiled back.

Taking on the tone of a strict schoolmaster, Rolf quizzed his son. "Ben, what time is our train from Prague Main tomorrow?"

Before the boy could answer, Oskar interrupted. "Son, they know the plan. Everyone knows the schedule. You've gone over it a thousand times now."

"Keep your voice down, Papa. The neighbors don't need to hear every word," Rolf clipped.

Minna pressed a smile. "That boy of mine. Born with a list of worries in his hand. Six o'clock, six o'clock, Rolf, so you can be at the station an hour and twenty minutes before your train to Vienna."

"Mama," Rolf shot back. "This is serious."

"It is, but repeating it over and over doesn't do anyone a bit of good. Let's enjoy our evening together. Make nice memories to last the next few months."

Hannah nodded, then quickly reached under the sleeve of her grandmother's dress and tried to memorize the feeling of her skin, like a silk sachet, soft and loose. Her eyes scanned the scars of their dining and living rooms: the nails in the wall where paintings once hung, the empty spot on the coffee table where the art deco ashtray had sat for years, the curio case stripped of tchotchkes from their travels together. The only thing left inside was a large chunk of pyrite Hannah and Oskar brought back from one of their earliest digs near Weissenberg, worthless to anyone but them. She remembered her eleven-year-old self working the rock from the earth with a hand shovel, imagining the castle she would buy for her family with the block of gold she had unearthed. But Oskar told Hannah that pyrite had no value. "It's fool's gold," he'd said, amused. Hannah had no idea why she felt acute loss over treasure that never truly existed, but Oskar's comment cut through her.

In preparation for their migration, the Kaufmans sold most of their belongings. It took funds to get a family of four out of the country. There were train tickets to Vienna, then to Bucharest. They needed bribe money in case Romania allied itself with the Reich, as the news was predicting. Before she fled for London, their friend the Czech social worker Marie Schmolka had given them a contact in Bucharest who would shelter them for the night before the first of their trains to Turkey at dawn the following day.

One missed train and the Kaufmans would not make it aboard their ship from Turkey to Palestine.

Oskar opened his arms wide. "Oma's right. Let's stop with all the worrying and be thankful that we are here together tonight," he insisted.

Hannah nodded, rubbing her head to soothe the pain.

———◇———

Hannah wasn't sure which tormented her more: the sharp cold or the roiling movement of the ship churning her stomach with every swell. She curled her body in a tight ball and wrapped her arms around her knees, hoping it would warm her. Had her family booked a cabin in an icebox? Hannah knew what the prickling sensation in the back of her mouth meant—she had moments to make it to the toilet down the corridor. She prayed there wouldn't be a line.

Reaching for a wall to steady her balance, Hannah staggered toward the water closet. Her vision was hazy, but images began to come into focus. The crystal knobs on the wooden doors were exactly like the ones in their apartment on Karpfengasse. A small bud vase held two white flowers on a narrow table just like at home. She padded past them, her bare feet sinking into the hall rug she had grown accustomed to for five years.

Wait…where am I?

When Hannah pushed open the WC door, any confusion vanished. She knew that the lace curtains muting the moonlight were a family heirloom passed down to Oma Minna. Hannah fell to her knees and gripped the rim of the toilet before her dinner left her stomach with a bitter slurry.

Hannah didn't need to turn her head toward the doorway to

know that the approaching footsteps were Oma's. After a decade as Hannah's primary caregiver as a child, Minna was acutely attuned to her granddaughter's distress. In turn, Hannah recognized the rhythm of Minna's gait. Ingrid had always worked beside Rolf at Kaufman Apotheke in Munich, then when they moved to Prague, she got a job at Hospital Na Františku. In Hannah's earliest memories, it was Minna who nursed her through her colds and bandaged her scrapes.

"*Mamaleh*" was all Minna needed to say. She grabbed the side of the sink, then lowered herself, bending her knees far quicker than she should have. "*Oof*," escaped from Minna's lips as her tuchus landed on the floor tiles. Sometimes Hannah forgot that although her grandmother liked to show the world a dignified elder, the truth was that her body had been riddled with joint pain for years. But there was no room for pretense in the middle of the night sitting beside a toilet.

As heave after heave produced nothing more than bile and tears, her grandmother combed Hannah's hair, smoothing down the curls and gathering the mass into a tail in the back. Minna slipped the ribbon from the collar of her nightdress. "There now, *shayna punim*," she offered, tying Hannah's hair.

"Aren't you freezing?" Hannah asked, wiping her nose against her sleeve.

Minna pressed her lips on Hannah's forehead and frowned. "You're burning," she said. The lines deepening around her grandmother's mouth told Hannah the situation was more serious than she was letting on. Minna maneuvered herself onto her hands and knees, then managed the laborious task of standing—kneeling, pulling, straightening.

"Let's get you back to bed, and I'll cool some rags," Minna said, turning toward the medicine chest and plucking out the clear bottle of aspirin. She worked the cork from the glass neck and reached down to Hannah, still sitting beside the toilet. "How long have you had that headache?"

"A few days. I need blankets, Oma," she whimpered, a little girl again, her teeth chattering and body shivering. "Can I wear your woolly socks?" All Hannah's clothes were packed in a valise by the front door.

Minna did not respond, because of course Hannah could wear her socks. "Let me bring you a nice cup of ginger ale," she said as she led Hannah back to bed. "And we will have you in top form for your big adventure tomorrow…later today," Minna added, gritting out a smile.

Minna must have moved with miraculous speed, because she appeared at Hannah's bedside moments later with a metal basin with cold, damp cloths. She wrung out the excess water and began to press the fabric onto Hannah's forehead. The cold was torturous when all she wanted was to curl herself in front of a roaring fire. It was equally agonizing to know that until Minna was able to join the family in Palestine, Hannah would never feel cared for this deeply. Her parents loved her, she knew that. But Hannah and Minna were tethered by something she could not quite explain, as if they had been together longer than this lifetime. Hannah knew that this was a silly notion, but it was the only way she could describe how fully connected she felt to her grandmother.

"Sip, sip," Minna said, holding a glass of ginger ale to Hannah's lips. "I put a little oregano in. It'll cure all that ails you."

After the second coat of cool water had been patted into her skin, Hannah knew what was coming next and inched her body closer to the wall to make room for Minna on the bed.

Minna sat on the edge of the bed frame and worked her legs onto the mattress. She lay back onto a pillow and turned to face Hannah beside her. "We humor your *Vati* and Opa with their scientific *Hokuspokus* and medicines, but we both know the real cure for what ails us is a good snuggle."

"I'm going to miss you, Oma."

"Miss me?" She waved a hand dismissively. "You'll be sick and tired of me underfoot night and day in Palestine." She raised her pitch, imitating herself nagging. "*Mamaleh*, grab a book and snuggle next to your old Oma," Then lowering her voice slightly to play the role of Hannah, Minna continued, "Oma, come now, I'm busy. I'm digging a hole in the ground, looking for dinosaur bones. I've got children of my own. Leave me alone." The two smiled, too tired to laugh at the absurd notion. "Now close your eyes and get your rest."

Hannah drifted to sleep, Minna by her side.

—◦—

From her sickbed, Hannah watched the window lighten to violet and looked at the clock on her bedside table. Quarter after five. Her pounding headache and chills told Hannah that her fever remained high, but what troubled her more were the dark red pinheads that appeared on her stomach and arms. She didn't need a mirror to know that a handful more were brewing on her face.

She reached for the empty space beside her just as Hannah heard Minna and Rolf arguing on the other side of the door.

"Smallpox," Rolf opined. "Don't go back in there. You need to stay healthy, Mama."

"I never get sick. You worry too much," Minna replied.

"And you don't worry *enough*," Rolf returned with urgency. "I have plenty on my mind without you getting yourself sick."

"The *mishegoss* never stops with this one. Let's worry about getting Hannah's fever down."

"And the spots you saw on her? You want to get rid of them in less than an hour too?"

"You don't have to leave at six. Seven will be fine."

Hannah tiptoed to the door and opened it a crack. She saw her mother and grandfather sitting at the table, Ingrid's face buried in her hands. Oskar listened attentively, nodding his head in agreement with every word Minna spoke.

"Mama, we cannot wait," Rolf offered solemnly. "Our tickets are for the seven twenty train."

Ingrid looked up and shook her head. With a tone of both incredulity and protest, she rushed, "They'll never let her on the first train looking like—"

"Without Hannah," Rolf interrupted, tossing a copy of *České slovo* onto the coffee table with force.

Hannah struggled to stand so she could see the newspaper through the crack of the door. On its front page was the Eiffel Tower with the letter V mounted beneath the lower platform.

"The Nazis took Paris on Friday," her father continued.

"Meh," Oskar interrupted. "If Hitler's busy in France, maybe—"

"Don't be flip, Papa!"

Hannah rarely heard Rolf shout and certainly never expected to hear him snap at his own father, but she understood his annoyance. In the last nine months, the Nazis had occupied Poland, Denmark, Norway, Belgium, the Netherlands, and Luxembourg. And now major parts of France, including Paris. This was no time for Oskar's insistent jest.

"We are leaving in an hour." Rolf glanced at his wristwatch. "In forty-five minutes."

"I'm not going without my daughter!" Ingrid's voice pitched high. "I'll stay behind with Hannah."

"Ingrid, please." Rolf inhaled deeply, seeming to collect his patience. "Nearly every koruna we have was spent on these transit papers and tickets. Think about Benjamin. Our son deserves a new life just as much as Hannah."

"No, no, I'm not leaving her," Ingrid rushed. "Call Marie. She can help."

"She's in London now, remember?"

"Then go to Jáchym. He can…he can change Hannah and my papers." Ingrid nodded her head frantically, begging the men to agree. "He'll make them for Oskar and Minna. They'll go to Palestine. Hannah and I… We can stay behind."

Oskar held up his hand to interrupt Ingrid's plea. "Have him change the papers? I should have him turn an old man and his wife into a young woman and her mother? The man is a forger, not a magician, Ingrid."

Rolf hurried to add, "It's dangerous for two women alone in Prague."

Especially Jewish women. Hannah understood what no one said aloud.

Rolf paused, then continued, "I'll stay behind with Hannah. Papa, you go in my place."

Hannah wanted to return to her bed, pull the blanket over her head, and disappear. To ease her family's burdens, she'd spent her life following rules and never complaining. Being a Jew in Europe was a struggle; that she couldn't help. But if she earned top marks at school and stayed out of trouble, at least she would give her family *naches*. Now, Hannah was the source of their problems; her illness was the only thing that stood between them and freedom.

Minna suggested she stay behind with Hannah.

Oskar sighed loudly and stood from his chair. "Rolf is right. Two women alone in Prague right now is dangerous. Better that he stay behind. Or…" He lifted his finger and started to pace the floor as he always did when thinking. His left foot thumped the wooden planks despite the special shoe he wore to even the length of his legs. "Hannah was born in 1921, correct?"

"Yes," Ingrid replied. "What are you thinking?"

"Minna's birthday is 1881. This could work," Oskar said. "If the nine becomes an eight, and *oof*, changing that two into an eight won't be easy. Rolf, grab me Hannah's visa. Minna, get me your passport and your mother's emerald ring."

Minna pointed her finger, stabbing downward to remind her husband that they had hidden their jewelry under the floorboards.

Hannah closed the door so Oskar would not see her eavesdropping when he hobbled past the bedroom on his way to wake Ben.

Rolf whispered, "Papa, you need the jewelry for your own passage. It's safer if I go. I—"

"Let's take care of today's problem today and worry about tomorrow then. Rolf, bring both sets of papers, and we'll see what

Jáchym can do," Oskar said, glancing at his watch. "It's five thirty. We need to make it to Jáchym and back before… You can leave at seven, can't you?"

"Papa, I'll stay behind with Hannah," Rolf demanded, and Hannah could practically feel the burning in the pit of her father's stomach. There were no good choices. However well intentioned Oskar might be, he wasn't someone equipped to care for a young woman in the protectorate, nor was he the best travel companion for Ingrid and Ben. Oskar's judgment was often clouded by unrealistic optimism, which might have been charming in peacetime but now put his loved ones in danger.

At the sight of her father's terrified expression, Hannah felt a wave of nausea, and the rug began to sway. She turned to make her way back to the bed, but the world went black, and she fell to the floor.

2

Hannah

Prague
June 1940

WHEN SHE WAS HALFWAY UP THE APARTMENT BUILDING stairwell, Hannah heard a telephone ringing from inside one of the six homes on the second floor. She was almost certain it was hers and began to run up the steps and down the corridor, reaching for her key. The soles of her shoes clomped the tiles, and her breath became heavier. Hannah wasn't ill any longer, but she certainly wasn't in top form after spending more than a week in bed. She was especially worn out today, her first working as a housemaid for Paní Božiková, a wealthy Christian woman who was friends with one of Hannah's former schoolteachers.

Ever since Germany's Nuremberg Laws had been applied to the Protectorate of Bohemia and Moravia last March, companies were required to purge Jewish employees from their payrolls, and bank accounts were frozen, so after the rest of the family left for Palestine, Oskar and Hannah had to find jobs in the shadows of public life. A Czech chemist hired Oskar and tucked him away in the back of his shop to mix ointments and medicines. Oskar made far less than what he had earned at the pharmacy he and

Rolf had owned, but the money kept body and soul together. They could not manage on Oskar's earnings alone, so even when kindly Paní Božiková suggested that Hannah take a rest, Hannah pressed on, scrubbing more vigorously than before, desperate to remain in her new employer's good graces. Hannah was paying for it now in exhaustion.

The ringing telephone meant good news, and Hannah couldn't afford to miss it. She'd watched Oskar place dozens of telephone calls, reminding friends of favors they owed him. Before work every morning, Oskar limped to the office of the Jewish Ältestenrat, pressing the council for exit papers for Hannah and himself. "It's called *Persisténz*," he'd told Hannah. "It's only a matter of time before that telephone jingles with someone telling us it's our lucky day."

Hannah fumbled with her key outside before the ringing stopped. *Scheisse!* She'd missed the call. Then she gulped with relief when she heard Oskar's voice inside the apartment.

"Rolf?" Oskar called out.

Hannah rushed inside, watching Oskar lower his brows with confusion. "I can barely hear you with all that crackling. Oy, there's an echo."

Hannah ran to Oskar's side, where he tilted the receiver toward her. She pressed her head against her grandfather's so the two could listen together.

Oskar continued, "You were going to write a letter when you arrived. Why the phone call? You're such a big shot now and can telephone just to kibitz?"

"Hallo, Papa!" Hannah shouted into the telephone mouthpiece.

Rolf's voice was faint, strained. "We're here, but…" He sniffed.

But what? What's going on?

"*Mutti*," Rolf continued.

Hannah clutched the receiver, hands overlapping Oskar's.

"She...she became ill on the boat."

Hannah turned to check her grandfather's expression and saw the reality hadn't registered.

"Papa, I'm sorry," Rolf continued. "*Mutti* didn't survive."

Oskar pinched the flesh that hung from his neck and shook his head. He pulled the receiver away from Hannah. "Rolf," he said, his voice quivering.

Placing her hand on Oskar's back, Hannah felt his breath ripple beneath his rib cage.

Hannah reached for a chair. "Sit, Opa," she offered, but he swatted her away.

"How did... Minna was fine," he protested, his voice cracking.

When Hannah dropped onto the wood seat, she felt it slap her bottom. She rested her elbows on the kitchen table and buried her head in her palms.

Oskar began fidgeting with the telephone cord as he listened intently, shaking his head. "What illness? My Minna's healthy as an ox," Oskar shouted into the phone as if debating his son could change the truth. Hannah watched her grandfather's face contort and tighten as Oskar listened to Rolf. "Oh," he said, then, "I see," glancing at Hannah. "Where did you... Where is she buried?"

Hannah looked at a nail in the wall where Oma Minna's favorite painting once hung, an apple tree with a young woman standing on her toes beneath it, reaching for fruit that was just out of grasp. The square patch of wallpaper was slightly lighter than the rest.

When the call ended, Oskar kissed Hannah on the forehead. Tears in his eyes, he swallowed hard. "It's not your fault," he whispered.

Hannah's best friend Míša always said that whenever someone offers absolution before you've asked for it, it means they really blame you, but they wish they didn't. Hannah watched Oskar limp toward his bedroom stoically.

"I need a little..." He didn't finish the thought and waited until his back was toward Hannah before reaching into his shirt pocket for a handkerchief. She felt the slam of the door echo through her body.

—◦—

One of the worst parts of losing Oma Minna was not being able to mourn properly. They could not attend a funeral, comforted by friends who would help shovel dirt onto her casket and share stories of her life. Neither Oskar nor Hannah could afford to miss a day of work, so they sat shiva and recited the Mourner's Kaddish only after returning from their respective jobs. Hannah was grateful for an excuse to drape black cloth over the mirrors so she wouldn't have to see the pockmarks her illness had left on her face.

Hannah wondered when Minna first started showing symptoms of the smallpox she had given her, if she had suffered. Rolf assured Hannah and Oskar that Minna had a peaceful passing, but Hannah knew her father was sparing them, a fact she simultaneously felt grateful for and resentful of. She would never know the truth.

By winter, Hannah stopped crying every time she thought of

Minna and began smiling, occasionally laughing with the memories. At supper one evening, Hannah stepped lightly into new territory with Oskar. "Remember how she rolled back the rug and danced to her old swing records?"

Oskar was silent for a moment, and Hannah wondered if she'd made an error in judgment. Maybe he wasn't ready. Then he surprised her, offering a melancholy nod of his head. "How about the way she'd insist she wasn't wincing in pain, that she was trying some new, *meshuga* dance move?"

Hannah took a chance and pressed on. "What do you think she'd be doing now if…if she were in Palestine?"

Oskar knit his brow, pondering. "Oma would be working in a schoolhouse for Jewish immigrants and teaching the children Hebrew. You remember how she was when you were a little one?"

"Do I ever!" Hannah disappeared into the memory of Minna rewarding her with a gumdrop whenever she learned to pronounce a new Hebrew letter.

"You should be glad for it now," Oskar said with the first smile Hannah had seen since they got the call from Rolf six months earlier. "We were lucky to have her, *Mausi*. You know it was Oma who started calling you that? A month early, you were born. Such a little thing."

"I miss her so much, Opa."

"Me too. Every day. I think we always will, but…" He paused to tap his chest. "May her memory be a blessing."

Hannah forced a smile for the sake of her grandfather.

3

Hilde

H ILDE KRAMER-BISCHOFF WAS FINISHING HER MORNING bread at the kitchen table when she heard the soft knock on the front door. She rolled her eyes. The roosters had barely crowed, and the farmhands knew Hilde always got her chores done, even if she was often late to make her way to the henhouse. Let the broody old birds have a few extra minutes with their eggs before Hilde came to snatch them away. Normally, Hilde was a stickler for punctuality, the childhood memory still vivid: her mother's loud clap as she trilled "*Schnell, schnell, schnell*" at Hilde and her siblings when she woke them for school. As a grown woman, dragging her heels in the morning was Hilde's small rebellion, a way to show her mother-in-law, Frederike, that she cared little for the family farm. As soon as her husband, Max, returned from defending the Fatherland, Hilde would beg him to take her back to civilization, ideally Berlin.

It had been nearly two years since her husband brought her to live on the Bischoff dairy farm, and Hilde wished the workers would show her some deference. *That's a laugh*, Hilde thought, realizing that the knock at the door was surely at the direction of old Frederike. If the head of the house had no respect for her son's bride, neither would the farmhands.

When Hilde pulled back the curtain of the door window, she saw that the male silhouette wasn't Ernst or Herbert after all. It was Herr von Braun from the local office of the National Socialist Party.

Milk soured in Hilde's stomach. There was only one reason for a visit like this, especially at such an early hour. She opened the door, and the man lowered his head and removed his cap. Hilde's eyes traveled down and caught the wooden box in von Braun's hand, no larger than a cigar humidor with an imperial eagle and Hakenkreuz engraved on its lid.

Max is gone, Hilde realized silently, reaching for the box.

Herr von Braun pulled it back, clutching it protectively. "Please ask Frau Bischoff to come to the door."

"I *am* Frau Bischoff," she returned, strangely comforted that her fighting spirit had not abandoned her in the face of tragedy. She would need it more than ever now.

He sighed softly, kindly. "You know what I meant. Frau Bischoff, his mother. The first…the other Frau Bischoff."

The officer used his free hand to retrieve a letter from the pocket of his jodhpurs. Before Hilde could respond, she heard the whip of the back door open and the clipped footsteps of Frederike fast approaching. She must have seen the car parked in the driveway or heard the dog barking at von Braun's arrival.

Not waiting for the officer, Frederike grabbed the letter and tore it open, burying her eyes in the text in front of her. She seemed unflappable, but Hilde could hear the whistle in

Frederike's moist nostrils. *Fweeet*. Hilde recognized the sound of her mother-in-law hiding her heartbreak.

The officer cleared his throat and gave Hilde a wide-eyed look of sympathy. "He was shot in battle near Leningrad," von Braun reported, seeming relieved that he now had a script to follow. "His captain said he did not suffer. He was buried at Sologubovka Cemetery with comrades who also fell in Operation Barbarossa."

Hilde shook her head as if to tell von Braun he was mistaken. She had received a letter from Max just yesterday saying that the worst was over and the war would end soon. Bischoff was a common name, Maximillian even more so. He had it wrong. "How…how can they be sure it was him?" Hilde asked, scratching for reasons the Wehrmacht had made an error.

Before Hilde could suggest that Max was simply injured and now at a military hospital amusing the nurses with his *kitschig* card tricks, Frederike stepped in. "Thank you, Herr von Braun," she said, her chin tilted up slightly. "Hildegard and I could not be more proud of Max." Frederike glanced at the framed, sepia-toned photo of Max's father in his Luftstreitkräfte uniform that hung above the wall calendar. "Herr Bischoff would have…" Frederike did not finish, instead lifting a string of her apron and dabbing her eyes.

Soon Hilde was back at the kitchen table with Frederike, the small box of Max's belongings between them. Hilde pushed her plate to the side. Frederike lifted the lid and pulled out an oval aluminum identification tag that, only days earlier, had pressed against Max's beating chest. Hilde reached inside the box for her husband's gold wedding band and slipped it onto her thumb, examining the scuff marks and wondering where he had been when each occurred. Or maybe all the scratches had happened at the same time. A photograph of Hilde and a small wedding portrait browned and curled at the edges like autumn leaves. Max's Wehrmacht toothbrush with worn bristles and the word GARANTIE etched on the handle.

How had her life been upended over the course of breakfast? One moment, she was grousing about farm chores, and the next, she was a twenty-year-old widow. She stood stock-still, the tick of the grandfather clock in the hallway taunting her with the reminder that time could only move forward. She wished she could rewind life like a reel of film.

Hilde had no recollection of von Braun leaving but knew he must have because the door was closed, and he was no longer there.

Frederike sat across from Hilde, looking as though all her breath was trapped in her chest. Hilde knew this feeling all too well. When trying to gather her strength, Hilde often inhaled deeply as if to bolster herself but forgot to exhale.

She decided to try something she'd never done and extended her arm across the table to grasp Frederike's hand. "Max was the most wonderful—"

Hilde's mother-in-law flicked her wrist and interrupted. "I don't need you to tell me about my son." Frederike stood, walked toward the kitchen hutch, and pulled open a wooden drawer. She returned with a small pad of lined paper and a stubby pencil and jotted the words "death card" on the first line.

"I can fill out his death card," Hilde volunteered. She knew Max would have been proud of her for refraining from striking back at his mother. How many times had he promised that she would come around? She heard his voice reminding her, *Mutti was the same way with Gustav's wife, and now Ani is like a daughter to her.*

Hilde suspected Max was wrong. From the first time Frederike set eyes on Hilde, when her new husband carried her over the threshold of his childhood home, Max's mother made a show of narrowing her eyes as she scanned Hilde from head to toe. "Such news," she had said before a loud *fweeet*. Now, Hilde would never know if Max was right, if Frederike would have grown to love her. Hilde and Max would never get to adopt a child and make an oma of Frederike. They would never be able to enjoy the new Germany they helped build. She wouldn't see Max's hair go gray or his face line with time.

Hilde strengthened her resolve to help Frederike; she owed it to Max to extend kindness to his mother, even if it meant faking it. "I can help with the paperwork."

"*Ach*," Frederike muttered with a wave. "Do you even know where Max was born? You hardly knew my son. I'll call on Brigitte this afternoon."

Frederike had a hundred different ways of reminding Hilde that she was not her first choice for her son, unlike Brigitte Kaltenbrunner, Frederike's best friend's daughter who lived on the farm adjacent to the Bischoffs'. "I always thought those two would marry," Frederike often muttered.

It wasn't just her words; she spoke to Hilde as if she was chopping cabbage. *Sort the beets. Till the soil. Patch the fence.*

"In the meantime, Hilde, start thinking about where you'll go once you leave Bamberg. The Wehrmacht has been telling us for months that the *Kaserne* is full, and they need rooms for soldiers.

We'll have a service on Sunday at Saint Stephan's, then you can be on your way Monday."

How this beast raised a sweet young man like Max was beyond Hilde's comprehension. "*Ja, ja,* I will leave after the funeral," she said, wondering if they would bury an empty casket. More urgently, where *would* she go? There was no way in hell she could ever return to her parents' house in Munich. Their disdain for her, combined with the shrines to her brother and sister, would be unbearable. She wondered if the Women's League in Berlin would take her back after the incident with Obergruppenführer Werner Ziegler. One little indiscretion didn't make a girl useless.

Hilde trudged upstairs to the bedroom she had shared with Max and scanned her surroundings. She remembered how they both laughed when they moved in after their wedding. The walls were still plastered with childish posters from Max and Gustav's days in the Hitlerjugend. Toy Wehrmacht soldiers and tanks crowded the top of their bookcase, above which was a photo of a sweaty Herbert Runge holding his boxing gloves overhead and an Olympic medal around his neck. Hilde had been relieved when Max promised they would soon move into a home of their own, devoid of the detritus of his *Grundschule* years. Everything in the Bischoff home looked as though it were stuck in the last decade except for the barn, which had been rebuilt after a fire burned it to the ground three years earlier. Max and Gustav helped their father, Wilhelm, rebuild it, but days before they completed the project, the boys watched their father clutch his chest and drop to the ground. Frederike put on a pair of canvas trousers and work gloves and helped her boys hammer nails, build walls, and paint the farmhouse the same shade of sage it had been before.

Every night, the three would visit Wilhelm at the hospital and tell him about their progress; the unspoken agreement was that they would finish the job and he would come home to see it. Two days later, he had another heart attack, this one fatal.

Max saw that his new bride didn't care for their accommodations, but instead of calling her spoiled or ungrateful, he promised they would not be there long. "I will build you a house worthy of a queen," he had told her on their wedding night. Now he was gone, and Hilde lay on her back on the blanket covering their twin bed, the horse hair of the mattress beneath her clumping on the left side. "I'll sleep on the lump," Max had said after their first night of tenderness as a married couple. He patted his chest. "I'm all the mattress you'll ever need." Instead, she nestled herself into the side of Max's body, resting her head on his shoulder and wrapping a leg over his. She felt a tear slide down her temple, wondering how she was lucky enough to find such an adoring man. Hilde knew she didn't deserve Max, but she was grateful for him nonetheless.

Now, she wiped away tears for the opposite reason. She was alone. Hilde held her hands over her mouth to mute the sound of her sobs, removing them briefly to wipe her nose with her dress sleeve and catch her breath.

Where would she go after the funeral? It was too late to chase her youthful dream of being a cabaret comedienne, the pluck and wobble of a violin string punctuating her punchlines. Those ambitions were more frivolous than ever now that Germany was reclaiming its place in the world. As a grown woman, she was needed on a different stage. On Monday morning, she would return to Berlin and report for duty at the Women's League. Surely they had forgiven her by now. Two years had passed, and with Germany now at war, the Reich needed all good patriots on hand.

She would simply show up at the office and pretend the ugliness with Werner never happened. Her former supervisor, Lotte Brack, once shared that a woman's best assets were her pretty smile and a terrible memory. Grudges were for men to hold.

Hilde hadn't realized she had fallen asleep until she heard the knock on her bedroom door and jolted upright.

Brigitte peeked her head inside and asked if she could come in. "I just heard," she uttered, barely a whisper. "Oh, Hilde, I cannot believe… I hope you take comfort knowing he gave his life for the Fatherland."

"*Ja, ja,* I do," Hilde said, waving her friend inside. Patting the bed, Hilde watched Brigitte place a palm on her lower back, the other on the mattress, as she carefully lowered herself to sit.

"She wants me out. Monday morning after the service."

Brigitte cast her gaze downward; Frederike must have already told her.

"I'll never get to meet your baby," Hilde continued.

"Oh, Hilde, you'll come visit," Brigitte protested, though they both knew the truth: Their friendship was built on their connection to Max and proximity to each other. Once Hilde's train departed from Bamberg, she would leave this part of her life behind. "Hilde, I'm so sorry, but I still need to walk to the market this morning. Won't you come along?"

"I don't think so, Brigitte."

"The fresh air will do you good."

"All right," Hilde said, resigned, unable to decline an invitation from someone who enjoyed spending time with her. It

seemed whenever she made a girlfriend, something came along
to spoil it. Her best friend from childhood had left Munich after
Mittelschule. When Hilde was in her last year of *Gymnasium*,
Jutta Klinger, her former Bund Deutscher Mädel leader, got married and became less available. Then, just as Hilde was beginning to make inroads with Lotte, the most senior office girl
at the Women's League, Hilde got pregnant and was sent to a
Lebensborn home in Bavaria.

Hilde and Brigitte walked in silence as they left the Bischoff
farm, the rhythm of their steps in the sticky mud accompanied by
a small flock of geese honking overhead. Wings spanning wide,
they seemed pleased that the rain had finally let up after three
days of downpour.

The young women made their way from the dirt road to the
paved Siechenstrasse. Hilde took in the sight of Brigitte, just a
pace ahead of her, and admired how her pinafore apron dress
swung as she walked. The two were both framed tall and broad,
but Brigitte had a delicate carriage that Hilde could never imitate. Brigitte walked lightly, even at seven months pregnant, while
Hilde lumbered. Hilde jutted her chin despite reminding herself
to relax her face into an open, welcoming expression like Brigitte.
They even sneezed differently: Brigitte's a birdlike chirp, Hilde's
a mule's bray—or so her mother always told her.

Why was she thinking about this? Her husband had been
killed in battle. Shouldn't she be wailing in grief?

"I really did love him," Hilde told Brigitte.

"I know you did. I admire how strong you're being. If
Jürgen… I can't let myself think about that. Our soldiers are safe
in Copenhagen."

What a luxury it was for Brigitte to choose not to imagine her own tragedy. Was Hilde mistaken in thinking there was the slightest hint of smugness in Brigitte's declaration?

Hilde may have married Max out of desperation, but she had grown to care for him deeply. After she miscarried her first pregnancy, she seduced Max, who was working as a guard at the Heim Hochland Lebensborn home where she had been staying. She became pregnant with his baby but claimed the child belonged to her married lover, Obergruppenführer Werner Ziegler, presuming that a child would secure her place in his life. Instead, she was quickly cast aside by the obergruppenführer, and Hilde needed the escape hatch Max provided when he proposed. The choice had been as clear as dumpling broth. Max really was the baby's father, and he'd never learned of Hilde's deception, so he was none the wiser. At the time, Hilde felt cursed, but now she realized it was fate intervening on her behalf.

What started as a marriage of convenience grew into real affection. The letters Max had written to her, the notes he jotted to their unborn baby, his promises of their future softened her. Max's kindness disarmed Hilde, and she wondered who she would be now without it.

Hilde and Brigitte continued toward the Main-Donau-Kanal, passing two shuttered storefronts. To the right, a single rowboat dotted the brown water. A burly man began opening canvas umbrellas on the row of tables outside the biergarten, then poured a bucket of water on the cobblestones to wash away spilled brew from the night before. A soldier from the *Kaserne* whistled, and Hilde couldn't help but feel flattered. Though Brigitte was the prettier of the two, Hilde knew the attention was for her, because no German soldier would dare flirt with a pregnant woman.

No, Brigitte got her approval from the hausfrau wearing a Mutterkreuz medal, pushing a baby carriage toward them on Siechenstrasse while three little ones scrambled beside her.

"*Heil* Hitler," Hilde and Brigitte greeted her. As adults, they were no longer required to salute child-rich mothers, but they had become accustomed to it over the past two years. It was a nice way to show respect for women who had answered Reichsführer Heinrich Himmler's call of duty to repopulate the Fatherland.

Brigitte turned to Hilde. "Why don't you stay in Bamberg with me until Jürgen returns from Denmark?" she suggested. "You'll help me with the baby."

Hilde felt her chest tighten at the thought of being Brigitte's nursemaid. Of all the people Hilde had known, only Max and Brigitte understood that Hilde was made for a bigger life than ordinary people.

As they reached the Kettenbrücke, Hilde remembered the first time she saw the bridge with Max. "As a boy, I thought the entrance was two giant chess rooks," he'd told her. Hilde didn't see it, but she remembered feeling a flush of warmth realizing that Max had an endearing ability to view ugly nothings as stately and important. She wished she could look at the world through his lens. *He would have been a wonderful father*, she thought, placing a palm on her barren womb.

Brigitte stopped and grabbed Hilde's hand intently. "Stay, Hilde. Frau Bischoff will squirm every time she sees you in town," she offered, curling her lips mischievously. "You'll get practice for when you adopt a baby someday. After you remarry. Plus, everyone will know what an old witch she is to turn away her son's poor widow."

Poor widow? The words were an assault. Hilde pulled back her shoulders and lifted her head. "I have to pack," she offered before turning abruptly.

"We haven't even gotten to—"

Hilde interrupted and continued walking back toward the farm. "I need to pack my things." If she clenched her jaw any tighter, she might chip a tooth. Hilde was not about to have a bunch of small town *Hinterwäldler* pity her.

"All right, I'll help you—"

Hilde held up a palm. "Brigitte, I practically ran the Women's League for the reichsfrauenführerin. I can manage my valise." Looking at bewildered Brigitte, Hilde's anger abated. "Thank you. I don't need any help, that's all."

Keeping her eyes on the ground, Hilde found a small stone and kicked it a few meters ahead, then did it again when she caught up with it.

She reached her hands into her skirt pockets and used her thumbnail to cut into the flesh beneath the nail of her pinkie, then switched to digging her pinkie nail into her thumb. She had tried to quit this nervous habit dozens of times, but the relief it offered was addicting. Yes, it brought her pain, but it was a satisfying discomfort, a soothing agitation. Hilde once tried to explain it to Jutta, but her friend just scrunched her face and suggested Hilde use her willpower to stop.

By the time Hilde arrived home—rather, back to the Bischoff farm—she had broken the skin of her small finger and drawn blood. She walked through the front door and heard the

Volksempfänger on full volume. Frederike always turned up the radio so the sound would carry from its stand in the living room to the kitchen, where she spent several hours each day scrubbing, peeling, and ironing.

"The führer is expected to return to Berlin next week for a grand parade celebrating Germany's recent victories in the east. It will be a celebration like no one's ever seen before!"

Hilde gripped the banister post cap and lifted her foot onto the first stair before hearing the sound she hated most—Frederike's trilling holler.

"Hildegard!"

She'd almost made it. Hilde sighed, defeated.

"Come into the kitchen. I need a word."

Hilde stood at the doorway watching Frederike lift the lid from a cast iron pot of boiling potatoes, a pan filled with sizzling onions frying beside it. The aroma momentarily fooled Hilde into feeling cared for.

"You're...*cooking?*"

Frederike's eyes were swollen and red, and strands of hair fought to break free from her tight bun. Hilde knew better than to try to offer her mother-in-law comfort, though. Clearing her throat, Frederike told Hilde, "My sister and her husband will be here this evening, and Ani and the boys are arriving by train tomorrow morning. You'll have to share Max and Gustav's bedroom with her. I have two cots I'll unroll for the children."

Hilde nodded her agreement.

"And no hysterics from you. You know Gustav is on the front, and I can't have anyone filling Ani's head with fear."

For a moment, Hilde and Frederike shared a mission, and

Hilde couldn't help yearning for more of a connection to Max's mother.

"Hildegard, you and I have never gotten along the way Max hoped, and for that, I am sorry," Frederike said, standing guard over her stove.

Hilde wanted to ask Frederike to sit with her on the love seat and show her photos of Max as a child. Her mother-in-law wasn't the sentimental type, but Max had once shown Hilde a cloth photo album Frederike had made. It was soft and cushioned with a baby photo slipped into a small frame on the cover and held closed by a dark blue ribbon. The delicate creation had surprised Hilde, as Frederike's kind words did now.

Hilde had seen the glaze of her mother-in-law's eyes threatening to well with emotion before she turned to face the stove again.

"I trust you can pack on your own."

"Yes, yes, Frau Bischoff."

"*Gut*," she said, back still turned to Hilde. "I will have Ernst drive you to the train station on Monday morning. Where will you go?"

"Berlin."

"That's what I figured. You'll return to the Women's League then? You always speak fondly of your days working for Reichsfrauenführerin Scholtz-Klink. I'm sure she will be pleased to have you back at the Frauenschaft. There's a train that leaves for Berlin just after ten. Ernst should be done with most of his work by then."

"Oh." Hilde groped for the right words but could only manage a quick thanks.

Frederike turned to face Hilde and reached for a handkerchief to dab her eyes.

"He cared for you, Hildegard. And I...got used to having you around."

———◇———

After Max's funeral, Hilde fell onto the bed and buried her face in the pillow, pulling the sides up to cover her ears. She considered screaming but didn't want to draw attention from Frederike or Brigitte and her mother, who were still downstairs sharing memories of Max with the Bischoff family. In many ways, Frederike was right—Hilde hardly knew her own husband. She had no idea that he'd chipped his front tooth when he fell from a tree trying to save the cat Brigitte found by the canal and spooked by chasing it. She didn't know he was allergic to strawberries or had started a science club with boys from the village.

When she finally fell into a deep sleep, Hilde's mind returned to the day she lost her second pregnancy, Max's baby, more than a year earlier. The hospital was nearly identical to the one she'd been transported to in real life—stark white walls, bright under fluorescent light tubes, metal instruments on a rolling table, men with cotton masks covering their noses and mouths. A doctor approached Hilde, who was now on a four-post bed that looked like it should be in a castle, not a hospital. He handed Hilde a metal bucket like the ones Ernst used to milk the cows. "What a handsome boy you have!" he exclaimed. But when Hilde looked inside the bucket, it was a jumble of bloodied limbs, Max's adult face rising to the surface flashing his chipped tooth as he smiled at Hilde.

"*Mein Gott!*" Hilde bolted upright, gasping as though she had stayed under water too long. "I need to get out of here."

———◇———

Hilde stood by the train door while the locomotive was still in motion and other passengers were seated. She watched thickets of maple and linden trees give way to open fields, and she could hardly wait to see the city appear in the distance, then grow larger as she got closer. Every seat was filled. Mothers wore floral frocks with white shawl collars. Their little boys sported Hitlerjugend or Deutsches Jungvolk uniforms while girls donned dresses with tiered flouncy skirts and puffed short sleeves. Older girls wore their Bund Deutscher Mädel uniforms, locks pulled into two low braids the way the führer liked. Hilde saw a Hitler Youth troop, all of whom styled their hair like Reichsführer Himmler, shaving the sides nearly ten centimeters higher than the tops of their ears.

Holding a metal bar with one hand and her valise with the other, Hilde made sure she'd be the first to step onto the platform at Berlin Anhalter Bahnhof. The Women's League would close in less than two hours, and Hilde still needed to walk to Frau Sauer's boardinghouse, where she had leased a room a year earlier. Hilde had sent a letter alerting the landlady of her arrival, but there hadn't been time for her to reply, so she would have to keep her thumbs pressed for good luck. She would have just enough time to set down her bag and get to the office.

As the train belched to a halt, Hilde took a deep breath and remembered Max showing her the elaborate electrical train set he and his brother and father built in their cellar together. He'd asked, "Do you ever wonder if we're just toys of space aliens, and every time we take a train ride, it's because some Martian kid is playing with his railroad set?" She hadn't, but for some reason, she thought of his silly musing now. It was hard to imagine never hearing his voice again.

The train doors opened, and Hilde stepped out of her memory and onto the platform, sunlight illuminating the rib cage ceiling. The station clock was perched on a tall pole, a lone soldier leaning against it as he puffed a cigarette. Hilde watched a cluster of nuns, maybe a dozen or so, gathered on the opposite track, waiting to leave Berlin.

Hilde inhaled deeply and wondered why she smelled flowers inside the station.

What the hell? Two men pushed a rolling hand truck filled with enormous circular wreaths packed with gardenias, roses, and lilies through an arched doorway from the lobby onto the platform. Another two carts followed with arrangements in multiple bursts of yellow and orange; four men balanced a two-meter Hakenkreuz of red roses and carried it toward the track as disembarking passengers gave them a wide berth.

Hilde remembered what she had heard on Frederike's radio—Berlin was preparing for a victory parade. The train station was being festooned with flowers for those visiting the city to celebrate the führer's return from visiting troops in Latvia and other battlegrounds in the east.

The buzz of energy fueled her. As she clipped down Bernburger Strasse, Hilde looked up at apartment building windows. She watched a woman straightening a swastika flag that the wind had wrapped around its pole. In the window three stories below, a man unfurled a sheet that draped against the stone face of the building. On it was painted DEUTSCHLAND ÜBER ALLES, Germany above all others.

Hilde hadn't realized how much she'd missed the sounds of the city—the honk of automobile horns, the clop of police horse hooves, threads of conversation tangling with one another in the air. The scent of Berlin in the summertime was a familiar comfort too. Fresh grass and sausage carts mingled with the slightest hint of motor oil. She'd been born in Munich, but Berlin was home.

"*Guten Tag!*" Hilde said to a man sweeping the sidewalk in front of his housewares shop. He nodded pleasantly in return. A pair of Hitlerjugend zigzagged the boulevard, eagerly offering pedestrians handheld flags. Like every good German, Hilde wanted to show her patriotism and accepted the small cloth stapled to a slender wooden dowel. Passing a row of cylindrical columns of street kiosks, Hilde smiled at the diligent girls of the Bund Deutscher Mädel brushing a final coat of glaze onto their posters.

There was a crackle in the air over the führer's return to Berlin. As she continued, Hilde smelled the slightest whiff of fresh paint and hoped the pristine coat of white on the furniture store was just a sprucing rather than covering damage. Hilde knew that the city had endured a few nicks and scrapes to streets and buildings from a handful of minor air raids by the British Royal Air Force.

She made her way to Frau Sauer's and knocked on the door, hoping her old landlady wasn't at the market or preparing the streets for tomorrow's parade. Hilde saw the peephole open, then darken as someone peered through.

"There she is!" Frau Sauer's voice sang from inside. She

opened the door and told Hilde she had been waiting for her. "You never mentioned what time you would arrive so I've been here all day," she said, waving her hand as if to say it didn't matter now. "Come in. Welcome back." She bent to pick up Hilde's valise. "Don't you worry yourself with that."

Hilde followed the landlady inside, surveying the living room from where she stood in the foyer. It hadn't changed since she'd lived there two years earlier: mounted antlers hung above the fireplace mantle, which was cluttered with postcards of German landscapes. Hilde smiled at the sight of Frau Sauer's glass candy bowl filled with butterscotch drops. She felt a pang of nostalgia for her old life, when she worked at the Women's League and had just started dating Werner. She didn't miss her relationship with the obergruppenführer, but she longed for who she had been then, fresh out of *Gymnasium* and beginning a new life as part of the Reich administration.

"My heartfelt condolence over your husband," Frau Sauer said, pursing her lips. "And the…" She pointed at Hilde's stomach. "You're young. You'll have your babies yet."

Hilde shook away the unpleasant thought. This wasn't the time to correct her, to share that she was no longer able to have a child of her own blood.

"Thank you, Frau Sauer," Hilde replied, looking at her watch. The Women's League closed in a little over an hour. She looked up the staircase she used to trot down every morning for breakfast. "Is my old room available?"

"*Ach nein*, Hilde. I wish I had a bed for you," the wizened woman said with an exaggerated pout, her fist pressed firmly onto her chest. "Every last room is full. In one, I've got girls doubled up in a bunk bed, but my cousin had a tenant who just married and left her with a spare room. Frau Schwammberger lives on Oranienburger Strasse. In the Mitte. Would you like me to telephone her?"

Hilde nodded gratefully.

"You'll be working for the Reich now that you're back, won't you? My cousin only rents to Reich girls."

Without thinking, Hilde lied, "*Ja, ja*, of course. I'm returning to the Women's League." She felt a twinge of guilt for her fib but quickly assured herself that a lie was simply a wish that hadn't yet come true.

Frau Sauer walked to the kitchen, Hilde in her wake, then picked up the telephone receiver and started to place the call. "I remember how fond of you the reichsfrauenführerin was. She'll be delighted you're back at the Women's League."

"She was like a second mother to me," Hilde returned. Hilde had been as insignificant to the reichsfrauenführerin as she was to her own mother. That wasn't entirely accurate. Reichsfrauenführerin Gertrud Scholtz-Klink had barely noticed Hilde's presence in the Frauenschaft office, whereas when her mother got angry with Hilde, she sniped that the girl could test a mother's limits.

Twenty minutes later, Hilde was at her new home where the smell of boiling cabbage choked her from the moment she stepped through the doorway. The landlady was built like a farmworker, thick and sturdy with legs the shape of logs. She had wrapped a kerchief over a head full of curlers, gray hair held onto the black cylinders with metal clips. She placed a hand on her hip and outstretched the other to invite Hilde inside.

"Thank you, Frau Schwammberger," Hilde said, brushing past her and setting down her valise. The heavy curtains were drawn closed, and cigarette smoke had worked itself deep into the room. She noticed small strips of cellophane self-adhesive tape repairing tears to the edges of the wallpaper, electrical tape patching an armrest of the pilling sofa.

"I have only three rules: Lights off at ten. Eat everything you are served. And absolutely no entertaining men in the bedrooms."

Hilde nodded in agreement.

"Frau Sauer says you're a good girl, but I still feel I should warn you... Break any of my rules, and you'll find yourself on the street."

"Of course. I need to get to the Women's League before they close," Hilde explained. "The reichsfrauenführerin wants to see me right away so we can discuss a new project," she lied again.

"I will take your bag upstairs to your room," Frau Schwammberger said, seeming proud to play her role in this important reunion between Hilde and the reichsfrauenführerin. "Don't keep her waiting."

Hilde knew it was unladylike to run through the streets of Berlin, so she walked with long strides and knees nearly locked. *They will want me back. Of course they will find a job for me.*

She smelled the slight odor of hay and animals from the zoo as she rounded Tiergartenstrasse and heard the squeal of children's laughter. Max would have been the type of father who let his children ride on his shoulders so they could get a better view of the elephants in their enclosure. Hilde reached into her blazer pocket and pinched her palm with a fingernail, a reminder to focus on what was ahead.

Nearly at the villa that housed the Frauenschaft, Hilde passed the headquarters of the Aktion T4 euthanasia program and remembered Lotte explaining how Germany would weed out its bad blood. "Imagine a world without cripples or imbeciles draining our nation's resources," she'd said. Hilde nodded, figuring someone like Lotte, nearly a decade her senior with far more experience in the Reich, must understand the world better than she. Hilde simply hadn't matured enough to see the difference between cruelty and mercy. The drapes were closed, but Hilde watched a nurse in a starched white hat step outside and reach for the wrought-iron handrail as she began her descent down the front stairs.

Now in front of the Frauenschaft headquarters, Hilde tried to catch a glimpse inside the large front window of the office. Stationed at her old desk was a woman Hilde's age holding a telephone receiver, brows knit as she listened and bit her bottom lip. Hilde quickly flashed her old identification badge at the guard, who barely glanced at it and nodded that Hilde could go inside. *He really should be more cautious*, Hilde thought, though she was grateful for the man's carelessness.

Pulling at the bottom of her jacket, Hilde checked nervously to make sure her buttons were aligned properly. Her brown skirt matched the jacket perfectly and had remained miraculously wrinkle-free despite her five-hour train journey.

She climbed the steps and reached for the doorknob, silently repeating to herself the positive feedback she had received from Lotte two years earlier. *Diligent. Bright. Clever and crafty.*

Hilde stood in the doorway, observing the women at work before they noticed her. The emblem of the Frauenschaft—a large black triangle with a white cross and a red swastika at its center—was still displayed on the back wall so it was the first thing people would see upon entering. Since she'd been gone, the Women's League began framing the covers of its monthly magazine, *Frauen Warte*, and lining the walls with them. *Mein Gott*, she missed this place: the clacking of the typewriter, the hum of the overhead light fixture, the shuffle of papers.

Lotte's head lifted from behind the mimeograph machine, and she grimaced at the sight of Hilde, then glanced anxiously toward the closed door to the reichsfrauenführerin's private office. "Hilde, what are you doing here?"

The woman at Hilde's old desk averted her eyes, and the other worker remained bent over the filing cabinet, continuing to sort papers, but Hilde could tell they were both eavesdropping.

Lotte walked toward Hilde and placed her hand on her back, gently leading her out into the foyer. "You can't be here. The reichsfrauenführerin thinks you're insane, totally turned through after what happened with the obergruppenführer, and honestly, I can't say I blame her. What were you thinking?"

"I thought—"

"No, Hilde, it wasn't a real question," Lotte returned.

Hilde took a breath before speaking so her voice wouldn't quiver like the insides of her stomach. "I made a mistake."

Lotte crossed her arms over her chest. "You could have ruined a man's life. That's more than a mistake."

Outside in the Tiergarten, Hilde heard a marching band begin practicing for Hitler's procession the following day. The jubilant notes from the brass horns felt painfully at odds with the ache in Hilde's heart. "I'm sorry. It was a long time ago. I wasn't thinking straight."

"Exactly why you are a liability to the cause," Lotte said. "You'd better go."

PART II

4

Hannah

Protectorate of Bohemia and Moravia
December 1941

EIGHTEEN MONTHS AFTER THE FAMILY'S FINAL SHABBAT dinner together on Karpfengasse, Hannah stood in the hallway of their emptied apartment, straightening her knit beanie in the gilded mirror they would leave behind. It was still dark outside from the night that had passed, but Hannah could see the scarring on her face and touched her cheek with her fingertips. She wondered if Oma Minna's face had pebbled like this, if there was a cream or ointment that would smooth the pockmarks. Her face had also thinned a bit, making her look more like her mother than ever. Like Ingrid's, Hannah's face was heart-shaped with a widow's peak and sharp chin. Combined with their penetrating brown eyes, Hannah and her mother were the sort people pegged as kind souls. They were quick to tilt their heads and nod sympathetically when others spoke; Hannah and Ingrid were the women that beggars would always approach on a crowded street. Hannah wondered if the similarity between them seemed more pronounced because Hannah's face had matured or because she was wearing the hat and coat Ingrid had left behind.

Reasonable or not, Hannah was seething that Oskar had given up on their immigration to Palestine last year. "I tried everything I could, *Mausi*," he said after his final attempt. Oskar did his best, but one evening last winter, he pulled off his scarf and tossed it on the table, and Hannah saw the resignation in his slow gait and slumped shoulders. Bushy white eyebrows growing wildly, he looked older than his sixty-five years. That night, Hannah watched Oskar through the crack between her bedroom door and its frame. Sitting on the couch, his elbows spiked his knees and his hands covered his face. Oskar's chest heaved, though he never made a sound.

Now, duffel bag in hand, Oskar emerged from his room freshly bathed and shaved, ready to be transported to a new settlement in the Czech village of Terezín. Under Nazi occupation, it was called Theresienstadt, a spa town just an hour north of Prague where they could wait out the war. "Hitler's gift to the Jews," a rabbi at the Ältestenrat had assured him, handing Oskar his deed to a lakeside cottage in Theresienstadt.

Seeing Hannah at the mirror, Oskar teased, "Not a hair out of place."

"I wasn't…" Hannah trailed off, knowing this routine all too well. She would tell her grandfather that she wasn't concerned with her hair, then he would give her a soft shove and tell her he was going to buy her a sense of humor for her birthday.

Oskar tucked his deportation notice into the pocket of his wool coat, then slipped on his leather gloves. "Ready for our big adventure?"

"I'm not," Hannah answered with unintentional candor. "I don't want to go."

"I know, *Mausi*," he said with a rictus smile. "Oma always said home is where you have a loved one by your side."

Hannah appreciated the sentiment, but she had loved ones in Palestine; they both did. *That* was home, not this Theresienstadt settlement.

Gesturing toward his bag, he reminded her, "We're taking a bit of home with us."

Oskar had heeded the advice of the transport notice and packed up the last of their belongings. Hannah had wrapped a knit jacket around a framed photograph of the family on a Sunday afternoon steamboat ride to Štěchovice. It was one of their last days of normal life together, and Hannah was grateful that Oskar had handed his camera to a fellow passenger to capture the moment for them. She often studied their faces in the photo to see if there were any clues that her parents or grandparents knew what lay ahead.

The Ältestenrat included a list of items they recommended for setting up their new homes: blankets, pots, books. No more than one hundred kilograms.

Oskar stared down at the floor for a moment, then lifted his head with a stiff grin. "Let's bid farewell to the apartment," he said, embracing Hannah as they took a final look into the living room, where their few belongings would remain, including Oma Minna's periwinkle velvet love seat. Hannah's eyes burned as she remembered afternoons resting her head on her grandmother's lap while the two read their novels and listened to the Ježek Orchestra on the gramophone. "You were a good home to us," Oskar called out before he returned his gaze to Hannah. "It's time. The war will end soon now that America has joined the Allies. We'll be safe in Theresienstadt. You'll see."

Days earlier, Oskar had handed over the key to their apartment and exchanged the last of their stashed jewelry to purchase a cottage by the lake in Theresienstadt. "It's a settlement for veterans and the elderly. Other prominent Jews too," Oskar had assured her, winking. "You're lucky your old opa was a *Jäger* for the Imperial German Army." He mimed lifting a rifle and shooting. "I gave a good hip for Germany. The least they should do is keep us safe during this war."

When Hannah told Paní Božiková that she and her grandfather had received a transport notice, her employer kissed her forehead and offered to take her in. "I know people," she whispered. "We will say you're my niece. I can get a birth certificate for a girl your age." Oskar would hear nothing of it.

Hannah slipped on her knit gloves as Oskar switched off the light and closed the door behind them. They showed the trolley driver their special pass for Jews to ride to Veletržní palác, where they had been instructed to congregate before sunrise. The SS wanted the transport of one thousand Jews out of Prague before workers started their morning commutes and children began their school day. There was no need to alarm citizens with the sight of the expulsion of their neighbors.

Hannah felt a pinch in her shoulder as she lugged her valise, so she alternated her grip with every block but wound up accidentally knocking into her legs with the brass edge bracket of the suitcase. She was grateful that her mother was a good fifteen centimeters taller than Hannah, because Ingrid's old coat reached below her shins, protecting her from the strikes.

Panting as she walked, Hannah's lungs burned, and her face felt slapped by the winter wind. She had seen the gray block building of Veletržní palác from several streets away, but when she and Oskar turned the corner, Hannah slowed at the sight on the sidewalk—a Milky Way of yellow *Judensterne* patches sewn onto hundreds of coats.

Hannah swallowed hard when she saw dozens of Czech gendarmes lining the sidewalk, rifles slung across their chests.

"Why are they armed?" Hannah asked.

"For everyone's safety, *Mausi*."

Oskar glanced at his watch and shook his head at the sight of faces he recognized from the synagogue and veterans' club. "Twenty minutes until five, and we Germans are all here with our trunks and carts packed and ready to go. Meanwhile, every Czech Jew with a transport notice is still reading the morning newspaper," Oskar said, loud enough for others to join in.

"In their nightdresses, no doubt!" shouted Herr Müller, the kosher butcher, before making his way toward Oskar to pat him on the back.

Spotting instrument cases, Oskar continued. "They say some musicians from the Prague Symphony Orchestra will join us at Theresienstadt. My Hannah will finish the war with a PhD in music appreciation."

Hannah was embarrassed by the spectacle. Why did her grandfather always appoint himself the person to spread cheer among crowds? No matter where they were—at temple, the Fair of St. Matthew, concerts—Oskar seemed to need to make a show of his gaiety.

Just before five o'clock, the crowd became dense. The transport was composed of mostly elderly men and women, but their younger relatives also lined the sidewalk with luggage. A few dozen children clutched the hands of their parents, clinging to stuffed dolls. Nearly all were Czech Jews, but like Hannah and Oskar, there were clusters of German-born Jews who had immigrated to Prague. Hannah recognized Cantor Fein from the temple and wasn't surprised to see his fingers curled around the handle of his cello case. Peeking out from a young man's burlap sack were slim wooden brushes bespattered with dried oil paint. Hannah had packed only two books: *The Magic Mountain* and *Berlin Alexanderplatz*. Oskar promised that Theresienstadt had an extensive library for residents.

Despite the thick layers of clothing people had bundled themselves in, Hannah could see that bodies were rigid with apprehension, faces engraved with worry. They seemed to wonder: *Are we really going to a spa town, or are they sending us to a labor camp in the east?* At least these were Hannah's questions. There were so many rumors that it was hard to know what to believe.

An old man called out to a younger one in a green uniform. "Tomáš! Tomáš, it's Pan Getzl from the conservatory. Over here!"

The gendarme stretched his neck and scanned the crowd. Hannah saw Tomáš's eyes spark with recognition, then quickly turn away.

Another gendarme with salted hair peeking from beneath his cap appeared before them and snatched Oskar's set of transport papers. He held them up to the light of the streetlamp, then nodded before continuing. "Identification."

Oskar handed over their burgundy canvas German passports, and Hannah looked away, praying the gendarme would not inspect hers too closely. She watched as he opened it, then flipped through the typed pages on his clipboard. "Kaufman, Kaufman. There you are. Hmm, my records show Oskar and Wilhelmina Kaufman as married sixty-six- and sixty-year-old Jews living at Number Thirteen Karpfengasse." He shook his head and continued. "She's your *wife*?"

"There must be a mistake. She's my granddaughter, *Hannah* Kaufman, and she is clearly not sixty years old." He'd been gone from Germany for six years, but Oskar could still muster a tone of indignation that said, *You people, so disorganized.*

A typed transport letter with Oskar and Minna's names had been slipped under the door by the Ältestenrat four nights earlier. Hannah had begged Oskar to report to the headquarters of the Jewish council in the morning and show them Oma's death certificate the family had mailed. Oskar snapped, "I couldn't get us out of Czechoslovakia with all my connections, but you think you can do it alone? Please, Harry Houdini, tell me how you plan to escape the Nazis?"

Oma Minna had been traveling under Hannah's identity, so her last gift to Hannah was priceless: a document declaring Hannah Kaufman dead. According to the SS records, Minna Kaufman was sixty years old, so they would pass right over Hannah during their search for the missing old woman. Hannah could stay behind in Prague and live with Paní Božiková until she could make her way to Palestine.

When Oskar refused, Hannah's guilt set in like a stain. How could she abandon her opa? Maybe he was right and Theresienstadt would be a decent place to be as the war wound down. "Six months," he'd promised. "The war won't last. You'll see."

The gendarme studied Hannah's young form. When he leaned in close, Hannah could smell years of tobacco on his breath. "I don't know who this girl is, but she's not Wilhelmina Kaufman," he said. After his eyes scanned the crowd, the man stepped closer and whispered, "Between our four eyes, if I were her, I'd tear off the yellow star and walk away right now."

Oskar narrowed his eyes at the gendarme. "Thank you for your concern, but no one is taking my granddaughter's spot at the spa town."

The gendarme shook his head and shrugged. He then penciled a check mark next to Minna's name. "Have it your way. Just be ready to walk to the train station in ten minutes," he said, pointing to lines forming on the sidewalk. "We need you people on board by six."

Once the mass of Jews was led to the train station blocks away, even Oskar couldn't mask his shock at what awaited them. Instead of a sleek commuter engine, a dozen rickety wooden cars for livestock lined the tracks. When the gendarmes slid open the door to the stock car and pointed inside to a space large enough for no more than eight horses, Rabbi Horowitz from the Maisel Synagogue spoke up. "There's only one bench in each compartment."

The gendarme whisked past him, saying nothing.

"Did you hear me, young man? This is inhumane!"

Another gendarme turned to the rabbi and said sheepishly, "It's a short ride."

The tendons in Oskar's neck tensed when he reminded Hannah that Terezín was only sixty kilometers north of Prague. "We'll sit on my bag."

Hannah gripped her suitcase strap with both hands and grunted as she tried to lift it into the train compartment. The luggage scraped the skin from Hannah's shin before dropping onto her foot.

"Watch it," a fellow passenger's voice clipped from behind Hannah.

Oskar bent to lift the suitcase, struggling for balance before steadying himself. "You go inside, *Mausi*," Oskar said, face reddening as he pulled the suitcase to his belly, then hoisted it to the edge of the boxcar opening. Finally, Oskar pushed it inside, where Hannah grabbed it.

"Stand it up!" said the man next to her.

"Don't lie it flat like that!" said another passenger.

Hannah wanted to shout at them to stop pestering Oskar. Given his state, he had just performed a miracle.

Once the allotted ninety people had been herded into the car, the passengers were so densely packed that Hannah felt an old man's beard on her forehead, and she could smell his metallic odor. Someone's shoulder forced Hannah to lean her head to the right. A little girl clinging to a baby doll wet herself, and Hannah knew that the stink of urine would soon fill the car. Hannah turned to face the opening of the compartment, dreading its closure but preferring to stare at the wooden door when it shut instead of the jigsaw puzzle of humanity inside.

A gendarme shouted to another, "There's room for two more!"

"There's room for *no* more!" Oskar grizzled as he struggled to turn his head to meet the gendarme's eye.

"I bet you people can squeeze a little tighter," the young man taunted, pointing his rifle at Oskar and poking the tip into his stomach.

All Hannah's nebulous worries solidified to acute terror. The slivers of space between people disappeared, and the bodies lined like matchsticks in a box.

"Meh, it's fine, *Mausi*," her grandfather whispered. "See how everyone worked together to make room? We'll all look out for one another. You'll see."

She nodded, knowing Oskar needed to believe that he was comforting her.

He managed a chuckle. "We Jews have been through worse than this."

When Hannah turned to look outside, she saw two men running toward the car. They were like twins separated by twenty years, both wearing corduroy pants and matching tweed caps. A father and son, Hannah guessed. As they got closer, Hannah recognized the younger of the set. "Pavel?" she called out to the man who looked like her former schoolmate. "Pavel, is that you?"

Pavel Černý and his father, Alois, were the first to jump from the wooden train car at Bauschowitz station, just outside Terezín. They planted themselves on the ground on each side of the door, and Pavel offered his muscular arm for the elderly passengers to hold like a rail. Pavel lifted Oskar's duffel bag onto his shoulder, and Oskar and Alois helped a group of men load blanket rolls and stuffed pillowcases onto a large wooden mule cart. Hannah didn't know where it had come from, but the men seemed grateful for the acquisition.

Despite their circumstances, Pavel held himself with his usual confidence, removing his cap and shaking his flop of blond waves from his eyes rakishly. From the day Hannah first spotted Pavel in *Gymnázium*, she could tell he was the sort of person who'd grown accustomed to life going his way. It always had, and it seemed he couldn't imagine otherwise. He was square-jawed and athletic, and the world typically yielded to the desires of his type. Pavel greeted classmates with a nod of his chin, which Hannah initially mistook for arrogance. Later, as they became friends, she understood that Pavel had simply internalized a sense that the world was rooting for him, a harmless enough assumption that had been bolstered by years of the world, in fact, rooting for him. Even now, when his own nation had betrayed him, Pavel carried himself with the assuredness of someone who knew he would always come out on top. It was no wonder he and her best friend Míša had gravitated toward each other. They were both the sort of people that others stepped aside for, while Hannah had always been the one to move out of the way, praying she wasn't a bother. When anyone accidentally bumped into Hannah, it was she who rushed to apologize.

"Hey, Hannah, wait for me, and I'll help with your bags," he promised.

Oskar accepted the offer on his granddaughter's behalf. Hannah wondered how difficult it had been for Pavel not to flinch when he first saw her face in the cattle car. Míša must have mentioned that Hannah's cheeks had been scarred from her bout of smallpox a year earlier. Still, seeing her mottled skin was a different story. Hannah was thankful that Pavel had been able to mask his reaction.

Oskar leaned closer to Hannah and whispered, "Is that the boy you and Míša went to school with?" His breath formed a fog of chill.

Hannah confirmed with a discrete nod. Pavel had been in his third year of *Gymnázium* when Hannah and Míša started at the high school. He was active in organizing student protests against the National Socialist Party. Although Míša's interest in revolution was sparked by her desire to spend time writing speeches and distributing pamphlets with Pavel, she soon became a student leader in her own right. Before the Nazis shuttered Czech universities, Pavel had been able to attend Charles University for one year, and Hannah and Míša often visited him when their high school classes ended for the day. Hannah had dreamt of attending Charles University to study archaeology. She imagined Míša carrying a stack of political science books to meet her at Albertov, where she would be examining minerals that she might encounter on digs. If Hitler hadn't marched into Czechoslovakia, the young women would be in their second year at university now. Pavel would be out in the working world, maybe employed in the parliament, perhaps aspiring to become a minister of interior affairs himself someday.

When Hannah last saw Míša three weeks earlier, her friend told her that she and Pavel had sneaked out after curfew and chalked the sidewalk with one word she hoped would lift the spirits of her fellow Czechs: *Svoboda!* Freedom! Hannah gripped Míša's shoulders and begged her not to take such a foolish risk again. "You'll be arrested. It's not worth it," Hannah implored.

Míša had also confessed that she and Pavel had come torturously close to having sex recently. "If my father hadn't come home early, *pfft*, I know it would have happened," she confided.

Five days later, when Hannah knocked on Míša's door so the two could go to the market during Jewish shopping hours, there was no answer. A neighbor told Hannah that Míša and her parents had left earlier that week but had no other information. Hannah knew that Míša's father was trying to get the family to Shanghai, but the three of them wouldn't have left without trying to say goodbye.

On the transport to Terezín, Pavel told Hannah that he hadn't heard from Míša either. Hannah hoped the family was in hiding somewhere safe. A teacher once explained to the girls that if the earth stopped spinning, people would be flung into space. This was how Hannah's new reality felt: those she loved just disappeared without warning, out there somewhere.

As the deportees walked from the Bauschowitz train station toward Theresienstadt, Oskar continued. "That's the boy Míša's sweet on, isn't it?"

"Shush, Opa!" Hannah snapped, trying to shield her best friend from the embarrassment of Oskar's loose tongue. If she no longer cared about Míša's secrets, it would feel as though she had given up on finding her.

Oskar shook his head. "He can't hear a word I'm saying."

Hannah's eyes shot toward Pavel, who was smiling as he walked. He and everyone around them had heard Oskar's blustering voice. Now beside his son, Alois elbowed Pavel as if to tell him he'd told him as much. It was odd, Hannah thought, how people could think about romantic love even as they marched toward the ominous unknown. Was it a frivolous distraction or emotional salvation? Hannah had no idea.

The curved road through the town of Terezín was covered

in cobblestones, though years of wear had displaced some of the bricks and left only black soil beneath. Small shops with pitched roofs lined the street: a tavern, an inn, a livestock feed shop. Hannah stepped gingerly, careful not to dampen her leather boots with the freshly melted snow covering the ground. Her fingers wrapped tightly around the handle of her suitcase. Strapped to her back was a stuffed bundle, bound together with rope, that was too heavy for the elderly woman beside her to carry. Signposts offered directions to other streets in Terezín, but the sea of one thousand people flowed in the same direction, passing spindly trees and electrical poles sparsely lining the road. With a shiver, Hannah pulled down her hat to cover her ears.

In the distance, Hannah watched a fortress come into focus— brick walls, barred windows, and an arched gateway. Czech gendarmes surrounded the perimeter, feet planted on the ground, rifles strapped across their chests, motionless and uniform. When the road ended, three kilometers from the Bauschowitz train station, Hannah could see that the walls of the fortress were equipped with gun embrasures, and barbed wire lined the top of the entrance.

The group narrowed to pass over a bridge covering a deep moat. Hannah took note of the height of the brick walls below.

"Nine hundred sixty acres, an eight-point star from a bird's-eye view," Pavel said. He explained that Emperor Joseph II of Austria built Terezín in 1790 as a holiday resort for Czech nobility and named the fortress after his mother, Empress Maria Theresa.

They made their way to the other side of the moat, and a chill rushed through Hannah's body as she read the words above the entrance—ARBEIT MACHT FREI.

Work sets you free? Oskar hadn't said anything about work. Was this a labor camp? And weren't they already free?

The group was instructed to leave their luggage at a two-story building with garage doors lifted open that revealed a vast space that appeared to span the entire ground floor. A young gendarme told the new arrivals that their belongings would be *processed* and delivered to their residences. A dozen pale, disheveled men emerged from the building and began moving the bags inside.

A raspy male voice protested. "I can carry my own suitcase."

Oskar called out jovially, "Where was this concierge service when we got off the train?" He looked at the others for affirmation. *Am I right or what?* No one laughed, though, and Oskar looked at his feet, embarrassed. "We'll be all right, *Mausi*," he said, his vigorous nodding only making Hannah more anxious.

Two gendarmes passed the building and eyed the suitcases being swallowed into the open doorway. "It's a good day at the *Schleuse*," one said, rubbing his gloved hands for warmth.

The sluice?

Hannah stood on her toes and lifted her chin, shifting her weight from side to side, hoping to catch a glimpse at what was happening inside. What she would give to be tall like her mother right now.

A row of male bodies hunched over open suitcases, fingering through the contents and plucking out items. Lace and fur were placed in crates on the ground underneath the tables. In the corner, a mound of silver grew as a crookbacked man tossed a picture frame into the pile.

"Pavel," Hannah said, her voice trembling. "Stay with me."

He grabbed her hand, then turned to look for Alois and Oskar. The older men were being slowly absorbed into the sea of bodies, heads covered in wool hats and babushkas. "Papa! Herr Kaufman!" Pavel called out when he spotted them. "Hey, let's stay together!"

They took in their unwelcoming surroundings, eyes flicking about with fear. Spa towns weren't filled with decaying barracks, nor did they smell like mildew and sweat.

A stiff gendarme pointed forward and shouted, "*Dělejte, honem!*" *Hurry along!* Three others, who looked younger than Hannah and Pavel, then led the new arrivals to the public square they called the *Marktplatz*, an open area surrounded by a municipal building, a church, and about a dozen two- and three-story barracks in various states of disrepair. Some were smaller and looked like apartment buildings with twenty or so units. Three were sprawling blocks that looked like dormitories in dismal shades like mushroom and phlegm.

They kept walking, the ground covered in a thin layer of slush.

Oskar smiled broadly, though Hannah could see him fidgeting, tapping his fingers against his legs. "Don't worry, *Mausi*. We've got a waterfront cottage."

Hannah bristled. There was no sign of any lake, and the Ohře River flowed outside the walls of Theresienstadt.

At the center of the *Marktplatz*, a man with a doughy face and round black eyeglass frames stood on a wooden crate, coaxing the crowd to gather around him for an announcement. He wore a black peacoat with a yellow star. "Welcome friends. I am Jakob Edelstein. I've just been appointed chairman of the Council of

Jewish Elders of the Theresienstadt settlement. Our first group of residents arrived two weeks ago. You are the second." His eyes shot toward the six men in SS uniforms observing the intake, then swallowed hard before finishing, "Theresienstadt is... It's Hitler's gift to our people."

"Pavel?" Hannah whispered. "Opa purchased a cottage by the lake, but... There's no lake here, is there?"

"No, my friend," Pavel returned. "I doubt there's a lake. Or cottages."

Between the buildings surrounding the square, Hannah could see more barracks behind.

"Eleven barracks in all," Edelstein told the group.

"Barracks?" someone shouted, while others murmured similar questions.

"*Housing*," Edelstein corrected himself.

Hannah rubbed her gloved hands together and tented them over her nose and mouth, exhaling warm breath. Nothing helped the chill that crept under her sleeves and penetrated her skin like a blade. Her feet were covered in wool socks and sheepskin-lined leather boots, but the tips of her toes stung.

Clustered in front of Hannah, dozens of knit caps, fedoras, and babushkas tilted upward to watch Edelstein. It wasn't as though they looked to him as a leader or even trusted him. Rather, he seemed to be the only one among them with answers about the wretched place they had landed. When Hannah turned to look behind her, she saw the faces of hundreds of more people, some creased with apprehension, others clenched in terror. The handful of elders with vacant eyes troubled Hannah the most. Their jaws hung loose as if it was too much trouble to open or close their mouths. They were neither listening nor horrified. Hannah couldn't tell if they understood what was happening.

She felt the jostling of a few others from the back of the crowd who were jockeying for a better position to hear Edelstein. A woman shorter than Hannah looked at Edelstein standing on his crate and muttered, "I can't hear a word he's saying."

Hannah grabbed Pavel's hand and reached for Oskar's so they would not be separated in the crowd, a horseshoe around Edelstein's wooden box.

Focusing on Edelstein again, watching his eyes move from the new arrivals to the SS officers surrounding them, Hannah squeezed Pavel's palm. They glanced at each other, taking in the dozen men in blue police hats and jackets, yellow *Judensterne* sewn onto the left side.

Edelstein gestured to the line of men. "The Ghettowache, our own Jewish police force, lives here in the…the settlement to keep us safe," he explained to the group. He told them that Jewish police officers patrolled the interior of Theresienstadt.

"And outside, many of you saw the Czech gendarmes." He swallowed again. "The gendarmes patrol the perimeter to ensure that no one comes in to harm us. And," Edelstein paused, "to make sure we don't…um, wander off into town where it isn't safe for…us."

"Moment," a man's voice called out from somewhere in the back. "We can't leave?"

Others grumbled, their words unintelligible. People spoke over one another, mostly Czech, but Hannah could hear clips of German and Yiddish from people like her—Germans whose families had immigrated to Czechoslovakia years earlier, thinking they would be safe from Nazi rule. Their questions were all the same: *We cannot leave? Is that right? Are we prisoners?*

She felt her body trembling, then turned toward Oskar, who was listening intently. He must have noticed his granddaughter's glare and gave her a shrug. "Who would want to leave a Jewish settlement in the middle of a war?"

"The *middle*?" she bit back. "The war began more than two years ago!"

Oskar shook his head and huffed a laugh, dismissing Hannah's rebuke. "Just like my Minna, parsing every word. You both should have been jurists," he said, placing his hand on Hannah's shoulder. "*During* a war, *during*, not the middle. Are you happy? America has joined the Allies. Hitler will be finished in six months. You'll see."

Maybe Oskar was right. She tried to remember what Oma Minna always advised her about listening to her elders: *Sometimes we* alte kakers *know a thing or two.*

Edelstein was now instructing residents to line up at one of the two dozen tables stretched across the *Marktplatz*. "You will get a housing assignment, and"—he looked down—"and if you brought money, we will exchange it for Theresienstadt currency."

Before Hannah could respond, a man's voice barked. "I bought a cottage on the lake. Where are those?"

Hannah raised her eyebrow at Oskar skeptically. "We'll be fine," he assured her with a pat on her head. "They told me it would take another week or two to finish our cottage. Until then…" He shrugged. "Meh, we'll stay somewhere else."

After glancing at the SS officer closest to him, Edelstein

straightened his back and cleared his throat again. "Today, the *Judenrat* will assess your skills and assign you work detail. You will also be given a postcard to send to your family, to let them know you are safe and happy at Theresienstadt. Once you hand in your postcard, you may get in line for bread."

"Hannah," she heard Oskar whisper. "I'm going with Pavel and Alois to see about work. I overheard someone say the men who do manual labor get more rations."

"Manual labor?" Hannah shook her head. "You can't do manual labor with that hip."

"My hip, my belly." Oskar shrugged. "Meh, today I choose my belly. We'll meet right back at this spot for lunch. We'll tell each other about our new jobs."

Look for a madhouse. You'll fit right in, she thought, immediately regretting her impatience. She knew his brave face was partly for her benefit. Hannah could hear Oma Minna's voice chide her gently. *Let Opa be Opa and Hannah can be Hannah. I don't want any changes to my two favorite people.*

Hannah waited outside in a single line for over an hour, arms folded, rocking on her feet from front to back. She sensed that the SS men overseeing the intake process would reprimand her for jumping in place to warm herself.

A frail woman at the folding table motioned for Hannah to step forward and asked for her last name. "Kaufman," Hannah replied.

"Wilhelmina Kaufman?"

"No, I'm… The paperwork is wrong. I'm *Hannah* Kaufman."

The woman nodded her head, incredulous at the error. "Stupid Nazis," she grumbled, barely audible. "You're in the

Dresden Barracks for women. First, head to the Magdeburg Barracks for your work assignment."

"Oh…um, I thought I would live with my opa."

The woman opened her mouth to speak, then decided against it.

Hannah's eyes began to glisten, but she quickly steeled herself.

"Don't forget your transport number."

Knowing that she was L-939, one of a thousand people on transport L, would be important during her time at Theresienstadt. The woman pointed toward the Magdeburg Barracks, which was past the church, then down the next block. Her head was covered with only a thin scarf, and bare fingers wrapped around a pen. Hannah noticed that the woman's knuckles were swollen and wondered if the condition developed at Theresienstadt or if she had gout before she arrived. The woman then gripped a rubber stamp, pressed it onto her red ink pad, and marked Hannah's identification papers. "Next!"

———◇———

Hannah's stomach grumbled as she waited her turn in another line, this one to meet with a member of the Council of Elders who would place her in a job. Seven men sat at children's school desks in the stone-walled cellar of the Magdeburg Barracks and were responsible for interviewing the thousand transports who arrived that morning. Hannah could only see a back view of the new arrivals, arms gesticulating wildly with questions. As for the men of the council, Hannah watched their faces for clues, but they revealed little. They appeared sympathetic but also exhausted by their burden.

Finally, Hannah made her way to a metal chair, where she sat, then immediately leaned close to the man across the table and whispered, "This place… Is this a ghetto?"

He looked like a turtle to Hannah: his bald head sinking into his round shoulders. "Theresienstadt is Hitler's gift to us," he said flatly before his eyes darted toward the officers standing at the door.

"Is it a gift we can return? If my opa and I want to leave…" She trailed off as she noticed a woman in the next chair turn to hear the answer.

The man looked down at Hannah's paper. "What was your work in Prague?"

"I was a student. Just *Gymnázium*, but I planned on studying archaeology at university."

He looked uninterested. "Can you sew?"

"I cook," Hannah offered.

"You and every other woman here. What languages do you speak?"

"German and Czech." Hannah glanced at the two SS officers, one of whom was now offering the other a cigarette from a silver box. "I know Hebrew too." Hannah smiled stiffly and tried to whisper without moving her lips. "Please help me. I need to know if—"

The man interrupted swiftly. "You can read Hebrew? How is your penmanship?"

"My penmanship?"

"The SS is making a museum of Jewish culture in Prague, and they have a workshop here. They need girls with nice handwriting to create tomes for display since so many were destroyed in…you know, the troubles." He slid a piece of paper and a pen toward her.

This baffled Hannah. Why would the SS have encouraged the Kristallnacht riots that burned synagogues and ravaged ancient Torahs, then replace them all? And why in the world would they build a Jewish museum when they planned to deport Jews to other lands?

After writing the alphabet and several words from a booklet, Hannah looked up. "Can you at least tell me if we're safe here? Is this a labor camp or a ghetto? Where are we?"

The man smiled ruefully as his eyes traveled to the back of the room where the SS men were smoking. "You are very fortunate to be at Theresienstadt. We are treated well and have everything we need in our self-governed settlement."

At the sound of the man's stilted delivery, Hannah was unable to hold back tears. She lifted the cuff of her coat sleeve and wiped her cheeks, feeling the scratch of wool against her face.

"Report to work at the museum at seven tomorrow morning."

Her lips formed a straight line as she fought back more tears. Hannah nodded in agreement, though her breath sputtered. "Seven. All right."

He handed Hannah a tin mug and told her to bring it with her to meals.

He then looked at her with mournful eyes and beckoned her close with the pull of his index finger and whispered, "*Gam zeh ya'avor*, my sweet." *This too shall pass.*

Oskar didn't show up to the meeting spot, but Pavel hurried toward Hannah. "Your opa's fine. He's in the Magdeburg Barracks with me and my cousin Luděk, who I just found out is here. Anyway, your opa doesn't have to work because of his age, but he's talking to Jakob Edelstein right now, trying to get himself a spot on the leisure time committee. He says he'll find you later."

Pavel went on to tell Hannah that he was chosen to join Luděk on a new work project: an extension of railroad tracks from the station at Bauschowitz directly into Theresienstadt. Other men had been assigned to work in the carpentry shop, where they would build everything from kitchen cabinets to dining room furniture. About a dozen women were selected for *Glimmerwerke*, cutting mica stones into slivers. He explained, "The girls who work there call it the glimmer factory because of how mica sparkles."

"Why do we need mica?" Hannah asked.

Looking away from Hannah, Pavel hesitated. "They're… it's not for us. The furniture and cabinets aren't for us either. Everything we make here is for the war effort. The Nazis will use it or sell it to fund the war."

Prisoners also made boots, saltshakers, fountain pens, inkwells, and lampshades. Some women were assigned to the tailor shop, where they sewed Wehrmacht uniforms and women's dresses. Artists worked making maps and propaganda for the Nazis. Doctors and nurses would have plenty to do at the ghetto hospital. The luckiest of the prisoners were cooks or kitchen workers, since they could steal food.

"Luděk says the ghetto gelt is worthless. Food is the most valuable form of currency."

Most valuable? "There are others?"

"Cigarettes and…nothing a nice girl like you needs to know about."

Then, quick as Pavel arrived, he caught sight of a Ghettowache officer watching the conversation. "Be careful of them. They're

Jews, but they're not like us." Noticing Hannah's confused expression, Pavel explained. "You give some guys extra rations and a badge, and they forget who they are." He bent down to bring his face closer to Hannah's and whispered, "But Luděk told me he's part of a...a *group*. You know what I mean."

A resistance group? Hannah asked silently with the raise of her eyebrows.

Pavel nodded to confirm.

"I don't think..." Hannah trailed off before she could finish the thought. Pavel should have known better than to tell her that. They'd been friends for nearly four years, and Hannah had never taken part in any of their rabble-rousing. She often thought Míša and Pavel's activities were foolhardy and told them so, though she sometimes secretly admired their courage. Still, she wanted no part of their group.

———◇———

That night after a meal of radishes in potato broth, Hannah's new home became the third floor of the Dresden Barracks for women and mothers with young children. Constructed with unfinished timber, triple-decker bunk beds were arranged in two configurations: most jutted from dormitory walls like the teeth of a comb; others were flush against walls. Hannah shared a stall-like area with five other women and the little girl who had peed herself in the cattle car. Between their two bunk beds was a small, open space where the women could change clothes or brush their hair. The six women, all of whom arrived in Theresienstadt on the transport that day, decided that it would be safer for the mother and daughter to share a bottom bunk.

Olina Vyštejnová was a Jewish woman whose Christian husband divorced her, leaving both his wife and their four-year-old daughter, Danuše, who under the new Nazi race laws was classified as a *Mischling*. He abandoned them in their hometown of Telč after the Nazis gave gentiles the choice to divorce their Jewish spouses or risk sharing their fates.

The other bottom bunk went to Klara Schneider, a grouchy old woman who said she was afraid of heights. Like Hannah, she was a German Jew who had immigrated to Czechoslovakia. "Mistake," she bristled. "I should have gone to England like my brother and his wife."

Hannah was relieved that the others agreed to let her have a third-level bunk. It would mean climbing down a ladder every morning, but there was a bit of privacy. Just below her was Friedl Dicker-Brandeis, a Viennese artist who had been assigned to work with the children.

In the bunk directly across from Hannah's was Iveta Čapková, a Czech teen with a thick mane of chestnut hair that Hannah could imagine capped with a floral crown, tresses spilling onto her red *kroj*. The girl reached into an orange purse that looked as though she had crocheted it herself, the stitches clumped in spots and the strap sewn on with black thread. Iveta retrieved a photo of a boy in swim trunks and bathing cap.

"Your sweetheart?" Hannah asked her in Czech.

The flush of red was Iveta's confirmation. "Vladislav. My mother disapproves," she said with a smile. "She thinks I'm still a baby." Iveta explained that her mother was a nurse and lived on the first floor of the barracks. "I can't see why we were separated. My father and brother are together at the Hanover Barracks."

Beneath Iveta lived Alice Herz-Sommer, a Czech pianist who others whispered was famous. She had a little boy only a bit older than Danuše, but he had been assigned to the boy's house. Her suitcase was half-filled with sheet music and she smiled impishly, saying, "Where there is music, it cannot be so terrible."

Fifteen hours earlier, Hannah had awakened in a sleigh bed in Prague. Now she lay on a pallet with a hay-stuffed mattress and a coarse blanket she'd been issued in the barracks. Unlike the satin duvet that gently enveloped Hannah at home, this was practically stiff across her body, allowing the winter chill to work its way underneath. She curled into a fetal position and exhaled into the collar of her nightdress for warmth.

The ceiling hovered above, too close. When she slapped a bug on her arm, Hannah accidentally bumped her elbow into the wall, causing insects to rain from the ceiling. Spitting them from her mouth, Hannah tried to hold back tears, but her eyes and nose were prickling uncontrollably.

Hannah heard a woman in a nearby stall sniffle. Another bleated like a lamb until the whimpering spread like wildfire. Olina sounded as though she was gathering her strength before she eked out a lullaby in a thready soprano for her little Danuše.

Hannah held her hands over her ears as tears escaped from her eyes. The tenderness was unbearable.

5

Hilde

Berlin
December 1941

LIFE HAD NEVER BEEN KIND TO HILDE, BUT SHE WAS BEGIN-
ning to feel as though she'd been cursed. Since her arrival in
Berlin that summer six months earlier, Hilde had visited every
office of the Reich in the city at least twice. She wrapped her
hands around the gate bars at the Ministry of Aviation and called
out until an officer emerged from the building. Realizing the
stance made her look like a prisoner in a jail cell, Hilde stepped
back and straightened her posture. "I have an appointment with
Reichsmarschall Göring," she lied.

Heart racing, Hilde silently reminded herself to breathe. *Just
get in front of Herr Göring, and you'll convince him to hire you.* She
closed her eyes, hearing the voice of her *Grundschule* teacher telling Hilde's mother, "Your daughter often speaks without thinking. I do admit her wild stories can be amusing, but she will need
to outgrow this sooner rather than later."

The officer at the ministry peered at her, hawkish.

Hilde's chest tightened with anxiety, so she rushed to fill
the silence. "I work at the Women's League," she explained

as she flashed the badge that had let her past the guard at the Frauenschaft.

This gatekeeper, however, was more cautious and shook his head as he examined Hilde's card. "The reichsmarschall is not in Berlin this week," he said through the gate. "And this badge is no good."

There was a time, before the assassination of German diplomat Ernst vom Rath three years earlier, when an officer of the Reich would have been charmed by Hilde's gumption and let a harmless girl inside. Now, though, Germany was a nation at war, and Hilde was finding the Reich nearly impenetrable.

Every morning, Hilde left Frau Schwammberger's house for a fabricated job at the Luftgaukommando. Thankfully, neither of her housemates worked for the Luftwaffe, so there were no attempts at gossipy exchanges about officemates. Before anyone could ask questions about her work, Hilde spoke first and tried to appear well versed in Reich news by reciting what she'd read in the latest edition of *Der Stürmer*:

Reichsminister Goebbels announced a winter clothing collection drive for troops on the eastern front.

Lightning victory in Soviet Union inevitable.

Anti-German terrorists apprehended in "Night and Fog" directive.

Hitler gives Czech Jews settlement in the Protectorate of Bohemia and Moravia.

Honestly, it was all a swirl of details that didn't interest Hilde. The only thing she cared about was the future Hitler promised, one where she was valued, important, and part of something noble. Until she was a teen, she had no idea she was part of the master race, but it was welcome news to her after a lifetime of feeling cast aside by just about everyone: her parents, teachers, boys. The only three people who hadn't made Hilde feel as though she should be grateful for their meager attention were gone. Max had fallen. Her sister, Lisa, had died. And Hilde's best friend left Munich after *Mittelschule* ended without so much as a goodbye. Death was understandable, but abandonment was unforgivable.

Now, Hilde was on her own and had to pry open the locked doors of the Reich administration, where they needed her, even if they didn't realize it.

Hilde's charade of employment managed to satisfy her landlady, who seemed to have no idea how her tenant really supported herself. After three humiliating months as a house cleaner, Hilde was dismissed, her boss saying that Hilde's incessant chatter made her a nerve saw. Hilde moved on to serve beer at the Zur letzten Instanz near the Ministry for Propaganda, hoping to eavesdrop on conversations that would help her land a job making films for the Reich. She heard snippets but little that proved useful.

Then there was the incident when Hilde's housemate Vilma Pfannenstiel, who worked at the Reich Chancellery, stopped in for a beer with her *Schatz* and spotted Hilde balancing a tray of *Deutsches Reichsbräu*. For the price of a silver locket, Vilma kept her mouth shut but frosted toward Hilde. Thankfully, she held up her end of the bargain and did not share her secret with Frau Schwammberger, or even Nora Rösener, the mousy little thing who also rented a room in the house and worked with Vilma at the Chancellery.

Shuttling drinks was not how Hilde imagined serving the

Reich, but anything was better than returning to her family home in Munich. When Hilde's younger sister, Lisa, died at the age of ten, her mother could have clung tighter to Hilde. They might have become close, sharing memories of the little girl they had both loved. Instead, Hilde's mother became a bitter turnip who had nothing but disdain for her middle child. Now that Hilde's brother, Kurt, had been killed in battle, Hilde's mother appeared to resent her even more. When Hilde telephoned Johanna to give her the details of Max's funeral, her mother stiffly told her that she was attending a service for a friend's son in Munich on the same day. Plus, if Hilde returned home, it would be as though her last two and a half years were spent running in a circle. She had been a valued member of the Women's League, had a love affair with a high-ranking officer, then married Max. These were steps forward, not ones that should set her in the same place she was in her last year of *Gymnasium*.

Hilde knew if she persisted, she would find her place in the National Socialist Party.

Finally, her perseverance paid off. Engel, the manager at Zur letzten Instanz, loved to bolster his own importance by dropping the names of Reich officers whenever they came in for beers. Other servers rolled their eyes, watching Engel twist himself into a pretzel trying to impress the men in uniform. Not Hilde, though. Laying her fingertips lightly on Engel's sleeve, Hilde cooed, "You know everyone, don't you?" She followed with a series of questions that left the poor dummkopf feeling flattered instead of manipulated.

When Engel pointed out the deputy director of the film department at the Ministry for Public Enlightenment and

Propaganda, Hilde watched Herr Otto Mazuw's every move for clues about how she might work her way into his life. Finally, she spotted a box of matches on his table after he lit his cigarette. Glancing down as she passed him, she read the swirling golden letters ZUR GERICHTSLAUBE, a restaurant on Poststrasse.

Hilde spent her free time parked on a bench across the street from the restaurant, pretending to wait for the tram or read the newspaper like a spy in a film. Luck was finally on her side one evening in November when she watched Herr Mazuw enter the restaurant alone. Folded newspaper in hand, Hilde walked toward the WC at the back of the restaurant and, at just the right moment, pretended to twist her ankle and fell to the ground beside Herr Mazuw's table. She felt his meaty hand on her elbow and heard him ask if she was all right. Hilde looked up with tears in her eyes. "Nothing has gone right for me today," she whimpered. "I'm sorry to disturb your meal."

Herr Mazuw shook his head and tut-tutted his sympathy. Minutes later, she was his guest at the table with a bowl of hot hasenpfeffer on its way. Herr Mazuw took the bait so easily it was a wonder Germany was winning the war.

———◇———

On her first day as a secretary to Herr Otto Mazuw, Hilde made her way up from the S-Bahn station steps, careful to avoid patches of thawing snow on the boulevard. Safely grounded on Unter den Linden, she adjusted her hat and turned up the collar of her brown mouton coat to shield herself from the wind pushing at her back.

When Hilde rounded the corner at Wilhelmstrasse, it was

as though a stage curtain opened to reveal the ministry's lime-stone palace with its embellished pediment and regal columns. Hilde grinned with satisfaction as she spotted the New Reich Chancellery across the street. *Life is good when the führer is your neighbor.* Yes, yes, she'd seen these buildings nearly every day, but now that she was part of the Reich—rather than scrapping for her place in it—she could take a moment to appreciate their grandeur. Mein Gott, *what a time to be a young German living in Berlin!*

Reaching for the iron railing of the ministry steps, Hilde pulled back her shoulders and lifted her chest before entering the building. The inside of the ministry looked even more impressive than it did on the days she had come for her interview and security clearance. She loved the sound of her boots clacking against the marble floor as she walked down the long hallway in the lobby. Two other secretaries clopped toward Hilde, already armed with files in hand. Behind her, Hilde heard two men discussing an upcoming meeting about a board game in development; she had to resist the temptation to turn and ask about it, so she just listened. A woman in a tailored suit stepped out from an office and into the hallway, nearly crashing into Hilde. The workday did not officially start for another twenty minutes, and Hilde had prided herself on being early. Now she felt as though she had arrived late.

The path to her new office was lined with painted portraits of Reich cabinet members as well as historic photos and artist renderings. Her favorite was a painting of the famous Beer Hall Putsch in her hometown of Munich nearly twenty years earlier, Herr Hitler's first attempt to save Germany from hyperinflation and the impotent Weimar Republic. A fresh-faced Adolf Hitler was perched on a stump, red Hakenkreuz flag behind him as he leaned forward in earnest, speaking to a few dozen men seated in wooden chairs. The artist illuminated young Adolf and bedimmed the faces of the others for a messianic effect.

Those who dismissed Hitler's uprising as a ragtag insurrection weren't laughing anymore.

She didn't want to look like a newcomer at the ministry, so Hilde masked her giddy smile at the photo of the führer as a younger man. Beside it was a revamped front page of the notoriously liberal—and now defunct—*Berliner Tageblatt*, its headline proclaiming Germany the victors of the Great War. *How clever*, she thought. *Frankly, we did win the war. It was the backstabbing Jews and their lying news, the* Lügenpresse, *that really lost the Great War, not Germany.*

Hilde saw the words "Department of Film" painted onto the smoked glass window of the office door. She turned the brass knob and entered to find a woman about her age sitting at a reception desk. "You must be Hilde," she said eagerly. "I'm Susanna Röthke. Looks like we're working together."

What the hell? "*Ja, ja.*" Hilde nodded, as politely as she could muster. She hadn't realized there would be another secretary at the office. The last thing she needed was another young woman trying to climb the ranks of the Reich. Herr Mazuw had told Hilde she would be replacing a young woman named Erna who left to start a family. "*Ja*, I work for Herr Mazuw."

"I do too, silly," Susanna replied with a hiccup laugh. "Here, let me show you where you sit." She glided from behind her desk like a dancer instead of a secretary for a nation at war. Even the way her belted plaid dress swung as she moved seemed frivolous given the seriousness of their work.

Waving her arm across the room, Hilde asked, "Is it just us?"

Susanna pointed to the closed doors of three private offices and replied, "Out here in the reception area, yes, but the others are here when they're not out shooting."

Hilde squinted her eyes to read the name on the door in the far corner. "Leni Riefenstahl?" She fought to keep her composure but wanted to flutter her hands and jump like a little girl. All her rejection and humiliation would be worth it if it led her to the doorstep of *the* Leni Riefenstahl. Imagine if she groomed Hilde to be the next great filmmaker of the Third Reich?

"She hardly comes into the office," Susanna said with a shrug.

It was beyond Hilde's comprehension how anyone could say those words with such indifference. At least Hilde wouldn't have a competitor in this girl. "Susanna, what kind of films are we working on now?"

Walking Hilde to her station, Susanna let out another of her hiccup giggles. "Oh, we don't work on the films. We type letters and set appointments for Herr Mazuw."

Hilde pressed a smile at the young woman, a pretty face as dumb as a bean straw. How in the world did she land a job here when Hilde had to try every trick in the book? "Are you... Does your father work for the Reich?"

"Did Herr Mazuw tell you that?" Susanna asked. "*Vati* oversees the cultural office. You know, emblems, architecture, music, all that."

Hilde mentally sighed in relief. This girl was no threat to Hilde. She knew these types: the ease of life with family connections weakened them. Susanna had as much ambition as a ladybug.

Hilde settled into her new seat and arranged the supplies on her desk. A stenography pad and staple gun lay beside a wire tray for papers. On a rolling metal table beside Hilde's desk was her typewriter, a brand-new Wanderer-Werke Continental, ready for her to tap out new scripts for the *Volk*. She looked out the window at snow frosting the corners of the glass panes, icing tree branches, and blanketing the lawn outside. Yes, Berlin was beautiful in the winter, but the expanse of whiteness meant something more to Hilde. It would soon be a new year and a fresh slate for her.

—◦—

What was going on with Herr Mazuw? Hilde had been working for him at the ministry for an entire week, and her supervisor had hardly said a word to her other than *Type this* or *Deliver that*. It was like being on the Bischoff farm all over again. He had seemed so interested in her ideas when they first met at Zur Gerichtslaube. Herr Mazuw had even taken notes when Hilde described her feature film idea about the sinking of the *Titanic*, placing the blame for the accident squarely on British incompetence and American arrogance. She'd even suggested a fictional character—a German engineer who happened to be a passenger—who would try to warn the captain that the *Titanic* would hit an iceberg if they sped the ship. Herr Mazuw had been so impressed.

Hilde poked the tip of a letter opener against her thumb as she ran through the events of the last five days. Had she done something to upset Herr Mazuw? Had someone from the Frauenschaft telephoned to warn her new boss about her?

"Yoo-hoo, Hilde," Susanna sang. "Is anyone home in that noggin of yours?"

Huh? "Do you need something, Susanna?"

She giggled. "I've been calling your name, but your head's somewhere else today."

No, my head is on my job, Hilde thought. She held her tongue, not because she was being kind but because she didn't want to give Susanna any ideas about taking her own work seriously.

"All right then, you've got my attention. What do you want?"

"Oh," Susanna said, her delicate eyebrows arching with surprise at Hilde's sharp tone. "I wanted to say that I like your new blouse. The blue looks pretty with your eyes."

Muffling her frustration, Hilde nodded. "Thank you," she replied. No use making enemies at work. "Yours is nice too."

Hilde returned her focus out the window, where she noticed a few brave sparrows flitting between the tree branches. She was not going to waste her time wringing her hands about Herr Mazuw. No, she would wait until Susanna left for the evening, then knock on her supervisor's door and ask if he had given any more thought to her film idea. She was twenty-one years old now; she could assert herself. Hilde had allowed the incident with Lotte at the Women's League to rattle her confidence for long enough.

Placing her palms on her desk to ground herself, Hilde closed her eyes and remembered the praise she'd received at the Frauenschaft before the incident with Werner. They called her a model worker. Hilde never simply typed memos; she offered creative input on their content. If another secretary was out for the day, Hilde jumped in to fulfill her duties. Maybe Lotte could dismiss Hilde over one little lapse in judgment, but she would never give up on herself.

Newly bolstered, Hilde waited until after seven that evening. When Herr Mazuw opened his office door to leave for the night, he looked surprised to see that Hilde had outlasted him. Loose jowls folded into his collar. What did he expect? He'd agreed that afternoon to meet with Hilde after work when she told him she had an important matter to discuss. When would people learn to take Hilde seriously?

Herr Mazuw bunched his face, pushing his walrus mustache into his nostrils. He walked to Hilde's desk, resting his palm on her upper back. She could feel the heat of his hand permeating through her office jacket, the clasp of her necklace pressing into her spine. "You wanted to talk?" he said, extending his arm toward his office. "Let's talk."

Herr Mazuw's door closed, and the latch sounded like the cocking of a gun.

He sat on his sofa and touched the spot beside him, an invitation. "You want to discuss the *Titanic* idea?"

She nodded and sat, grateful that he was so direct. It was rare that a man did not talk around the hot porridge with Hilde, so she did not interrupt.

"It's a fine concept, but I'm under pressure to make a film about Jewish settlements in the new Reich territories. Every country that refused to take in Jews is now haranguing us about rumors of their mistreatment."

Hilde relaxed as her supervisor confided in her. He hadn't

forgotten about Hilde; he was busy, that was all. "Hypocrites," she huffed, relieved to mend their connection.

"Exactly," he smirked, tapping her forehead with his index finger. "Smart girl. The Jews are doing well, as you know…as everyone knows." He looked down at his steepled fingers and asked Hilde if she'd heard of Theresienstadt. "It's a new settlement in the protectorate. Beautiful, really. There's music and culture every night of the week."

Hilde let out a light snort. "Lucky them."

"Would you care for a drink?" Herr Mazuw asked.

She nodded and looked down as he rose and stepped toward the liquor cart next to his desk. Hilde didn't want her superior to see her smile, both relieved and excited.

When Herr Mazuw handed Hilde a crystal tumbler of scotch, his eyes scanned her body. Hilde could tell that her supervisor was interested in a more intimate relationship, and she grinned internally at the power this gave her. She could string him along until he assigned her to the crew of the film. Theresienstadt. Warsaw. Łódź. Whichever settlement the department wanted to film, Hilde could play an integral part. Herr Mazuw's desire for her was Hilde's secret weapon.

She took a sip of the amber liquid and felt its warmth spread through her chest, knowing her mood would soon loosen. Hilde wished she could come up with something coy to say, but instead, she lifted her eyes and whispered, "Tell me how I can help, Herr Mazuw."

A moment passed between them, Hilde never breaking Herr Mazuw's gaze. When he moved close to kiss her, she could only muster a weak excuse, a lie at that.

"I'm sorry. I have a *Schatz*," she said, trying to sound confident but not too forceful. She couldn't afford to offend him, so she smiled broadly as she stood and stepped back.

"And I have a wife. We'll be discreet," he said, standing from the couch, then clamping his hands around Hilde's waist.

She was unprepared with a retort as he moved her back as though they were dancing a clumsy tango. What had she done? How did her offer to help on the film about the ghetto sound like an invitation to Herr Mazuw?

He lifted Hilde onto his desk and looked down toward her skirt eagerly.

"Herr Mazuw, we probably shouldn't—"

"Otto. Call me Otto when we're alone," he said, now nuzzling into her neck like a pig digging for truffles. He pushed up her skirt and then looked down, sighing at the sight of the garters holding up her stockings.

Soon, Herr Mazuw placed his hands over Hilde's and pressed them into the hard oak of the desktop. Her slivered pinkie began to throb with pain. It was odd, she thought, that she could slice into her own finger with satisfaction, but it hurt when someone else touched the same cut.

Herr Mazuw stepped back and pushed Hilde's knees apart roughly, then reached for his belt buckle, the imperial eagle in silver filigree. A moment later, Hilde heard the clank of metal as it fell and dangled from the leather belt strap.

"I don't think we should—" Hilde pled, her voice fluttering.

"Shh, no hysterics." Herr Mazuw placed his fingertip on Hilde's lips. Riesling and *Fischbrötchen* mingled in the smog of his breath.

She closed her eyes tight, hoping her supervisor would relent. Hilde knew she could only suggest they stop, not insist on it. Not if she wanted to keep the job she'd fought long and hard for. If she was dismissed from the ministry, surely her reputation would be unsalvageable. She was an insider now, part of Germany's renaissance, and she wasn't about to return to a life of invisibility.

"Maybe we should finish our drink?" Hilde made a final attempt. Then she felt it. The push of his flesh working its way into her body.

Hilde's face twisted with the pain of his penetration. She didn't want this, not in the least. But how awkward it would be to tell him that now, once he was inside her? And what exactly would she say? *Please remove your* Schwanz?

No, Hilde would keep her eyes shut and endure it. She had learned how to tolerate aggressive sex during her months with Werner. Oddly, this experience with Otto didn't remind Hilde of the obergruppenführer, her first lover. Instead, she thought about her husband, Max, the person who cared about her pleasure, her feelings. She would think of him to get through this.

Mercifully, it was over quickly. Herr Mazuw grunted and pulled himself from Hilde, then wiped his penis with a handkerchief before stuffing it back into his undershorts. She felt tarnished by Herr Mazuw's saliva on her neck. Then there was the awful mess he left inside her. He buttoned his pants and gave an approving nod. "You really are something, Hilde."

"Thank you," she said, wondering if that was the right response. Should she have told him that *he* was really something too?

An hour later, Hilde squatted in the bathtub at the boardinghouse and poured a cup of water onto her stomach and let it run down to where Herr Mazuw had been. The water barely covered her toes as Hilde did not plug the drain, wanting to make sure any evidence of the night went straight down the bathroom pipes. She couldn't clean herself quickly enough, working the soapy washcloth into her reddened flesh. Nothing could erase Herr Mazuw from her body. She looked down and saw that the insides of her thighs were spotted with a bright red rash that reminded her of the tender skin of a child who had fallen off a bicycle.

Hilde startled at the sound of her housemate Vilma shouting as she pounded on the bathroom door. "You've been in there forever! Some of us need to use the toilet."

"We have two bathrooms, dummkopf!" Hilde called back.

"Frau Schwammberger wants us to use the toilets on our own floor. Should I just come in and *pipi*?" And without a moment's notice, Hilde heard the wriggling of a hairpin in the keyhole. The door flew open too quickly for Hilde to cover up. Vilma held her hand to her chest, and her expression fell with distress. "*Scheisse*, Hilde," she whispered. "Are you all right? Your eyes... Have you been crying?"

Had she? Hilde had no idea, but she was certain that she hated the cold breeze Vilma brought in when she opened the door. Worse, she despised being seen naked like this.

Hilde unwrapped the ball of soap from her washrag and held it up as if she were going to throw it at Vilma. "Get the hell out of here before I tell Frau Schwammberger what a demented pervert you are!"

Vilma held up her hands in surrender. "Are you all right?"

"Get out!" Hilde shouted.

"Hilde." Vilma's voice was now soft with sympathy. "What happened? Were you…"

Raped? That was what Vilma was thinking, wasn't it?

"No, no, I wasn't…*that*!" Hilde shot back with fury. "My new *Schatz* is a passionate lover. I'm sorry you wouldn't know anything about that. I swear if you don't get out of here—"

"Fine, Hilde, fine," Vilma said, stepping back.

Hilde's body relaxed at the sound of the door cracking shut. There was no way Vilma or anyone else was going to pity her.

There were many ways to see most everything in this world. Hilde could have viewed the night with Herr Mazuw as her boss taking advantage of her. Or she could decide that what she told Vilma was true. She had a new boyfriend she had simply driven wild with desire. *This might have been the best thing*, Hilde told herself as she decided to plug the drain and let the water rise after all. Soon she held her breath and let her body slide down the porcelain tub until her head was fully submerged in cold water.

6

Hannah

H ANNAH WALKED OUTSIDE TOWARD THE LATRINE IN THE morning. As she stood at the back of the line, she lifted her hands to cover her mouth and nose as her stomach lurched with disgust at the stench filling the wooden hut.

"Mama," Danuše whined to her mother as she crossed her thighs. "I need to go."

"We're next," Olina assured her. "Hold it a little longer."

Before Hannah could see the child's reaction, she turned at the sound of a gasp behind her. Her bunkmate Iveta pressed her knees together and gripped the fabric of her skirt. "*Ach!*" Iveta cried, lowering her head.

"What's wrong?" Hannah asked.

"My…it's my monthly." Iveta began pulling at the seam of her skirt pocket and, after working the thread loose, was able to tear it off. When she removed the swatch, Iveta folded it into a rectangle to use as a menstrual rag. "At least I'm not…" Iveta didn't finish the thought.

Pregnant? As bad as it would be to bleed for a week

in the ghetto, Hannah could not imagine having a baby at Theresienstadt. She looked at the women around her and wondered if any were carrying children, whether they knew it or not. Hannah tried to find some words of comfort for the girl but realized the kindest thing would be to turn away and say nothing. Iveta seemed embarrassed enough already.

Finally inside, Hannah watched a woman shake her bottom over the makeshift seat, one in a long row of circular holes cut into a plank of wood that hovered above a pit. The woman's eyes searched in vain for toilet paper until she curled her lips in disgust and pulled up her underpants. The next in line hurried to take her place as soon as she stepped away.

The longest wait wasn't to use the toilets. It was the handwashing area that would slow Hannah. A dozen women stood tapping their toes restlessly as the latrine attendant spooned chlorine from a bucket into the cupped palms of a cluster of school-age girls before her. Hannah couldn't begrudge their caregiver for singing a happy song about the importance of good hygiene, but some of the women behind Hannah called out impatiently.

"I can't be late."

"We have quotas."

"Pour a separate cup for the children and take them aside."

Hannah wondered how the poor woman doling out the chlorine in the stink of the toilet room got stuck with the job.

Eating her morning bread on the way to work, Hannah reached the door of the museum workshop, where an older woman stood at the threshold, arms crossed with annoyance. "You're late." The straight line of her mouth barely opened as she delivered the reprimand. "I cannot have that in my workshop. Do you understand?"

The woman had somehow managed to find time to set her wavy silver hair and place her combs in perfectly. Even her *Judenstern* appeared bright and pressed. She wore low black heels as though she were working in the finest law office in Prague instead of as a slave laborer for the Nazis.

"I'm sorry," Hannah said, noticing that her coworkers were already at their spots on the benches, squinting through their eyeglasses and dipping pens into inkwells.

"I'm Griselde Benzbach. When the Ghettowache or gendarmes are here, address me as Frau Benzbach. Otherwise, it's Griselde."

"And the SS?"

"If the SS is here, child, don't speak at all." She extended her arm and pointed to the workstations at the far end of the room. "You're at the transcription bench. Here's your folder. Don't be late again, or we all pay the price."

Hannah focused her gaze out onto the snow carpeting the ground and frosting the chestnut tree branches outside in the *Stadtpark* across the street, one square block of nothing more than six trees jutting from the earth.

Griselde followed Hannah's eyes and explained. "I keep the shades lifted so my workers remember the beauty of the world," she said, offering a self-satisfied grin.

Hannah found the notion cruel. If the women at the museum looked out a different window, they would see police officers patrolling the ghetto. Should their eyes wander past the maple tree at the far corner of the park, they would be faced with the reality that they were trapped by ramparts and moats. Hannah wished Griselde would pull down the shades. The beauty of the world no longer belonged to them.

In the cavernous room, light bulbs hung from wires on the ceiling. The space was filled with women stationed at long wooden tables carrying out their assignments.

Hannah walked past a table filled with women polishing silver: cutlery, tea services, and empty picture frames. She suspected she would never see her family portrait again, and a soft whimper escaped through her nostrils. *They can keep the frame. I just want the photograph*, Hannah silently negotiated with God. At the end of the bench, a woman held up a serving spoon she had cleaned, inspecting her work. Her reflection was upside down in the sterling curve.

Hannah eyed an empty spot at the end of a workbench, took a seat, and opened the folder with her transport number penciled on the tab. Inside were fresh sheets of parchment along with five charred and cockled pages sliced from the Torah. She and four other women were tasked with hand-penning the holy scriptures so beautifully that the calligraphy would rival royal wedding invitations.

Klara from the Dresden Barracks worked there too and looked far better than she had the night earlier, hours after their arrival in the ghetto. She'd combed her white curls into a low bun that accentuated the roundness of her face. Adjusting her wire-rimmed eyeglasses, Klara grumbled that she couldn't wait to transcribe the plagues on Egypt. "There'll be a lot more than frogs falling from the sky, I'll tell you that." She flashed a smile that revealed a missing top bicuspid tooth.

"Because you know better than God?" a Czech woman next to her returned.

Klara looked at Hannah and muttered in their native tongue. "*Gehirnverweigererin*," she called the other woman.

The way Klara winked at Hannah when delivering the German barb reminded Hannah of the secrets she shared with her oma, though Minna would never insult someone's intelligence like that.

Klara held out her hands and swept the area like a showroom model. "I wouldn't mind giving God a few pointers right now." She turned her attention back to Hannah and, switching back to Czech, introduced the woman who had chided her. "This is Helena. No one more pious."

Helena pulled her lips to the side, her expression a resigned, *What can I tell you?* Helena Nováková had arrived on the first transport earlier that month and had glassy brown eyes with a thick red streak in the white of the right one. She sucked her teeth the same way Oma's father used to fidget with his dentures.

"And that's Alena and Petra," Klara offered, gesturing across the table at two women in their late fifties. Alena Pospíšilová's wiry black hair was held down with a red kerchief. "Alena's deaf, so make sure she's looking at your lips before you say anything to her," Klara whispered.

Hannah thought it a cruel irony that the woman who could not hear had oversize ears.

"Petra is new too," Klara said of the woman whose face was weathered like a shrunken apple doll.

"I saw you at Veletržní palác yesterday," Petra Dědinová told Hannah.

"Are you from Prague?"

She nodded. "Yes, in Vinohrady," Petra replied, brown bangs framing her face as she continued gliding her pen across the parchment like a painter. Her letters were sharp and elegant; Hannah could imagine her as a girl practicing her penmanship by candlelight long after her parents believed she was sleeping.

Helena nodded her head toward the papers on the table. "You'd better get to it. If you don't make your daily quota by the end of work, you stay late, and you don't want to miss supper at Theresienstadt."

Hannah sighed with relief. "Oh, thank goodness. It's better than breakfast then? All I got was a slice of bread."

When Helena lifted her eyes to meet Hannah's, she held both pity and envy in them. Hannah suspected she knew what the woman was thinking: *This girl has no idea.*

The sound of Hannah's pen hitting the side of her inkwell was slightly different from what Petra produced. Hannah clinked, almost as though she was trying to get the attention of dinner guests to make a toast. Klara rolled the metal pen nib around the glass rim to shake off excess ink. Hannah had never noticed people's idiosyncrasies before, but now she was aware of the way Helena cleared her throat, how Petra hummed.

Other women in the museum sorted items apparently stolen from inmates at the *Schleuse.* Two young men wheeled in large carts filled with silver scroll crowns, finials, and pointers. Later, Hannah watched women unload ornate candleholders and chalices, then catalog each item. Hannah remembered how she used to complain about what difficult work it was to polish her great-grandmother's filigree kiddush cups. If she'd only known then how perfect life really was. She wondered if the women at the sorting table ever came across their own belongings and thought about the lives torn from them, their children playfully welcoming Rosh Hashanah by holding the hollowed ram's horn on their heads before blowing into it, like Ben always had.

Hannah suspected that Obersturmbannführer Adolf Eichmann was not creating a museum of Jewish culture in Prague. The Nazis were probably melting down precious metals, plucking out jewels, and plundering the art to enrich the Reich. Or maybe they would host a traveling exhibition like the degenerate art show they had produced four years earlier. No one at Theresienstadt knew what Eichmann's plan was, but it certainly wasn't preserving Jewish heritage.

Hours passed, and Hannah watched from her bench as the windows framed a sky that turned burnt orange with streaks of black clawing at the heavens. Reading the word of God hadn't untangled the coils of dread she felt, but the verse from the Book of Deuteronomy offered a bit of relief. She tried to imitate the fluid strokes that produced Petra's delicate stems, curves, and nikudot, desperately wanting to believe the words she put to paper.

> Be strong and courageous. Do not be afraid or terrified because of them, for the Lord your God goes with you; He will never leave you nor forsake you.

Before she stood to leave, Hannah looked at her fingers, blackened with ink, and sighed. Thankfully, the museum workshop was one of the few buildings with running water, so she could wash up. It had been a long day in Theresienstadt, with only a short break for a midday slice of bread, and Hannah longed to reconnect with Oskar, who she hadn't seen since shortly after their arrival when he hobbled off to find manual labor a day earlier.

Oskar was nowhere to be found among the crowd at the food lines in the *Marktplatz*. Nor did she see Pavel or his father, Alois, just hundreds of prisoners waiting for their tin cups to be filled with lentil soup—or rather brown water with a spoonful of lentil husks.

From the moment Hannah's lips touched the cold rim of her cup, she could smell a fetid odor that reminded her of rotting leaves. Still, she needed to fill the empty drum inside her body, so she stepped to the side of the serving vat and tilted her head back to swallow the soup quickly. A gritty film coated her mouth and crunched against Hannah's teeth.

Wood pigeons flew overhead squawking, taunting Hannah, and she wished she could shoot one from the sky and roast it. The realization that she would not eat again until morning felt like talons digging at her insides, dragging down slowly.

"*Mausi!*" Oskar called out, and Hannah whipped her head around, grateful to see him waving his hand as he made his way to her. Hannah began walking toward Oskar to shorten his way, and she noticed his hand tucked deep in his pants pocket. Finally together, Oskar grabbed Hannah's hand and discretely slipped a bread crust into her palm.

As Hannah's hand eagerly rose to her mouth, she accidentally slapped herself. The sting was quickly forgotten as Hannah felt the relief of baked dough settle on her tongue. She closed her eyes as she chewed, grateful for the momentary satisfaction. "Where did you—"

"Meh," he returned, kissing his granddaughter's cheek. "You know me. I make friends with all the big *machers*. I have good news, *Mausi*!"

The war is ending? We're going to Palestine?

Oskar opened his arms wide, palms facing the dark sky. "You are looking at the newest member of the leisure time committee."

"The leisure time committee?"

"Concerts, lectures," Oskar explained. "We're going to make the best of our time here. You'll see!"

Casting her gaze down at her ink-stained fingers, Hannah sighed, curbing the impulse to tell Oskar he had tomatoes on his eyes. What was the point? He was content with delusion. Before the pain in her chest produced tears, Hannah kissed Oskar's cheek and bid him a good night.

All Hannah wanted to do was set her weary body onto her wooden pallet, however uncomfortable it was. Before long, the cramping of her right hand would abate, and she could escape into dreams of digging through the ruins of Pompeii or reading hieroglyphics on the walls of King Tut's tomb. For as long as she could remember, Hannah had wanted to dig up lost civilizations, gently dusting off the skulls of early man. She envisioned putting their broken pieces back together, if not immortalizing them, then at least giving them a second chance to be in this world. Hannah had always been drawn to the idea of relics as messengers from the past, as teachers to future generations.

Hannah pulled her body up the first flight of stairs at the Dresden Barracks and heard the lilting voice she'd recognize anywhere after listening to it nearly every day for the last six years. "Hannah?"

She turned. "Míša?" she called out, a burst of energy helping her rush down the steps to meet her friend.

"What are you doing here?" Míša cried out, climbing the stairs to meet Hannah.

"What are you... Oh my God, I thought you left—"

"Why aren't you with Paní Božiková?"

"Long story. Short story, really. Opa," Hannah replied before jumping down the last three steps. "I'm so glad you're here," Hannah said as she wrapped her arms around Míša. "That's not what I mean," she said, and they both laughed self-consciously, afraid someone nearby might feel smacked by their momentary happiness.

"I know, I know. It's good to see you, even though—" Míša stepped back and gestured to their surroundings.

Hannah pulled her friend close again, but when she felt the blades of Míša's shoulders through her work smock, she flinched for fear of breaking her. She gripped a bunch of Míša's short russet hair and pressed their foreheads together as if to consume her.

Hannah examined more closely when they unlocked from their embrace. Míša's eyes were framed with dark circles. Hannah wondered if her friend had just covered them with makeup before or if the shading was recent. Míša still reminded Hannah of a lioness with her hair pinned back like a mane, drawing attention to her hazel eyes.

Then the reality set in. If Míša was at Theresienstadt, her family hadn't made it to Shanghai. "You didn't... What happened?"

"We only got to Main Station before we were arrested for

using false identification papers. They think Papa's part of a communist spy network. He's in the small fortress now." Seeing the look of confusion on Hannah's face, Míša clarified. "It's the prison."

"Isn't *this* a prison?"

"Officially, no, this is the ghetto. The small fortress on the other side of the river is the prison. We were the first transport two weeks ago. They say we're lucky to be here, that it's better than the camps in the east."

"Who says that?"

"*Pfft*, I don't know, the Council of Elders, I suppose," Míša said. "Hey, where were you assigned to work?"

"The museum workshop. What about you?"

"I'm at the glimmer factory," Míša offered, holding up her palms as though in surrender, which were slashed with cuts. "We slice mica. It's hard on the hands, but it's one of the better jobs for women here."

Hannah sparked, remembering that Míša probably didn't know that Pavel had arrived in Theresienstadt. "Pavel and his father were on yesterday's transport with Opa and me."

Closing her eyes and knitting her brow, Míša said, "I thought they got out."

Hannah shook her head, watching Míša wrap her arms around her shoulders as if she were cold.

"Did he say how he… I guess it doesn't matter now. He's here." Míša's gaze drifted through the arch of one of the Dresden Barracks' many arcades. "I liked thinking of him out in the world. London, Palestine, somewhere safe."

"He's working on the rail extension with his cousin Luděk."

"Hard labor and youth." She nodded with satisfaction. "Both will get him better food rations. I'll look for him tomorrow. Let's go somewhere else," Míša whispered. "Eyes and ears are everywhere in Theresienstadt." She reached for Hannah's hand and led her down the stairwell toward the ground level, out the door, then found cover behind a nearby bush, bare of leaves but dusted with snow.

Moments later, safely camouflaged, Míša promised, "Don't worry. I'll tell you everything I know—who you can trust, where to find food."

Hannah's body sprang to life. "Do you have food?"

"Not now, but Mama works in the kitchen. I'll teach you how to get by here."

Despite her harsh reality setting in, Hannah felt a flicker of joy at the thought that Markéta was cooking in the Theresienstadt kitchen. And although Míša's father, Šimon, was a quiet man she hardly knew, once he was released from prison, his familiar presence would be a comfort to Hannah. More importantly, he could help his daughter and wife. Hannah felt warm relief knowing she had Míša by her side in this hell.

Hannah remembered when she met Míša, on their first day at Gymnázium Jana Keplera in Prague. Míša spotted Hannah from across the schoolyard and squinted her eyes to see who the new girl was. The fifteen-year-old then walked with her arms pumping as she made her way toward Hannah and asked her a question in Czech. Hannah had no idea what the girl was saying. It could have been *Are you new? Are you a Jew? Would you like a punch in the face?* Hannah didn't know, so she smiled and said the one word she knew in Czech: *děkuji*, thank you.

At the end of the school day, Míša tugged at Hannah's sleeve and said loudly and slowly, "*Pojd' se mnou.*" She curled her fingertips toward herself until Hannah understood that Míša was inviting her somewhere. Soon they were riding the trolley around Prague, Míša eavesdropping on conversations and acting out important words for Hannah.

"*Jídlo,*" Míša said, popping an invisible treat into her mouth and making exaggerated chewing noises. She finished by patting her stomach with satisfaction and exclaiming, "*Mňam, mňam, mňam!*"

Eight months later, Hannah had a firm grasp on the Czech language and a best friend who enjoyed being in the know about everything from school gossip to events around Prague. Every teacher needed a student, every leader a follower. Hannah had always attracted friends with strong personalities like this. When she was growing up in Munich, it was a best friend who always craved the spotlight. These relationships worked for Hannah, because what her friends suggested usually seemed like fine ideas. Her father always called her the world's most agreeable child, less in the way than wallpaper, though Hannah sometimes wondered if her accommodating nature was merely a response to the constant message that Jews were a burden. The more she saw the posters—*The Jews are our misfortune!*—the smaller she became. Her brother, Ben, had a different response, making himself the loveable jokester in his classes and loyal supporter of clubs. Either way, the Kaufman children became who they needed to adapt to the shifting cultural terrain.

"Hannah," Míša whispered as they crouched behind the whitened branches. "If I tell you something, you have to swear to keep it a secret."

"On my naked belly button," Hannah replied.

Míša then used her palms to create a tunnel between her mouth and Hannah's ear. Barely audible, she whispered, "There's a resistance group that—"

Pulling away, Hannah shook her head, a vehement no. She leaned close to Míša and whispered, "Opa says the war will be over in a few months. I don't want any trouble here. We're going to Palestine."

Míša looked at the ground. "*Pfft*, if you believe that…" she said.

Hannah softened her face. "We must have hope, Míša."

Míša bit her bottom lip and shrugged. "That's what the Nazis want us to think, Hannah. Hope is their accomplice."

———◦———

Hannah felt eyes lingering on her as she sat beside Opa Oskar in the cellar of the municipal building, listening to her bunkmate Alice play the delicate notes of Beethoven's Moonlight Sonata. The fifty folding chairs had been filled quickly once word got out that a piano had been discovered in a storage room and that Alice would perform that evening. A dozen or so others stood along the back wall of the room, including two Czech gendarmes, who removed their caps when Alice began to play. An hour earlier, Alice had winked at Hannah and said, "I am Jewish, but Beethoven is my religion," as she buttoned her white blouse and tucked it into her black skirt, readying herself for the concert.

Alice's profoundly soulful rendition of the Beethoven classic washed over the room, each note played with passionate finesse and a deep connection with the music. Hannah turned to her right and saw a young man about her age looking at her, his eyes withdrawing with embarrassment once he realized that Hannah had caught him. She knew him from somewhere, though Hannah could not recall where she had seen him before.

Hannah had been at Theresienstadt for five days, and the empty pit of her stomach was never satisfied with the meager rations of watery broth or potato peels served for supper. Oskar was able to palm bread crusts for his granddaughter, but even that was not enough to quiet the riot of hunger within Hannah.

Like many of the elders, Oskar embraced the idea that creating a vibrant cultural life with Theresienstadt's abundance of talent would nourish the souls of prisoners. As much as Hannah often resented Oskar's delusional optimism, it was preferable to the choice two other old men had made upon their arrival in the ghetto. Seeing the conditions at Theresienstadt, each climbed to the second floor of the Magdeburg Barracks, made his way to a window, and jumped to his death. One made a point of ending his life dressed in his gray Deutsches Heer uniform from the Great War, a row of freshly polished silver buttons lining the front.

Hannah felt eyes lingering on her as she sat beside Oskar in the packed cellar of the municipal building, listening to her bunkmate Alice play the delicate, haunting notes. She glanced behind her and saw the familiar-looking boy, who quickly turned away before Hannah could remember how she knew him. She returned her attention to the music. Some pianists involved their entire bodies as they played, but Alice remained still, save for her curled fingers traversing the keys.

"A piano, such a gift," Oskar said, patting Hannah's leg. "You'll see. Things are always better than how they look at first."

She gritted her teeth, muffling her annoyance with her grandfather. Guilt settled in soon after, as it always did. How was it possible to want to wrap her arms around him for comfort and pound her fists against his back in rage at the same time?

The second movement began, the music gaining lyricism and levity, and Hannah felt the grip of anger loosening. Earlier that day, Alice told her bunkmates that music was the closest thing to being in the presence of God, and Hannah thought she may be right.

Moments later, it struck her. The boy who was watching her—it was Kryštof Horák from Gymnázium Jana Keplera. She hardly knew Kryštof; he was two classes behind her, though he was only a year younger. A friend had once whispered that Kryštof had been a sickly child, so he had to repeat a school year. Kryštof had the same pale skin and mushroom cap haircut he sported at school but now sprouted a dozen or so chin hairs. He looked at Hannah again, so she waved with a polite smile, but Kryštof looked away and fixed his gaze on Alice at the piano.

"You have an admirer," Oskar loudly whispered, nodding in Kryštof's direction.

"Shh," Hannah scolded. "Don't humiliate the boy."

An hour later, when Alice stood and bowed, Hannah caught Kryštof turning to look at her once more. Oskar tapped Hannah's back and told her to go and say hello. "Make new friends while you're here," he urged, then called out, "Young man, over here!"

Kryštof checked over his shoulder and pointed to himself with a questioning shrug.

"Come, meet my granddaughter Hannah. You two are about the same age."

Her old schoolmate made his way toward Hannah and Oskar, his long legs moving with an awkward stride, like the baby giraffe Hannah had seen years ago at the Hellabrunn Zoo. "*Ahoj*, Hannah, I thought that was you. It's been a long time," he said, his ears reddening.

"You're from Prague?" Oskar asked.

Hannah offered Kryštof a smile, hoping it was friendly enough to put him at ease but not so encouraging that he would get the wrong idea. "Yes, Opa, Kryštof and I went to *Gymnázium* together. Nice to see you again, though I wish it were back in the lunch hall instead of here. How long have you been at Theresienstadt?"

"I came in November with the building crew," he replied, eyes widening as though he sought approval from Hannah and Oskar. "I work in the *Schleuse* now."

Oskar must have seen the spark of excitement from Hannah and mistaken it for interest in Kryštof, so he excused himself with an exaggerated yawn. "Time for me to hit the sack. I'll let you two get reacquainted. Kryštof, it was nice to meet you."

Before Oskar made it to the exit, Hannah stepped closer to Kryštof and gripped the sleeve of his flannel work shirt. "The photos. What happens to them?" At her friend's perplexed expression, Hannah pressed. "I had a picture of my family. In a silver frame. It was taken at the *Schleuse*. Do you think… Can you get it back for me?"

Kryštof's eyes scanned the room as people left the cellar,

and Hannah could tell he was deliberating by the way he bit the inside of his cheek as he had at school. He leaned closer and lowered his voice. "Hannah, I…I may be able to find the photo, but you can't have the frame. It's not worth getting caught."

"All I want is the photo. Please, Kryštof, my bunkmate has a picture of her *Schatz*. I know it's allowed."

Placing his hands deep into his pockets, Kryštof continued gnawing his cheek, then grimaced. "I want to help, but it's dangerous. I mean, can't you just remember what they look like?" At the sight of Hannah's eyes beginning to well, Kryštof relented. "You were always nice to me at school. Not like that friend of yours. She's been here two weeks, and she looks at me like she's never seen me before."

"It's been two years. She probably forgot—"

"*You* remembered me," he said.

"Míša has a lot on her mind."

"We all do."

Hannah sighed internally. She didn't want to waste any more time soothing Kryštof's hurt feelings or defending Míša's good name. The photo of her family was the last picture she would ever have of all six of them together. Once the war ended and Hannah and Oskar joined the family in Palestine, they would snap new shots of their life together, but none would ever include Oma Minna again. "Míša can be like that," Hannah said, knowing her best friend would approve of the benign betrayal.

Kryštof hesitated for a moment, then nodded. "The *Schleuse* is locked now, but if you come early in the morning, maybe twenty minutes till six, I'll be there. My friend lets… Never mind. The less you know, the better. You can look for the picture there, but you need to be quick. Meet me at the side door."

"Thank you," she whispered, refraining from hugging him.

———◦———

The next morning, the sky was still dark when Hannah approached the *Schleuse*. She flinched when she saw a circle of yellow light flash from a rod before realizing it was Kryštof signaling to her. "Hurry," he whispered, so she quickened her pace, hoping the falling snow would cover her tracks before the ghetto came to life.

Walking through the side door of the unlit *Schleuse* felt as though she had been swallowed whole into the belly of the beast. The sharp stink of silver polish needled through the moldy stench of damp wood, and Hannah heard the sound of tiny claws scampering across the stone floor. The beam of Kryštof's flashlight revealed rows of small wooden crates filled with silver cutlery tossed inside haphazardly, trailed by other boxes loaded with dishes, pots, and pans. The illumination did not travel far enough for Hannah to see an end of the row, adding to the gloomy effect of the *Schleuse*.

"Come with me," Kryštof said, grabbing Hannah's hand and leading her toward the back of the cavernous room. Then they turned left and rounded a corner until they reached a bookshelf stacked with picture frames. He lifted one and flashed his light onto the glass and smiled. "You're in luck. We haven't removed pictures from their frames from Tuesday's transport. It was silver, you say?" He scanned the collection on the top shelf.

"Yes," she replied, already running her fingertips down the

sides of the frames stacked on the shelf beneath the one Kryštof was inspecting. Thankfully, Oma Minna had selected a unique silver trim for their family portrait: a repoussé bow intricately curling beyond the rectangle shape of the edges. Hannah rifled through the selection as she described it to Kryštof, and her heart sped as she pulled it from the stack. "I found—" She interrupted herself at the sight of the faces of a bride and groom looking back at her.

"Hannah, we need to hurry," Kryštof said. "If you're here when the workers arrive, I don't know how I'll explain it."

But before Hannah could answer, she spotted another frame, one she was certain was hers by the slight bend of the tip of the silver ribbon at the corner. Hannah pulled the frame from the shelf, and her eye was immediately drawn to the image of Oma Minna sitting in a tufted velvet armchair at the center of the photo. Behind her stood Opa Oskar in a bow tie, resting a hand gently on his wife's shoulder. On each side of the chair were Ingrid and Rolf, Hannah's father placing Ben in front of him; Hannah stood beside her mother.

Hannah dropped to the floor and placed the picture frame in her lap, flipping it over and pulling back the aluminum fasteners with her fingernails to remove the wooden backing. Moments later, Hannah's fingertips delicately held the white edges of the sepia-toned photo. She tucked it under her coat, hoping it wouldn't bend or warp too much when she ran back to the barracks before breakfast. Still, it was them. Whole. Together. A family.

"Thank you, Kryštof," she said, eyeing the door.

He shined his light, a pathway for her to leave, when Hannah caught a word printed in red ink on the side of a wooden crate. *Portugal?* Hannah reached for Kryštof's hand and aimed his beam directly at the box. PRODUCTO DE PORTUGAL, it read.

There were no prisoners from Portugal in Theresienstadt. "Why... What's from Portugal?"

Kryštof looked nervously toward the door, and Hannah could see his mouth twitching, wanting to share the secret but knowing he shouldn't.

"Come on, Kryštof. You can trust me."

He sighed, defeated. "The SS doesn't just send *our* things to Germany for sale or...I don't know, gifts for officers. They take most of the packages the Red Cross sends for us, medical supplies, food, that sort of thing. For some reason, I have no idea, we get lots of sardines from Portugal."

"Wait! Those are sardines?" Hannah's stomach growled at the mere mention of food.

"It all goes back to the Fatherland or SS headquarters in Prague, I'm sorry to say."

Hannah heard voices outside in the distance and knew she had to act quickly. "Give me a can. Please, Kryštof, I'm starving."

"Everyone's hungry, Hannah. If I get caught..." He trailed off.

She swallowed hard, hating what she was about to say, what she had to do. The low notes of male voices grew louder as workers approached the *Schleuse* for another day of scavenging through prisoners' suitcases, forced to vulture for the SS. There was no time for subtlety, for gazing into his eyes and waiting for him to kiss her. Hannah held her family photo with her left hand, then reached for Kryštof's palm with her right and pulled it toward her blouse and placed it on her breast. He widened his mouth and gasped, a soft wheeze escaping as he squeezed Hannah's full cup. "You won't get caught. I won't tell anyone about us, Kryštof. It will be our little secret."

He nodded and opened the crate, handing Hannah a can of sardines.

Kryštof was a sweet boy who she hated deceiving, but the hollow in her stomach pained her, as did the sight of her best friend withering away. What was the harm in a friendly barter that helped both Hannah and Kryštof make their time in Theresienstadt bearable? She pecked his lips and ran to the door.

7

Hilde

Berlin
December 1941

AUF *WIEDERSEHEN*," Susanna sang out as she buttoned her coat, then tossed her scarf around her neck. "Are you sure you don't want to come to Café Kranzler with the girls tonight?"

"So sorry," Hilde returned sweetly. "I have a date."

"Oww, that's right, your mystery *Schatz*," Susanna replied, reaching for her cloche hat on the rack by the front door to the office.

Mimicking Susanna's playful tone, Hilde winked and said, "A girl can have a few secrets." She had learned to button her lips after her experience with Werner two years earlier. Hilde wasn't about to let that happen twice. Plus, she didn't want to give Susanna any ideas about advancing her own career and making a move on Otto. Hilde was the one who'd endured her supervisor's boorish behavior for the past week, so she would be the one to reap the benefits.

On several nights, Hilde lay awake in her bed, haunted by the look on Vilma's face when she barged into the WC and found Hilde in the bathtub. What simpletons like Vilma didn't understand was that adult relationships were complicated. Hilde hadn't been raped, not even close. *Vati always said you can't rape the willing. I was willing. I just hadn't realized it yet.*

Now, she and Otto had developed a routine: Otto would ask her to stay late to discuss film ideas, but soon he found himself unable to control his desire for her. Hilde's dilemma was that Otto wasn't merely a brute; he also listened to her ideas intently and added his mustard to it. They worked well together, and she could see how much he respected her artistic vision. Life was a series of trade-offs, she reminded herself. She could endure his spongy flesh and whiskey breath for a few minutes every evening if it helped launch her filmmaking career.

Susanna reached for the doorknob and turned back toward Hilde. "You know where we are if you change your mind!"

The silence of the office tore at Hilde, so she turned on the *Volksempfänger*, hoping to fill the room with holiday music. Hilde peered out her window and felt a pang, knowing she was stuck inside, missing Berlin's Christmas festivities. The opening piano chords of Hilde's favorite carol floated from the radio speaker. A male voice crooned.

"Silent night, holy night, all is calm, all is bright. Only the Chancellor stays on guard, Germany's future to watch and to ward, guiding our nation aright."

Hilde reveled at the sight of women in long fur coats and beaded felt caps gliding along the streets reflecting light from electric lamps. They linked arms with men in black leather trench coats and stiff boots.

Then Hilde lifted her gaze and admired the night sky. Despite the city lights, dozens of stars managed to glimmer through, ornamenting the heavens like a holiday Jul tree. Hilde would never admit it aloud, but she often scanned for signs of Allied planes overhead. News reported minor RAF attacks on German cities, but Hilde couldn't help worry that the recent bombing of Pearl Harbor and America's entry into the war might mean aggression aimed at Berlin. There was little she could do to protect herself from a bomber, but Hilde would take some cold comfort in knowing she hadn't been caught off guard.

Hilde hadn't realized she was digging into her thumb when it began to bleed.

Forty minutes later, Otto's office door opened, and he emerged with a face pinched with consternation. He trudged toward the coatrack and turned only when Hilde cleared her throat. He widened his eyes at the sight of her. "You're still here."

"I was hoping we could talk more about the Theresienstadt film," she said eagerly.

"I'm sorry," he said, making his way back to Hilde's desk and kissing her on the forehead. "I'm late getting home for our Jul tree trimming."

Forcing a smile, she reminded herself that a successful mistress was one who didn't place too many demands on her *Schatz*. "Let's discuss it at the meeting with Frau Riefenstahl tomorrow."

"Hilde," he said like a father gently scolding a child. "Remember that the meeting is to advance the Reich through film, not further your own career."

She lowered her tensed shoulders. "Advancing the Reich through film *is* my career."

Hilde could hear the ticking of Otto's wristwatch when he pulled his hand from his coat pocket and glanced down.

Maybe she would join Susanna and her friends after all. It had been two years since Hilde had one of the café's scrumptious desserts. Now, she had been employed by the ministry for two entire weeks; she was young and hardworking. Hilde deserved a night of holiday fun.

———◦———

As Hilde passed under the striped awning of Café Kranzler, a man behind her rushed to hold the front door. Just as she registered the musical chatter of Berliners enjoying a night out, she was enveloped by the aroma of sweet honey bread and cinnamon. She patted her purse where she kept her ration card, knowing she would likely spend her entire two-month sugar allowance that night.

Café Kranzler was exactly as Hilde remembered, with its clusters of tables with Tiffany-style lamps hanging overhead. Above a round four-top near the front was a clear glass shade with chocolate ice cream cones adorning the rim. Of the two dozen tables, there wasn't an empty one in the café, and with the mirror covering an entire wall, the dining area looked twice as full. She was proud that Berliners wouldn't consider letting war keep them at home with their curtains drawn. And why should they? Hitler had made good on his promise that Germany would be on the offensive, not cowering under attack. *Or checking the skies for bombers*, Hilde silently chided herself.

Pulling off her new kidskin gloves, Hilde stopped at the glass display cases at the front of the shop and studied the café's dozens of offerings. What would she order? Chocolate rum balls dusted with cocoa powder? Honey-soaked almonds atop slices of cream-filled *Bienenstichkuchen*? Apricot, cherry, and plum tarts, each sprinkled with thick grains of sugar?

"Hilde, yoo-hoo!"

She turned toward the back of the dining area and saw Susanna waving. Also gathered around the crescent-shaped booth were three young women Hilde recognized from the ministry. At the next table was a young man from the graphics department on a date with a petite woman with blond braids rolled to the sides of her head like earmuffs.

"You came!" Susanna exclaimed, and Hilde felt a flash of warmth, realizing that she had made the right choice. Women friends could be a source of strength. Real strength, not the close proximity to power that older men offered. Another bonus was that rum balls were already on the table. Susanna noticed Hilde eyeing them. "Help yourself. We're already stuffed."

Before she even sat, Hilde plucked the treat with her fingers, then rushed to explain her presence to Susanna. "My poor *Schatz* caught a cold and didn't want to get me sick." The women slid closer together on the booth bench to make room for Hilde, and she lowered herself onto the seat, grateful for the inclusion.

"I'm Margarete," said a young woman. Margarete, who worked in the children's books department, had a tight roll of brown bangs that clung to her forehead and wore a red ribbon bow around her collar that she twisted nervously.

Susanna gestured with her hand. "This is Ida from the board games division," she said and turned to the blond with plump cheeks and a chest that looked like it was storing treasure.

"And I'm Julia," said the slender raven-haired woman with icy blue eyes. Julia grinned and lifted her penciled eyebrow, appraising Hilde. "I work on *Volksempfänger* programming. Musical talent, comedy shows, that sort of thing," she said with a wave of false modesty.

The moment the chocolate hit Hilde's tongue, she melted into her seat, tasting the bitterness of the powder give way to sweetness inside. She heard the crunch of vanilla wafer crumbs, their light flavor mingling with the earthy sweetness of chocolate. Walnut pieces added an even more complex flavor and texture. And oh, how it all absorbed the nip of rum mixed in. Hilde was in heaven.

"How could we possibly go skiing this year?" Julia continued. "It feels disrespectful with so many of our boys in the east."

Hilde chased away an image of Max in his Wehrmacht uniform the last time she saw him, perfect and alive. He cast his gaze at her small belly and said, "Take good care of your *Mutti* while I'm away, little one." Six months later, Hilde had to write to Max with the news that she'd not only lost the baby but would not be able to bear children in the future. She often wondered if the news drained Max of his will to fight. Perhaps she should have waited until he safely returned home.

Around the table at Café Kranzler, the women nodded. "We're staying in Berlin too," Ida added, joining Hilde in just one more rum ball.

Julia turned to Hilde. "What about you? Is old Mazuw giving you some time off to go home to… Where are you from?"

"Munich," she replied, feeling smacked by the characterization of Otto. Yes, he was forty years older than the women around the table, but Julia said his name with a harsh tone of derision.

Margarete leaned in and whispered, "You should get extra

holiday time for having to work for that old *Schwein*." She laughed at her own joke, eyes pecking around the table for approval.

"Combat pay," Julia added.

"Come now. He's not that bad," Susanna said. "Right, Hilde? He's started trimming the hair on his ears lately."

They all giggled, and Hilde smiled tightly. Loath as she was to admit this to herself, Hilde was flattered that Otto seemed to be paying closer attention to his grooming. She would have to remember to compliment his shorn earlobes next time they were together.

The young man from the graphics department laughed, and for a moment, Hilde thought he was joining their conversation about Otto.

"Who is that boy? Doesn't he work at the ministry?" Hilde snapped her fingers as though she was trying to remember where she had seen him. Best not to appear too interested.

"Him?" Julia asked. "That's just Martin from graphics."

"Is that... Are they married?"

Susanna swatted Hilde's forearm. "You rascal. What would your *Schatz* say?"

"Or Martin's?" Ida looked up from her straw.

Hilde felt her face flush with heat and glanced away.

"We're sorry, Hilde." Susanna gave a hiccup giggle. "We're teasing. I've never seen that girl before, and knowing Martin, I never will again."

What does that mean? Is Martin a heartbreaker, or is he socially inept and never gets a second date with women? It was hard to tell during wartime when so much more than a man's looks went into evaluating his appeal. In Hilde's eyes, rank in the party was far more attractive than broad shoulders and a square jaw. Not that Martin had either of those features. He wasn't classically handsome with his thin brown hair and a receding chin, but the way he locked eyes on his date and flashed a perfect smile made him good-looking in a goofy way. There was something about him that drew Hilde's attention.

"What are you doing for Christmas, Hilde?" Julia asked.

"Oh," she said, biting into a walnut shell. She wished Café Kranzler would be more careful when making its confections. "My parents keep pestering me to come home," she lied. "But I'll stay in Berlin."

Susanna tilted her head and offered, "You can join our family gathering. We have plenty of—"

Urgently, Hilde shook her head. "No, no thank you. My *Schatz* and his family live in Berlin. I'll celebrate with them."

"Good, as long as you aren't alone for Christmas."

Hilde reminded herself to smile and wave a hand blithely. "No, don't worry about me. Honestly, I enjoy his family more than my own."

"I know that feeling," Ida added, reaching for another rum ball. "We should order some more."

"We can use my ration card for this round," Hilde offered.

"Thanks," Ida said and leaned on her elbows and smiled conspiratorially.

"Can you girls keep a secret?"

Hilde watched Ida's gaze land on each woman at the table. She had to give this Ida girl credit—she knew how to dangle a treat.

Susanna scanned the table, urging the others to agree. "Promise, we won't breathe a word, right, girls?"

"All right, I'll spill. Karl's mother told me that he asked to see the wedding band his *Uroma* left for him."

Dim-witted Susanna looked like a silent film actress with her arching brows and mouth agape.

"I mean, Karl hasn't asked me to marry him yet, but it's a good sign that he wants to look at a wedding band, don't you think?"

Julia nodded. "It can only mean one thing."

Maybe he wants to sell the ring.

Hilde hated when women were so smug, as if they couldn't imagine any other outcome than the one they desired.

She hoped her smile looked more natural than it felt.

"As long as we're telling secrets," Julia said, looking around the café as though someone might care to eavesdrop on a bunch of silly office girls. "I won't be returning to the ministry in the new year." She gave an impish grin and lowered her eyes to her stomach.

"No!" Susanna slapped her hand over her mouth.

Julia replied, "Yes!"

Actually, it's maybe. You may be pregnant today, but things happen.

"What good news!" Margarete exclaimed.

Listening to these braggarts made Hilde feel as though she was in a burning building, frantically searching for an exit as smoke choked her. "Oh no," she said, slapping her forehead. "My housemates are waiting for me to...go figure skating tonight."

"Figure skating?" Susanna asked. "I thought you had a date."

"Yes, we were all going skating at the lake together. When... Uwe got sick, I forgot all about the girls back at the house. I hope they're not waiting for me," Hilde said, feigning exasperation with herself. "It was nice to meet you all," Hilde managed as she grabbed her coat and placed it over her shoulders.

———◦———

"Did you have fun last night?" Susanna asked as Hilde strode into the office the next morning.

"Loads. Sorry I had to leave early. Your friends are very nice," Hilde said, making her way to her seat. They were frivolous girls, blissfully oblivious that their only influence came from the man they'd attached themselves to. Hilde would forge her own way.

"How is Uwe feeling?"

Uwe? Who the hell is Uwe? Oh right, my Schatz. "Still sick, poor dear."

Glancing at the wall clock, she scolded herself silently for being ten minutes late. Hilde hated when Susanna beat her to work, but she had uncharacteristically slept through her alarm clock after struggling to fall asleep the night before. When she finally did, it was a fitful slumber plagued by bizarre dreams of babies on skates, blades gliding over Hilde's body. It must have been from eating too many sweets. Wanting to avoid Susanna's nattering, Hilde sped toward her desk and kept her eyes down.

"...the lighting of the tree," Susanna finished and looked expectantly at Hilde. "You're not listening to a word I'm saying, are you?"

She raised her hands in surrender. "Guilty. I need to get my work done before the meeting with Frau Riefenstahl." *You know...work!*

"That's right. I forgot," Susanna returned. "Herr Mazuw asked me to take notes at the meeting this morning."

What the hell? Hilde felt her head rattling as she shook it too quickly. "No, he asked *me* to sit in on the meeting."

"I know. He said his plans changed, so I'll be filling in for you."

"But I don't need you to *fill in* for me. I'm here now, see?"

Susanna shrugged. "I'm not sure why he made the decision, and to me, it's a sausage."

To her, it's a sausage? How dare she be so flip about my career!

"But I do care," Hilde exclaimed. "Very much!"

"I'm sorry, Hilde. I know you wanted to meet Frau Riefenstahl, but I've talked to her a few times, and she's not that friendly to girls like us. I once told her how much I enjoyed *Olympia,* and she practically ignored me. I guess she's heard it a million times, but really, she still could have—"

"Susanna!" Hilde snapped. "You know meeting her meant the world to me. *Mein Gott,* what are you up to? Are you carrying on with Otto?"

Susanna stepped back and clutched her chest. "Herr Mazuw? That's disgusting! What's gotten into you?"

Hilde stood to meet Susanna's eye. "I'm sorry. I don't know… I just don't understand why he would do this to me. I was supposed to…meeting Frau Riefenstahl… Can you keep a secret?" She saw last night how sharing confidences bonded women; they were currency. Maybe Susanna would help her if she told her the truth. After nearly a month of working together, Hilde could see that Susanna had no ambition as a filmmaker. Yes, she would do her part for the Reich while she was needed, but once the war ended, Susanna's career would too.

Nodding eagerly, Susanna assured Hilde, "You can trust me."

"When I came to the ministry, I had this idea that Frau

Riefenstahl would take me under her wing. How can that happen if I never meet her?"

"Hilde, there's nothing I can do. Herr Mazuw needs me in ten minutes."

Hilde rushed with an answer. "Pretend to be sick."

"What?"

"Come on. Didn't you ever get out of school by faking an illness?"

Susanna giggled nervously. "Sure, I guess, but I can't just leave work."

Hilde grabbed Susanna's hands and squeezed them tight. "Please, I'm begging. Pretend you've come down with something." Pleading felt so powerless and humiliating, but what choice did she have?

"If it means that much to you," Susanna replied.

"You…you'll do it?"

"Sure, anything for a friend."

Hilde's entire body relaxed. Until it softened, she hadn't realized that her face had been a fist of tension. From the corners of her eyes, Hilde could see her own shoulders drop, like tires quickly deflating. "Thank you, Susanna. I really owe you for this."

"Don't be silly," Susanna returned with a light swat of her hand.

As she heard the doorknob of Herr Mazuw's private office turn, Hilde watched Susanna clutch her stomach and bend over.

"Oww, the pain, it won't stop," Susanna whimpered to Hilde. "I feel so, so sick."

Not so obvious, Susanna!

"What's the matter with her?" Otto asked.

"Susanna's not well, Herr Mazuw. It's probably best if she goes home to rest."

Otto made his way toward the women. He reached for Susanna's shoulders, then turned her to face him. Placing a hand on her forehead, he rolled his eyes. "She's fine. Susanna, in my office in two minutes."

Hilde wished Susanna hadn't let Otto see her scrunch her face apologetically, an expression saying, *Sorry, I tried.*

"Herr Mazuw," Hilde whispered through gritted teeth. "Susanna needs to go home and rest. She's having…female problems." That would do it. Yes, Susanna looked mortified, her bottom lip curled down, but Hilde needed to say something rash, something that would make Otto uncomfortable. She had always found that the slightest suggestion of a woman's monthly cycle made men want to end a conversation.

"Don't mistake me for a dummkopf, girls. We all know Susanna's only female problem is you, Hilde. Susanna, in my office now."

Susanna made things worse by shrugging at Hilde and walking toward Otto's office, visibly pain-free.

But why? Why would Otto treat me this way after all I've done for him?

She began following him toward his office, but as soon as Susanna made it through the door, Otto turned and held up his hand. "Stay," he commanded.

Hilde made her way back to her desk and dropped into her chair with her full weight.

When Hilde heard the turn of the front doorknob again, she realized she was wasting time wondering about Otto's motives.

He is selfish. He feels threatened by me. He knows I'll outshine him in the meeting. Who cares? That's all his problem, and I will get nowhere trying to figure him out. The important question is what am I going to do when Leni Riefenstahl walks through that door?

Hilde rose to her feet and turned toward the entrance, ready to greet the filmmaker and tell her how much she admired her work. *Triumph of the Will* had changed her life. It had been released when Hilde was fourteen years old, and the world was coming to accept that Aryans, Germans in particular, were the master race, poised to reclaim all that had been stolen from them by the Jews. Hannah's spirits soared when she watched Riefenstahl's scenes of rallies for the führer, the largest crowds the world had ever seen gathered to support a leader. It was a promise of a future in a gleaming new world, and Hilde wanted to thank the filmmaker for her part in making Germany great. In Hilde's fantasy, Riefenstahl would be so charmed by Hilde's passion that she would insist on including her on the Reich's next film. *This girl should be behind the camera, not a desk!*

A man's voice was the first Hilde heard. She recognized it as that of Reichsminister Joseph Goebbels. Hilde could only see the sleeve of his jacket and the tip of his polished boot. "…could be a problem. If Theresienstadt looks too nice, won't the *Volk* want to know why the führer gave them such a gift?" He opened the door and held out his arm.

The first thing Hilde noticed about Leni Riefenstahl was her athletic build; Hilde imagined this was from the filmmaker's years as a swimmer. Riefenstahl's eyes were also closer together than they appeared in magazine photographs. Hilde loved the statement Riefenstahl made with her brown chin-length bob pushed back with a headband. She was too productive to fuss with her hair.

As the two made their way toward Otto's office, Hilde stood and began to introduce herself. "*Guten Tag*, Frau Rief—"

Goebbels's voice ran over Hilde's like a train. "Then again, resentment of the Jews is never a bad thing."

Neither Frau Riefenstahl nor Herr Goebbels seemed to notice Hilde. They were now steps away from Otto's office door.

Hilde's heart sped, and she watched the officer's hand reach for the brass doorknob. "*Heil* Hitler," Hilde tried again, her greeting still unacknowledged.

Otto appeared at the door and held out his arm to hail the führer. Hilde could see Susanna inside, left arm wrapped around a notepad, right extended in salute.

Hilde dropped back into her chair, replaying the past moments in her mind. *Did Frau Riefenstahl ignore me, or didn't she see me? Did Herr Goebbels interrupt me on purpose, or was I invisible to him?*

She remembered seeing an article in *Frauen Warte* with a photo of Frau Riefenstahl shooting a particularly difficult scene in *Olympia*. The filmmaker twisted her body behind the camera-man on a large cart being rolled by a production assistant. The message to German women was that when situations are hard, get creative like Leni.

Hilde knew what she had to do. She stood and straightened her skirt, then headed down the corridor.

—◦—

Two and a half hours had passed, and Hilde was starting to wonder if Leni Riefenstahl had used another toilet in the building. As far as Hilde knew, the three-stall women's room on the main floor was the closest to the film department. If the meeting had already ended, Hilde would certainly be in the devil's kitchen for leaving her post for so long.

Hilde heard the door open and peeked under the divider between stalls. Instead of the shoes she had watched all morning—pointy-toe flats and T-strap heels—Hilde saw Frau Riefenstahl's lace-up burgundy spectators and heard her sigh. Hilde bit her tongue to stop herself from asking what was wrong. She wondered, though, if Riefenstahl had been frustrated by the meeting. Or was she annoyed that someone else was in the toilet stall beside her?

Sitting in the bathroom had been torture, the smell of urine lingering after women relieved themselves. Hilde shuddered, remembering the sound of a plop of *Kacke* hitting the toilet water and the stink of rotten egg that lingered.

Once Hilde heard the flush next to her, she pulled the chain over her toilet seat and walked toward the sink. "*Heil* Hitler, Frau Riefenstahl," Hilde said, looking at her idol's reflection in the mirror.

Hands pushing the dispenser for soap powder, Riefenstahl returned the greeting. She pursed her face and tilted her head. "Aren't you the girl from Herr Mazuw's office?"

"I am," Hilde replied, hoping she didn't sound overeager.

Riefenstahl lathered; Hilde lathered. Riefenstahl rinsed, so Hilde did too. Riefenstahl shook the excess water from her hands, and Hilde did the same.

"Hmm, you didn't want to attend the meeting about Theresienstadt? It's going to be an important film."

Hilde had no idea why Frau Riefenstahl cared whether she was at the meeting or if she was just making polite conversation, but she decided not to question her good fortune.

Heart fluttering, Hilde hoped her voice would not catch. "Frau Riefenstahl, I am your greatest admirer, not only as a film-maker but as a woman," Hilde began, reminding herself to take deep breaths so she didn't pass out from nerves. "I've seen *The Victory of Faith* eight times, and it's…it's genius. I mean, every-thing you do is great, and I've seen all your films at least ten times." *Ach! Eight times is not at least ten times. Slow down.*

Riefenstahl smiled. "Clearly a smart girl."

"Do you…do you think I could ask your advice?" Hilde saw Riefenstahl glance at her wristwatch and decided to press for-ward. "I keep asking Herr Mazuw to work on films, but he never lets me, no matter how many times I ask."

"Why do you keep asking?"

"Because I know I could do a good job. Frau Riefenstahl…" Hilde's voice hitched. "With your guidance, I could become the Reich's second-greatest propaganda filmmaker."

Riefenstahl never turned to look at Hilde directly, instead con-tinuing the conversation with her image in the mirror. "You mis-understand. If this is something you're destined to do, do it. Insist on working on the Theresienstadt film or next year's *Titanic* film."

"The *Titanic*…" Hilde could not finish, blood pumping so hard she heard pounding in her ears.

"Some silly idea he came up with about how the sinking ship could have been saved by a German engineer." Riefenstahl waved a hand dismissively. "That will be a large-scale production with hundreds of people involved. If you really want to make a name for yourself, create something of your own."

Hilde's thoughts raced. *Otto stole my* Titanic *idea? Leni Riefenstahl thinks it's silly?* She fought to return her attention to the woman she had been waiting a lifetime to speak with, who would be gone in a minute.

"The Reich needs short children's films right now. Write a script, check out a camera from the office, and shoot it yourself."

"Don't I need his permission?"

"Do you?"

"Herr Mazuw is in charge," Hilde replied. "He's my superior."

Riefenstahl raised an eyebrow. "What's your name?"

"Hilde. Hilde Bischoff."

"Hilde Bischoff, you're a German woman. No one is your superior. Don't let any man tell you otherwise." She turned and began walking toward the door.

Yes, when you're Leni Riefenstahl and the führer adores you, it's easy to call the shots, but Hilde was just a secretary. Just a mistress. Just someone whose silly ideas Otto could steal.

"Frau Riefenstahl," Hilde called out desperately. "I can't just *tell* my supervisor I'm making a children's film."

Riefenstahl turned around and faced Hilde. "Not directly. Make him think it's *his* idea."

8

Hannah

HANNAH AND MÍŠA CLIMBED THE BACK STAIRWELL AT THE Dresden Barracks and hurried toward Míša's stall, bumping shoulders with a knot of women descending. Then the pair sped down the corridor, dodging women and girls moving slowly in both directions. "Careful!" an old woman shouted. "You're making me dizzy!"

They turned into the area where Míša slept. "We need to be quick," Míša said, pulling Hannah onto her bottom bunk.

"Not so rough," Hannah protested as she swatted her friend's hand away from her arm. It was the first night of Chanukah, and the two had only a few minutes to exchange trinkets before others would start to wonder why they were late for the lighting of the candles in the secret synagogue. And Míša's mother would surely scold them if they didn't get to the food line soon.

"How can I save for you anything solid if you're not here?" Markéta had asked earlier that week after Hannah had to stay late at the museum workshop to finish her transcription. She had clucked her tongue at Hannah. "I cannot say no to the old people wasting away. You must be smart, Hannah. Baked pigeons don't fly into your mouth."

Markéta was right; after their first few days at Theresienstadt, prisoners figured out that they were more likely to get a chunk of turnip or potato if they asked the cooks to lower their ladles to the bottom of the vat. There was no way she could live with her guilty conscience if she denied the request.

Míša's mother wasn't the only one who would be on the lookout for the two women that evening. Oskar and Griselde, Hannah's work leader, were expecting to see them at the secret synagogue. They had recently started attending cultural events together and promised to save spots for the young women at the evening service. Oskar swore that he and Griselde were old friends from their school days in Munich, nothing more, but Hannah suspected something deeper was developing. Like the Kaufmans, Griselde and her late husband made the mistake of moving to Prague, thinking it was safer than Munich for Jews. Over the past few days, Hannah noticed Griselde had begun referring to Oskar and her as *we*. *We can't hold seats in the front row for long… We loved* Tevye the Milkman… *We cannot believe you live with Alice Herz-Sommer.* It reminded Hannah of the postcard she received from her mother earlier in the week, the first mail that had arrived for her in the ghetto. *We have our own apartment now, and it is constantly bustling with Ben's school friends… We met a nice family from Munich who has a son your age… We pray the war will end soon and you will join us.*

Hannah sat on Míša's mattress and tried to create some privacy by pushing herself all the way back against the wall. "Let's be fast then. Better than gelt, *ah lichtigen Chanukah*,"

Hannah offered with a kiss on Míša's cheek. She reached into the pocket of her jacket and wriggled out a green tin of Memphis brand cigarettes. Seeing her friend bite her bottom lip with anticipation, Hannah needed to temper expectations. "I couldn't get a whole pack. It's only eight—one for each night of Chanukah."

Míša leaned into Hannah's arms and hugged her tight. "How did you get these? Everyone's cigarettes are taken at the *Schleuse*."

"I have my ways," Hannah said with a shrug of her shoulders, feigning nonchalance. If Míša knew the price Hannah had paid, she would have never accepted her gift. Kryštof had poached cigarettes and four cans of sardines for her. In exchange, she allowed him to run his hands over her bare breasts for a few minutes in the back of the *Schleuse*. She was selling her body, but there was something oddly tender about the reverent way the boy touched her flesh. He closed his eyes with pleasure and breathed heavily through his mouth. Both then and now, Hannah tried to focus on being grateful for the chance to get her hands on provisions and pushed aside the guilt of knowing they had been stolen from new arrivals and parcels from the Red Cross.

Míša reached into the bib pocket of her dress and pulled out a soft aluminum package the size of a deck of playing cards. Hannah unfolded the neatly sealed edges and lifted the flap. *Dear God, I've gone to heaven*, Hannah thought as her mouth moistened at the rich aroma. She peeked outside into the large room to make sure no one else caught a whiff. Hannah had never seen a latke made with only potato peels and margarine, but the dark patty was a beacon home. Oma Minna had always peeled and grated her potatoes, letting them pop and crackle in a pan filled with schmaltz until they browned on the outside. Míša's was far smaller and would not taste the same but would be equally delicious because, like Minna's, they were prepared with love. Hannah asked, "How did you…"

"I have *my* ways."

Although her friend was teasing, Hannah swallowed hard, hoping Markéta had helped her daughter rather than resorting to Hannah's black-market currency.

"Thank you, Míša," Hannah whispered. The gift was a reminder that though Míša had a tough exterior, she also had a generous heart. Even when she was a student, she shouted the loudest at demonstrations, but always on behalf of the vulnerable. How difficult it must be now for Míša to be among the persecuted instead of their advocate.

Míša winked. "Keep your mouth shut at service so no one smells your potato breath and wants to know your source."

Hannah broke the small latke in half. "I want to share *with* my source."

Míša waved her hand. "*Pfft*, Mama has a special meal planned for me later."

Secretly relieved, Hannah ate the latke in two bites. She had meant to savor the potato pancake, crisped by oleo, but hunger ruled her actions. Hannah licked her fingertips for any last traces of margarine.

"A Chanukah miracle," Hannah said as she stood and nodded her head toward the door, signaling that it was time for them to make their way to the food line.

Míša rose from the bunk and scrunched her mouth to the

side, "*Pfft*, I don't believe in any of that nonsense anymore. We have to make our own miracles."

———◇———

Hannah remembered watching Míša accept a birthday gift from Pavel two years earlier at a small party with their friends at Míša's family's apartment in Prague. Hannah and four of their classmates watched Pavel hand Míša a satin pouch at the end of the evening, and one of the boys teased by making a kissing noise. Trying to ignore the playful taunt, Míša pulled out the colorful necklace made of small glass beads separated by slender copper disks. Pavel helped Míša fasten it around her neck, and Hannah blushed at how her friend lowered her head and closed her eyes when Pavel's hand grazed the back of her neck.

On that night, Markéta had made her specialty, *the fluffiest dumplings you will eat ever*. Šimon rubbed his belly and lifted his half-full beer mug to toast his wife. "When I first tasted Markéta's cooking, I knew she was the woman I would marry!"

"You said to me it was my charming personality," Markéta quipped, swatting her husband. "Míša, I made *medovník* for dessert, your favorite."

When it came to her daughter, Markéta always went to great lengths to ensure her only child, her miracle baby, had what pleased her most. Markéta frequently told the girls that on the day Míša was born, she made a deal with God. "I held in my arms this perfect little baby and promised, I will do everything this child needs and wants, but you, my God, you must do your part and keep her healthy." Markéta said she knew she would recover from all the other losses—three miscarriages and a stillbirth—if Míša survived.

When Hannah and Míša made it to the food line, they unfastened their tin cups from their belts and eyed the contents of Markéta's soup pot. It looked like dishwater inside, but Markéta could only do so much with what she was given. "Potato soup," she said, stirring the bottom of the pot with her ladle.

Hannah knew the scraping sound of a near-empty soup vat all too well. It reminded her of a metal gate closing. She tried not to look too disappointed, but Míša's face crumpled with despondency.

"I'm sorry, *děvčátka*," Markéta replied, eyes downcast with embarrassment for what she, a former restaurant chef, was forced to serve. "Tonight, let the candle lighting feed your soul, since I cannot fill your bellies."

"I'm not hungry," Míša told her mother.

Hannah felt a pang of guilt for not realizing that there was no feast for her friend that evening. Stomach roiling with regret, Hannah watched Míša's face quivering, fighting off an expression of disappointment.

"Everything tonight went into making soup," Markéta said, voice cracking with the shame of being unable to feed her own daughter. A wrinkle formed between her eyebrows, and she looked down toward the pot. Just as the musicians and artists shared their gifts, Markéta told stories in the barracks about the three-course meals she prepared for foreign dignitaries visiting Prague. Meat so tender that you only needed to press a fork into it before it broke into delicate threads and absorbed the gravy. And forget about a dollop of cranberry sauce atop a bit of *smetana.* Markéta mixed the thick cream and berries and placed the sweet whip at the side of the plate. "I had to make a note on my menu that you may have as much sauce as you want, no need to keep begging," she had boasted with a lilting, playful bravado. "Per Albin Hansson himself told me my *svíčková na smetaně* was the very best he tasted ever. The man never returned to Sweden without first visiting Vila Hančová for a meal."

Míša lifted her head and smiled at her mother. "It's fine, Mama. Our work leader gave me a whole loaf of bread for exceeding my quota today."

"Can you believe this child?" Markéta asked Hannah. "Even here, she is such a perfect girl. More than your quota?" She leaned in and whispered to the pair, "The Nazis should burn in hell, but it is never a bad thing to be known as a good worker."

Hannah and Míša quickly drank their broth and headed toward the secret synagogue, a recently converted storage room beneath some of the private *prominenten* apartments where the Council of Elders and a handful of others lived with their families. Each unit had its own kitchen area and small closet. Children often slept in the same room as their parents or grandparents, but at least they were together.

The underground synagogue had low, arched ceilings that were newly adorned with orange Stars of David surrounded by smaller, five-point stars. An artist's skilled hand had painted Hebrew prayers along the top of the side and back walls.

V'techezenah eineinu b'shuv'cha l'tzion b'rachamim.

Let our eyes look upon your return to Zion with mercy.

The floors were unfinished wood, but Hannah could see that they had been cleaned with care. An image of Oma Minna flashed in her mind: Hannah and her grandmother bent on hands and knees on the kitchen floor, wiping their freshly swept floor with hot, damp rags. "The water picks up dirt that slips through bristles of a broom," Oma explained.

The room was packed with around seventy prisoners of all ages, sitting shoulder to shoulder along benches and standing against the walls. Oskar sat in the front row beside Griselde, whose hand was busy brushing away dandruff from the shoulders of his forest-green knit jacket before she patted his back tenderly. Oskar wore a sky-blue yarmulke that Hannah had seen Griselde admire at the museum earlier that day. Oskar turned and gestured by curling his index finger quickly, then pointing to the two empty seats beside them. His silver hair seemed as if it had been recently trimmed and tamed by a comb, his face clean shaven. Hannah swallowed a stone in her throat, noticing that Oskar's bushy eyebrows had been trimmed, something that hadn't been done since Oma Minna left for Palestine.

Next to them was Klara, still in her work dress, a dark blue frock with white embroidered flowers. Her head was turned toward Alena, and she exaggerated the movement of her lips as she spoke to her friend. Hannah thought it was in bad form for the young woman beside Alena to take a seat instead of offering it to an elder, until the woman struggled to stand and looked toward the back of the room, hand resting on her full belly. Hannah wondered when the pregnant woman was due to deliver and prayed the war would be over by then.

Hannah and Míša made their way to the front of the room to greet Oskar and Griselde but opted to stand against the wall with Iveta, who rested her head on the shoulder of a woman

Hannah assumed was her mother. The two women had the same thick waves and chiseled facial features; the older wore the muslin red cross armband of the ghetto nurses. "Let someone else have the seats," Hannah told Oskar, eyeing the elders entering the synagogue. She turned toward the door and waved them over, pointing to the empty seats.

Olina and Danuše stood directly across the synagogue from Míša and Hannah, the little girl clutching her new cloth doll, a gift Friedl had made in the studio that the council established to provide art lessons for the children. The doll had a long, dark braid like Danuše and two dimples stitched into the cheeks to match the little girl's. "What will you call her?" the artist had asked when she presented the child with the doll earlier that week. Friedl paused as the girl whispered in her ear. "Good choice! Adélka is a beautiful name. Children tell me that when they are afraid, they tell their *puppen* about it, and they feel better."

Hannah noticed Míša scanning the room for Pavel, who told her they would meet at the service, but he was nowhere to be found. "He's fine," Hannah whispered. "You know he's always late."

Jakob Edelstein rose from his seat and stood by a music stand at the front of the synagogue. "*Ah lichtigen Chanukah*, my friends."

Hannah and Míša had made it just in time.

"Many of you know that last week's transport brought the revered and respected Rabbi Leo Baeck to our community," Edelstein said, gesturing to the rabbi standing beside him. Baeck gave a small nod.

Hannah's eyes settled on Rabbi Baeck, who the Council of Elders invited to lead the prayer for the lighting of the candles.

"He's been arrested five times," Míša whispered. "Resistance. Some of us think he's a hero, but a few of the elders, *pfft*, they worry he'll bring trouble."

"How do you know this?" Hannah asked. Míša whispered that a group of prisoners smuggled a radio into the camp and listened to it secretly and passed on news to trusted friends. From there, information was transmitted by gossip, what they called "mouth radio."

Rabbi Baeck wore a clipped white beard that matched the sparse hair trimming his nearly bald head, which was covered in a simple black yarmulke. Hannah figured Rabbi Baeck would borrow one of the finest menorahs from the museum workshop, but when she searched the room for the candleholder, all she saw on the table before the rabbi was a small spoon with margarine, a curl of thread, and a single match. Hannah wondered if the rabbi saw her knitted brow as she surveyed the items, because he pointed to the table.

"We have a very special *chanukiah* to light this year," Rabbi Baeck announced. "Two gifted artists in our community carved it from a block of wood they…*found*." He exaggerated as he cleared his throat, then grinned mischievously. He looked to his right and nodded toward the door where Pavel appeared, carrying a *chanukiah* about fifty centimeters high and wide, but its presence filled the entire room. A Star of David was ornately carved into a linden wood disk at its center. It was about the size of a phonograph record. The star wasn't simply etched into the wood; it was hollowed through entirely. The artists chiseled in relief the Hebrew letters for *Mi kamocha ba'elim adonai*: Who is like you, God?

Hannah couldn't imagine how many hours it must have taken the men to create. *How did they find the time and energy?*

As the rabbi held a single match to the candlestick holder for the shammash, Hannah watched with wonder as a piece of thread caught the flame and ignited the margarine. Rabbi Baeck moved the match to the holder at the far right and lit the other. "I'm bending the rules, but I believe God will forgive me."

The group laughed softly, some people sounding as though they forced the response out of respect for the rabbi.

Pavel lifted his eyes to meet Míša's, and the two smiled, then quickly looked away before anyone else noticed.

A man in the front row stood and tucked a violin under his neck. He guided the bow carefully from the frog to the tip, producing a soulful longing sound, the rich melancholic music transporting Hannah to holidays past. In Munich, their synagogue offered the Chanukah prayer with two violins and a harp, engulfing the sanctuary with an ethereal comfort, like peaceful slumber. In Prague, Cantor Fein played his cello, and the sound of his wife's flute floated above the pluck of strings. Here, the secret synagogue was awash with the melody of "Maoz Tzur." Hannah could see others were drifting into their own memories, times of freedom with loved ones around the glow of candlelight. The vibrato was a quivering weep, outstretched hands shaking as they reached for something beyond their grasp. Still, it was beautiful.

Alice closed her eyes and swayed to the melody, the corners of her mouth rising, her chest filling. Hannah wondered if her bunkmate was aware that she was moving her fingers in silent accompaniment. Probably so, Hannah realized, remembering how Alice told her that she heard music everywhere. At bedtime, when little Danuše had been frightened by the winds outside, Alice assured her that rustling leaves were nature's wind chimes and that raindrops on the rooftop were angels playing tambourines. "Music is magic, but you must listen closely or you will miss the symphony God has composed for us," she had whispered to the girl.

Hannah heard a sniffle and glanced to her side to find Iveta, head still resting on her mother's shoulder, turn her face in toward her mother's dress sleeve. The sixteen-year-old liked to present herself as a grown woman of the world, often inserting unrelated facts or experiences to show how much she knew. Here, though, as the girl nestled into her mother, Hannah could imagine what Iveta looked like at Danuše's age, holding a rag doll of her own.

Griselde held her palms against her lips, and Hannah watched the wooden candleholders darken as they burned. For a moment, the flames from the *chanukiah* flickered in time with the chitter of the violin.

Oskar placed his right hand on Griselde's arm and outstretched his left one toward Hannah. Their fingertips barely touched, so Hannah stepped closer and bent to kiss his forehead.

By the end of the service, Markéta tiptoed into the synagogue and gently pushed through the crowd to make her way to Míša. "*Ah lichtigen Chanukah*, girls," she whispered. "Next year in Jerusalem." It was the wrong holiday for this wish, but the words felt like a gift to Hannah.

9

Hilde

Berlin
December 1941

H ILDE COULDN'T STOP LOOKING AT HER NEW WRISTWATCH, a *Rauhnacht* present from Otto, an apology for taking credit for her film idea. "The party would never have taken it seriously if they had known it came from a secretary," he explained. "You must start with small projects and work your way up, my dear." All day at the office, Hilde admired the way the diamond chips glimmered when she held the rectangular face under her desk lamp.

Now, in the darkness of the evening, Hilde pushed up the velvet trim of her coat sleeve and squinted at the watch hands as she made her way back to the boardinghouse. Hilde could not be late for Frau Schwammberger's Jul tree trimming. She quickened her pace, and the cadence of her leather boots against the sidewalk reminded her of the ticking of the hall clock at the boardinghouse. Her housemates Vilma and Nora were both heading to their respective families near Berlin for the holiday, and the landlady insisted that the women celebrate together before the house was all but empty. *You girls are the daughters I was never blessed with*, she often reminded them.

Passing the dress shop, Hilde turned to the window display and watched a woman in a slick bun straighten *Deutsche Weihnachten* figurines: a cow, two deer, and a family of rabbits. Next to the store was a news bulletin board with headlines promising that the winter relief program would ensure that no German would freeze or go hungry. "The entire German people have become one great family," another headline blasted.

Across the street, a furniture shop hung a large banner in its window:

Down with a Christ who allows himself
to be crucified! The German God
cannot be a suffering God! He is a
God of power and strength!

In the early years of the Reich, the National Socialist Party updated the Christmas holiday pantheon to better reflect its values: Odin the Norse god replaced Sankt Nikolaus, peace on earth became peace in the Fatherland, and of course the birth of Christ, a Jew, was eliminated entirely. The *Volk* continued with their dated ways of seeking comfort in the church, so the ministry developed propaganda that directly took aim at Jesus. *The führer is our true savior!* It was important for a nation to be unified in its beliefs.

Pushing open the front door to the boardinghouse, Hilde melted into the warmth of the living room with a fire snapping in the brick hearth. The scent of fresh pine and sweet dough wafted through the air. She adjusted her headband to neaten her freshly bobbed hair. A bare Jul tree stood by the front window, hovering above three open red ornament boxes. The first was filled with gold tinsel; another contained slender white candles and brass holders. The sight of the third made Hilde step back. She had forgotten about Frau Schwammberger's cache of aluminum busts of Hitler. Germans were forbidden from using party symbols—especially images of the führer—as tree ornaments, yet Frau Schwammberger owned at least ten. They were placed in sectioned compartments that looked like egg crates alongside iron crosses, toy grenades, and imperial eagles, all of which were now verboten as holiday decor. Odin's sun wheel and birds were the modern symbols of the season.

Before Hilde could consider reminding her landlady of this, the kitchen door swung open, and Frau Schwammberger emerged in a white apron, holding a tray filled with ginger snaps made with her new cookie cutter in the lightning bolt shape of the *Siegrune*, the symbol for the Deutsches Jungvolk. Trailing behind was Nora gripping the handle of a glass pitcher of hot apple cider.

Frau Schwammberger's face brightened at the sight of Hilde removing her coat and hanging it on the rack. "*Juchu!* Everyone is home now." She placed the tray on the table and turned her head toward the stairwell. "Vilma, come downstairs," she called out.

Hilde looked at the tray and exclaimed, "Mmm, ginger snaps, my favorite."

With an incredulous laugh, Frau Schwammberger replied, "Why do you think I made them?"

Maybe Hilde wouldn't say anything about the ornaments after all. It was the season of forgiveness, and who among them didn't break a few rules? Even a fanatic Hitler girl like Hilde had a secret pot of rouge she applied on special occasions, despite the führer's disapproval of makeup.

Frau Schwammberger turned the knob of the *Volksempfänger*, and a deep male voice filled the room with Hilde's favorite holiday song, "Exalted Night."

Vilma's feet pounded the steps as she ran downstairs.

"Oh good, Hilde's here. Now, can we open our gifts?" Vilma asked, gesturing to the burlap sack next to the door. She winked. "Some of the girls at the Chancellery say Odin was very good to them this year. Anna got a mink muff, and Rita got a gold locket."

"The tree, girls, the tree!" Frau Schwammberger scolded playfully, then swept the room with her open palms. "You girls are so fortunate. When I was your age, we had nothing."

Vilma shot Hilde a knowing glance. Everyone in their generation had heard this lament a dozen different ways. *Germany had just lost the Great War. We were a broken nation. Fleeced by the Jews. Demilitarized and forced to pay reparations. No hope for the future. Then a worldwide economic depression.*

Hilde knew she should politely agree with her landlady, especially after the woman had prepared her favorite treats. At the same time, she couldn't afford to alienate Vilma. The two had forged an unspoken truce after Hilde's first night with Otto; Hilde knew that Vilma had grown to admire her once she hinted that her secret *Schatz* was a high-ranking member of the Reich. "Good to hear," Vilma had said softly, backing away from her usual aggressive stance. "You can always count on me as a friend, you know, Hilde." But Hilde wasn't interested in friendship with a jealous girl who only wanted to latch on to her rising star.

Still, she could not afford to have Vilma as an adversary when she knew that Hilde had lied about employment in the Reich for so long. She waited until Frau Schwammberger turned toward the tree, then rolled her eyes. *This again?*

Conflicted, Hilde backtracked. "We *are* fortunate, Frau Schwammberger. I don't know how you all pulled through."

"It wasn't easy, but life is no pony farm," she replied, bending down to lift a box onto the coffee table. She pulled a plain red ornament and continued. "Start with the solid red balls deep in the bush, then work your way out with the more detailed ornaments."

Hilde looked at Vilma and raised an eyebrow. She reached for a glass ball, disappointed that it would be a while before dusting the branches with tinsel, Hilde's favorite part of the tree trimming. When her sister, Lisa, was a little girl, Hilde would place her on her shoulders so she could toss "icicles" onto the tree.

Stepping close, Hilde took in the scent of pine as she searched for sturdy branches. The soft needles tickled her arm as she reached in and found a place for a red ball.

Frau Schwammberger moved about the Jul tree the same way Hilde's mother did, placing an ornament on a branch, then stepping back to evaluate. "One more on the left side, Nora," Frau Schwammberger instructed. "A beautiful tree is balanced, not too much on one side or the other." She sighed. "I wish I'd known how promising the future of Germany would be back when I was young like you girls. Not five years ago, I lived in a crummy little apartment, and now..." She swept her arms across the room.

Hilde nodded in agreement and opened her mouth to speak, but Nora beat her to it. "And our children will have it even better."

"We *all* will," Hilde said, hoping the bitterness she felt hadn't seeped through in her tone. Yes, yes, children were the future of Germany, but all their lives mattered.

Her fingers froze as she searched for a branch for her tree ornament. Maybe that was what the children needed from a propaganda film. They should see how magnificent cities like Warsaw and Prague and Stalingrad would look as part of the new German Reich. Right now, these were just names of far-away places, but if a beloved goddess like Frau Holle introduced German children to *Lebensraum*, they would see the promise of a brighter future. *Yes, there are rations, but look what's ahead for you. Be patient,* Kinder. It was a simple idea, perfectly digestible for little minds. Even better was that Hilde had the day off from work on Christmas—no, no Julfest—so after supper with Frau Schwammberger, Hilde could get to work on a script.

10

Hannah

MARKÉTA WORE AN APRON AS SHE STOOD BEHIND HER IRON vat and tucked a loose tendril of hair back into her kerchief. A long line of prisoners spilled into the *Marktplatz* behind Hannah and Míša, but only nine were ahead of them. When she arrived at Theresienstadt three weeks earlier, Hannah started timing how long it took each cook to serve supper so she could count out the seconds until she had food. Míša's mother was the fastest server, taking six seconds to dip her ladle into the vat and pour it into a tin cup, another two to hand a person a slice of bread. The cook who stood next to Markéta took eight seconds to serve and had a smaller drum, so his service came to a halt every time a kitchen hand had to refill the vat. Somehow the wait felt longer in the dark of the winter night.

Míša coughed just as she and Hannah reached the front of the food line, and Markéta shook her head with irritation at the sound. "Will you talk some good sense into her?" Markéta urged Hannah. "That cough is only getting worse," she said, tilting her ladle and pouring thin brown liquid into Hannah's cup. Beef stew, the kitchen called it, though it offered no meat; the potatoes were rotten, so the cooks overboiled them to dull the taste and kill bacteria.

"It's winter, Mama. *Pfft*, everyone has a cold," Míša replied as Hannah wrapped her hands around the tin mug, hoping her gloves would hold the warmth of the broth.

"Your mama is right," Hannah added, licking her lips for remnants before a Ghettowache officer blew his whistle.

"Keep the line moving," he shouted, the demand riding on the frost of his breath. He moved from side to side, rubbing his hands together.

"I'll keep trying," Hannah assured Míša's mother before the two stepped aside for the next prisoners in line.

As they walked toward the Dresden Barracks, Míša hacked again. "*Pfft*, a tickle in my throat, that's all," she assured Hannah.

"Go to the hospital, Míša. The nurse can give you some medicine to sooth your throat," Hannah insisted. "If not for yourself, then go for the sake of everyone else on the third floor. We can hear you from all the way on my side." Hannah hated to lie, but she knew her motives justified it. There were nearly a thousand women who slept between Hannah's stall and Míša's bunk, and a good quarter of them rumbled with coughs and moans.

"All right."

All right? That was it? None of Míša's usual arguments about not wanting to waste precious resources? No lecture about how the best place to catch a virus was in the hospital? Míša was a lot of things, but agreeable wasn't one of them. She was up to something.

"What time will you go?"

Míša shrugged. "In about ten minutes."

"Good. I'll walk there with you."

Shaking her head, Míša insisted it wasn't necessary. "You shouldn't be around all those germs."

"I want to make sure you actually go, Míša. I'll meet you at the stairwell in ten minutes," Hannah said, knowing her friend would not wait for her. The two walked the rest of the way to the barracks in silence until they made it to the top of the steps, and Hannah turned left toward her end of the third floor. "Ten minutes. Maybe fifteen," she reminded Míša.

Míša sighed, exasperated, and agreed. "Fine."

Hannah knew her friend was appeasing her.

The only good thing about living in a crowded ghetto, Hannah thought, was that she could follow Míša unnoticed, blending in with the human landscape that looked like Prague Main train station at the end of a workweek. As Hannah expected, Míša hurried down the stairwell. But what Míša didn't know was that Hannah had immediately descended the back stairwell and remained twenty meters behind her as she predictably passed the hospital and continued toward the moonlit *Marktplatz*. Hannah tucked her hair into her wool hat and turned up the collar of her jacket so she would look like any other bundled prisoner at Theresienstadt.

After Míša crossed the *Marktplatz*, she made her way down a narrow side road that led toward a grove of trees. The crowd thinned so Hannah had to be more discreet. Finally, she saw the glimmer factory, a converted red barn, in the distance set back in trees. *Why would Míša go back to work at night?*

Hannah trotted behind, quickening her pace as she watched

Míša run toward the back of the glimmer factory. She clung to the side of the building and followed Míša's path before she stopped, realizing she was probably about to interrupt her friend's secret meeting with Pavel. When they'd all been in the audience of *The Bartered Bride* three nights earlier, Hannah noticed how Míša and Pavel leaned toward each other as soon as conductor Rafael Schächter began playing the overture on the baby grand piano. During the second scene of the opera, when characters Mařenka and Jeník vow their faithful love, their voices in duet, Míša and Pavel laced their fingers. As the piece came to a close, soprano and tenor notes intertwined, Pavel lifted Míša's hand to his lips and kissed it gently.

Now, Hannah wrapped her arms around herself as she watched Míša tap on the back door to the glimmer factory. It slid open, just a crack, and Míša stepped inside. Hannah had made a mistake and intruded on a private moment.

"Hello, Hannah," a voice from behind her said.

When she turned, she startled at the sight of her friend, illuminated by the blue light of the moon. Hannah gulped for air and felt a rush of pinpricks cover her body. "Pavel…what are you…" *If Pavel is out here, who let Míša into the glimmer factory?* "I don't… What's going on?"

She pointed to the rucksack strapped across Pavel's chest, but he didn't explain. Instead Pavel looped his arm through Hannah's and led her to the barn door, where he tapped in the same pattern as Míša had. *Knock. Pause. Tap, tap.*

"Come with me," he whispered.

Hannah dropped her head when she spotted Míša inside.

"Hey, look who I found," Pavel said.

"*Oy Gotenyu*," Míša said, shaking her head. "Did you follow me?"

"Sorry, I didn't know you two were—"

The click of a switch was followed by a soft white glow coming from Pavel's flashlight. Hannah couldn't help noticing the dust sparkling, illuminated in the beam of light. Laid out similarly to the museum workshop, long wooden tables were clustered throughout the room, three long rows that could seat a dozen on each side. But unlike Hannah's tidy workplace, the walls of the mica-splitting plant were the color of rotten teeth with chips of paint hanging from the ceiling like stalactites. Small knives the size of letter openers lay neatly on tables, next to cutting boards and whetstones. Stacks of pans, empty save for a layer of glitter coating the bottom, sat ready to collect new mica flakes the next day.

The same series of knocks sounded, and Míša opened the door for someone else.

"Who's she?" a male voice asked.

Hannah turned to see a young man with similar looks as Pavel, hair trimmed short on the sides with a shock of loose sandy waves at the top. Not only did he have the same athletic build as Pavel, but he wore the identical style of flannel work top and also rolled his corduroy pant legs above his ankles.

Pavel sighed with irritated resignation. "You're here now, so, Hannah, this is Luděk, my cousin."

Hannah had seen Luděk once, when she passed the work site for the railroad extension from Bauschowitz into the ghetto. She remembered him because he and Pavel seemed to be the most experienced laborers of the group, shouting instructions to the crew leader and teaching teens and grown men alike how to properly use a railroad jack and mallet.

"She'd better be here to help us. I told you to be careful," Luděk said with a stern tone.

It all came rushing back to Hannah. Pavel said his cousin was involved in a resistance group. Míša told Hannah she was part of one too. Hannah's skin began to prickle, and she wanted nothing more than to run back to the Dresden Barracks and forget what she'd seen.

Míša jumped in before Hannah could reply. "She's my best friend. I…I invited her to the meeting. Stop wasting time, and get upstairs." Widening her eyes at Hannah, Míša's message was clear: *Don't argue. Just follow me.*

Trailing behind Míša, they all walked to a supply closet in the back of the room. The door was ajar, and Luděk pushed it open and held out his arm, gesturing for Hannah and Míša to enter first. Inside was lined with shelves holding metal canisters the size of barrels, embossed with imperial eagles and swastikas, about twenty in all. Each bore a single word beneath the Nazi symbols: LUFTWAFFE. Míša reached her hands up to grip the second shelf and climbed up as Hannah's stomach swirled with nausea. What had she gotten herself into?

"Míša, what is this?" Hannah asked.

"The mica? I wish I could tell you, but the Luftwaffe needs it for something, because we're splitting tons of it."

When Míša reached the top, she pulled on a crate until it swiveled and revealed an attic door. "Come up," Míša whispered.

"Need a boost?" Pavel asked from behind her on the ground.

"I've got it," Hannah returned, gripping the wooden post of the shelf, then flinching when she felt a splinter lodge itself into her thumb. After she made it to the top, she followed her friend, who had already pulled herself through the attic door.

On all fours, Míša poked her head out. "Do you want my hand?"

Hannah reached toward Míša. "Please." She felt the muscles of her arms stretch as Míša pulled. A sharp pain made Hannah acutely aware of the connection between her shoulder and clavicle. At the top, Hannah felt her stomach lunge at the stink of mold, like wet socks and spoiled vegetables. She turned back to see Pavel scaling the shelves with ease, Luděk on the floor beneath them, shining his flashlight upward.

Hannah's gaze was quickly drawn inside the attic, toward the center of the space where two female faces were illuminated by the light from an oil lantern, which they gathered around like a campfire. There was Iveta, hugging her knees into her chest for warmth. Beside her was Klara, ending a story. "They wouldn't want to disturb this Garden of Eden," she said, pursing her lips, then pretending to spit on the ground.

Some of the women in the Dresden Barracks gossiped that Klara complained too much, but that was exactly what Hannah liked about her. There were enough well-meaning elders who tried to comfort the younger women and assure them that Theresienstadt was bearable. Ironically, it was Klara's barbs that brought Hannah real solace by letting her know that her feelings of sadness and disgust were valid. Though the others had good intentions, Hannah would have gone mad trying to bridge the gap between what she heard and what she saw with her own eyes.

Still on her hands and knees, Hannah struggled to keep from bumping into the wall as she crawled on the wood floor toward the tight circle. Míša followed, then tucked herself between

Hannah and Klara. "Hannah, you know Iveta and Klara from the barracks," she said, pointing to the women. "Hannah's here to help us."

Wind whistled through a warped slat of wood of the attic wall and felt like a whip against her face. Luděk made his way inside and sat next to Hannah, then reached into his jacket pocket and removed a small loaf of bread broken into pieces. Hannah remembered that manual laborers received extra rations and pressed her lips together, remorseful that she had already made her choice to accept Luděk's offer to share his bread when she knew that he needed the nourishment more than she. And did she really deserve the rewards of this resistance group when she wanted no part of it?

None of that mattered once Hannah felt the pinch at the sides of her tongue that came from eating when she was famished. Soon the pain relented, and the sensation of chewing doughy goodness filled her with relief. Hannah closed her eyes, wanting to block out the rest of the world and experience nothing other than consuming bread.

Míša clapped her palms together softly, not making a sound. "We have a lot to cover tonight, so let's get started. Pavel, you have the letters?"

He confirmed by patting the rucksack on his lap.

Hannah remained silent as they reviewed the plan: Pavel would meet a Czech gendarme who agreed to help the prisoners at the back entrance of the ghetto at the shift change at four in the morning and hand him the satchel of letters addressed to the International Committee of the Red Cross, the League of Nations, and the Vatican, along with dozens more to family members still in Prague. Unlike the scripted postcards prisoners sent through the ghetto postal system—or the censored letters that came in—these would tell the truth about the conditions at Theresienstadt, including that a credible source had told them that a transport bound for a work camp in Riga was scheduled for later that week. After the gendarme had the bag in hand, he would deliver the letters to a contact in Prague, who would somehow get them to Switzerland, where they could be mailed. The whole thing sounded loosely planned and ill-advised, and Hannah could not hold her tongue any longer.

"I don't understand. Why don't you use the ghetto postal system?"

Iveta rolled her eyes. "And say what? Dear Red Cross, we are slave laborers being starved and sleeping in vermin-infested barracks without running water?"

"She's right," Míša added, looking at Hannah. "You've seen what the censors do to the letters coming in. More words crossed out than left on the page. And you know the Nazis read all our postcards that leave the ghetto."

"So send a message in code. One misspelled word from Pavel, and anyone would know something's wrong."

"Yeah, because Pavel has so many friends at the Red Cross and League of Nations," Iveta snapped.

What was Iveta's problem? The two had been friendly in the barracks, but now the teen was downright hostile. It was as though Iveta resented Hannah's late involvement in the group or suspected her motives altogether, which Hannah could not begrudge her for. Iveta was young and passionate, and Hannah did not actually support what the group was planning.

Hannah sighed, exasperated. "I know you want to take action. So do I, but the war will be over soon and—"

Míša interrupted. "Stop! No one knows when… We can't wait till then."

Hannah inhaled deeply before continuing, then looked at the others, trying to make her case. "But the Americans have already… Save your energy for survival, not these…these…heroics that could get you people sent to the small fortress."

"You people?" Luděk asked. "I thought you were here to help us."

Hannah shot back, "I am. But every action you take has consequences."

Iveta shook her head with disgust. "Every action we *don't* take has consequences, Hannah. You'd think if anyone would get that, it would be a German."

"What's that supposed to mean?"

"If you Germans fought back against Hitler, maybe we wouldn't be here now."

Who was Iveta to give Hannah a history lesson? A wrong one at that! This girl knew nothing about what it was like to live in Germany as a Jew during Hitler's ascent to power.

"You Czechs didn't exactly rise up when the Nazis annexed the Sudetenland or created the protectorate. You rolled over almost as fast as Austria."

"Very convenient of you to forget Jan Opletal and the other Czech students protesting the occupation."

"And very convenient of you to forget they were killed," Hannah snapped back.

"Hey, hey." Pavel jumped in to defend Iveta. "She said they fought back, that's all. You can't say we Czechs didn't try."

Thankfully, Klara jumped in before Hannah could return with a childish swipe that Iveta was the one who started this line of accusation.

"Enough with the *Fingerzeig*! The Nazis are the enemy. We mustn't point fingers at one another."

"We're all on the same side," Míša reminded Hannah, then turned her head to Iveta.

"Are we?" Iveta raised her pitch.

Luděk held up a hand. "All right, girls, take off the gloves. We're not here to fight each other."

Iveta snapped back, "That's *exactly* what she's here for!"

"Hush," Klara hissed. "Keep your voice down."

At the sound of boots clomping across the workroom of the glimmer factory, each of the six prisoners sat upright and turned toward the opening they had crawled through to enter the attic. The sound of the steps was heavy and unafraid, growing louder as it came closer, climbing up toward the secret entrance. Hannah curled her fingers around Míša's and squeezed, forgetting how raw her friend's hands were until she flinched. Iveta's teeth began to chatter, and her body rocked slightly, her eyes locked forward as if the girl had been transported to another place. They all heard the crate begin to slide, the sound of wood scratching against the grainy shelf.

Hannah's eyes were searchlights focused on the open hatch to the attic. A dark shape appeared. It was the rounded top of a Ghettowache policeman's hat pushing through the small opening. Hannah saw the glint of metal jacket buttons catch the lamplight, followed by the red shoulder stripes of the police uniform jacket.

"*Oy Gotenyu!* Radek, you scared the life out of us!" Míša whispered. "You said you couldn't make it tonight."

The others were all visibly relieved at the arrival of the Jewish policeman. Shoulders dropped and bodies unclenched. Hannah understood that this Radek person was a member of their group, but she couldn't convince her body of this. Her heart beat so fast it was practically vibrating, and her pores opened wide, sweat coating her back.

"Sorry, sorry," he replied, removing his blue Ghettowache cap, then looking at Hannah. "Who's she?"

Hannah tilted her head to the side and twisted her mouth with confusion. To Pavel, she asked, "Didn't you say not to trust them?"

"What was I going to tell you, that some of them work with us? Hey, the less you know, the better for everyone."

Hannah shuddered, remembering Kryštof telling her the same thing. She didn't know whether she was insulted or grateful for both men's attempts to shield her from the truth.

Hannah had seen Radek before and always thought him a brute because of his harsh tone when he shouted orders at prisoners. *Move along! Stay with your work group. Quiet!* He seemed to enjoy his authority, and Hannah had assumed it was to compensate for his stubby build and chipmunk cheeks. She offered him a quick smile as she recast him in her mind.

Radek interrupted. "I'm afraid I have some bad news."

Lifting her head quickly, Iveta began shaking it. "Don't say a word in front of her! People here will sell their mother's right arm for a potato. We don't know if she's an informant."

"Enough, Iveta!"

Hannah sighed with relief when Míša defended her.

"She's misguided, but she's not selling information. What's your news, Radek?"

"It's your father, Míša." He looked down. "He'll be on the transport to Riga. It's leaving sooner than we thought. Tomorrow." Radek explained that the SS assigned the Council of Jewish Elders the wretched task of choosing one thousand names for the transport list.

Míša held her hand to her chest and bunched the collar of her blouse in her fist. "Does Mama know?"

He nodded. "She's relieved he'll no longer be in the small fortress."

"Right," she said. "Mama's right. He's a hard worker. He'll be better off in Riga."

Hannah watched Míša sit on her hands and knew she was trying to stop their trembling.

Míša turned her focus to Hannah. "Look, we've got work to do."

"Don't tell her our plans—" Iveta interrupted herself with a loud huff that said, *You people are so damn stupid!*

"I just don't want anyone to get hurt," Hannah said, her voice pitching high with apology.

"What would you call this?" Pavel held out his arms and turned to show their surroundings.

"Maybe it's better if you leave," Míša suggested.

"Make sure nobody sees you," Luděk added.

Radek turned to Hannah and gave a warning look that resembled the one he gave prisoners. "You know if you say anything about this group or these letters, we'll all be sent to the small fortress."

"I won't breathe a word," she promised.

Iveta crossed her arms over her chest. "You'd better not."

—◦—

When she returned to her barracks, Hannah climbed the ladder to her top bunk and picked up the dog-eared copy of Thomas Mann's *Buddenbrooks* she'd left beside her hairbrush that morning. Hannah had already read the novel and needed to return it to the library but wanted to escape into the pages of another era in Germany when her friends weren't prisoners planning to smuggle letters from the ghetto. Exasperated, she sighed. Míša and the others were completely turned through! Hannah tried her best to disappear into the prose but wound up reading the same line four times. Tonight would have to be one for falling asleep to her own thoughts.

As she lay on her pallet each night, Hannah usually closed her eyes and returned to her favorite memories. On this night, though, when she tried to transport herself to the Klementinum Library in Prague or the ski slopes of Oberstdorf, Hannah's thoughts pulled her back to growing up in Munich. The question that haunted her was one that had no answer, yet Hannah could not stop wondering if there was a particular moment when Germany descended into madness.

Hannah first noticed changes in Germany on her first day of the eighth year of school, the month after President von Hindenburg died and Chancellor Hitler became the führer. It was 1934. Hannah was thirteen years old and had never been particularly interested in politics. Few people her age were. A year earlier, she'd heard about the fire at the Reichstag and saw her parents fret about the boycott of Jewish businesses, but these things were the province of adults. They had assured Hannah and Ben that they needn't worry about the Nazis, so the Kaufman children turned their attention to more pleasant things. Dancing to records with Oma Minna. Reading new books and going to the cinema.

Soon, though, like smoke slipping through the crack of a window, Nazi ideology found its way into German schools. When Hannah entered her *Mittelschule* classroom after summer break, she noticed a large poster titled *Bilder deutscher Rassen*, "Pictures of German Races," unfurled on the blackboard behind Frau Borsig. It was a grid of nine faces, both male and female, front and profile views. Beside it was another poster with the same layout, only this one was titled *Untermenschen*, "Subhumans." On it were photos of Jews, Africans, and Romani, all with hideously exaggerated facial features. Hannah had spent her entire life around Jewish people, and she had never seen a nose as big as a pickle or eyes as beady as a rat's.

Oma Minna had always armed Hannah with a bouquet of flowers to give to her teacher on the first day of school. "*Guten Morgen.* These are from my oma's garden, Frau Borsig," Hannah said, offering the instructor a dozen poppies tied together with a red ribbon.

Narrowing her eyes, Hannah's teacher accepted the flowers and threw them in the trash can beside her desk. "The proper German greeting is *Heil Hitler.* Sit in the back of the classroom."

Hannah couldn't understand what she had done wrong to go from one of Frau Borsig's star pupils to the object of scorn over the course of one summer. "Oh...um...all right," Hannah said, looking at her shoes. Hannah raised her arm as she had seen others do.

She struggled to see the blackboard all year, though Frau Borsig moved Hannah to the center of the room during final exams. The teacher always found fault in Hannah's reports. She never gave her more than partial credit on her written responses to test questions in history and racial science, but she could not downgrade the girl's answers to mathematics questions. There were only right and wrong responses, and Hannah's were always correct.

Hannah had grown accustomed to her spot in the last row and found it unsettling to be suddenly relocated to a place where she could not see her classmates behind her. On the day of the final exam in mathematics, Hannah sat erect with her hands folded on the desk. Frau Borsig handed out the test booklets, then turned her back to the class and began erasing the chalkboard. Soon, she sat at her desk and began leafing through a magazine as Hannah felt the shadows of her classmates leaning close to copy her answers. Hannah was certain that Frau Borsig would have to intervene when Hans Delmotte snatched Hannah's exam booklet from her desk. Everyone had heard the hiss of Hannah's pencil being dragged across the papers, the *whoosh* of the pages plucked away. Even Hannah's best friend copied her answers that day.

Was that when her life as a normal German schoolgirl ended? Or had Germany changed earlier, more quietly, and Hannah simply hadn't noticed?

Lying on her pallet in the bunk in the Dresden Barracks, Hannah bunched her fists, willing herself to sleep. Rest was a precious commodity at Theresienstadt, and a full night's sleep wasn't easy to come by, because Hannah never knew whether it was the hay-filled mattress or bedbugs causing her skin to itch. She knew she should try to allow her mind to idle, yet she could not stop her racing thoughts from revisiting the last time she saw her best friend in Munich, two years after she'd taken answers from Hannah's math exam, then stayed silent when Hannah was punished for cheating.

Hannah's lungs stung from the cold as she walked to her friend's house for her fourteenth birthday party in November 1935. When she reached the front door, it opened before she could knock. Her friend's mother had always been kind to Hannah, but standing at the threshold of her home, Frau Kramer's eyes were vacant and aloof. Before Hannah could say a word, Frau Kramer held up her palm, "I'm sorry, dear, we…" She looked back into the house and quieted her voice. "I tried to telephone your mother. We… Hilde needs to broaden her circle of friends." Frau Kramer remained in the doorway for a moment, then stepped inside and closed the door.

Paralyzed with humiliation, Hannah stood on Hilde's doorstep, the one she had crossed hundreds of times over the years without a second thought. Had Frau Kramer always felt this way? The hollow sound of the door slamming echoed in Hannah's ears. Hannah turned to her left and spotted a handful of girls from their class turning the corner with wrapped gift boxes and dashed off in the opposite direction. After that, she did not dare venture within a block of Hilde's home, not even to say goodbye when her family left for Prague the following week. She considered going late at night and tossing pebbles at Hilde's window, but anxiety got the better of her. She was terrified of seeing Frau Kramer again but more afraid that Hilde might feel the same way her mother did.

On her walk home that day, Hannah tossed the gift she'd brought for Hilde in a rubbish can on the street. Oma Minna had taught Hannah how to make a papier-mâché mask like European nobility wore to masquerade balls. Once it had hardened, Hannah painted it gold and adorned it with rhinestones and a long violet feather. She sat in the park for hours so neither her parents nor grandparents would ask why she had returned early from Hilde's party.

11

Hannah

THE YOUNG WOMEN LINKED ARMS AS THEY STEPPED FROM
the Dresden Barracks onto the morning snow as they made
their way toward the *Marktplatz* for their breakfast ration. "That's
never going to work, you know," Hannah said, mustering a smile
as Míša tried to blow smoke rings with the condensation from
the cold morning air. She let out a cough as though she'd taken
too long a draw of a cigarette.

"Let a girl dream," Míša said, bumping Hannah with her hip.
"I smoked all the cigarettes you gave me."

"Not by yourself," Hannah teased. "You had a little help from
Pavel, didn't you?" Hannah knew Míša and Pavel had been sneak-
ing off to steal moments of intimacy in a *kumbál* like many others
in the ghetto. She could hardly pass judgment; at least Míša was
in love. Hannah had only engaged in mild petting with Kryštof
from the *Schleuse*, but the sole feeling between them was gratitude
that they could satisfy each other's desperation—his for the soft
skin of a woman's breasts, hers for food.

When Hannah saw Míša blush over her teasing about Pavel,

she changed the subject. "Opa gave me two tickets to *The Magic Flute* tonight. Want to be my date? It got a great review in *Vedem*."

"We're relying on the opinions of teenage boys now?" Míša said with a snort.

"Their magazine happens to be excellent," Hannah replied playfully.

"All right," Míša said, clearing her throat.

Hannah was relieved that her friend was not angry with her about speaking out at the glimmer factory resistance meeting the night before. "You did what you thought was right, just like I'm doing," Míša said when she saw Hannah later. "*Pfft*, how can I blame you for that?"

Iveta hadn't been as generous, making a big show of ignoring Hannah as they prepared for bed. She locked her jaw and glared, shaking her head at Hannah, her expression saying, *I don't trust you one little bit.*

Returning to the present, Hannah told Míša that *The Magic Flute* began at eight that evening. "You don't have a date with Pavel tonight, do you?"

Míša said nothing but quickened her pace to hide her mischievous grin as the two turned the corner to the *Marktplatz*. Hannah stopped so abruptly that she lost her footing. She considered that her eyes were playing tricks on her in the blue hour before sunrise. Perhaps her wits were dull from another night of restless sleep. Míša's arm tightened, and Hannah regained her balance.

They froze at the sight before them. At the center of the public square was a row of lifeless bodies, all men, hanging from newly erected gallows.

"*Oy Gotenyu*," Míša whispered as she placed her hand protectively over her neck.

The two stepped back around the corner and hid behind the side wall of the town hall, Hannah counting quickly. Nine men.

Heart pounding, Hannah watched hundreds of fellow prisoners slow their pace as they walked through the square on their way to their morning meal. They peered up at the faces of the men, shaking their heads with sadness. Low whispers of mourning hung in the air like fog. *What a shame. To je strašný, tut, tut, tut.* Ghettowache officers barked at the prisoners to hurry along to the breakfast lines outside the Engineer Barracks. It was almost time for their work shift.

Hannah had never seen an actual dead person. Now she was facing nine, their heads slumped forward or to the side of their broken necks. Their bare feet were limp, a waxy sheen of purple covering one man's toes, bruises staining the swollen face of another. Hannah shivered at the sight of blood soaking through the shirts of two more, darkening their yellow stars. The men had surely endured a brutal interrogation before the Nazis strung them up in the square for all to see.

"No!" Míša screamed before she lost her balance trying to run toward the men. She'd fallen onto her elbows and knees, and the crack of bone against ice terrified Hannah. Had she broken an arm or leg? But Míša bolted upright and rushed toward the men.

"Míša, what are you—" Hannah called out, reaching for her friend's coat sleeve, causing them both to topple onto the ice.

"Let go of me!" Míša shouted, pushing Hannah away and running toward the gallows.

When Hannah lifted her head from the frozen ground, she squinted her eyes and realized one of the silhouettes looked familiar: the waves of hair curtaining the man's face. When she saw the way his pants were rolled at the bottom, she knew it was Pavel.

Beside Pavel was his father, Alois, who had let a beard start to grow since their arrival three weeks earlier. He had wet the front of his pants, and Hannah shivered at the thought of how frightened he must have been. Hannah noticed his eyes were still half-open.

Hannah ran toward Míša, who was already standing beneath the bodies, tugging at the sleeve of a Ghettowache officer, demanding that he cut the ropes. "Get them down from there! What is wrong with you? How can you just stand there?"

Hannah wondered if Míša thought the men could be saved or if she wanted to preserve their dignity.

Hannah wrapped her arms around Míša's shoulders and pulled her in for a hug. Turning Míša away from the sight, Hannah whispered, "Don't look." Hannah desperately wanted to replace the horrid image of Pavel with the one of him alive in the glimmer factory attic the night earlier. Better still, Hannah closed her eyes tight and tried to remember the way Pavel looked when she and Míša ventured to Charles University to see him after their *Gymnázium* classes ended for the day. She disappeared into the recollection for a moment. There he was, in Hannah's mind, alive with his eyeglasses fixed on a political science textbook as he ate lunch. "Let's think of him the way he was," Hannah offered, her throat tightening. She thought about the way Pavel's pronounced Adam's apple rose and fell when he was absorbed in his books. Hannah sniffled. "Remember how he always forgot his cigarette burning in the ashtray and the ash got so long?"

Míša nodded as Hannah slowly coaxed her away from the scene, walking her back to the town hall, where they had been minutes earlier. "That's our Pavel. Not this."

Radek, the policeman who had been at the glimmer factory meeting, blew his whistle, and Hannah wondered if it was he who had betrayed the group. "Move along," he called out. She searched his face for clues, but he remained expressionless.

Her back pressed against the wall of the town hall, Hannah heard steps approaching and turned to see little Danuše and her mother, Olina, making their way to breakfast. "You two shouldn't dillydally," the mother advised.

"Don't…don't go that way," Hannah tried to warn them as they reached the corner.

Hannah began to step in front of them but didn't move quickly enough. She watched Danuše's long brown braid whip Olina's leg when the girl turned away and buried her face in her mother's hip. "Mama, why are those boys—"

Her doll, Adélka, dropped to the ground.

"Hush!" Olina demanded as she quickly reorganized her face. She glanced down at her daughter and inhaled deeply. "You're safe. We are safe," she said, scooping her child into her arms, then picking up Adélka. She hurried to cross the square, shielding Danuše's eyes with the doll.

Hannah swallowed a cry as she leaned back onto the wall, pained for the mother forced to make false promises to help her child bear the moment.

After Olina clipped across the *Marktplatz*, Míša wiped her

eyes with her sleeve. "I thought if they were caught with the letters, they might be sent to the small fortress with Papa. Locked up but not…not…oh God, not…*this*."

"Did you see the others?" Hannah asked. "Was Luděk…"

"I don't know. I couldn't see. I…I hope not."

Hannah understood that her timing was insensitive to Míša's loss, but she had to ask, "Why were there nine men? Who else was involved?"

"There were others," Míša whispered.

Hannah gasped at the next thought. "Will they come for the women? Are you and Klara and Iveta going to…" She could not finish.

Míša's arm gestured toward the gallows. "The men took our names to the grave with them. Otherwise, we would be up there… They protected us, Hannah."

The cold stone of the municipal hall pressed against Hannah's back. She curled her hands into fists to keep them from shaking and clenched her jaw to trap her screams. *Why had they gone through with this foolish plan?* Then guilt set in. *Why didn't I try harder to dissuade them?*

"Don't miss our morning feast," Klara said with a bite of sarcasm, breezing by Hannah and Míša as she made her way to the square. When she stopped, she didn't say a word or make a noise; her hand reached for the smooth facing of the town hall and splayed her fingers against the wall. Hannah watched her bunkmate sink to her knees, then rest her palms on the ground before vomiting onto the footing of the building.

"Do you need a handkerchief?" Hannah asked before realizing that she didn't have one.

Hannah pulled Míša's arm toward the *Marktplatz*. Reluctantly, Míša nodded and began to walk toward the breakfast line, trying to appear no more distraught than any other prisoner. "Should we say a prayer for them?" Hannah asked.

"*Pfft*, who exactly do you think is listening to our prayers?" Míša wiped away her tears.

As they stood in line for breakfast, Hannah reached for Míša's hand, but her friend shook it away.

"Sorry, I just don't want to feel…" She searched for the right word, then took a deep breath before she labored to speak. "Bound."

Hannah tightened her fists again. She knew the plan to smuggle letters out of the ghetto would fail. Why couldn't they have been patient? Everyone knew that America had entered the war a month earlier, just before Hannah and Oskar had been deported. If the men had survived, they could tell the world about the Nazi persecution of Jews in the war crimes trials that would inevitably follow. She felt a heavy weight of guilt for being angry at a friend who had died, especially one who was murdered fighting for what he believed was right. Hannah couldn't help it, though. She was furious that she would never see Pavel again. And that her best friend had just endured an unimaginable loss.

In the food line, Markéta handed her daughter and Hannah a slice of bread and used her ladle to fill their tin cups with ersatz coffee. "My sweet baby" was all she could say, looking at her daughter's quivering hands. Hannah could not tell if Markéta knew that Pavel was one of the men hanged or if she was simply pained knowing what Míša had witnessed.

"I'll be all right, Mama." Hannah saw her friend's fingers tighten around her cup.

"The transport," Markéta said, eyes glazed. "It left for Riga this morning."

"Papa's a hard worker," Míša reminded her mother. "He will do well at the camp."

Hannah wondered if that was true. Did Markéta know of her daughter's involvement in the plan to smuggle letters from Theresienstadt? Did she have any idea how close she'd come to losing her only child? Hannah shook away the thought, the chilling image of Míša on the gallows.

As they walked from the food line, Hannah and Míša stuffed large slices of bread into their mouths and cupped their free hands under their chins to catch any crumbs that fell. "Míša," Hannah whispered, her voice shaking. "You have to promise me this is the end of your… Míša, if anything happens to you, I'll never survive it."

"I can't do that, Hannah." Míša looked down as they continued walking, nearing the spot where they went their separate ways to their workshops. "If we stop now, Pavel's death will have been for nothing."

Before she could reply, Hannah gasped. "Míša, look!"

It was Luděk standing beside the railroad extension, lifting a spike maul overhead before lowering it with a grunt. He must have felt their gaze on him, because he looked up at the young women and shook his head. He averted his eyes and got back to work. They all knew it was too dangerous to reveal any connection to one another, lest someone see it and suspect they were involved with the failed letter-smuggling operation.

———◇———

Hannah saw Griselde's hands clasped behind her back as she stood at the entrance of the museum workshop, offering each worker a solemn greeting. Once the women took their places at their stations, Griselde cleared her throat. "Ladies," she called out. "Ladies, this morning, our community suffered a terrible loss. Before we begin our work today, shall we recite the Mourner's Kaddish for the men?"

Hannah's eyes scanned the room and saw the women around her nod. Klara dragged her fingertips down her forehead as though she were trying to wipe away the image in her mind. She removed her glasses and began cleaning the lenses with her shirtsleeve. They began.

Yitgadal v'yitkadash sh'mei raba b'alma…

Hannah's thoughts drifted between the Hebrew words. She found it difficult to pray when she wondered if Míša was right—that God had abandoned them. Or maybe He never existed in the first place.

Once the prayer concluded, Griselde glanced at the clock on the wall and grimaced. "I'm sorry, but we still must meet our quotas if we are to eat tonight."

Before the women could make their way back to their stations, a Ghettowache officer entered the workshop with a slip of paper in his hand. Sheepish, he looked at Griselde and apologized for interrupting. He was more sorry, it seemed, for what he said next. "Eliška Brazda, Věra Beran, please come with me."

Griselde spread her arms as if to block the man from coming closer. "What is this about?"

"I'm sorry. I don't know. I was told to bring them to SS head-quarters immediately."

Eliška and Věra were two old women who polished silver and glued loose gemstones back onto Judaica. They had nothing to do with the letter-smuggling operation. Why were they being called to Nazi headquarters?

Věra reached for Eliška's hand, and Hannah watched their fingers intertwine and squeeze together, knuckles whitening and fingertips reddening with the pressure. Eliška's face was a road map of broken blood vessels on a thin sheet of white flesh. Her loose bottom eyelids revealed the slick pink inside. The woman quickly scanned the room, a flash of an expression that seemed to say, *We're not coming back.*

At the end of the work shift, the door to Griselde's office opened, and she emerged. "Hannah, may I see you?"

Hannah stepped inside Griselde's office.

"Close the door, please," Griselde said.

"What happened to Eliška and Věra?" Hannah asked, but Griselde just shook her head and swallowed hard.

"I don't know, child. They… The council sent a note saying they would be replaced by new workers tomorrow morning."

"Are they…"

"Hannah, please." Griselde looked down and dabbed her eyes with a handkerchief. "They tell me nothing, but…it's not good." She inhaled deeply, then reached into a basket under her desk and retrieved a thick wool scarf and handed it to Hannah. "I chose plain black so no one would pester you and say it was theirs, stolen at the *Schleuse*."

Hannah held the smooth purls against her cheek. Then, she

felt a jolt of alarm as she remembered the price of small infrac-
tions. "You stole from the Nazis?"

"Goodness no, child," Griselde returned, pressing her fingertips against her chest. "As a work leader, I am allowed to claim a
few items for myself."

"Oh," Hannah said. "Um…thank you. It will certainly keep
me warm. Thank you for thinking of me."

"I always think of you, Hannah. As does your opa. You haven't
come to see him in a few days."

Now Hannah understood Griselde's cause for generosity.

"Maybe you'll pay him a visit tonight after the show?"

The show? Hannah had forgotten about her tickets to *The
Magic Flute* that night. How was life going on—operas being
performed, no less—after the brutal sight in the *Marktplatz* that
morning?

Hannah resented Griselde's meddling, though she was grateful that someone else in the ghetto had her grandfather's interests
at heart.

Griselde raised her eyebrows, imploring. "You're the only
family he has here in the settlement."

"Oh…I…I'm not sure I'm going to the show," Hannah
said. "It feels… It doesn't feel right after…what happened this
morning."

Sighing, Griselde shook her head. "A horrible sight. Oskar
warned Alois their scheme was dangerous."

The words landed with a thud. "What…what do you mean
Opa warned Alois… He *knew* about this? When did he… When
did Opa tell him it was a bad idea?"

"I don't know, Hannah. Your opa told me a few nights ago."

"Did he say—" Hannah stopped, not sure she wanted to finish the question. "Did he say where he was when he warned Alois?"

Oskar wasn't a fool, but he didn't always know how far his voice carried. Hannah shuddered with the thought of someone overhearing his warning in the shower room or the food line. She burned with rage at the image of a faceless man gobbling up a can of sardines after selling the news to the SS.

"Hannah, many people knew about the plan," Griselde said. "Don't you dare blame him. It was not his fault. Your opa is a good man. He was trying to help them stay out of trouble here. The war will be over soon, and you'll be safe if you follow the rules and don't do anything foolish like Pavel and Alois."

"But, Griselde, what if—"

"Not another word about this, child," she snapped. "He wasn't responsible, and if you start planting seeds of doubt, you will kill him, do you understand?"

Hannah pressed her lips together, knowing Griselde was right. Oskar would be shunned by the community and racked with guilt over something he likely did not cause, something that could never be undone anyway. Hannah decided she would never breathe a word to anyone. Like Pavel had protected his comrades, Hannah would shield Oskar from the truth. Or what was possibly true. What was probably not true at all.

PART III

12

Hilde

W HEN HILDE FIRST CONFRONTED OTTO IN DECEMBER
about stealing her *Titanic* film idea, he agreed to let her
make a short children's film. Hilde knew he was appeasing her,
but what could she do—quit and go back to serving beer? Return
to Munich and live in a house of ghosts and their bitter mourn-
ers? No, Hilde was vested in this relationship, and ending it now
would be shortsighted.

"Take a friend from the ministry, and shoot a little film," Otto
had suggested, hoping to end their argument and ease into something more pleasant. Hilde swallowed her rage and smiled, cob-
bling together a plan. She would enlist the help of Martin Bohle,
the boy she had seen at Café Kranzler, and film a sweet story about
the expansion of the Reich. It was only a matter of time before the
party appreciated her talent. Then she would tell Otto to go to hell.

Hitlerstadt was a simple concept for a children's film: Hilde as
Frau Holle would fly above the shining new city of the Reich—
Hitlerstadt—and explain to the *Kinder* how the territory became
theirs.

First, Martin would use the latest camera magic to superimpose a floating Frau Holle onto the gray skies above modern-day Stalingrad. *Here's what the city looked like before it was part of the Reich*, she would say as images of Stalingrad appeared on-screen. Martin could use a filter to darken already-bleak images of the city square and remove people from the benches and paths. She would instruct him to edit out the trees and pave the grass with cement. Then Frau Holle would flick her wrists, and Martin would later add the special effect of glimmering fairy dust sprinkling down, as if Frau Holle was anointing the city. Moments later, the photos of Stalingrad would transform into the gleaming new Hitlerstadt. German mothers pushing baby carriages through parks. Children with colorful balloons. Sausage carts on every corner. Swastikas would be engraved into stone building pediments, and red and black flags would snap in the breeze. *Now look how beautiful the city became when the führer claimed it for the Reich*, Hilde would add in a playful voice, high notes that would appeal to young viewers.

The enhanced images would allow children to see what the Soviet city would look like after it became German. Yes, this was a perfect way to see the Reich of the future. How wonderful it was that they had the technology to help Germans envision what was to come.

—◇—

Martin had been right: sunrise was the best time to shoot film of Hilde in her gossamer Frau Holle costume. The golden light filtering through her trumpet sleeves created an ethereal effect. No one had ever called Hilde a great beauty, but in her flowing gown and cape, a freshly trimmed blond bob wrapped in a long silk scarf, she felt as though the goddess of land and fertility would be pleased with her portrayal.

Hilde had waited three months for the snow to melt so she could set the film in her favorite green of Tiergarten. As usual, though, luck was not on Hilde's side. She hadn't accounted for how cold and abrasive the dirt path would feel against the thin slippers on her feet, but she continued to endure the discomfort of sharp pebbles and twigs needling her soles as she glided across the park terrain. Hilde had been through worse. One day, she would look back at this project as the precise moment that launched her career as a propaganda filmmaker.

"Keep going, Hilde," Martin called from behind his film camera. "I'll definitely shoot more than we need."

Continuing to sweep her arms open and gaze down adoringly, Hilde imagined how mesmerizing this scene would look on-screen.

Not only was the aureate sky heavenly, but there wasn't another person in sight at the park. Hilde had never seen Neuer See without children at its shore, pulling strings that attached to their toy boats along the water. Tiergarten felt as though it belonged only to Hilde and Martin.

"Move faster, and you'll get a breeze against those sleeves," Martin directed. "You're a goddess, not an office girl," he suggested.

She couldn't help but smile before she ran, reminding herself that she wasn't trying to win a race but appear as a fairy leaping between clouds. "How can I say no to a man who calls me a goddess?"

"It would definitely be cruel," he replied with a wink. Martin wasn't classically handsome; he had a face that drooped like a basset hound and wide, eager eyes, but Hilde had to admit that the way he listened to her without dismissal was attractive.

Hilde scampered down the path, this time silently cursing her lot. Why couldn't she be with a nice young man like Martin?

She continued waving her arms, letting the sleeves billow, but quietly sighed, knowing very well why she couldn't be with Martin. She belonged to Otto. Hilde wished she'd never taken up with her supervisor but regretted it even more last month when Frau Mazuw visited the office to deliver her husband's briefcase, which he had left at home. The elfin woman in white gloves untucked two jars of raspberry preserves from her purse and handed them to Hilde and Susanna. "We all know the Reich would be lost without its secretaries," she said, leaning in conspiratorially. Otto had painted an entirely different image of his wife, a demanding nag who never showed a droplet of appreciation for anyone. Frau Mazuw seemed like the opposite. And frankly, even if Frau Mazuw *was* a miserable woman, maybe it was years with Otto that made her that way. The glass jar of preserves felt heavier than a brick in Hilde's hand.

After they finished shooting footage for *Hitlerstadt*, Martin slipped a wool blanket over Hilde's shoulders. She felt a bit like a horse after a ride in the cold but assured herself that Martin was only being considerate. Sitting on a bench, Hilde pulled on a pair of wool socks and leather boots.

"You were definitely born for the screen," Martin said with a hint of flirtation, then dared her to walk with him to Brandenburg Gate and sing "Horst Wessel Lied" under the columns dressed in her Frau Holle costume. "If you do it, I'll take you to breakfast anywhere you want," Martin promised.

She wished he had wagered a kiss, but a meal would do. She could pretend it was a real date, that Martin was her *Schatz*, and Otto Mazuw did not exist.

Hilde was shocked when Martin agreed to treat her to breakfast at the fashionable Marmorsaal at the Hotel Adlon. She had been half-joking when she suggested it, but Martin didn't flinch. He commended her on her good taste, and they headed back to the ministry to return the film camera.

"You're sure?" Hilde asked, hating the high, uncertain pitch of her voice.

"Hilde, you threw your whole self into that song. A deal's a deal," he said. "A good breakfast with a brilliant woman. I'm definitely hitting two flies with one swat."

The dining room was elegant and modest, clean and orderly. Solid, rectangular pillars reached a ceiling painted with dark black trim that defined the space. Round tables were covered in white linen, surrounded by sturdy chairs. There were frivolities like the plaster frieze of German gods and elaborate brass sconces on the pillars, but Hilde's overall sense was that this was a place of substance.

"The film will be great, don't you think?" Hilde asked Martin a second time. She hated sounding needy, so she quickly tacked on, "I mean, if we succeed, it could be a real feather in your hat."

"We have a winner," Martin replied.

Hilde reminded herself not to rest her elbows on the breakfast table or lean forward toward Martin as he spoke. Yes, that was exactly how his body was positioned, and it was a dead giveaway that he hung on her every word, but she didn't want to seem as eager as him.

"Old Mazuw is definitely going to love your film. Don't you worry," Martin said as a waiter set down their shared plate of apple pancakes.

"After you."

The scent of baked apples and cinnamon reminded Hilde of the winters of her childhood when she and her brother, Kurt, returned to their mother's kitchen after a long morning of snowball fights with the twin boys who lived next door. Hilde took a bite, noticing that she always thought about her next forkful of food even while her mouth was full.

She closed her eyes, taking in the blend of dough and soft apple slices. The pancake needed syrup, so Hilde picked up a delicate porcelain pitcher on the table but refrained from licking her lips at the sight of buttermilk syrup drizzling over the pancake.

"Tell me, how are you certain Herr Mazuw will love my film? *Our* film, I mean."

Martin chewed for an unbearable few seconds. "It lets children see the world not how it is today but how we want it to be."

"How it *will* be, Martin."

"Right, how it *will* be."

Trying to mask her smile, Hilde lifted her napkin and dabbed the corner of her mouth. She wanted more. Her brother, Kurt, used to call her a bottomless pit of need because she could never settle for a simple word of praise. Hilde could practically hear her mother's voice urging her to ask Martin about himself. *Boys don't like girls who talk too much, Hilde. Remember you have two ears and one mouth.* Hilde never dared to remind her mother that the same was true for boys.

"How long have you worked for the ministry, Martin?"

He shrugged shyly. "Since the war started. I want to do my part, but after our victory, I definitely want to get back to painting."

"You're an artist?"

"A painter. I mostly do portraits. I did a few of the führer. My *Mutter* sent him one of my early paintings. I was ten years old, and she had it framed and delivered it to Hitler's office herself." He laughed and cringed, then shook his head as if to say, *Mothers. They can't help embarrassing us.*

"*Mein Gott!*" Hilde laughed along. "That's awful. Were you mortified?"

"Completely!"

"Did you find out what happened to your painting?" Hilde asked, "I mean, did the führer return it, or do you think his secretary tossed it in the garbage bin?" She raised her lip with mock disgust and placed her finger horizontally under her nose, imitating Hitler. "This *Kinder.* This Martin Bohle, he has committed treason with this awful portrait of me. Bring him to me at once!"

Martin smiled. He was on the brink of laughter, so Hilde continued, balling her free hand into a fist and holding it to her chest before pumping it with increasing intensity. She quickened the cadence of her speech but refrained from spitting, though she knew the move was a crowd pleaser. "I don't care if Martin Bohle *is* in *Grundschule.* You bring that boy to me now!"

Martin's face flushed to match his ears, and his eyes teared from laughing. "Hey, you do a great impression!"

I can do others, she did not say aloud. Instead, she turned the spotlight back to Martin. "So what happened to the painting? Did you ever find out?"

Martin shrugged modestly, pulling his lips to the side. "I got a nice letter saying I should keep painting 'cause I definitely had talent. He said he hung it in his office to remind him that the party is fighting for the children."

The gaiety Hilde felt quickly sank. "Are you...are you serious, Martin? The führer wrote you a letter?"

"Technically, he was the chancellor back then, but yes. *Mutter* framed it and hung it on the wall."

Of course she did. Hilde refrained from rolling her eyes. "That must have been some painting."

With a hand wave that Hilde thought looked like false modesty, Martin returned, "I'm sure it was just a secretary who wrote it. It's not like the führer still has my painting on his wall."

Just a secretary? Hilde nodded. "I'm sure he doesn't." The syrup curdled in her stomach. Hilde had spent her entire life tap-dancing for the recognition that a little boy gained effortlessly.

After a half hour of Martin's talk of his love of hiking, horses, and wood whittling, Hilde nearly forgot the sting of his boasts.

"What's your favorite trail in Berlin?" she asked.

"Anywhere in Spandauer Forst."

Agree.

"Best place to ride?"

"Definitely out in Hohenschönhausen."

Right again.

Martin smiled, then took another bite. The silence, however short, felt like a connection unraveling.

Hilde curled her toes in her boots, trying to come up with another question to extend their meal. "Favorite dining spot in Berlin? I love to know where the natives go."

Scooping the creamy liquid into his mouth, Martin grinned. "Marmorsaal. Definitely Marmorsaal. Their breakfast is the best."

"Thank you, Martin," Hilde said. "I had fun this morning."

She watched him chew and nod his head in agreement. Hilde waited for Martin to swallow before she continued. "I work so much, I don't get to go out and enjoy the city as often as I'd like."

"That's too bad. You should get out more."

She opened her eyes wide, resisting the urge to bat her lashes. "I really should."

13

Hannah

T HE MORNING SKY WAS A GAUZE OF RED AS HANNAH AND
Míša walked to health services, housed in the Hohenelbe
Barracks, where Iveta promised that her mother would slip Míša
a spoonful of cough syrup. Markéta had stolen as much cognac
from the SS kitchen as she could without the officers noticing, so she could no longer brew her own concoctions. Handing
her daughter a fistful of potato peels the night earlier, Markéta
demanded, "Stop being stubborn, and see Nurse Jana!"

Hannah agreed. She had no idea why her friend would
deprive herself of relief. Míša had also declined invitations to
concerts and plays and even refused Markéta's tickets to a lecture on the Habsburg Empire, a topic Míša typically couldn't
get enough of. From the looks of her thinning frame, Míša had
not been eating the food Hannah passed along after her nights
with Kryštof.

On the walk toward the health services ward at Hohenelbe,
Hannah eyed the line for the latrine, taking in the faces of the
new arrivals and noting who had disappeared. Four transports,

four thousand people in all, had been lost to the east since January. Each time, she saw poor Jakob Edelstein posting lists on the public message boards and handing copies to Ghettowache officers to distribute to residences. With each transport list the council was forced to draw up, Edelstein looked as though he had aged another decade: dark circles around his swollen eyes, sallow skin sagging on his face. Still, serving on the Council of Elders kept these men and their families in Theresienstadt. Within days of their departures, transported prisoners were replaced by new ones who'd been forced from their homes in the protectorate. The shift of humanity felt like quicksand beneath Hannah's feet.

"I need a favor. I wouldn't ask unless it was an emergency," Míša said, clearing her throat. Hannah remained silent, so Míša continued. "Remember Dominika's baby?"

Of course Hannah remembered the little girl born in the ghetto in February, Alena's granddaughter. Like the seven others born in Theresienstadt, baby Anna died soon after birth. She had made it three weeks; most didn't last that long.

"Another child was born on Saturday, and we're going to… We need to get him out of here," Míša whispered.

Hannah shook her head frantically. "Didn't you learn anything from Pavel?"

"I did, Hannah," Míša said, steeling her jaw. "I learned what's worth fighting for."

"So did I," Hannah snapped. "My life is worth fighting for. Seeing my family again is worth fighting for."

Míša crossed her arms over her chest and coughed. "And what will you tell your family when you see them? When they ask what you did to help others, what will you say?"

Hannah's gait felt heavier against the earth with every step she took.

"We have a pipeline of people who will help get this baby out of the ghetto tonight. I just need you to do one small thing."

"Míša!" Hannah hissed. How she wished she could shout, but prisoners were everywhere—coming toward them, passing from behind, and crossing their path. She whispered, "You couldn't get a bag of letters out. This will be harder."

"I know!" Míša shot back. "Don't you think I know that? But last time, we were betrayed." She coughed into her fist.

Fighting to maintain an impassive expression, Hannah swallowed hard. She hadn't noticed how dry her throat had gotten. *Griselde said many people knew about the letters. It couldn't have been Opa's fault.*

"This is a small thing, but it will mean a lot. I need you to go to the cabaret tonight, and before the ventriloquist finishes his act—"

"Can't someone else do this?"

Míša bit her lip, looking distressed. "Iveta was supposed to, but she's in the typhus ward."

Typhus? Iveta seemed fine the night before. Hannah hadn't seen her that morning but assumed she rose early to get to the latrine or breakfast line. She complained that she was exhausted and her stomach hurt, but that was everyone's condition in the ghetto, so Hannah didn't think much of it. Hannah had also noticed Iveta scratching her arms in the barracks, but they all had trails of bug bites on their arms and legs. She should have kept a closer eye on Iveta, but after their altercation at the glimmer factory, Hannah tried to avoid the teen. She didn't want any more harsh words between them, but now Hannah chided herself for taking the easy path. Hannah wished she had learned sooner that prisoners did not have the luxury of harboring petty grievances.

"Even when she gets out," Míša continued, "I don't know if… The betrayal with the letters, it was pretty hard on her."

"It was hard on all of us, Míša. You especially."

"I know, but it just reminded her too much of… You know what happened with her father?"

"Her father?"

"Oh," Míša said, looking down. "I thought you knew. Maybe I shouldn't—"

"You have to tell me now!"

"Iveta's father, he's why she and her mother are here. Iveta didn't even know she was Jewish until… Her father was carrying on with another woman, and the mistress reported Jana to the Gestapo. Told them she was Jewish and Iveta was a *Mischling*. And now…" Míša shrugged. "Imagine. Your own husband, your father?" Míša paused and switched back to their original conversation. "That's why I need your help. I know I can trust you and—"

"I can't," Hannah interrupted.

"It's a baby, Hannah." Silence hung between them before Míša pled, "She who saves one life saves the world."

"Now you're quoting the Talmud?"

Hannah and Míša stared at each other for a moment that Hannah knew would shape their friendship. Míša had sworn off faith in God, but Hannah hadn't. The Jewish principle of *tikkun olam*, repairing the world through good deeds, was something Hannah still believed in, even if Míša's reminder of this was wholly manipulative.

"What do you need?"

Míša pulled Hannah in for a hug. "Thank you!"

"I haven't agreed. I asked what you need."

"You'll deliver a baby bottle filled with formula Mama made."

Markéta's access to the SS pantry meant she could steal condensed milk and water down the officers' cans. She could poach a spoonful of cod liver oil from the commandant's personal supply.

Míša gripped Hannah's shoulders. "If we don't do this, a baby *will* die. I can't live with that, and I don't think you can either."

Maybe Hannah could deliver a baby bottle just this once. Monday nights were busy in Theresienstadt with the cabaret and *The Magic Flute* still running. No one would notice a bottle tucked under her arm.

"Can you promise this won't get me killed?"

"You're doing a mitzvah. That's all."

"A mitzvah that won't get me killed?"

"Deliver the bottle. That's it. If we do nothing, the baby has no chance. He will die like the others."

———◇———

Hannah stood in the hallway outside the Magdeburg Barracks cellar, breathing deeply but unable to calm her nerves. She could not see the Ghetto Swingers but could tell that most of their musicians—maybe six or seven—were onstage blowing life into saxophones and clarinets, sliding trombones, and grinding an organ to their signature number, George and Ira Gershwin's "I Got Rhythm."

Hannah leaned against the stone wall and laid her palms against the cool surface, trying to steady herself by closing her eyes and remembering better times hearing this song. Oma Minna placed a black shellac record on their player, the soundtrack to the musical *Girl Crazy*, and said she had seen it in New York City with Ethel Merman and Ginger Rogers when it first opened. Hannah inhaled again, trying to slow her pulse as she envisioned Minna swaying to the opening notes in front of Hannah, who was planted on the velvet love seat, book in hand. Minna plucked the novel from Hannah's grasp and placed it on the coffee table, extending and curling her fingers, an invitation to dance.

"I got rhythm. I got music," the two sang out, facing each other and kicking their shins back to the tune. "I got my man. Who could ask for anything more?" Minna liked to tuck her elbows into her ribs and outstretch her bobbing forearms and snapping fingers.

At the Terezín cabaret, only the music of the instruments filled the room, but everyone knew the lyrics, and she imagined some mouthing along. Who could ask for anything more? Was it cruel to ask such a question, delivered on flitty notes, in the ghetto?

Though Hannah could not see the musicians, she knew what was happening when the saxophonist began improvising a solo. She had watched band leaders Eric Vogel and Pavel Libensky before and enjoyed when they held out a hand in the direction of one of the musicians, a cue to take a minute or two to play whatever moved him at the moment. Tonight's extemporization was an offering of languishing, low notes that felt playful and sultry. *Who could ask for anything more? I can, that's who. Let me make it through this evening's task without getting caught. Let the war end! I could ask for a lot more.*

Hannah's plan had been to remain out in the hallway to avoid Griselde seeing her and beckoning her to join Oskar and her in the front row. Before the war, Griselde had been a schoolteacher, and she had not lost the eyes in the back of her head. It was easy to imagine her writing on the chalkboard and scolding misbehaving students behind her, because she did the same thing at the museum workshop.

Hannah's strategy was to mill about the hallway and listen until the ventriloquist act began, but Jakob Edelstein arrived late and insisted Hannah come inside with him. "Don't be shy, Hannah," he said. Before Hannah could object, the head of the Council of Elders led her inside and raised his hand, gesturing to Oskar, who was standing to the side of the makeshift stage. *Look who I found*, Edelstein's wide eyes seemed to say.

Dear God, please don't let Opa make a big production of my arrival.

Thankfully, Hannah's prayers were answered. Oskar took his job as host far too seriously to go off script. The last thing she needed was for Oskar to make every person at the cabaret aware of her presence. She needed to be discreet, if not invisible.

A prisoner who worked in the Reich mapmaking office had stolen a sheet of damaged paper and painted the words KABERETT TEREZÍN in black.

Hannah turned to Edelstein. "I'm feeling a bit dizzy, so I'll just… I'm going to sit in the back," she whispered. It wasn't a lie. After four months on a meager diet of bread and diluted soup, Hannah had recently started needing to grip the sides of her seat when she stood. If she turned her head too quickly, objects around her formed comet tails. Even with Markéta's stolen potato peels and Kryštof's pinched sardines, Hannah felt the constant pang of hunger.

"I will sit with you," Edelstein offered.

"That's very kind, but—"

"Nonsense," he replied, settling into the chair next to Hannah. "Part of my job, comforting the ill."

She smiled tightly, knowing that another objection would raise suspicion.

Oskar wore a wrinkled white shirt and wilting red bow tie. He clapped his hands, holding them out toward the audience to rally more applause. "One more time for the Ghetto Swingers," he said, extending his arm toward the band. Each musician turned to both sides of the stage to ensure he acknowledged all fifty people surrounding the nine-square-meter wooden board that was typically placed in front of the window to shield drafts. As the men packed their guitar, saxophone, trombone, bass, and clarinets back into their cases, Oskar continued. "Next, we have the grand illusions of Vojtěch Flatow from the Hanover Barracks. Please welcome Vojtěch to Kabarett Terezín!"

Vojtěch looked as though he was barely out of *Mittelschule* and wore a top hat too big for his head. He pushed it from his eyes twice before uttering a single word.

The young man removed his hat and showed it to the audience, first the inside, then the outside. "Can I have a volunteer from—"

Before he could finish, Danuše jumped from her seat next to her mother and ran onto the stage, her cloth doll in hand.

The joy of a child was like a sliver of chocolate for the adults, who clapped as Danuše stood proudly beside the magician. It

wasn't the rousing applause Hannah had heard in the world outside, but it was everything some prisoners could muster. A few
opted to shout a quick hurrah rather than lift their labored hands.

"What's your name, little one?" Vojtěch asked as he leaned
down toward the girl, his striped necktie dangling too far beneath
his beltline.

"I am Danuše Vyštejnová, and I just turned five," she said,
splaying the fingers of her open hand. "And this is Adélka. She's
just borned."

"Mazel tov!" Edelstein called from the back, and Hannah's
heart sped, knowing that some of the audience would turn to see
who had called out. The fewer people who saw Hannah, the less
likely her disappearance would be noticed later.

"Now, Danuše," Vojtěch continued, "these fine people can
trust you to tell them the truth, can't they?"

The girl nodded vigorously.

"Good, because I want you to take a look inside my hat and
tell me what you see."

Danuše placed her face close to the rim of the hat and
inspected. "Nothing. Nothing's in there."

"Not so fast, Danuše," he urged. "Stick your hand inside, and
feel around a bit. Are there any hidden pockets or zippers?"

Now elbow deep in the top hat, Danuše's tongue poked from
the corner of her mouth as she searched in earnest.

"No, there's nothing," she said, nodding once with authority.
"Nothing but hat."

Vojtěch raised an eyebrow at the audience, then slipped a
whittled twig from his back pocket and tapped the hat three
times. "Danuše, can you say *abrakadabra* with me?"

"*Abrakadabra*," she said, wide-eyed.

"Not just yet. First, we need to say the magic spell together. When I say *abrakadabra*, you repeat after me."

She nodded again, looking up at the boy.

"My top hat was empty, that much is true. But now it has a gift for you. *Abrakadabra*."

Danuše stood on her toes and looked at the top hat with wonder. "*Abrakadabra!*"

Vojtěch asked the audience to join in. "Can everyone help Danuše?"

"*Abrakadabra*," voices called out, some robust, others soft and raspy.

"All right, my little magician's assistant, reach into the hat, and see if it has a surprise for you."

Danuše's tiny mouth formed a circle as she pulled out a striped, brown men's tie. Knotted to the end was another, yellow with geometric shapes. Then a dark red tie with small blue dots. She looked at her mother, Olina, in amazement, her expression asking, *Did you see that?*

From the back, an older man shouted, "Can you do that with my soup bowl, kid?"

A few people chuckled at the bitter joke.

After a card trick, the act finished. "Thank you, Vojtěch," Oskar said, walking onto the stage again. "Next up is Jaroslav Hruška and his little friend Jirka." It was time for the ventriloquist and his dummy.

Hannah clutched her stomach and turned to Jakob Edelstein. "I'm going back to the barracks," she whispered.

"I can walk you to the hospital if you need assistance," he offered.

"No, no, it's just…female problems."

Hannah felt her entire face flush red. She couldn't believe she had just said such a thing to a man—a ghetto elder, no less—but there was no way she could let him follow her to the hospital. She remembered her friend Hilde once saying that anytime a woman needed to end a conversation with a man—and send him running—she should allude to menstruation.

"Ah, I see. Get some rest, Hannah."

"Thank you," she said, eyes down.

From the stage, Hannah heard Jirka the puppet cry out, "What do you mean I'm not telling the truth? You're the one with your hand up my back, pal."

Hannah located the bottle stuffed into a black sock behind a loose brick in a corner of the basement floor of the barracks as Míša had promised. She tucked it under her arm and walked outside into the crisp night air, where she immediately saw Alice and her six-year-old son, Štěpán, heading toward her.

"Did we miss the Ghetto Swingers?" the boy asked with the disappointed whine of someone who already knew the answer.

Alice gently teased her son, correcting his manners. "Good evening. I hope you are well, Miss Hannah."

"The ventriloquist just started," Hannah replied.

She decided to turn onto the side road behind the church toward Magdeburg, hoping to avoid running into anyone else she knew.

Hannah looked toward the sky and wondered what her family was doing in Palestine at this very moment. Her mother had written recently and spoke of a Purim festival in Haifa. "Ben dressed as Queen Esther. His friends thought it was very funny, but Papa was not amused." Entire sentences had been blocked out with ink, and Hannah ached to know what the SS had redacted. She imagined her mother sitting at a kitchen table, looking out the window at Haifa Bay and seeing the same moon that hovered over Theresienstadt.

Ten minutes later, Hannah had made it into the courtyard of the Hohenelbe Barracks, a building almost as large as the one where Hannah lived. It was a three-story U-shaped building with large chips of mustard-colored paint peeling from its exterior. Of the dozens of windows Hannah could see, only a handful were lit, but the full moon illuminated vines wrapped around the base of a skeletal linden tree.

Hannah soon found herself at another doorway, on the second floor of the hospital. She knocked four times in the pattern Míša had instructed, then opened the door to a large supply closet dimly lit by a candle. In the center was a young mother on the floor, curled into the fetal position, her baby tucked close to her belly as though she was trying to envelop and protect him as she had when he was in utero. Míša sat on the floor beside the woman, trying to comfort her by caressing her head. The young mother was as thin as the elders who didn't work—from her hollowed eyes to her bulbous ankles. Hannah cringed at the bitter irony of this mother resting her tearstained face on a pillow made from remnants of clothing made for SS officers and their wives.

Míša spotted Hannah and said, "*Pfft*, don't just stand there. Get inside and close the door."

When she walked in, Hannah spotted Radek, the Jewish policeman, sitting on a step stool beside an empty shelf. Across his chest was the strap of a rucksack. His broad shoulders and muscular forearms hadn't registered with her before, and Hannah wasn't sure why, but she pretended not to notice him.

He nodded in Hannah's direction and asked Míša, "Where's Iveta tonight?"

"I told you, Hannah's filling in while Iveta's sick," Míša replied, nodding her head toward the ceiling. *Upstairs in the typhus ward,* her gesture said.

"Where's Luděk?" Hannah asked.

"If you didn't see him, that's a good thing," Míša said, sounding pleased. "He's outside. Making sure we don't get any uninvited visitors."

Hannah knelt to hand Míša the warm bottle. Míša rubbed a hand over the woman's legs, then punctuated the movement with a series of pats to let the mother know the time to say goodbye to her baby was drawing near.

The baby's cheek was pressed into his mother's stomach, and his hand was balled in a fist, looking almost as though he was knocking on the door to return to the womb. Hannah always thought the closed eyes of newborn babies looked like walnuts in their wrinkled shells, protruding slightly and finely slit at the center.

Míša looked up at Radek. "Grab the Veronal for him."

"František," the mother lifted her head to say. "His name is František."

"Of course," Míša offered. "František is a beautiful name for a beautiful boy." She then whispered, "I'm sorry, but it's time." She dipped her pinkie into the small brown bottle Radek had handed her, and slid it into František's mouth like a nipple.

"No, not yet," the mother wailed as Hannah watched Míša gently pry the baby from her mother's arms.

"Shh," Míša returned in a soothing tone. "You're doing what few mothers have the chance to—you're giving your son life twice."

There was too little of Hannah left to absorb the flood of sorrow, so she averted her eyes as the mother rolled onto her back, crying. She couldn't help peeking, though, as Míša lifted the spindly baby into her arms and moved toward Radek's rucksack. He and Míša exchanged a worried glance as the baby squawked like a sparrow.

"The Veronal should kick in any moment," Míša assured Radek. In Míša's arms, the child began to flail about, legs cutting through the air as though riding an invisible bicycle. "Now, now, sweet František, we're going to get you all wrapped up for your... journey to safety."

With the baby now safely in Radek's bag, Míša knelt to the ground and placed her hands on the woman's face and whispered, "Sometimes the best choice is the hardest one."

"Your mama loves you, František," the mother whispered. "I wish..." The woman's voice caught, and she did not finish, though Hannah could guess what she wanted to say. *I wish we lived in a different world, where babies weren't taken from their mother's arms because it was the only way for them to survive.*

"Thank you for saving his life," she whispered.

The words were like a knee pressed against Hannah's chest.

The woman turned toward Radek and cleared her throat. Then, to no one in particular, the mother wondered, "Do you think his new parents will tell him about me?"

14

Hilde

Berlin
April 1942

HILDE'S BREATH FLUTTERED WHEN SHE HEARD THE TICK-
ing of the film turning from one reel to the next. Every
muscle in her body was in a twist of excitement.

In a moment, the white square projected on-screen would be
filled with the image of her as Frau Holle, flying above the new
Reich city—Hitlerstadt.

With a snap, the projector flashed a backward number four
encircled in black. Looking at Otto beside her, Hilde couldn't
help reaching for his hand. He wasn't a perfect man, but he had
come through for Hilde, and she was grateful for that. She was
a filmmaker now.

The number three flashed on-screen, and small splatters of
white appeared and faded in seconds. Her heart sped.

Otto turned his head and smiled. "I'm proud of you, my dear."

They were alone in the ministry screening room, so Hilde
leaned over and kissed his cheek.

Two.

One.

Then, finally the brass fanfare, the triumphant trumpet call of the opening notes of "Ride of the Valkyries" by Richard Wagner, the führer's favorite composer. The full orchestra of strings, brass, and percussion ushered in the image of snow falling from the sky, swirling to the center until the film screen was covered in glimmering white. Bold and dramatic, the sound was urgent, preparing the viewer for a tale of conquest and victory. Suddenly, like the stomp of a boot, the title appeared in block letters—*Hitlerstadt*.

There she was—Hildegard Kramer-Bischoff, floating over the gray city of Stalingrad, its dreary square with a round area with six spokes of paved paths sectioning the dead lawn. Frau Holle scrunched her face with disgust and shook her head as she flew toward All Saints Church on Mamayev Kurgan. The three onion domes were ugly reminders of the Soviet era.

What a wonderful job Martin did superimposing Hilde's image into the sky. She could not look more natural floating past the clouds.

The narration began, "Long ago, before the führer gave Hitlerstadt to the *Volk*, the Bolsheviks and Jews overran the land, spreading disease and filth."

Hilde was grateful she had taken Martin's suggestion of speeding the audio recording so her voice would sound more childlike and appealing to the young audience.

Then Hilde's favorite part: the camera zoomed in on her as she flicked her wrist to release glittering dust. Frau Holle gazed down at the old city, then looked directly into the camera. Her little voice squeaked, "When the city became part of the Reich…"

As Martin pulled the camera back to show the city below, Hitlerstadt went from black-and-white to Agfacolor. Bright red

Hakenkreuz flags now hung from stately buildings surrounding the verdant square. A sculpture of the imperial eagle topped a seven-story structure with rounded edges and elegant columns.

Hilde glanced at Otto, who nodded his head and turned to Hilde and winked. "A woman with many talents."

———◇———

A week had passed since Otto viewed Hilde's film, and he still hadn't shown *Hitlerstadt* to Reichsminister Goebbels. At first, he mumbled that the timing wasn't right. Days later, Otto told Hilde that he wanted to add some special effects of his own. He finally admitted that he had no intention of showing her film to anyone in the Reich. "I'm sorry to say this, my dear, but *Hitlerstadt* isn't ready. *You're* not ready."

Hilde sank into the chair across from his desk, the leather cushion sighing beneath her weight. "You said it was great!"

"I said you have talent. *Hitlerstadt* is a nice first attempt."

Attempt?

She reminded herself to stay in control of her emotions, not to cry or yell but to simply ask, "What's wrong with it?"

"I'm sorry, but…it's too simplistic. Frau Holle flies over Stalingrad, and suddenly it becomes Hitlerstadt? We can't have children think this happened by sorcery. Where is the glory to the führer? Where is the blood of German soldiers in all this?"

Hilde could not help but raise her voice, her throat a taut rope of anxiety. "You want blood in a children's film?"

She slouched into the seat and crossed her arms like a little girl on the verge of an outburst. "Let Herr Goebbels decide. Show it to him and see what he says!"

"My dear." Otto spoke with a soft tone and tilted head, as though he were addressing an imbecile. "I cannot waste his time showing him a subpar film made by an office girl."

Hilde tamed the impulse to pick up the crystal eagle paperweight on his desk and hurl it at him. She forced the corners of her lips into a smile. "At least I'll get experience working on the Theresienstadt documentary," she said as she feigned resignation while thinking of ways to get to the reichsminister without Otto knowing. Perhaps Martin could help her.

"About that," Otto hemmed. "The competition for the production assistant is going to be stiffer than I first thought."

Hilde fought to maintain her smile and adjusted her tone to sound like a woman who was merely curious. "Meaning what?"

"Meaning there will be several people applying for the job."

"You said it was mine."

"Because I thought it was."

"And what do you think now?" Her patience was eroding.

Hilde often asked questions that had already been answered, hoping for a different response. She knew what Otto meant. The job she assumed was hers wasn't and, with her luck, would never be.

"You could still get the job, my dear."

Could? Could! Hilde swallowed her rage. She needed to get out of Otto's office immediately, breeze past Susanna, and splash cold water on her face at the WC sink before the car arrived to take Otto and her to the Ministry of Aviation for Reichsmarschall Göring's speech. "Excuse me," she offered and looked at her watch. "I'll be back in a few minutes."

"No hurry."

No hurry?

"Doesn't the car arrive at ten?"

"Right," Otto returned after a beat. "I need you here at the office. I'll be taking Susanna to the ministry."

"What are you saying?" There she went again, asking him to clarify what was already abundantly clear. "Is this because of *Hitlerstadt*, because—"

Otto held out his hand to interrupt. "Hilde, don't make a big fuss about this. I promised Susanna's father I'd take her, that's all. She's been working diligently, and we thought it would be a nice little treat."

Hilde felt dangerously close to begging Otto to take her to the speech, but there was no way she would give him the satisfaction of pitying her. Such weakness was crippling, and she needed to get herself into the privacy of a toilet stall before she lost control of herself. "Please excuse me," she said, speeding from Otto's office.

"Yoo-hoo!" Susanna called when she walked out, but Hilde rushed by without acknowledging her.

Making her way down the corridor, the fast clacking of typing coming from the offices reminded her of gunfire, and she felt like the target.

Thankfully, the WC was empty, and Hilde stood in front of the row of sinks, turning on the cold water spigot. She hadn't realized how flush with heat she was until she felt the stark contrast of frigid water chilling the flesh of her palms. Hilde pulled her hands from the stream and placed her fingers on the back of her neck. *Do not cry. I will not cry.* Splashing her face with water, Hilde felt the choke of tears forming and ran into the toilet stall.

She might not be able to manage her emotions, but she could control who would be witness to them.

A half hour later, Hilde was drained. Maybe she didn't need to cry in the bathroom after all. Perhaps what she really needed was to talk to Martin.

After Hilde climbed the staircase to the second floor of the ministry, she knocked on the door of the Office of Mass Propaganda. A man's voice shouted for her to come in, so she pushed the door open to the sight of Martin and his colleague, each seated at his own drafting table, plumes of smoke rising from ashtrays. The *Volksempfänger* was already playing, a news announcer reminding listeners that Reichsmarschall Göring would begin his speech shortly.

Martin lifted his head and smiled when he saw Hilde, and she couldn't help but grin, thinking of their first date tobogganing in the park during the late snowfall last Saturday. He'd sat behind her and wrapped his arms around her waist as he steered them downhill by shifting his weight from one side to the other. The fresh cold air had felt baptismal, and recalling it now managed to melt away Hilde's anger toward Otto.

"Come here, Hilde. Let's get a woman's opinion on this," Martin said, waving a hand to beckon her into the office.

As she reached their workstation, Hilde saw that each of the graphic artists was sketching propaganda poster ideas—different representations of the same theme: the threat that America and Britain posed to the *Volk*. Martin's design was an illustration of a cherubic German baby, his arms pulled in opposite directions, one wrist bound by an American flag, the other by the Union Jack. The baby's toes were pointed downward toward a map of the Reich, a sea of weeping mothers grasping in vain to save the child. It was a crucifixion without the cross. Hilde immediately knew the party would frown on imagery filled with Christian symbolism.

Martin turned to Hilde, "Bodo here thinks my poster will frighten children, but they definitely need to know the threat Germany is facing."

Bodo Schmidt held up his hand to disagree. "Nah, that's not it, Martin. You didn't connect the Jews to the Allied forces, and that's your mistake," he said, pointing to his sketch pad. In Bodo's illustration, the American and British flags were two panels of a stage curtain. A shadowy Jew peeked from behind, baring his pebble teeth and hook nose.

Hilde hated to admit that Bodo's sketch was better. It was less morbid but still appropriately menacing. "I love them both," she offered cheerfully. "You boys are doing such important work here. I'll bet the ministry uses both of your designs." She would give Martin her feedback privately; there was no use embarrassing him in front of his colleague.

Hilde turned to Martin and asked if he could spare a moment in private.

"For you, two moments." Martin slid from his stool and held out his arm toward the hallway, where he and Hilde could have more privacy.

Before they reached the door, a roaring sound from outside made all heads turn to the window. The glass began to rattle, threatening to shatter within its panes. Hilde reached for Martin's arm and gripped the fabric of his sleeve. "Are we—"

She could not finish her question before the same sound followed. Then a third.

Bodo shouted, "*Scheisse!* Planes! Flying way too low. Get down! Take cover!"

Martin grabbed Hilde's arm and pulled her toward a large oak desk. "Down, down!" he shouted, rushing, "Underneath, go, go, go!"

The wail of three low-flying RAF de Havilland Mosquitos came through both the *Volksempfänger* and the window. Hilde felt Martin's hand push her onto the floor beneath the desk and lay his body over hers.

"Cover your head!" he shouted.

Hilde wondered if Martin could feel her heart pounding or her body trembling as he blanketed her.

"Stay put. This will all—"

A thundering explosion, the sound of an artillery round.

Bodo shouted from under the drafting table, "They're attacking! The damn Tommies are bombing us!" They had never flown through the heart of Berlin in broad daylight.

Hilde lifted her head, keeping her eyes trained on the window. There was no way she would allow herself to be blind to what was happening outside.

Another blast was followed by a cloud of black smoke. Hilde heard high-pitched screams outside, the whine of engines above and terror of Germans below.

"It's coming from the ground," Martin shouted. "They're not bombing us. *We're* firing at the planes." He brushed Hilde's hair from her ear and whispered, "Don't be afraid. Our antiaircraft batteries will take them down soon. We're safe."

"That's us? We're shooting at them?" Hilde asked, confused.

"I won't let anything happen to you," Martin said, covering Hilde's head with his palms.

Suddenly they were jolted by another sound, one completely at odds with the circumstances. A wave of classical music, woodwinds and brass, floated through the room, and for a moment, Hilde wondered if they had died and the Pearly Gates of heaven were beckoning them.

No, it was coming from the *Volksempfänger*. Anton Bruckner's Symphony no. 7 in E Major played through the radio as the blasts continued outside. Hilde imagined how confused listeners at home and work must be.

The buzz of the planes dulled as they flew farther from the city center, then grew stronger as they returned.

Hilde shouted, "What the hell are they doing?"

"They're gonna bomb us this time," Bodo shouted.

Hilde opened her eyes wide and intertwined her fingers with Martin's. She held her breath as the planes flew directly over the ministry and waited for the next blast. "Martin, please tell me we're going to—"

A deafening blast sounded, rattling the walls and shaking the overhead lights. Outside, sirens blared, and voices cried out in terror.

15

Hannah

TWO WEEKS EARLIER, MÍŠA REPORTED BACK TO THE GROUP that Baby František's exodus from the ghetto was a success. He was safely delivered to the nearby farming village of Kamýk, where the little boy became the newest addition to a Christian family. Ghetto informants had not betrayed their network, and no one had been caught. The plan had gone perfectly.

Hannah would never admit this to Míša, but she felt a wave of excitement with the news. A child's life had been saved. That was of primary importance, she knew, but Hannah silently confessed that it was exhilarating to beat the Nazis, even on this small scale. If she shared her thoughts with Míša, though, her friend would see it as a crack in the door, then try to kick it open. Hannah knew her will was no match for Míša's, so she buttoned her lips.

Even after hearing the good news, Hannah had been in a heightened state of anxiety. As she transcribed her Torah verses at the museum workshop, her mind raced with alternate scenarios that could have happened and surely would if Míša and her friends continued with their reckless actions. She startled awake every night at the reoccurring nightmare of infants hanging in the *Marktplatz*. The sound of her own voice roused her, and the moment she remembered where she was, she frantically asked Klara what she'd said, hoping she hadn't divulged anything. Then there was the vomiting, the violent heaves of bile that struggled for release from Hannah's empty stomach.

—◇—

Iveta had been in the typhus ward for two weeks. Hannah walked through the gauntlet of cots filled with bodies in various stages of the disease. Attenuated legs were half-draped under thin blankets, open black sores marking the flesh Hannah could see. An old man slept with his mouth open, white paste forming in the corners. Wisps of hair covering his head made him look as fragile as a dandelion weed. Was he alive? Was the skeletal woman in the bed next to him still breathing?

Since Hannah's last visit the day earlier, Iveta's lips had turned pale blue, her eyes now rimmed with a wire of red.

"I brought you something," Hannah said, forcing an upbeat lilt and holding out a tin cup filled with oregano tea. "Compliments of Markéta. It will cure all that ails you."

"*Bleech*," Iveta's voice scratched.

"I'm glad typhus hasn't robbed you of your charm," Hannah said, desperately trying to mask the horrified look on her face. She placed the lip of the cup at Iveta's open mouth and tilted it.

Iveta cringed as she swallowed. "Hannah," she said weakly. "Will you do something for me?"

Hannah nodded. "What do you need?"

"The doctor says I have an infection."

An infection? Typhus and an infection?

"If I die—"

Hannah interrupted, "Don't talk nonsense!" But it wasn't nonsense. In this upside-down world, it was normal for a seventeen-year-old young woman to make a deathbed plea.

"All right, but if I do, you'll…" Iveta turned her head to the woman sleeping beside her and lowered her voice. "Take my place."

That afternoon, Hannah had received a letter from her mother reporting that the Kaufmans had moved into a new, three-story apartment building. *We have a balcony that overlooks the busy street below, and Ben's bedroom window looks out onto Mount Carmel. We miss you terribly but are pleased to hear you are happy in Theresienstadt. I cannot believe you live in the same apartment building as Alice Herz-Sommer. Tell her that Oma attended one of the Herz family salons in Prague when we first moved to the city. Maybe she will remember the meeting. I dream of a day when we are all together and can sing stage show tunes around the piano. Won't that be something? Opa was right; avocados are delicious and plentiful. We are all praying for your safe arrival very soon.*

How could Iveta ask Hannah to risk her own life to save the children of strangers? The thought pressed painfully against her forehead.

"Hannah," Iveta whispered and reached for her leg. "They're babies."

"None of this matters, because you'll be better in a few days."

Iveta smiled weakly. "Then promise."

The truth was that Hannah wasn't sure of anything anymore.

How could she be? But saying as much to Iveta seemed cruel. The girl needed to hear that Hannah had no doubt she would recover, so she lied, "All right, Iveta, I promise."

"Thank you," she whispered. "I'm sorry about what I said at the... I know you're not..." She looked to her side again and stopped before she finished the thought.

"Please," Hannah scoffed. "It's forgotten." She tried to ignore the voice in her head that reminded her that Iveta might not be as forgiving if she knew that Oskar could have been to blame for the hanging. *He wasn't. He couldn't have been.*

Iveta smiled and closed her eyes.

Hannah turned to leave and saw Nurse Jana in her white smock and stiff nurse's cap approaching her daughter's bed. "She's asleep," Hannah offered.

"Good. Rest is the best medicine," Jana said, rubbing her eyes, as if the words reminded her of her own exhaustion. "Iveta is a strong girl. She will be good as new in a few days."

Hannah left the hospital and cut through the *Stadtpark* as she headed back toward the Dresden Barracks, when she heard a male voice call her name. She turned and saw it was Radek, and she felt guilty for the jolt of excitement over how appealing he looked out of his Ghettowache uniform. Ever since she'd watched him tuck Baby František in his rucksack and hurry down the hospital corridor, Hannah saw him in a new light. His face looked kinder, his carriage more confident. He wore a plain flannel shirt and work pants, and for a moment, she imagined Radek walking through the front door of a home they shared. *Hannah, my love, I missed you while I was at work. Mmm, do I smell brisket?*

Hannah had always thought of herself as a good person, but

now she questioned if that was true. How could she think about such things when her friend was gravely ill? Worse, Hannah knew she was lying when she promised to take Iveta's place in the glimmer factory resistance group.

"Where you going?" Radek asked.

Hannah wished she had something clever to say to impress him with her wit, but all she could muster was the truth, that she was returning to her barracks.

"Can I walk with you?" he asked, and Hannah nodded, then turned away so he wouldn't see her face flush with color.

"Míša told me you're from Prague."

"Munich actually. We moved to Prague when I was fourteen," she replied, lowering her eyes. "What about you? Where are you from?"

"Brno. I was a law student. Masaryk University. Before these bastards shut the place." He gestured in no particular direction, but Hannah understood. The Nazi bastards. "My father taught there. He's a tutor now. Rich parents always want their children to be the smartest of the smart, even in wartime. At least that's what Papa says."

"What about you? What did you do when you couldn't study law anymore?"

Radek shrugged. "Farm work. Factory labor. These are good times for people who need strong young men willing to work illegally. They can pay us crap, and we can't do a thing about it."

"And the rest of your family?"

"Mama's in Brno writing letters to her aunt in America, who she's hoping can sponsor us. Both of my sisters are married. Anička is pregnant with her first child in Edinburgh. Her husband, Sammy, flies for the RAF, and she's worried sick about him. Dagmar is in Prague with her husband and two babies."

"How...why are you the only one here?"

"I volunteered. Part of the building crew that came in November. That's how I met Luděk. The Nazis were looking for men to work and made a lot of promises that sounded pretty good."

Hannah refrained from asking what Radek was offered, because she knew he had to regret the decision. Opa Oskar had finally given up on his lakefront cottage. He always seemed pleased with himself when he discreetly pressed bread crusts into Hannah's palms, but she could tell that he felt ashamed that he'd been so misled.

Radek shook away the unpleasant thought and asked Hannah, "What are your plans for after the war? Míša said your family is in Palestine. She said you want to study archaeology."

Hannah always felt more comfortable talking to people when it was harder to see her pockmarks, but on this night, she was grateful that the darkness of night hid her reddened face too. She couldn't help but feel flattered that he had asked Míša about her.

"That's right."

"What do you think archaeologists will make of this place when they dig it up in a thousand years?"

"I suppose it depends on who wins the war," Hannah replied.

"You have to believe Germany will lose the war. That's what keeps me going—thinking about prosecuting the Nazis for war crimes."

After her visit with Iveta and after seeing Pavel hanging from gallows just four months earlier, she wasn't so sure the Nazis hadn't already won.

"The good guys always prevail in the end," Radek said, bumping his shoulder against Hannah to lighten the mood.

"You're right," Hannah returned, though she did not believe her own words. Maybe it was simply that the victors wrote history and cast themselves as the heroes. Still, why argue to convince Radek of this? Let him have hope.

The next morning, Hannah walked to the *Schleuse* to visit Kryštof, whose eyes widened with excitement at the sight of her. "What do you need today, Hannah?"

Suddenly, Hannah began to question her decision to come to the *Schleuse*. Her stomach was crying out, and she could see a wooden crate with canned peaches peeking through the slats. *Just do it quickly*, Hannah silently coaxed herself. *This takes nothing away from what you and Radek could have.* Yet she could not imagine lifting her fingers to unbutton her blouse for Kryštof again. "I…I appreciate our…friendship, Kryštof, but I can't…" She tore her eyes away from the crate behind him. "I can't do our…our bartering anymore." She didn't explain that she'd fallen for Radek and wanted their first kiss to be pure and uncomplicated like so few things were at Theresienstadt. And in order for her to truly have hope that her imprisonment would soon end, Hannah needed to imagine a day when allowing a man to touch her actually meant something.

"Aw, really?" Kryštof groaned. "That's too bad, Hannah. You were my favorite girlfriend."

Your…favorite? "You…you have others?"

"None as pretty as you," he said.

Hannah lifted her hand to her cheek, feeling the scars on her face. "Oh, I didn't realize…" She forced a smile, not fully sure why she felt taken aback.

He turned and grabbed a jar of peaches he must have noticed her eyeing. "You can have these anyway. And I know you like reading, so I got you a present." He turned and walked to a supply shelf and reached his arm toward the very back.

"A book?" Hannah said. "How…how kind of you, Kryštof." She looked at the cover, tan and cream with an illustration of a man standing trial. "Franz Kafka? Never heard of him. Any relation to Georg?"

Kryštof nodded. "His cousin. Dead. Never really made it big, but I think his writing is interesting. Maybe you'll tell me what you think after you read it. We don't have to… I just… Here's another jar of peaches, just…just to say thank you for…um…everything."

———◇———

Weeks later as she climbed the side stairwell of the Dresden Barracks, Hannah used her last bit of strength to stay a few paces ahead of her new bunkmate, Lenka. She knew it was wholly unfair of her to dislike the new arrival, but the mere sight of her lying on Iveta's old pallet every night filled Hannah with molten rage. It wasn't Lenka's fault that Iveta never returned from the hospital. Lenka bore no responsibility for any of the deaths that had stripped the barracks of its women. In the five months Hannah had been at Theresienstadt, nine hundred had died in the ghetto. Hannah knew better, but she couldn't help feeling that the presence of new women erased the memory of ones who had come before.

"Give Lenka a chance," Klara had urged Hannah.

Friedl joined in. "The children loved her when she helped with their collages yesterday. She's a very sweet girl who needs a friend."

In another world, Hannah might enjoy Lenka's company. About the same age as Hannah, Lenka was bookish and quiet. She too had been deported with her veteran grandfather, though she had no other living family. She was even chubby as Hannah had once been, a mirror of Hannah's image not long ago. But in Theresienstadt, Lenka was merely a blight on the bunk across from hers. Not only was she taking Iveta's old space, Lenka asked too many questions about navigating life in the ghetto. *When do we get the rest of our luggage? What do we do about the bedbugs?*

"Hannah!" Lenka called out once she caught up with her.

"What do you want?"

"Oh." The young woman seemed surprised by Hannah's curt response, but she pressed on. "I wanted to say goodbye. My opa and I, we're going to another settlement in the east. I'm sorry we won't have a chance to get to know each other."

"You're leaving? When?"

"Tonight." She shrugged. "I don't know why we were picked, but our names were on the list the council posted yesterday."

A lump formed as Hannah remembered perusing the transport list, searching for her name, then Oskar's and Míša's. She checked on Griselde and Markéta. Radek and Luděk. Olina and Danuše. Alice and her little boy, Štěpán. Alena, Petra, and Helena. Never, though, did it occur to Hannah to see if Lenka was on the list. She pulled Lenka in close and hugged her. Why hadn't she been kind to this young woman?

"I'm sorry too," Hannah said.

"Klara told me you want to be an archaeologist. I'm going to be an engineer. You're always with a book. Have you ever heard of Katharina Paulus?" When Hannah shook her head, Lenka continued. "She was a German engineer. Invented the parachute. I just finished reading her biography, so bringing it along would be silly with the luggage weight limit and all," she said. "I'll leave it behind for you. There aren't too many of us women scientists. We need to stick together, right?"

Hannah looked down. "Right. We do." Until that moment, Hannah had no idea what any of Lenka's interests were. She didn't know where she lived or what her family name was because she never bothered to ask. Yet emotionally cauterizing the artery to her heart did not keep her from feeling the pain of yet another loss.

That night, Hannah pulled her blanket over her head and pretended to sleep as she heard the whispers and sniffs of twenty or so women stepping lightly on the creaking floorboards toward the exit. "*Pospěš si*," a gendarme demanded. *Hurry up.* The pounding of a baton against the wooden bunk startled Hannah. She closed her eyes tight and forced her mind to take her somewhere else.

Remember something wonderful, she begged herself until she heard her opa's voice in her mind. "Guess who is going on her very own excavation? They may have already found King Tut, but there's a lot more digging to do."

———◦———

Hannah was eleven years old when her *Mittelschule* teacher rolled out his slide projector and filled a white screen with images of

Egyptian King Tutankhamen's tomb, which had been unearthed a decade earlier. Like all her classmates, she made sounds of awe—*ooh*s and *aah*s—at the sight of the polished mask that the teacher explained was made from ten kilograms of gold with inlaid lapis lazuli and eyes of obsidian and quartz. "The Egyptians believed in life after death and buried valuables to take with them to the afterlife," the instructor said.

The next slides were Tut's jeweled diadem, golden sandals, spears, and cups. Hannah had so many questions: What did the hieroglyphics on the chalice say? There were two trumpets found in King Tut's tomb. Did he play the instrument himself, or had he expected someone else to entertain him in the hereafter? Would he still be a king there, or would he bow to the others who had come before him?

Twenty images later, Hannah could see her classmates' interest waning. She couldn't get enough. All this had been buried in the earth for three thousand years. What else was hidden underground?

"You can tell a great deal about the values of a culture or an individual by what they take with them," the teacher continued. "What is it we learn about King Tut and Egyptian mythology?" he asked.

Hannah's friend Hilde didn't bother raising her hand. "He has good taste in jewelry," she said, her eyes darting around the room to see who was laughing at her joke.

Hans Delmotte tried to top Hilde and called out, "King Tut's going to have no trouble finding a Queen Tut in heaven."

After that, Hannah knew there would be no serious discussion of Egyptian artifacts in class. To try to answer the teacher's question now would only get groans and snide comments from her classmates.

After school, Hannah returned to her apartment and told Oskar and Minna about the photographs she'd seen. "You and your digging. You've always loved that sort of thing," Oma Minna said. Sitting on the couch, she pointed to the small piece of amethyst in the curio cabinet. Then she gestured toward Hannah's room, where there were dozens of stones she had collected over the years.

"You want to learn how those archaeologists excavate, you don't need some *shmendrik* of a teacher who can't control his classroom," said Oskar. "I know a thing or two."

That Sunday, Oskar instructed Hannah to wear a long-sleeved shirt, old pants, and her mother's straw hat. He filled their canteens with cold water from the faucet and placed rope, stakes, and a spade into a rucksack. "Bring your school bag for our treasures," he said, handing her a garden shovel with a hollow-grip handle. "Can you carry this to the Hofgarten?"

"We're digging at the park?"

Oskar pulled on his boots and started lacing them at the kitchen table. "I know the groundskeeper. They're replanting one of the gardens next month, so we can poke around. Anything of value belongs to the city."

"Of course," Hannah said, her heart pounding with excitement. *Does Opa really think we could discover something valuable?* Maybe she would find Mad King Ludwig's lost medallion. Better still, something no one even knew existed.

As Hannah buttoned her jacket, Oma Minna placed a half loaf of bread and a jar of blueberry preserves into a lunch box. "So my favorite archaeologists shouldn't get hungry."

That afternoon, Oskar showed Hannah how to set up their excavation site. "Think of this space as a grid," he began, waving his hand across the area. "We want to keep track of where we're digging, so we're going to use these stakes and ropes to create a square. When you're in charge someday, you'll decide where to dig, but for today, we can poke around this little spot here where there's no grass."

When I'm in charge? Oskar had told Hannah about female archaeologists like Maud Cunnington, Kathleen Kenyon, and Tessa Wheeler, so she knew women could work in the field. But *in charge?* The thought was both thrilling and terrifying. Hannah had always assumed that people in charge were outgoing personalities like her friend Hilde and her brother, Ben, but Oskar assured her that some of the best leaders were quiet ones who said little but did a lot.

After the pair successfully roped off their site, Hannah plunged her shovel into the soil, then jumped onto its step to sink the blade farther into the ground.

"Take your time, *Mausi*."

"I want to get to the good stuff," she explained before trying to move the shovel to scoop away the soil. She wiggled the handle, but it would not budge, so Hannah gripped the wooden shaft and pulled down. Then she moved to the opposite side of the shovel and tried to push it forward. When that didn't work, she clasped her fingers around the neck of the shaft and used the full weight of her body to pull back. The wood bent slightly, but the blade remained fixed in the earth as though it had been cemented there.

Oskar set down his spade and placed his hands on his hips.

"All right, big shot. That's what happens when you go wild and don't listen."

Hannah exhaled through her nose angrily. She hated when her grandfather called her a big shot, especially when he was right. "I'm sorry, Opa. Can you get the shovel out for me, please?"

"What if you were out in the desert and I wasn't here? What would you do then?"

"Um…get another shovel?"

"Hannah, I'll help you, but I want you to look at what's around you and see if you can use what our surroundings have already given us."

She scanned the area.

Oskar shook his head. "Think about what *nature* has provided for us."

"Um…water. Should I pour water on it to loosen the soil?"

"You'd need a lot of water to loosen that soil," he replied and pointed up.

"The tree?"

"That's my *Mausi*! Let me show you a little trick I learned in the war," Oskar said, picking up the rope from the ground. "See that branch, the nice thick one sticking straight out from the trunk?"

She turned her head upward at the old lime tree.

"*Mausi*, I'm going to put you on my shoulders, and you are going to toss this rope over the branch."

Hannah did as she was told, and minutes later, two ends of rope were hanging from the branch directly over their site. Oskar looped them both through the opening of the shovel handle, tightened the slack, and tied a knot. Oskar pointed to the wooden stakes on the ground and told Hannah to bring him one.

"I'm going to show you a trick, Hannah," he said. "Place that stick between the two pieces of rope, and use it to twist."

She could feel the rope getting tauter with every turn.

"Keep going. Keep twisting." As Hannah followed Oskar's directions, her grandfather explained that with each turn, the rope grew in tensile strength and began to pull at the weakest points of connection. The bough would be pulled down and the bar of the handle up with every twist. "If you don't have a rope, use a piece of cloth," he said. "Dampen it, and it gets even stronger."

When Hannah freed the shovel from the ground, Oskar gave her a handshake.

"Nice work, *Mausi*. Now, let's dig deeper and discover some lost treasure."

16

Hilde

STURMBANNFÜHRER HANS GÜNTHER LIFTED HIS EYES FROM a sheet of paper and stood to greet Hilde as she entered the office at the Chancellery. "Herta Axmann?" he asked, pulling on his cigarette, then pointing to the chair across from his desk.

"No, it's… I'm Hilde. Hilde Bischoff," she corrected with a wobble in her voice. Steadying her stride, Hilde clutched the leather folder Martin had given her, holding her ideas for the Theresienstadt propaganda film: an opening scene with women playing cards as a maid served coffee. Another of a filled recital hall, Jews in their finery listening to a symphony. She could hardly wait to show off her concepts, especially since her story-boards had been sketched by Martin, a truly gifted artist. It was no wonder the führer had admired his painting all those years ago.

Herr Günther removed his eyeglasses and lowered his head to clean them with a flannel cloth, his shellacked brown hair reflecting light from above. Hilde had no idea why the head of the Central Office for Jewish Emigration in Prague would oversee a propaganda film instead of Leni Riefenstahl or Otto, but she did not ask for fear of appearing uninformed.

"Some stunt the Tommies pulled last week," he said, flicking an ash into the tray on his desk.

As it turned out, Berlin wasn't being bombed by the British. When the RAF ordered three planes to fly low over the city, their goal seemed to be making a lot of noise. They'd hoped to embarrass Reichsmarschall Göring and bewilder Germans listening to the speech on their *Volksempfänger* at home and at work. In the end, the Tommies' trick rattled a few nerves but proved the lengths the Allied forces would go to distort reality.

"Pathetic," Hilde replied, eyes discreetly taking in the framed photos on the wall, trying not to show how impressed she was. Herr Günther and the führer at Prague Castle. Günther and Obergruppenführer Reinhard Heydrich driving in an open-top automobile. Günther looking into the camera as the führer stood behind former Czech president Emil Hácha signing his resignation. And now, Herr Günther was a meter from Hilde, separated only by an office desk.

When Günther snuffed out his cigarette, Hilde noticed that the white ashtray on his desk had a low relief of a man's face at the center. She squinted to make out the image blackened by the ash of extinguished cigarettes. It was a Jew in a yarmulke, mouth stretched open with worry. Hilde thought it crass but fought to maintain a neutral expression. Men could be boorish, but it was unladylike to point it out.

Günther must have noticed Hilde's gaze linger on the novelty and held out a silver box with an engraved imperial eagle. "*Zigarette?*"

"*Ja, ja*, please," Hilde replied eagerly, hoping Günther hadn't noticed her revulsion at the ashtray. She could not afford to show even a hint of squeamishness if she wanted to make her way in the party. Hilde plucked the cigarette from the silver box and placed it between her lips, then leaned in as Günther flicked his lighter for her. She suppressed a cough and ignored the scratch in her throat, casting down her blinking eyes.

Günther got back to business. "Herr Mazuw says you are quite the Hitler girl but relatively new to filmmaking."

"To Reich filmmaking, but I made plenty of student films in *Gymnasium*. And home movies." *Why am I nattering on about home movies?* "Here, let me show you some sketches for a *Kaffeehaus* scene." She placed her cigarette in the ashtray and unlatched her folder, then opened it to the first page.

Herr Günther's eyes landed on the color pencil sketch Martin had created: a couple dancing the Lindy Hop joined at the hand, the woman in a teal dress, skirt spinning open as she leaned back, twisting at the waist. Her partner wore a crisp, white shirt with the sleeves rolled up to his forearms. His eyes were closed in delight as he crouched his body slightly, right hand fingers snapping.

Hilde began to read, "While the Jews learn the latest dance moves, Germans are busy making sacrifices for the Fatherland and—"

Hilde jarred at the ring of the telephone. Loud noises had frightened her for the past week, but they were typically doors slamming or plates dropping, never the trill of a telephone.

Günther held up his index finger and answered. "*Hallo, ja.*" He paused for a moment. "There's no need to… Really? He said those words? That's not just what you're making of it?" He was silent as he listened to the caller.

Several minutes passed, and Hilde looked down at her watch. The gift from Otto had stopped telling time weeks earlier, but it still made a nice bracelet. And at times like this, Hilde could glance at it, hoping the gesture was a gentle hint that she was waiting patiently.

"Uh-huh," Günther replied, not seeming to notice. "Hmm, I see. That *is* why it's called the Final Solution." His face relaxed into a smile as he listened intently, showing rings of coffee stain around his front teeth. "That's what I thought. You know, you're a bit of a worrier," he said, returning his attention to Hilde across the desk. "I have someone in my office now. I will call you later." He let out a boisterous laugh that jarred Hilde. "Now, that's the spirit."

Placing the receiver into the cradle, Herr Günther looked at Hilde's sketch pad. "I should explain the purpose of the film."

No, no, you shouldn't. I understand the purpose. We want to show the world that the Jews are living in comfort. I understand. There have been rumors of their mistreatment, but this film will dispel those myths. I get it, I get it. My drawings get better with each page!

Hilde left the book open, hoping Günther's commentary would be brief.

"The Reich is developing a documentary about Jewish life in the Theresienstadt settlement in the protectorate because Jewish sensationalists and the hysterics in the international news—if you can call it that—are twisting facts for political gain."

Mein Gott, *please stop.*

"Terrible," Hilde replied, wrestling for a chance to speak. "In preparation for working with you on the film, I read all the Reich reports on Theresienstadt and am very familiar with how—"

"Did you know those Jews are arranging concerts and theater every night of the week? Does that sound like mistreatment to you?"

"No, it doesn't," Hilde returned, flipping several pages ahead in her book to a drawing of a choir onstage as a conductor lifted his baton before a dozen singers. "I think we should go to Theresienstadt ourselves and have the commandant select the most promising performances for—"

"They have lectures every day, but those wouldn't be as visual," he mused. "A bunch of old men talking about whatever they talk about."

Herr Günther went on for nearly twenty minutes without pause, never stopping to ask a single question about how she would contribute to the film. Hilde was all too familiar with the feeling of interest in her waning, but she couldn't let this opportunity slip past her, so she interrupted and blurted, "I'm sure it will be useful that I speak Czech."

Günther looked at Hilde quizzically, as if remembering she was there in the room with him. "Herr Mazuw didn't mention that," he said, finally picking up his pencil and jotting it on the otherwise blank sheet of paper with her name at the top.

Because it's not true. Hilde's heart raced. "He must have forgotten. But most of the residents are Czech, aren't they?"

"At this point, yes."

Hilde smiled confidently, though inside, her hope wilted.

"You are a fine candidate, and Herr Mazuw speaks very highly of you," Günther said, steepling his fingers. "I will notify you next week."

Notify me?

"Herr Günther, if I could—" Hilde began, gesturing to her

sketches just as she heard a delicate knock at the door. Hilde turned, and a prim secretary poked her head in a sliver of open door.

"Your next applicant is waiting, Herr Günther."

The sturmbannführer stood from his chair and pointed his hand toward the exit. There was nothing more to be done, no more of a case to be made to Herr Günther.

As she made her way out the door, Hilde lifted her head at the sound of her name. "Yoo-hoo, Hilde!" Then that annoying giggle. "How did it go?"

"Susanna. I…I didn't know you were…"

Susanna shrugged and curled her lips in a way she had undoubtedly been told was charming. "Herr Mazuw told me to give it a try, so I figured what the heck." She stood. "Wish me luck."

Hilde felt the weight of every rejection, every slight she'd ever endured in her twenty-one years. There had been plenty, but she couldn't afford to take inventory of her failures now. She knew what she had to do.

"You'll be fine, Susanna," Hilde said, bolting out the door before her coworker could see how flustered she was.

Walking back to the ministry, Hilde silently rehearsed what she would say to Otto, deciding whether she would deliver her lines like a pouty teen or a sultry young woman.

———◇———

Finally face-to-face with Otto, Hilde turned her head toward the closed door of his office and took her usual spot on his sofa. "I've been thinking about the Theresienstadt film," she began. "Working on it would mean being apart from you for weeks, and the separation would be too hard on us."

Otto furrowed his eyebrows, and Hilde couldn't tell if he was confused or annoyed.

"I'd miss you too much," she said, daring him to believe her. "I've been thinking about us lately."

"Us?"

"Yes, our future."

His chin receded back into his neck. "Hilde, what in the world…"

"I'm in love with you, Otto. You must know that."

Hilde's toes pressed into the floor, and her calves bulged, knots of tension. She fought to keep from looking at Otto's face, locking her eyes on her hands clasped tightly in her lap, index fingernails digging into her thumbs.

"My dear—" Otto interrupted himself. "I didn't know you felt this way."

She pushed harder into her fingers. "Well, I do. I think about the two of us marrying and—"

"Hilde, I'm sorry, but I thought… Listen, you're a young woman with your whole life ahead of you. You don't want an old man like me."

"I do, Otto. And I don't want to risk losing what we have by leaving you for weeks to make a film in the protectorate."

Hilde wondered if Otto was aware that he had loosened his tie and tilted his head back to stretch his neck.

He softened his tone. "I know it doesn't seem like it now, but working on the documentary with Herr Günther would be the best thing for you."

"Oh, Otto, he probably won't even choose me."

17

Hannah

Theresienstadt
May 1942

THOUGH HANNAH WOULD NOT PARTICIPATE IN THE SMUG-
gling of the second baby, she knew it was happening that
night. Her mouth was parched, and her pores prickled with fear
as she sat next to her grandfather and Griselde in the basement
of the Hanover Barracks. Unlike the performance space in the
Magdeburg Barracks cellar, the dungeon-like stone walls and
floor were bare. The stink of mildew hovered in the cold, stagnant
air. Above, the ceiling bubbled with water stains that left rust-
colored echoes around them.

An audience of nearly one hundred prisoners dressed in
their best clothing created some illusion of normalcy. Oskar had
put on his green jacket and Alpine hat with a red feather, and
Griselde nearly matched him in a burgundy dress with a belt that
hung loose around her waist. Prisoners awaited the concert by
the Doctors' Quartet, one of the ghetto's most popular musical
ensembles. Oskar adjusted his necktie nervously as if it were he
who was about to play Haydn on the violin.

The musicians of the Doctors' Quartet tuned their

instruments, eyeing the first violin for the signal to begin. Soon, Hannah was flush with heat and wondered if anyone else felt as if the cellar was contracting. She eyed the door, trying to figure out how quickly she could bolt outside if she needed to vomit.

Breathing deeply, she tried to soothe her anxiety by focusing on the sounds of the musicians playing Haydn's most elegant and uplifting pieces for the strings, his Quartet in G Major in the first work of his seventy-sixth opus. After an opening of three bold, sharp tutti chords, Hannah's head started moving slightly to the rhythm. The rich, dense counterpoint harmony was a sound that usually transported her mind to an elegant affair, but tonight, nothing could deliver her from the ghetto.

Hannah was often saddled by guilt when she attended cultural events, though Oskar insisted that the best way to fight the Nazis was by living a life rich in beauty. "Joy is the greatest act of resistance," he advised. Oskar wasn't alone in his belief that art fed the prisoner's soul; elders often reminded one another of this. *A merry mind is half your health.*

Younger prisoners embraced this as well. "Music is saving my life," Alice had told Hannah as they stood in line for soup. In addition to performing, she now offered piano lessons. Luděk was among her students, sharing with Hannah that his childhood music teachers had always given up on him after the first few lessons, saying his hands were best suited for labor and sport.

Friedl instructed the children in drawing and painting away their sorrows in her art classes. "She's the Sigmund Freud of watercolors," Klara said of her bunkmate. On some days, the children drew their families and homes before the war, pleasant memories. Other times, Friedl focused on the little ones expressing their feelings, giving color and shape to emotions children were ill-equipped to articulate.

This was all well and good, but Hannah knew that music didn't stop the council from being forced to select prisoners for transports east. Other than the council and their family members, the only prisoners who were never sent east were the girls of the glimmer factory. But even their status couldn't protect them from the typhus epidemic ravaging the ghetto. Not a single case had been cured by an opera or a painting.

Just when the musicians reached the minuet and trio, there was a loud whistle from the back of the cellar. The musicians' bows froze, and the Doctors' Quartet ceased. One let his arms fall slowly to his sides; another kept his violin tucked under his neck.

Hannah turned to the back of the room and saw two Jewish policemen in blue and a Czech gendarme wearing green. "The concert is over! Everyone back to your barracks," instructed the gendarme.

Oskar looked at Griselde and lowered his brows quizzically. He stood and addressed the officers. "It's not curfew yet," he shouted.

"Quiet, Opa!" Hannah reached for his sleeve and pulled, urging him to sit. *His big mouth will get us all killed*, Hannah thought as the gendarme pulled his pistol from its holster and aimed it at Oskar.

The chorus of fear filled the room.

Ne, ne.

A gasp.

Mein Gott!

Hannah heard the slightest whimper from Oskar when he

lifted his palms in surrender, then the sound of him gulping and clearing his throat.

"Gentlemen," he began softly. "Might I ask—"

Oskar interrupted himself at the sound of the gendarme cocking his gun. The young man kept his arm rigid with Oskar in his sights. "Quiet." He raised his pistol and fired at the ceiling.

A storm of plaster bits rained on the prisoners in the middle section of the audience. A doctor huddled over his cello, protecting the instrument from the debris.

The gendarme shouted, "Back to your barracks at once!"

Oskar placed his hands protectively in front of Hannah and Griselde. "It will be fine," he said, his eyes focused on the gendarme. "Probably an air raid by the Allies," he said, nodding his head hopefully. "Let's get ourselves inside where we'll be safe."

Hannah didn't remind him that they were already inside. Soon enough, he would know the truth about the night's failed attempt to smuggle an infant from the ghetto. Hannah scanned the faces of other prisoners, some she recognized and others she'd never seen. They exchanged worried glances, clutched one another's hands. A young man remained fixed on a small cloud of dust hovering below the ceiling.

Hannah blinked away tears, trying to erase the image of Míša, Luděk, and Radek hanging in the square. And what would become of the poor baby girl who never got out of the ghetto? Hannah stood and held on to the back of a chair to find her balance.

The ghetto public address system began to crackle, and someone tapped on the microphone. Commandant Seidl. "All residents return to your quarters immediately. Failure to comply will be met with punishment," he said.

Hannah was fueled by fear and ran back toward the Dresden Barracks, finding small gaps between clusters of prisoners to squeeze herself through. Her arms bumped a few of the teens, but Hannah didn't bother turning back to apologize; she couldn't waste a moment or a breath. Climbing the steps two at a time, Hannah made it to the third floor and pushed through the crowd of women to Míša's bunk. She arrived breathless and scanned the area for her friend. There was Alena wiping her underarms with a rag. Helena reached for a muslin sleep dress that hung on a hook fastened to the bunk beam. No sign of Míša. Hannah felt her legs start to buckle beneath her, but a burst of adrenaline saved her from falling. She needed to find Klara. Fast. She would know what happened.

Hannah's footsteps drummed against the floor nearly as quickly as her heartbeat. What if Klara was gone too? She bunched her fists as she walked toward her side of the third floor where Olina knelt in front of tiny Danuše, whose mouth was open wide as her mother rubbed her small teeth with the hem of her own nightshirt.

Then Hannah heard a crumpling cough, a sound she never thought she'd be relieved to hear. It was Míša sitting on a crate between two bunk beds, Markéta by her side. Hannah could see there were others in the room, tucked into the bottom bunks. Klara's bare legs dangled over her side of the bed, and Markéta sat beside her inside the nook, cross-legged.

Nearly collapsing with relief, Hannah called out to her friend.

Why were Markéta and Míša in Hannah's stall? Why were Alice and Friedl sitting together on the bottom bunk, hunched forward listening to Míša?

"What's going on? Did everything…" *All these women weren't involved in getting the baby out, were they?*

Míša widened her eyes, a warning: *Don't say a word.*

"We have good news," Míša whispered, fluttering her palm, an invitation for Hannah to join them.

Good news? Hannah was relieved that the baby made it out of the ghetto, but why would Míša tell so many others about the clandestine operation, especially when the first betrayal had already cost her so much?

Míša must have seen the question on her friend's face and explained, "Heydrich was shot this morning." Obergruppenführer Reinhard Heydrich, the acting governor of the protectorate, the monster who spearheaded the pogroms the Nazis called Kristallnacht and created Theresienstadt, had been attacked in Prague.

"Is that why the gendarmes broke up the concert?"

Míša smiled. "It is."

Knitting her eyebrows, Hannah silently asked, *Did the baby get out?*

Hannah forced herself to suppress a sigh of relief when Míša gave a fractional nod. *All went well.*

Markéta patted a spot next to her. "Sit, sit. We're hearing from Míša the details. Mouth radio just gave the news."

Hannah sat on the floor as Míša resumed, leaning forward to whisper, elbows planted on her thighs.

"Is he dead?" Alice asked.

Klara added, "If there's any justice in this world, he's dead, I'll tell you that. They said it was a grenade."

"He's in the hospital right now," Míša said.

Hannah felt more awake and alive than she had since her arrival in the ghetto six months earlier. Her ears sharpened and heard the tap of bugs flying into the bare light bulb hanging overhead. The musk of the hay that stuffed their mattresses permeated the room; footsteps of women moving across the third floor vibrated through the wooden planks beneath them.

"Who did it? The Soviets?" Hannah asked.

Míša shook her head.

"America?" Friedl suggested.

"No again. It was two men from the Czech resistance. Two ordinary men took out one of the most powerful leaders of the Reich," Míša said, eyes landing on Hannah.

"They had help, no?" Markéta asked. "No two men could do this alone."

"I didn't say they worked alone," Míša replied. "They had friends."

Hannah felt a flood of emotions, understanding what Míša was saying to Hannah: *We have friends too.*

"We should only pray that he dies," Markéta said to the women.

"Mama, even if he lives, a message has been sent to the Nazis—we are coming for you."

Inhaling deeply to slow her breath, Hannah placed her palms on the floor. She needed to calm down, but the excitement rushed through her body. An assassination attempt had been made on Obergruppenführer Reinhard Heydrich. He had been injured, and who knew what other plans were brewing? Hannah understood that joining the resistance was dangerous, but suddenly, *not* fighting felt even more perilous to her. How could she take such a risk? Then again, how could she not? Partisans were striking back. And once in a while, they were making gains.

Dear God, give me the wisdom to do what is right, Hannah prayed. *Bestow upon me your knowledge, insight, and understanding to do what is best for my people, my family, and myself. Blessed are You, the grantor of wisdom. Amen.*

A sense of peace washed over Hannah, and her choice was clear. She couldn't wait to take Míša aside privately later and tell her she was ready to join the fight.

18

Hilde

Berlin
June 1942

I F HILDE WAS THE SORT TO KEEP A PERSONAL JOURNAL, SHE might write that she could not remember a time when she felt more satisfied and whole. Max had been a good husband, but marrying him had meant sacrificing Hilde's career. Now, she was back on track. She'd secured the position as the film production assistant for the Theresienstadt project. Hilde made a clean break from Otto—ideal, really. He let her keep her job but ended their late-night meetings. And finally, after months of frustratingly chaste dates, she'd begun a torrid love affair with Martin.

Hilde lay in a tangle of sheets before propping herself up on her elbows. She reached for a cigarette on her nightstand, then placed the tip into her mouth. Though she had only been a smoker for two months, Hilde was already addicted to how alluring it made her feel. She loved the way a cigarette crackled as she inhaled, then released sheer blue tendrils into the warm night air. The haze made Hilde's bedroom feel like a romantic oasis. She smiled, realizing that this sultry mood had far more to do with Martin sleeping beside her than the burning tobacco.

She watched her curtains billow in the spring breeze, brushing against the crystal figurines she collected on a small table by the window. Her favorite was a statuette of two girls in sea-glass green. The smaller child leaned on the older one's shoulder the same way her sister, Lisa, used to rest on Hilde during long trolley rides in Munich, the scent of gooseberry shampoo filling the air.

Hilde looked at Martin sleeping, the barrel of his chest rising and falling, the bristles of his new mustache fluttering as he wheezed lightly through his nose. She pressed a thumbnail into the pad of her pinkie, feeling a sting of relief as her skin gave way to the pressure. Yes, it helped to cut into her flesh, but it never fully took away the pain when she thought about Lisa's death. She tried to imagine carrying on her sister's memory through her work with the Reich. Someday, she would tell her grandchildren about how their idyllic lives were possible because of the sacrifices Hilde and Lisa's generation made. *When I was a girl, millions of* Untermenschen *lived among us, spreading diseases that killed innocent children. My own sister, Lisa, fell victim to something we called smallpox back then. But the Jews are far from Europe now and can no longer hurt good Germans like us.*

Hilde inhaled her cigarette deeply, feeling the smoke sear her throat.

A moment later, she heard an eruption of sound from downstairs, women speaking quickly in a higher register than normal. Had Martin left footprints on the back stairwell when they came in that evening? Had that bloodhound Vilma smelled Martin's cologne? Was Frau Schwammberger on her way upstairs to uncover Hilde's secret at that moment?

Hilde stubbed out her cigarette in her ashtray and slipped on a satin robe. She needed to make her way downstairs before Vilma—or worse, Frau Schwammberger—knocked on the door.

Tap, tap, tap, tap, tap.

Hilde checked the time, squinting to see the hands of her alarm clock on the nightstand. Nearly eleven, the worst possible time to sneak a man out the back door of the house. Hilde was certain that Frau Schwammberger was fond of her but also knew that there were no second chances after an infraction.

Scheisse! She startled at the sound of her housemate Nora's knock, a light but urgent tapping.

"Hilde, come downstairs quick," Nora said with a tone of apology.

Yes, she was in trouble.

"One moment," Hilde replied, rustling Martin. "Wake up," she whispered.

Martin let out a loud yawn, clearly forgetting he wasn't in his own bed. "What time is it?" he asked in far too loud a voice.

"Shh! Quiet. You need to hide."

"Hide?"

"Get under the bed," she suggested before realizing he would never fit. "I'll stall Frau Schwammberger downstairs for as long as I can. You go out the back."

Martin sat and nodded his head, then reached for his pants on the floor.

"Be right there!" Hilde called out. After belting her robe, she headed down the main staircase. Her two housemates and the landlady clustered together around the *Volksempfänger*.

"The Fatherland is in mourning tonight as we receive the tragic

news that Obergruppenführer Reinhard Heydrich has just died from injuries sustained in the attack in Prague eight days ago."

Hilde moved toward the radio receiver, shaking her head in disbelief. She reached for the circle of fabric screen at the center, trying to hush it as though it were a child's open mouth. "No, they said Herr Heydrich would make it," she muttered. "He was supposed to pull through."

Vilma wiped her eyes with a handkerchief while Nora rubbed her forehead with her fingertips. "Well, he *didn't*, Hilde," Vilma said, bending her thick legs to lower herself onto the love seat. She set her hands on her lap and began bunching her nightgown with her fists. "The wound became infected after those animals tossed a grenade under his car. Shrapnel and upholstery got into his leg, that poor man."

The whir of the news report continued with assurances to the German people that the assassins would be brought to justice. Anyone discovered giving the men safe harbor would be killed, as would their families.

Hilde joined Vilma on the couch and reached into the bowl of shelled peanuts Frau Schwammberger had set out on the coffee table. "Eat, girls. We all need our strength," she said, crossing her arms tight with worry. But who could eat at a time like this?

Quirking her mouth with incredulity, Nora shook her head. "Yesterday, the newsman on RRG said he would recover!"

Hilde recognized the unsteadiness in Nora's voice. She too relied on Reichs-Rundfunk-Gesellschaft for information; they all did. If RRG promised that the obergruppenführer was going to survive, he couldn't just die the following day. "He… Why didn't he…" Hilde shook her head, remembering the details of the attack that were reported the week earlier. "Why didn't his car have armored plating? Why didn't he have a bodyguard?"

Vilma chided Hilde with a huff. "A great man was murdered. His children don't have a father, and his wife lost her husband. Have a heart."

"And why don't you try having a brain?" Hilde snapped back. Yes, she was devastated over Herr Heydrich's death, just as she was grieving the hundreds of casualties and thousands of injuries the British caused when they bombed Cologne a week ago and Stuttgart earlier this spring. It was her heart—her loyalty to the German people—that drove her to ask questions about how the Fatherland could better protect itself from future attacks.

What nitwits like Vilma didn't realize was that Germany had not only lost a top party leader with Obergruppenführer Heydrich's assassination. The *Volk* might also lose confidence in the strength of the Reich.

Hilde told herself to brush off Vilma's criticism and focus on the job ahead of her. She couldn't retaliate against the Czechs who killed Heydrich, nor could she bring the obergruppenführer back to life. She could, however, work tirelessly to help the Reich make a propaganda film that would show the world that Hitler's cause was a noble one. Soon, she would do just that.

——◇——

It had been three weeks since Heydrich's death, yet Hilde's fingers still trembled as she read the internal Reich report about what the British called Operation Anthropoid. Czech terrorists Jozef Gabčík and Jan Kubiš had been trained by the British

Special Operations Executive in London and, with the approval of the Czechoslovak government-in-exile, parachuted into the protectorate for their heinous crime. Two dozen men were on the ground with them, but it was Gabčík and Kubiš who waited on a curve of V Holešovičkách in Prague and tried to shoot Heydrich as his driver slowed to round the turn. When Gabčík's gun jammed, Kubiš rolled a grenade under the car. Moments later, there was a minor explosion. The terrorists ran as Heydrich's driver chased them through the streets. He would have caught them if he hadn't been injured himself. Hilde could hardly believe the assassins managed to stay hidden at private homes and a church for three weeks after the attack. Thankfully, someone with good sense and decency turned in Gabčík and Kubiš, and the Reich brought the murderers to justice. The men were found in hiding and fatally shot for their offense.

Hilde stopped reading and opened the large window behind her desk, but nothing seemed to cool the prickling heat on her neck. Her body was broiling from within. Yes, Gabčík and Kubiš had been killed, but what if there were others like them plotting more murders? If two Czech partisans could kill the head of the Nazi Protectorate of Bohemia and Moravia in the heart of the region, were other SS officers vulnerable to attack? Might other *Untermenschen* try to shoot Reichsführer Heinrich Himmler or, God forbid, the führer himself? If partisans were able to assassinate the Reich's third-in-command, what would stop them from aiming higher?

The next words in the report were puzzling. More than puzzling, they were disturbing. After the attack, German soldiers retaliated by razing the Czech villages of Lidice and Ležáky, because the party suspected that residents of these towns had aided Gabčík and Kubiš. Men from these villages were killed, women and children imprisoned. Yes, the perpetrators and collaborators had to be punished, but what role could the children in these villages have played?

"Yoo-hoo, are you all right?" Susanna asked, now at her side.

Hilde tried to push away her apprehension. She reached for her glass of water and sipped, remembering what Jutta had always told her at their Bund Deutscher Mädel meetings: *It is us or them*. It wasn't simply us versus them like a sporting match; the threat of the Jews was an existential one. Today's harmless children would grow up to avenge their fathers' deaths. The Jewish problem had to be solved at the root. Hilde was a grown woman now, and it was time to let go of her childish sentimentality and accept the realities of war.

— ◇ —

After the four-hour train ride to Bauschowitz, Hilde walked from the lobby of the small station to the street outside, where she spotted a man about her grandfather's age standing in front of a black Mercedes-Benz. He looked up from his folded newspaper and tipped his old-fashioned bowler hat, then approached Hilde to proffer the requisite "*Heil* Hitler" and click of his boots. The man wore a tidy white beard that ended before reaching the wishbone of loose skin at his neck. He introduced himself as Herr Ludendorff, a veteran of the Great War who now served the Reich by chauffeuring dignitaries.

Hilde stifled a grin at the characterization. She was a dignitary now.

Reaching for Hilde's valise, Herr Ludendorff told her that the drive to Theresienstadt would take just a few minutes.

He held open the back door of the car and offered his arm to help her into the vehicle. Hilde caught her reflection in the window and thought she'd managed the perfect balance of femininity and competence: a simple khaki shirtdress with a blue striped silk scarf as a headband. As she left Frau Schwammberger's house that morning, Nora told Hilde that she looked just like Leni Riefenstahl in her outfit. *That's the point*, she did not say aloud.

The road was largely unpaved, with shoulders spiked by both skeletal and leafing trees. Hilde looked out from the back seat window and imagined the village flourishing once the war was won and resources could be used for improvements instead of defense. Smooth ribbons of black asphalt would lay over the dirt and gravel beneath the car. Fallen limbs of rotting trees would be removed from the ground, and sidewalks would bustle with life.

First, Hilde reminded herself, she needed to assist Herr Günther in scouting locations for the upcoming propaganda film.

From the window, Hilde spotted the brick fortress ahead, then watched it grow closer. The car passed a mustard-colored block of a building with an arched gateway painted with the words ARBEIT MACHT FREI. Leaning back in the seat, Hilde smiled at the sentiment. Work truly did set one free. Her own commitment to the Reich had transformed Hilde from an aimless schoolgirl to a woman with a purpose.

Herr Ludendorff drove over a small stone bridge directly into the settlement, then stopped the car in front of the stately SS headquarters across the street from a park badly in need of care. *Grass would do wonders for the grounds,* Hilde thought.

Sturmbannführer Günther briskly approached the parked car to greet Hilde. Shielding his eyes from the midday sun, he revealed wet marks at the armpits of his gray shirt. He tugged at his belt and looked as though he regretted wearing black wool slacks this time of year. Herr Ludendorff opened the car door, and Herr Günther extended a hand to Hilde. "Welcome to Theresienstadt," said Günther with a far more relaxed demeanor than he had shown Hilde in Berlin. "Come. Let me show you the settlement."

This is real. My film career is finally happening!

The driver announced that he would deliver Hilde's valise to the farmhouse in nearby Kamýk, where Hilde would stay for the next three days while the homeowners were visiting nearby family. While at Theresienstadt, Hilde would help Günther find the best locations to film. Barks of "*Sieg heil*" closed the exchange, and Herr Ludendorff returned to the driver's seat of the car.

Hilde turned her head at the sound of a man's voice behind her shouting, "*Schnell, schnell.*" With him were five women in aproned farm dresses. Each carried a wicker basket, two filled with beets, carrots, and onions; a teen carried an open creel brimming with cabbages and leeks. Two other women held smaller baskets with strawberries. Hilde noticed trails of red sores and scabs on the arms of three of the women and made a mental note to suggest that work gloves would help protect these women from garden pests.

Catching Hilde's curious gaze, Günther explained, "Every family has a plot of land to grow food. The women with the fruits trade their friends for vegetables and so on." She watched the women quicken their pace, and Günther continued on.

"*Schnell!*" The man in a green uniform shouted again, and Hilde jolted at the sound. He reminded Hilde of her Max, though she had to admit, her late husband didn't have the same commanding presence. They both wore their blond hair cropped close and had a similar, lanky build, but Max was softer, gentler than the gendarme escorting the group of women through the settlement. Hilde hated herself for the thought that followed: *Maybe Max was too meek on the battlefield, and that was how the enemy got the better of him.*

The street opened to a town square, the *Marktplatz*, Günther called it. In the center, dozens of young men assembled large shipping crates. No one spoke; the only sounds were the hammering of nails and grunts of exertion. A ghost of a man stood hunched, tapping spikes into the wooden frame, while a boy unloaded planks from a truck and hauled them on his shoulder to the worksite. Hilde tried not to stare at the men's leathered hands, metacarpals rising from flesh like islands from the sea. She held her breath to avoid inhaling the foul odor of unwashed bodies lingering in the stagnant summer air, thick with dust from boots moving about the dry ground.

Günther seemed not to register any of the residents in the crowded *Marktplatz*, instead focusing on the buildings surrounding it. "That's the municipal hall," he said, pointing to a three-story stone structure, a traditional European city hall, that stretched half the block. Beside it was a small, gated yard that it shared with a smaller building adjacent to it. On another block bordering the *Marktplatz*, a church stood. Dull white with four fluted pilasters and a pediment, a clock tower with a cross rose from the back of the building. "The hospital is behind the church," Günther droned. The barracks surrounding the *Marktplatz* were marred by black mold and eroding foundations.

Mein Gott, *this place needs work*, Hilde thought. *The Jews should take more pride in their community.*

Pointing beyond a building off to the right, Günther offered, "The bakery is directly behind the Hanover Barracks. Shall I show you where the bread and pastries are prepared?"

Hilde hadn't eaten in nearly three hours and could not accept the invitation more quickly.

Sturmbannführer Günther walked two paces ahead of Hilde and led her through narrow streets with rows of two-story residential complexes that were marked with painted wooden PROMINENTEN signs over their entryways. Along these blocks were small shops that were now used as workshops and offices for the Jews, Günther explained. Through a sheet of glass thick with dirt, Hilde saw a slim man sitting on a stool working with leather cutters, focused on a boot secured between his knees. A young woman stood in another storefront making final embellishments on a tulle gown on a mannequin.

Hilde removed her notepad from her purse and wrote, *Shopping district!* All this scene needed was a cluster of snooty Jewish women in fur coats, one fingering the fabric of the dress and making a snide remark to her friends, a reminder to audiences of how classist Jews were. Perhaps the film could highlight the differences between the rich and poor at Theresienstadt: a plump family feasting around their luxurious supper table, then a quick cut to a scraggly group sharing a small roast chicken and a few potatoes.

A dense crowd of older residents emerged from one of the buildings, then quickly parted to give Hilde and Günther a wide berth. Hilde watched an old woman, wrapping her arms around her chest, struggling with each step she took. She had sunken cheeks and bones protruding from both sides of her wrists. Hilde averted her eyes before realizing she needn't look away from residents; their heads were already downturned. Günther looked past the elders who saluted him.

Hilde's heart sank. There was no way they could shoot a film with the settlement and its residents looking like this. She perked up for a moment when she saw a strong and healthy teen boy carrying a roll of canvas darting through the crowd.

She grabbed her pencil. *Robust youth!*

"The residents are very proud of the little community they've created in Theresienstadt," Günther continued.

"*Ja*, it's…very nice," she replied, though the words tasted sour on her tongue.

As they walked, Günther told Hilde that their propaganda film would be the most important thing produced in Theresienstadt. "Next to mica," he added.

Mica? The rock?

"Very important," Hilde bluffed. Was she supposed to know about the mica production at Theresienstadt? Hilde clenched her jaw at the familiar frustration of not knowing what others were talking about. It was almost as if Günther was testing her, but she would not give him the satisfaction of asking. "Herr Günther, why do you think Theresienstadt is able to…to produce mica so efficiently?"

"I have a theory," he replied with a satisfied grin.

"Theresienstadt has a lot of musicians, and their women have an edge with those nimble fingers. They can cut the mica into flakes quickly."

Hilde nodded purposefully, as though she understood why the Reich needed mica flakes.

Her mood leavened when she walked into the bakery and smelled the comforting aroma of bread rising in the oven. It was an expansive space with four built-in brick ovens, arches over their cavernous openings that spilled volcanic heat into the room. Hilde felt the hair under her scarf begin to moisten and unbuttoned the collar of her dress. She watched a crew of diminished figures, women kneading and shaping bread on the metal counters just outside the oven doors. One wiped her damp forehead with her shirtsleeve before sliding a wooden peel inside to retrieve the fresh loaves.

"Grab one," Günther suggested.

Hilde plucked a loaf from the cooling rack and broke off a piece, noticing one of the bakers widen her eyes when Hilde took a bite.

The woman in the white apron twisted her lips and looked down in despair, so Hilde offered her praise. "Delicious. *Gut, gut!*" Remembering she had told Günther that she spoke Czech, Hilde threw in one of the few words she'd learned. "*Dobrý, dobrý!*"

"*Děkuji,*" the woman said softly, eyes still on the ground.

Hilde made a final attempt to find out what the mica was used for and asked Günther, "We must film the bakery, but shall I make note to shoot a scene at the mica workshop too?"

He waved away the idea. "We need action. Men working on crates, pounding iron, that sort of thing. No one wants to watch women sit in chairs and split mica. More important than that, we need to highlight the arts and cultural events. Rafael Schächter is here at Theresienstadt."

Hilde had no idea who that was, so she said, "That's wonderful. Which of his… What do you think is his…um…finest work?"

He stopped to place his finger on his chin and pondered Hilde's question. "I've always liked the man's piano playing, but I believe conducting is his true gift." Günther continued. "Friedl Brandeis is here too, giving the children art lessons."

Hilde was grateful she did not have to fish to find out the woman's vocation.

Günther shook his head slightly, remembering something. "Speaking of children, don't forget we're going to see the opera *Brundibár* this evening. The entire cast is children. Now that's something we want to include when we return with the crew."

Hilde sighed with relief. Finally, something uplifting they could film!

19

Hannah

Theresienstadt
June 1942

HANNAH USED TO LOVE SUMMERTIME. LATE INTO THE EVEning, Prague always held on to its ethereal glow as sun reflected on the Vltava River, bathing the city in amber tones that matched the medieval castle on the hill. At Theresienstadt, extended days only meant a longer wait for relief from the heat.

It was seven thirty, and the ghetto was still baking despite the sun sagging into the Sudetenland mountaintops in the distance. Hannah had finished her workday and eaten her potato; it was time to meet Míša at the Hanover Barracks to see *Brundibár*, the children's opera.

She began making her way from the third floor of the Dresden Barracks toward the back staircase. When Hannah reached the top step, she looked down and saw an old woman's body at the landing below. Her rheumy eyes were still open and her mouth agape, as if death had caught her by surprise.

The ghetto population had reached a record high. During one of their nightly walks, Radek told Hannah that a recent Ghettowache report logged nearly fifty thousand prisoners.

Forty people had already died in June, more than double May's toll. Many of the elders perished in their sleep. The ones who fell down steps or collapsed at work, exhausted and malnourished, often landed with broken bones and limbs akimbo. Older or sick prisoners collapsing in the food line was a common sight.

Now, she stepped over the old woman's body, troubled not by the sight of death but at how accustomed she had become to it in the seven months she'd been at Theresienstadt. She shuddered, imagining people passing Oma Minna dead in the street and going about their business without a second thought. Whipped by shame, Hannah turned back and smoothed the old woman's skirt to cover her exposed thighs. Gently, Hannah closed the woman's eyelids, which were as thin and brittle as onion skin. She deserved a funeral service. Family and friends to sit shiva. A candle and a prayer. But Hannah could only offer this small bit of dignity.

Hannah's stomach pinched as she realized that the woman might remain on the landing for several days until the ghetto workmen could transport the body to the newly constructed crematorium. A summer influx of elderly German and Austrian prisoners resulted in a death rate that work crews couldn't keep up with. The ovens burned once a week, filling the air with the odor of spoiled liver and old coins. It was more sanitary than burying the dead in the mass grave on the outskirt of the ghetto, but men were still needed to transport the bodies to the small brick building. The SS could reassign Luděk and some of the other men from the railroad extension project to the grim task of body removal, but they had a strict deadline they were intent on meeting. Starting next June, a spur of train track would stretch from Bauschowitz station directly into the ghetto. The Nazis would never sacrifice manpower from the railroad extension or any other work that contributed to the war effort or generated revenue for the Reich. Heaven forbid they produce one less Wehrmacht uniform or lady's ball gown. A clever carpenter recently saved himself from transport east by making a wooden toy dog that stood when its tail was pushed down.

Hannah shooed away images of young children of Nazis blissfully playing with their toy dogs, demanding they stand and amuse them whenever they desired. Quickly replacing those images was one that chilled Hannah even more—the shrinking collection of damaged tomes that she and the women at the museum workshop transcribed each day. Once she and Klara and the other women at the penning table completed their task, would they be sent east? Everyone in the ghetto knew that the women who split mica were never transported, but how could she get herself transferred when every other woman in the ghetto wanted a spot at the glimmer factory?

As Hannah walked toward the Hanover Barracks, she blinked her eyes and looked up at a cluster of clouds floating past her. Blackbirds fluttered above, landing on tree boughs, then flying away as they pleased, as if nothing had changed. Like it was any other summer evening. Nature taunted her, but it was humanity that had betrayed her. Where were the cries of outrage from the world? They had to know what was happening.

Hannah's footsteps became heavier with her thoughts. Her arms pumped and shoes pounded hard against the path as she turned her body and found open spaces to maneuver her way through the throngs of prisoners on the streets.

When she arrived at the Hanover Barracks, Hannah was out of breath, but the exertion had eased some of her rage at the world. She remembered that there were righteous gentiles like the gendarmes who risked their lives smuggling babies from the ghetto. Radek had told Hannah that the resistance members who delivered the babies to safety were Germans who had left the Nazi Party. "A married couple," he'd shared. "Rolf and Kathe, but I don't think that's her real name. I heard him call her Irma once." The Jews had allies, just not enough of them.

She looked for Míša in the entry line, then surveyed the surrounding area when she couldn't find her friend.

"Hannah!" a voice called out.

Radek?

He hurried toward Hannah, breathless, but wore a tentative smile. "I hope it's all right if I join you. Míša said her cough was acting up, so she gave me her ticket."

"Is she in the hospital?"

"No, nothing serious. She didn't want to disturb anyone."

With Radek's reply, Hannah's body unclenched, and warmth spread through her. She looked down to hide her smile and wondered if Míša was really such a considerate audience member—coughing throughout performances was common at Theresienstadt—or if she was giving Hannah a precious gift: time to feel like a normal young woman on a date.

As Hannah sat beside Radek in the Hanover Barracks cellar, their knees touched, and she imagined what it would be like to kiss him. They had been taking short walks before evening curfew for the past few weeks, but Radek had only gone as far as brushing a loose tendril of Hannah's hair behind her ear. The gesture was a tender one; he'd even whispered that she was beautiful, but he had yet to kiss her. She was embarrassed when she considered that she might have bad breath. Or maybe she wasn't sending the right signs. It had been so long since Hannah had properly flirted with a boy that she'd forgotten how.

I'm losing my mind, Hannah thought. *A half hour ago, I was closing the eyelids of a corpse, and now I'm worried about why my crush hasn't kissed me?* She imagined her brain as a tangle of wires, bent and fried.

Taking in the set of *Brundibár*, the audience of seventy waited for the children's opera to begin. Small homes were hand-painted on strips of paper against the back wall. A tall wooden fence stretched upstage, then extended forward on both sides. The open space in the center created a town square.

Peeking out from behind the curtain was Ela Steinová, a twelve-year-old prisoner Hannah recognized from Friedl's art class. With her straight, dark hair parted in the middle, Ela was costumed in black pants and a sweater, with cat whiskers painted on her face. Beside her, standing on his toes, was Alice's little boy, Štěpán, dressed as a sparrow. Hannah spotted an older boy wearing a white ice cream vendor's hat, holding a box marked ZMRZLINA.

She looked around at the audience and noticed that the children in their seats were dressed in their best clothes: suspenders with leather drops holding up cotton pants, frocks in shades of summer flowers, polished shoes.

"I'm glad you're here," Hannah said.

Radek placed his hand on Hannah's. "I'm glad I'm here too… you know, with you."

The single note of the piano sounded repeatedly, letting the thirty members of the chorus know it was time to take the stage. The tone also alerted the audience that it was time to quiet themselves, the show was about to begin. Four teens unfurled blankets over the two windows to darken the cellar.

The performance area in the Hanover Barracks finally stilled. Gooseflesh rose on Hannah's arms at the sight of Commandant Seidl along with a young woman and another man, all with the clipped gait of Nazi Party members. When they reached the front, the commandant faced three little ones in the first row and, with the wave of his finger, instructed the children to give up their seats and take a place on the floor. They complied quickly and found a spot off to the side, far away from the Nazis. Those in the rows behind them knew better than to complain about their now-obstructed view.

The show began, and Hannah was immediately drawn in to the predicament of young Aninka and Pepíček, whose ailing mother needed milk to restore her health.

"But we have no money!" Aninka exclaimed to her brother as the two skipped to the town center.

"Look at him!" Pepíček said, pointing at the titular organ-grinder, standing on a box in the bustling town square, wiggling his thick black mustache as he collected coins from passersby. Seeing Brundibár's earnings, the siblings tried their hand at busking, but neither played an instrument nor sang particularly well.

After failing to entertain the townspeople, darkness fell over the square, and Aninka and Pepíček fell asleep in despair over their failure. As the children slumbered, a cat, a sparrow, and a dog introduced themselves to the audience with musical solos.

Štěpán pecked about as he sang, soon followed by Ela's crooning cat. Her sweet voice reflected the gentle nature Friedl described when she talked about the children in her classes. Then the dog, a girl that the show poster listed as Hana Pollaková, joined the other animals in pledging to help Aninka and Pepíček.

Hannah was stunned to see the commandant moving his head to the tune of the music. He and his guests laughed along with the prisoners in the audience.

As the forty-minute performance went on, the SS in the front row continued enjoying the show, and Hannah wanted to scream. How could Nazis be entertained by people they hate? *They can see that we are creative, talented human beings, and they still enslave us. Even murder us for trying to send letters!*

For the final number, the cast marched into the town square onstage to the steady cadence of the piano and stood in a row. The milkman, baker, and policeman joined the chorus and began belting their victory song. They defeated the evil Brundibár. The message to the children in the audience was clear: Be brave and rely on friends, and you can make bullies behave. Hannah couldn't help wonder if the SS in the front row understood why the ghetto's most popular show was about the fall of a villain with a funny mustache.

The audience clapped with all their might as the cast took their bows. During the curtain call, the three Nazis stood and walked toward the exit. The men's faces were relaxed, not bearing their usual scowls. Commandant Seidl's shoulders even appeared a bit looser. As they approached, Hannah heard the man turn to the lone woman of the group. "This is perfect for the film," he told her as she nodded eagerly.

The young woman looked strikingly similar to Hannah's childhood friend Hilde Kramer, with the same way of jutting her chin as though she were ready to defend an accusation, the same wide blue eyes darting about the room.

The woman must have felt Hannah's gaze, because she turned her head and looked directly at her. Hannah no longer had any doubt. In a moment that felt infinite, Hilde glanced back toward Hannah and puckered her lips with an expression that said, *Do I…know you?* Hannah was no longer the chubby teen Hilde remembered. Although pretty as Radek said she was, Hannah knew the pockmarks on her cheeks were the first thing people noticed when they looked at her face.

Hannah's mind drifted into a memory of when Oma Minna let Hannah and Hilde help her bake challah for Shabbat. Between the tender images of Minna showing the eight-year-old friends how to braid the loaf and glaze it with egg white, another crept in. It might have never registered if not for Minna's reaction.

"It takes so long to make your bread, and it's so much work," Hilde said, then asked Minna, "How come you don't just get it from the bakery? If Jews have all the money, why don't you just buy your bread?"

Oma's hands stopped mid-braid. "What do you mean?"

"Oh." Hilde shrugged. "Papa said at the end of the Great War, Jews took all the money, and now there's a bank in America that just closed, and it's going to make the whole world poor. Except for the Jews, because they have all the money."

Oma Minna raised a clenched fist to her chest and excused herself from the room. She turned away in such a hurry that she spilled the bowlful of egg whites onto the kitchen countertop, the mixing spoon clattering as it fell to the floor.

The sound of Hilde's voice returned Hannah to the present. "Inspiring," she said with that same hesitant tone she used in school when answering a teacher's question. *Is that right? Is that what you wanted me to say?*

Hannah cursed the injustice of this world. *I am a prisoner, and Hilde Kramer is a filmmaker.*

"Hannah?" Radek's voice startled her. "Oh sorry, I didn't mean to scare you. I was hoping that maybe you wanted to take a short walk before curfew?"

"I would, but I should check on Míša." If Míša was feeling better, Hannah needed to tell her about seeing Hilde. There had to be a way to use this past friendship to her advantage.

———◦———

When Hannah made her way up to the third floor, she saw a blanket draped like a curtain over Míša's lower bunk. Whispers filled Míša's space, though Hannah could not hear what was being said. Who else was with her?

Fingers marked with burns curled around the hem of the blanket and pulled it back, an invitation. Then a voice. "Your date, it was good?"

"Markéta?"

"Come, come inside. I am telling Míša her favorite story. About the day she was born."

Before Hannah could ask about Míša, her friend's face appeared. "It's *her* favorite story, not mine."

"You're feeling better?" Hannah asked.

"Answer Mama's question," Míša pressed. "Did you have a good time on your date with Radek?"

Hannah crawled through the opening, Míša and Markéta moving their bodies to make room in the bunk. The space wasn't fully enclosed; light poured in from the uncovered foot of Míša's bed, but Hannah understood the appeal of the makeshift cocoon. She sat with her legs crossed and leaned in close. "I did," Hannah confessed.

"Then yes, I feel much better." Míša smiled.

Markéta reached for her daughter's face and patted her cheek. "She loves love, even when her own heart is heavy—"

Míša interrupted. "Mama, please. Let Hannah enjoy her night."

Hannah nodded, understanding. Míša needed her mother and best friend to lift her spirits, so Hannah would wait until tomorrow to share the news about Hilde. "Go on. Don't let me interrupt your story about the day Míša was born."

Míša tilted her head and smiled. She narrowed her eyes, a gesture that said, *Thanks a lot.*

"All week, it was rain, rain, so much rain, until I feel this little kick in my belly, my little angel saying to me that she is ready to come into the world. You would not believe it. The rain stops, and I look at the windows, and clouds are parting and the sun starts shining."

Míša leaned in toward her mother and rested her head on her shoulder. "Mama doesn't exaggerate at all. I am so powerful that my birth changed the weather."

"It is true!" Markéta protested. "Everything this child touches turns to golden treasures."

Hannah caught Míša's gaze falling to her lap and her lips pressing together, a look she recognized as her friend holding back tears. She knew Míša well enough to understand what she was thinking: *If that were true, why then was Pavel killed?*

———◇———

Opening the folder at her spot at the worktable, Hannah saw that the day's transcription was from the Book of Jeremiah. He had always been one of Hannah's favorites of the Latter Prophets, and his promise of a future in Israel was more precious to her than a cup of cool water today.

As she reached for her pen, Hannah looked at the callus that had formed on her middle finger where she lay the slender wooden barrel for ten hours each day. She saw that Klara had one too, as did Alena and Helena next to her. Before dipping the nib of her pen into the inkwell, Hannah looked at the papers in her folder and focused on the passage she would begin with that day.

Jeremiah 22:13: He who builds his house with unfairness
And his upper chambers with injustice,
Who makes his fellowman work without pay
And does not give him his wages.

Oma Minna had always told Hannah that God took care of them in ways that they often overlooked. Hannah never blamed the prisoners who lost their faith at Theresienstadt. She too felt abandoned by God but sometimes found morsels of faith that He had not forgotten her. That morning it was the cushion on her finger and the words she needed to hear.

A man wearing a green gendarme uniform stood in the doorway and cleared his throat. The women at Hannah's table stiffened, though they never looked up or stopped working. "Hannah Kaufman," he called out, his voice cracking like an adolescent.

Klara lifted her eyes and looked at Hannah, unsuccessful at masking her fear. Helena closed her eyes tight and hunched her shoulders, while Petra inhaled through her nose and chewed her bottom lip. Hannah was aware of every pore on her body prickling, but she felt the need to reassure the others. Hannah nodded her head and tried to signal, *it will be fine*. They all knew it wasn't true. Nothing was fine at Theresienstadt.

Griselde hurried toward the door before Hannah could reply. "What's this about? You know we have quotas, and Hannah has a great deal of work today." She crossed her arms, challenging the authority of the young man.

He lowered his voice to a whisper, but Hannah could still hear him, pitch raised as he pled. "Come on. You know I'm not in charge. The SS needs her at headquarters."

"No," Griselde swiped back with a dangerous mix of anger and fear. "Hannah isn't going anywhere with you."

Hannah watched Klara's fingers tighten around her pen, the silver tip pressing deeper into the paper. Griselde had lost her good sense. It was equal parts endearing and terrifying; her actions could land them all on the next transport east.

Shaking her head, Hannah's breath became a pant. Her heart pounded in her chest, and her legs felt like liquid. Griselde foolishly pushed again, seeming to forget her earlier admonition that they could only survive Theresienstadt by quietly obeying the rules. "No one is taking Hannah anywhere!"

"I'll go," Hannah cried out, then she placed her pen in its holder and screwed the brass lid on her inkwell. "I'll be back in no time."

She knew she wouldn't. Another prisoner must have implicated her in the baby-smuggling operation. Perhaps the SS wanted her to be an informant.

Hannah walked beside the boy. "What's your name?" Her voice fluttered, so she took a deep breath.

"Andrej," he replied.

"Do you know why…what's going on? Who wants to see me? Does the note say—"

"I was told to bring you to SS headquarters. That's all."

The two walked in silence until they arrived at the SS barracks, and Andrej opened the door for Hannah.

When she walked through the entrance, Hannah's eyes were assaulted by a Hakenkreuz flag larger than her blanket hanging above a framed color portrait of Adolf Hitler. An SS officer sat at a desk in the lobby. Barely registering the two, the man nodded his head toward the staircase to the right.

Before she reached the landing, Hannah heard the haunting weep of a single violin. Her chest hurt as she recognized the melancholy notes she'd heard dozens of times throughout her life. Kol Nidrei, the chant that traditionally ushered in Yom Kippur, the Day of Atonement, floated from an open door down the hallway. The plaintive opening phrase, played thrice, morphed into a gentle, sorrowful melody, like a sad lullaby, before moving on to the drama of the midsection, only to return, once again, to the opening phrase.

Why in God's name would Nazis play a phonograph of Jewish music? And why Kol Nidrei in June?

When Hannah passed the door, she spotted a prisoner inside, an older man with eyes closed as he played for the commandant. It was not a recording after all. The musician wore a loose-fitting black tuxedo, excess fabric from the pants puddling on the floor. Hannah wondered if the commandant had requested this piece or if the choice was one man's small rebellion.

Hannah and Andrej continued walking down the hallway, then turned into a small alcove with a single door. When Andrej knocked, a woman's voice returned that they could enter. Inside, sitting at a desk with a full glass of water beside stuffed folders, was Hilde Kramer. Behind her was an open window overlooking the *Stadtpark*.

Andrej pressed out a tight smile. "*Hodně štěstí*, Hannah," he whispered. "Good luck."

"Hannah," Hilde said tentatively. "I knew it was you. I'm so… It's so good to see you. I'm so glad you're… You look well." Hilde looked at the surface of her desk and straightened an empty basket. She pushed her chair back and stood, then reached into the pocket of her blue shirtdress to retrieve a gleaming silver case. "*Zigarette?*"

"Can I keep it for later?" Hannah knew Míša would appreciate an evening smoke. Or maybe she would trade the cigarette for bread.

Hilde shrugged, but her hands trembled as she plucked a cigarette from her case and handed it to Hannah. "Suit yourself," she said, rifling through her pocket before she found her lighter and sparked a flame.

The sound of the violin floated from the commandant's office as the young women looked at each other, Hannah silently instructing herself not to speak, to let Hilde set the tone for the conversation. Whether she liked it or not, her old friend was in charge now. The orange tip of the cigarette brightened as Hilde pulled her first draw.

Hilde pointed to the chair across the table from her. "Please sit," she ordered.

Hannah sank into the seat, relieved at least that this would not be an interrogation by the SS.

"So," Hilde began, a curl of smoke escaping with the word. "How are you?"

Hannah remembered when the two were in *Grundschule* and tossed a medicine ball between them. The question landed with the same weight, the same punch. *How am I? I've been a prisoner for more than seven months.* Hannah's lips began to wrinkle with disgust, but she quickly tamed them, knowing that showing her rage would serve no purpose.

"How is your family?" Hannah asked. "Do they still live in Munich?"

Hilde turned toward a painting of a castle hanging on the side wall, clenching her jaw, a gesture Hannah recognized from their childhood. She was holding back either anger or pain; the two always seemed closely intertwined with Hilde. "Lisa died four years ago," Hilde said, looking as though she were fighting to maintain her composure. She was unable to hold back a cough from the smoke. "Kurt too. He was killed in the war."

"I'm sorry to hear that," Hannah said, surprised that she felt genuine sympathy for Hilde. Not over Kurt's death. But Lisa was a sweet little girl, an innocent who hadn't been involved in any of Hitler's madness. "Your parents? How are they?"

"The same. How about yours? Are they here?"

Stiffly, Hannah replied, "Just Opa. Everyone else is in Palestine," she said, opting to withhold Oma Minna's fate. Part of her wanted to keep the truth to herself; Hilde hadn't earned this intimacy. Another part simply wanted to pretend it wasn't true and that Oma Minna was in Palestine, eating avocado with her morning toast. Hannah felt her back press against the wooden slats of the back of the chair. "Why are you here?"

Hilde shrugged with manufactured modesty. "I'm a film-maker for the...for Germany. We're making a documentary about the Jewish settlement here."

In her mind, Hannah heard Míša's voice: *Keep her talking. Get information.*

"A film?"

"Yes, yes, that's one of the reasons I called you in. We start shooting in a few months, and I'll need a helper. Do you speak Czech?"

"Of course I speak Czech," Hannah replied, barely hiding her irritation. "I lived in Prague for seven years."

Hilde's eyes narrowed. "I didn't know where your family ran off to. Remember? You left without saying goodbye."

And there it was—a reminder of what a self-centered person Hilde had always been. The Kaufman family had fled Munich for their lives after enduring years of persecution, but Hilde made it sound as though they had left on a holiday in the tropics without sending a postcard.

Hilde had once been a friend, but now she was a Nazi and deserved no further explanation. Part of Hannah wanted to spit the truth at her, that Hilde's mother had turned her away at the front door on the day of her party. Clearly, Johanna Kramer hadn't told her this, but Hilde hadn't come around to check on Hannah afterward either. "Of course I speak Czech."

"Good, then you can be my helper on the film. I'll need someone to translate what the Czechs are saying, and it will be...nice to spend time together again."

Had Hilde always been out of her mind, or was Hannah only noticing it now that they were adults? *Nice to spend time together?* Hannah could only nod in agreement, knowing that she had no choices in Theresienstadt.

Hilde stubbed out her cigarette, half-finished, and Hannah was disgusted by the waste. She did the calculations in her mind: one half cigarette could buy a small slice of bread.

Hilde crinkled her face and shrugged sheepishly. "So listen... I told Herr Günther, my supervisor, that I speak Czech, so we have to be a little sneaky about the translations. Like when you used to let me copy your homework," Hilde said with a nervous laugh.

Hannah heard Míša's voice in her mind. *This is a gift.* If the Nazis were making a propaganda film, it was because they needed to convince the world that the Jewish people were being treated well in Theresienstadt. Living in cottages by the lake. Enjoying their spa town.

Relief washed over Hannah. The world was asking questions. Maybe the war was finally coming to an end.

"Sure, Hilde. It will be a good time," Hannah said.

20
Hilde

Berlin
August 1942

"T HIS IS NOT TERRIBLE NEWS, HILDE! IT'S DEFINITELY A GOOD thing for the Reich," Martin assured her, his voice soft with compassion.

She couldn't fathom how Martin thought that the new plan—a prisoner making the Theresienstadt film—was a positive turn of events. Neither she nor Herr Günther would play any role in the documentary; they wouldn't be anywhere near the set. Hilde would watch *Hitler's Gift* in the cinema, like any other nobody in Germany.

A tuxedoed waiter appeared, placing a large bowl of *Kartoffelsuppe* before Hilde and a plate of diced pork, potatoes, and carrots in front of Martin.

Hilde startled at a wave of male voices from the back of the dining room, where four tables had been pushed together for a group of SS officers. She recognized the sound of men in agreement, low notes of *Mmm* and *ja ja* before they resumed clanking their silver forks against porcelain plates.

Martin tied a white napkin around his neck. He leaned

closer to Hilde. "I know you wanted to make the Theresienstadt film, but it's better if a prisoner shoots it. The Reich can spend resources elsewhere. Let the Bolshevik Jewess do the work, and you'll make another film. Now that more German soldiers are fighting in Stalingrad, maybe Herr Mazuw will let you have another try at *Hitlerstadt*."

"Are you stupid?" she spat, and without thinking, Hilde slammed her hand against the table, causing the silverware to clatter and a splash of soup to stain the white tablecloth. Horcher wasn't the type of place where diners raised their voices or pounded tables, but Hilde found Martin's suggestion exasperating. People like him assumed that opportunities came along effortlessly because the world worked that way for them.

"I'm sorry," she said when she watched his mouth drop at her reaction. Hilde hid the offending hand under the table for punishment, then began cutting into her flesh. "I didn't mean that, Martin. It's just that I worked hard for this assignment, and I can't believe the Reich would trust some Jewess to present the settlement in the best light. You know how they twist everything."

Martin could never truly understand Hilde's disappointment. How could he? As a child, Martin's painting of the führer hung in the Chancellery. Last month, he was promoted to head the graphic arts department. He was moving forward while she kept being pushed back every time life offered her the slightest promise.

She turned her head toward the window as the purpling light from outside bled through the lace curtains. There was no way she would let him see her fighting back tears. Not five months earlier, Hilde had wondered if Martin would feel threatened by her, a rising star in the Reich. She worried that she could never fully respect a man with a lesser rank. Now it was Martin who had the power, and she had taken two giant steps backward. Otto wasn't going to ask Hilde to revisit *Hitlerstadt*, she knew that. And this Jewess resident of the ghetto—this Irena Dodalová person—had been ordered to shoot the film Hilde would have given anything to create.

Hilde pressed her fingers against her forehead, trying to calm the headache starting to pulse above her eyebrows. It was foolish to alienate the one person who had been in her corner. None of her misfortunes were Martin's doing. She returned her gaze to her *Schatz*, who was forking his supper into his mouth, staring past Hilde coolly. When Martin glanced at his watch, Hilde felt a jolt of fear. She could lose him.

"I am sorry," she said with a pang to her chest that surprised her. "The truth is that I'm the one who feels stupid right now. I try so hard for the party, but half the time, I'm invisible, and the other half, I'm tossed aside like rubbish." The words were humiliating, but speaking them was oddly freeing. She hadn't even realized she felt this way until she blurted it out with her apology.

Furrowing his brow, Martin whispered, "Hilde."

She sniffed and nodded.

"Hilde, you have blood on your forehead."

"Oh." She panicked and lifted her napkin to wipe away the mark. "I didn't…" She trailed off.

Martin reached across the table and held Hilde's free hand. "Hilde." He paused until she met his eye. "I know this news was hard on you, but I want you to know you're never invisible to me."

With that, Hilde began to tear, realizing that she had been

waiting years to hear these words again. She'd been cherished by Max, but the short-lived comfort of knowing that, of feeling it, had been buried with him.

Martin laughed and shook his head as if to say Hilde was silly for not understanding this. "And you're definitely not rubbish."

Her relief was palpable, and Hilde let out a breath of laughter. "Thank you, Martin. I'm lucky to have you," she said and meant it.

"How'd you like to be even luckier?" he asked. "I mean, permanently lucky to have me?"

Was he asking what she thought he was? Her best bet was to remain silent and let him clarify. She didn't think she could bear the embarrassment of a misunderstanding this important.

"I was going to talk to you about this later, but maybe it will help you feel better if you were working to build Germany in another way. By starting a family. With me."

The proposal hung between them as Hilde considered the question. What did Martin mean by serving the Reich in *another* way? In addition to filmmaking or instead of it? Before she could consider this, Hilde gasped internally, remembering that she'd never told Martin she couldn't bear children of her own. She considered withholding the information, feigning surprise after they failed to conceive. What could he do after they were already married?

"My *Mutter* has been asking me to bring home a wife for years now. She'll be so pleased when she finds out it's a girl like you," Martin exclaimed.

Hilde warmed at the thought of a mother-in-law who would treat her kindly, perhaps even as a daughter. "A girl like me?" Hilde asked, fishing for praise.

"Definitely," Martin replied. "I can think of no one more dedicated to the cause than you, Hilde. You and me, we can build a real future together." He glanced over his shoulder and caught the attention of their waiter. "Shall I order a bottle of sparkling wine to…celebrate?" His voice shook with the final word, and Hilde found his nerves endearing.

"*Ja, ja*, Martin. *Ja*, order the wine, because *ja*, I will marry you!"

21

Hannah

H ANNAH FELT A STING IN HER NOSE AT THE SMELL OF ANTI-septic and urine as she entered the Hohenelbe Barracks and walked upstairs to the meeting spot, a large cleaning supply closet on the second floor.

Maybe Hilde should shoot her propaganda film here at the hospital. Or the morgue so the world can see the reality of Hitler's gift to the Jews. Where was Hilde anyway? It had been three months since Hannah had been summoned to SS headquarters with news of Hilde's film, and then nothing.

Shaking away the memory of the woman who was no longer a friend, Hannah reminded herself to remain in the present. She needed all her focus for the task at hand. A baby's life was on the line tonight. The group had successfully smuggled two infants from the ghetto, but this would be the first time Hannah delivered a child to the back gate of the ghetto and placed the infant into the arms of a friendly gendarme.

Twenty minutes before the 10:00 p.m. curfew, the hospital corridors were nearly empty, unlike after supper when hallways

were packed with prisoners arriving to visit loved ones in the
sick wards. Still, Hannah lowered her head for fear she would see
someone who might ask why she was there. *Is Oskar unwell? Did
Míša's cough turn out to be tuberculosis? Is dear Griselde all right?* Or
worse, Hannah imagined someone asking her to stop and pray
for a sick friend. How heartless she would feel refusing a person
comfort, but that was exactly what she would have to do. She was
on a tight schedule.

As she made her way toward the supply closet, Hannah
was grateful that she heard only a few sounds in the hallway:
a man clearing his throat, a child sniffling, footsteps clopping.
She knocked on the door—the soft, distinct rhythm of galloping
fingertips that Míša had instructed.

When Hannah pulled open the door, she found Míša seated
on the floor, holding a baby girl tucked into a burlap knapsack,
head peeking out from the top. Míša's hands waved Hannah
inside, then brushed the thin layer of the child's silken brown
hair. "This is Zophia," she whispered, tilting her head down to
kiss the top of the infant's head.

Hannah wasn't sure if she envied or pitied Zophia, who
would wake up the next morning in the Czech countryside
with parents who would adopt her as their own. Zophia would
never face transport east, but that protection came at a cost. The
faint memory of her mother's touch would evaporate like mist
at sunrise. Meanwhile, a young woman would spend the rest of
her life wondering if her daughter was safe, if she had brothers
and sisters, what she looked like swinging on the monkey bars
at the playground. Even now, Hannah had moments when she
thought she saw her family across the crowded *Marktplatz* before

remembering this was impossible. Would Zophia's mother search for her daughter's face in every girl her age long after the war ended?

Hannah stepped inside the closet and gently closed the door. "Has she been nursed and diapered?" Most importantly, Hannah asked if Míša had slipped her Veronal-coated pinkie into the infant's mouth so she would sleep through the night.

Míša teased, "All done, boss."

Hannah pulled a borrowed flashlight from her sweater pocket and slid her thumb up the ridged groove of the switch. A click released a beam of soft yellow light, and Hannah placed the flashlight on a shelf and aimed it at the ceiling.

"You're sure you want to do this?" Míša asked. "It's not too late to ask Radek to fly solo."

Hannah knelt before her friend and touched the baby's cheek with her finger. "Yes, I'm certain. You said someone walking alone toward the back gate would arouse suspicion. I want to protect him from that." She pointed to Míša's ankle wrapped in a bandage that Friedl made from nylon socks. "How's your…"

Míša shrugged. "It'll heal," she said of the sprain she had gotten when descending a ladder too quickly. "At least it wasn't my wrist. *Pfft*, can't afford to be replaced at the glimmer factory." At the mention of her workshop, Míša coughed lightly, holding her free hand over her mouth.

"Let me take the rucksack for you," Hannah offered, sitting next to Míša and inching her body close to her friend. After rubbing the baby's back, Hannah wrapped her hands around the infant's tiny body and transferred the rucksack onto her stomach.

Footsteps ascended the staircase with a quick cadence, and

Hannah prayed it was Radek instead of another Ghettowache officer who had been tipped off by an informant. Whoever it was, the person had reached the landing, and his heavy steps grew louder as he approached the closet.

Radek pushed the door tentatively and slipped inside the closet, pressing his back against a shelf stacked with canisters of cleanser and bottles of chlorine. At the sight of Hannah, Radek lifted his chin. "You ready?"

She nodded, feigning confidence. Hannah was not at all ready, but she reminded herself that they would have the child for fewer than five minutes as they made their way to the back gate. There, two gendarmes on duty would serve as lookout while an off-duty colleague whisked the baby to the meeting place. A few minutes, that was all.

"We need to go," Radek said.

Hannah held the rucksack close and tried to cover the front of her body with Oskar's cardigan as she and Radek walked toward the stairs. As they began their descent, Hannah looked down, making sure her worn leather boots landed squarely in the center of each step. This was no time for her to lose her balance.

On the ground floor, Radek and Hannah walked briskly, turning a corner of a brightly lit hallway with a mural of pine trees along a riverbank. After they passed the painted forest, bare windows scrolled by them as they made their way to the exit. The darkness of night against the door glass was their beacon.

When they were barely a meter away from the knob, a woman's voice called out from behind. "Moment!"

Hannah considered running but knew it was dangerous.

Maybe she should hand Zophia to Radek and tell him to sprint while she begged the woman not to turn them in.

The stranger called out again, "One moment! Stop."

Hannah saw Radek halt and did the same, though she kept her back toward the woman and remained focused on the door, just steps away.

"Can you help me, please? My patient, he's… I'm afraid to move him into another bed. He's…" The nurse's voice fluttered as she finished. "He's fragile. It's my first night, and the head nurse is with another patient."

Radek's eyes shifted toward Hannah before he lowered his brows. "Oh God, Hannah, I'm sorry," he said softly. "Can you handle…"

"I've got it," she whispered quickly. "Go."

"I'll catch up with you as soon as I can." Then he turned around to answer the nurse. "Glad to help," he called out, then began backtracking into the corridor.

The baby began to wriggle in her sack as if to remind Hannah that she had no time to waste. God forbid the baby started to fuss while she was still in the hospital; the sound would echo through the halls.

Hannah tightened her hold on the sack with one arm and used the other to push the door open.

It wasn't until she felt the cool night air on her skin that she realized she had been sweating. "Shh, little one," she whispered, adjusting the flap to cover Zophia's head. "You're going on a big adventure!"

Hannah took the path along the side of the home for the elderly where prisoners tended to retire well before curfew. Those who were awake were less likely to hear Hannah walking past their windows or the sound of her boots hitting the ground mixed with her heavy breath, crossing over the unfinished railroad tracks, until she finally saw the back gate of Theresienstadt.

A gendarme eyed Hannah running toward him and held out his palm. She shuddered, remembering that Radek hadn't told her the name of the gendarmes helping them. Hannah stopped and squinted her eyes as the guard flashed a light at her.

"What have you got there?" he asked with the deep, commanding voice of someone accustomed to shouting orders. "You got... Is that a baby?" the gendarme asked.

"No," tumbled from her mouth. "It's..." *What is it? What would make sense?* "It's not."

Andrej the gendarme walked closer to her, pinching his face in query as he examined Hannah, his eyes scanning the length of her. "You sure you don't got a baby in that sack?"

At that, the infant made the slightest yet unmistakable gurgle of a baby.

"Shit," he said. "They're supposed to be knocked out. You didn't drug him?"

Hannah flooded with relief. "She's a girl."

"Look, I don't care if this is a baby raccoon as long as it's quiet."

Hannah held on to Zophia with one hand while using the other to slip off the straps of the rucksack, then handed the child to the gendarme.

"Where's Radek? He was supposed to... *Ach*, never mind. We got to go now. Is she drugged?"

"She was given a bit of Veronal a few—"

"Got it. Don't need a whole report." He called out four short owl hoots, and a clucking noise soon replied. The gendarme ran, crossing the back gate, his green jacket soon absorbed into the dark of night.

Hannah followed a narrow, unlit path that ran parallel to the periphery of the ghetto. The route would take longer to get back to the Dresden Barracks, but it was less crowded and would give Hannah time to try to untangle the jumble of emotions she was experiencing. Elation that Zophia had made it out. Anxiety that Andrej would be caught. And, she was not ashamed to admit, she was proud of herself.

"Hannah," a voice whispered from inside one of Theresienstadt's many archways that led to brick-lined tunnels. This one was topped with a dirt road and festuca grass that led to an outdoor workspace. "Hannah, over here," she heard from the blackened mouth of the passageway.

She flicked on her flashlight to see Radek caught in a yellow beam with his arms shielding his face.

"Sorry about leaving you like that. I couldn't say no to the nurse without her suspecting."

Hannah felt the moist ground give way to her boots as she walked toward Radek, searching for an excuse to touch him. Anything would do: gripping the sleeves of his jacket, brushing the hair from his eyes.

Radek kicked the toe of his shoe into the ground and shifted his weight nervously. "I was hoping we could maybe talk for a few minutes before you go back to your barracks."

Had she done something wrong? Was there a problem with the nurse?

"Sure," Hannah said, swallowing her nerves and following Radek into the tunnel, the temperature dropping, the scent of damp earth growing with each step farther inside. She saw the silhouette of a couple pressed against the stone wall, locked in a kiss, the woman's arms wrapped around her lover's shoulders.

Radek reached for Hannah's hand and led her through the tunnel. "Let's give them some privacy…" He didn't finish the thought, and Hannah was relieved that he seemed embarrassed.

"Did you ever go to that sweetshop on Vodičková Street?"

Now under the darkness of a new moon, Hannah looked up at Radek, thoroughly confused by the question. "In Prague?"

"Yeah. My cousins used to take me there for *kremrole* whenever I visited."

"Cukrárna Myšák? Sure, I love that place. Everyone does." *What in the world?*

Radek looked down and tapped his toe into the soil beneath him again. "I guess I was wondering if I could maybe take you there once all this is over. I mean, we've been going for walks, and I thought it would be nice to look forward to…a real date once the war ends."

Hannah had no idea what had come over her—the thrill of their successful mission, the sweetness of Radek's nerves, the electric jolt of seeing the couple in the tunnel—but she felt like a different version of herself. She loved that Radek was thinking about life after the war. She loved that he saw her as part of it. Hannah would be in Palestine, but maybe he would relocate there too.

"I'd like that very much," she said, thankful that the dim sky hid her blushing cheeks. "I don't think we should wait until then," she said, reaching toward his shoulders and standing on her toes.

Eyes widening with understanding, Radek moved his head down and bent his knees to get closer to Hannah. Their noses bumped, and they laughed before they both tilted their heads to the same side, then laughed again. "I'll go right. You go left," Radek said.

"Wait, that doesn't make sense," Hannah said. "If I go to my right—"

Before she could finish, Radek cupped Hannah's face with his palms. "We'll work it out." And with that, he placed his lips on hers, and Hannah felt the warmth of his mouth spread throughout her body. The illusion of normalcy nearly made Hannah cry, but she blinked back her tears.

PART IV

22

Hannah

H ANNAH LIFTED HER SHIRTSLEEVE TO WIPE AWAY THE sweat forming on her forehead and felt the unforgiving stone of the footpath pressing against her bare knees as she and Míša knelt, scrubbing the sidewalk on the periphery of the *Marktplatz*. To the right of Hannah, also on all fours, were three young women she'd never seen before, two new arrivals from Denmark and one from Holland. On her left was an Austrian elder who shared a bunk with Míša on the third floor of the Dresden Barracks. The women were part of a crew of hundreds of female prisoners that new commandant Karl Rahm—the third after Siegfried Seidl and Anton Burger had been reassigned—had ordered to clean the walkways around the ghetto with their hairbrushes. The cleaning was one of the final steps in the nine-month *Stadtverschönerung*, the beautification of Theresienstadt in preparation for the June inspection by the International Committee of the Red Cross. If Hilde Kramer and her Nazi bosses had any sense, they would have made these improvements to the ghetto before they tried making their first two films about their paradise settlement.

According to mouth radio, shortly after Hilde visited the ghetto nearly two years earlier, the Nazis decided that instead of using their own film crew, they would order a prisoner who had been a film studio executive in Prague to make the documentary. Irena Dodalová's film was good, too good at showing the realities of life in Theresienstadt. Rumor was that Reichsführer Heinrich Himmler threw a fit when he watched the footage. It was hard to believe that type of information would make it back to the ghetto, but Hannah didn't care if it was true or not. She loved imagining a defeated Himmler.

Then the Nazis made a second attempt at a propaganda film. Hilde and her supervisor returned in January 1944 and left after only one day when they realized the scene was too chaotic. Hannah had gritted her teeth when she heard the news. *Oh, the irony. I hope it wasn't too difficult for you, Hilde, my old friend.* Not that she had said this. Hannah hadn't even seen Hilde, and that was fine with her. Hannah was glad the two films failed. Everything the Nazis did should be cursed.

Hannah scrubbed harder as she thought about Hilde, working out her frustration on the stone, but she reminded herself to conserve her energy for survival. After a lifetime of chubbiness, her belly had flattened and her collarbones now protruded. She didn't look sickly like Míša and so many of the others, but she was thin in a way that would make any grandmother run to her with a plateful of cake.

"Do you think Commandant Rahm will select us for the…" Hannah wasn't sure what to call the bizarre assignment. The inspection would be a well-orchestrated performance, every detail staged with precision. Prisoners selected to participate would be given lines of dialogue and strict direction. Cross Rathausgasse at exactly noon, whistling a happy tune. Let a ball roll from the new playground and onto the path as the commandant and inspectors arrive. All the children were to refer to the commandant as "Uncle Rahm" for the day.

Míša tried to help her friend finish the thought. "The show? *Pfft*, he may use you, but look at me. I'm a mess."

Taking in Míša's brittle hair and pronounced jaw, Hannah knew her friend was right. She was not the type of prisoner the Nazis wanted to spotlight.

The women continued washing dirt from the walkways, but Hannah looked up when she heard a chirp that sounded different from the finches that taunted her overhead. It was Griselde, trying to get Hannah's attention to wave hello. Her silver hair poked through the window of a two-story house, a *prominenten* home where women were filling flower boxes with tulips in candy-colored shades of pink and yellow. The scent of a thousand new rose bushes permeated the air, and it reminded Hannah of Oma Minna's perfume.

In the corner of the *Marktplatz*, young men assembled a music pavilion for outdoor concerts, and in the distance, Hannah heard hammering from the construction of the equipment at the children's playground. Benches were painted with a forest-green gloss. Whimsical signs featured wooden characters atop arrows that gave directions, like ZUM SPIELPLATZ, to the playground.

Other prisoners were busy dressing the window of a new toy shop with scenes from fairy tales: Hansel and Gretel skipping toward the witch's gingerbread cottage, a wolf dressed as Red Riding Hood's grandmother, and Rumpelstiltskin spinning straw into gold. Next to it was a butcher shop and coffeehouse where a handful of artists were painting letters and designs onto freshly cleaned glass. The words METZGEREI and KAFFEEHAUS were brushed on with an artful hand. If the inspectors failed to look behind the facade, they might easily think Theresienstadt was a normal European town instead of a Potemkin village. Yet Hannah clung to the hope that the Red Cross inspection would be the commandant's undoing.

Hannah lifted her head and shaded her eyes with her palm to look at the women on the other side of the square. She thought she recognized a few, but the glare of the sun made it difficult to tell.

"Stop daydreaming and keep cleaning," Míša warned. "*Pfft*, I can't have you getting in trouble now. We've made it this far without being sent east."

Sent east. These had become the most dreaded words in the ghetto. No one was certain what awaited them in the east, but rumor was that work hours were longer and food was even less than the meager rations they received at Theresienstadt. Some whispered that prisoners were killed upon arrival, though that made little sense, since the Reich depended on the slave labor of the Jews.

Olina had recently told Hannah that the stress of deportation burned her insides like acid. She wept, "I never know where my day will end. My Danuše, how do I explain this to a seven-year-old child?"

Overhearing the mother's sorrow, Míša gripped Hannah's hand. "I always know how my day will end," she whispered. "The same way it always does. I close my eyes, and I see Pavel on…" Míša didn't finish the thought. She didn't need to.

On her knees, under the hot sun, Míša whispered, "You can't drift off like that. SS is here today."

Hannah's mind snapped back to the present with Míša's warning. "Wait…did you say SS is here today? I thought they arrived tomorrow."

"When the commandant came to check with me, I told him today would be more convenient."

"All right, Míša. No need for sarcasm."

Hannah submerged her hairbrush into the bucket, then tapped it against the side to shake off excess cleaning solution, producing a hollow sound from the wooden brush handle against the metal.

A loud whistle followed by a series of short ones sounded behind the church. Every prisoner knew what that meant: *Put down what you are doing and stand still. Arms at the sides, eyes cast down.*

Griselde and the women at the windows made their way downstairs and lined up beside Hannah and Míša in the front row. Others stepped away from their construction and painting projects and joined the women in the square. In less than three minutes, two hundred forty prisoners lined the *Marktplatz* in rows of ten, separated by sex, as they had been instructed earlier.

The commandant was joined by a man with a tailored suit and boxy *Totenkopf* cap, who walked to the corner of the front row, where Griselde stood with Alice. An officer eyed Griselde carefully, then placed his fingertips on her chin and lifted her downturned head. He did the same to Alice. "These two look good. Put them in hospital beds for the visit."

Visit? Was it an inspection or a visit?

Rahm shook his head. "The younger one is one of our best pianists. We need her for concerts."

"All right, you know your Jews. Pick a few dozen for the hospital."

Three hours later, Hannah's body froze at the sound of rumbling in the distance. Voices. Footsteps. Men calling out orders. Hannah turned to her friend and widened her eyes with fear. Large groups of people only meant one of two things at Theresienstadt: a transport into or out of the ghetto.

Hannah stood and placed her hairbrush in her dress pocket. She gripped her bucket handle tight and turned toward Rathausgasse, where the sound was coming from. *It's new arrivals; it has to be. There was a transport east just weeks ago. These are new Danish Jews replacing them. The council is welcoming them in the* Stadtpark. *That's all.*

The *Marktplatz* was filled with prisoners, some standing motionless, others working tentatively as they turned their heads to see who was behind the barracks at the corner, soon to file through the streets of the ghetto. Seconds later, dozens of men and women lugging suitcases came into view, shoes and boots dragging as they walked toward the train tracks. Hannah dropped her bucket and splashed her skirt with dirty cleaning solution, then began running faster than she knew she could until she reached the end of the block and turned her head to the right. A mass of bodies was packed so tight that Hannah couldn't see a pinprick of light between them. This was no ordinary transport of one thousand. It was at least double, maybe triple. Lungs burning, she scanned the blue uniforms looking for Radek, but she couldn't wait. The Ghettowache would have answers, and she needed them now. Any one of them would do, so she gripped on to the closest police jacket sleeve as she struggled to speak.

"How many?"

"Seventy-five hundred."

"Seven *thousand*, five hundred?"

"Rahm wants the ghetto looking less crowded. The inspection, you know."

A soft whimper escaped from her lips as she stepped up onto the sidewalk and started moving against the flow of the crowd, desperately searching faces for Opa Oskar. There were older men and women she recognized from their transport two and a half years earlier. Herr Müller, the kosher butcher. Cantor Fein, no longer carrying his cello case. They were all *Muselmänner* now, skin and bones.

"Opa!" Hannah shouted as loud as she could, not caring if Commandant Rahm or the visiting SS officer saw her. "Opa Oskar Kaufman! Oskar Kaufman, are you here?" From behind her, Hannah heard the running footsteps of other prisoners making their way toward the thick stream, shouting names of their loved ones.

"Edith Laufer! Mama, are you here?"

"Ida Fleischmann! *Miláčkv, miláčkv*, where are you?"

"Georg! Georg Kafka!"

"Opa, it's *Mausi*. Call out if you hear me!"

A whistle blew lightly, and Hannah turned to see another Ghettowache officer furrowing his brow. "I'm sorry, but you can't walk up here. The sidewalks were just scrubbed."

Hannah's body flushed with heartbreak and rage. She stepped onto the street and screamed, "Opa! Oskar Kaufman. Oskar Kaufman, are you here?"

As Hannah called out through the crowd, she saw a man's head turn toward her. *Kryštof?* Worry lined his forehead, and he looked at Hannah with a rueful shrug before a young woman beside him slipped her arm through his.

"Why…" Hannah tugged at the sleeve of another Ghettowache officer. "Why would they take Kryštof? He's young and healthy."

"Maybe too young and healthy for his own good. The kid got caught stealing from the *Schleuse* to help his little girlfriend," the Ghettowache officer said, nodding his chin toward the flow of the crowd. "She's going too."

A familiar voice called to her from behind. "Hannah?"

She turned like a whip, grateful that it wasn't Oskar. "Luděk, have you seen Opa?"

They were both jostled by arms, elbows, hips, suitcases moving toward the railroad tracks, voices now cacophonous. Luděk gripped Hannah's shoulders and bent to meet her eyes. "He's not on this transport. They need him to set up the concerts for the inspection." His attention was drawn to an elder who had fallen on the path to the train station. Running to help the man, Luděk called back, "Oskar is still here. He's safe."

Hannah stepped back to give the poor souls more room. *Thank God. Thank you, God.*

"Hannah!" a woman's voice cried out.

"Klara?"

Klara fought her way to the side of the crowd of people moving toward the tracks, swatting away an old man who bumped into her.

"Klara, no."

"It's all right, *mamaleh*. I volunteered to join the children being sent to the Auschwitz family camp. The Red Cross is inspecting there next, so it won't be too bad." Klara's head turned quickly as she heard her name. Hannah recognized the voice immediately, then saw the face of another bunkmate.

Friedl? Friedl is going too?

"Who else are they taking?"

"I'll write to you," Klara promised.

"Who else is going?"

"Olina."

"And little Danuše?"

"I suppose she'll be at the family camp with us."

"Please let me know…" Hannah did not need to finish her sentence. The code had been established years ago, after the first transport to Riga.

Klara nodded with understanding. If rumors of the camps in the east were exaggerated and they were no worse than Theresienstadt, Klara would write her postcard in script that followed a straight line. If Auschwitz was worse, the lines of text would slant downward.

Hannah stepped back onto the grass of the *Marktplatz* and reached out for a tree to balance herself. The block-long run had dizzied her, so she lowered herself to the ground. Walking toward her urgently was Míša. "What's going on? Why so many?"

"The inspection."

"Did you see Mama?" Míša asked, voice catching.

"No, but she's kitchen staff. She should be safe."

"I don't like *shoulds* here."

Hannah stood again and pulled her friend into her arms,

hating that she couldn't offer anything more. No assurances. No information. Just her best guess about whether Markéta was still in the ghetto or had been transported east. A whistle blew, and a Ghettowache officer ordered workers back to their posts to continue work. They would have to wait another three hours to see who remained and who was on a train to the east.

———◦———

It was Radek who came to blow the whistle that ended the workday, his boots planted in front of Hannah's bucket. "How are you—" He stopped himself from finishing the question. "I heard the council spared your opa."

"For now," Hannah replied, lifting a sleeve to her watering eyes.

Radek extended a hand to help Hannah stand, but it didn't relieve her of the sharp pain in her hips as she struggled to unfold her body. He held on to her elbow and used the other arm to help Míša up, grimacing as he watched her wince.

"I need to check on Mama," Míša said and turned toward the barracks.

"We'll take your bucket," Radek offered. Then to Hannah, he said, "I figured you'd want to see Oskar."

Hannah nodded.

"I'll walk you there."

When they reached the Magdeburg Barracks, Radek asked if Hannah wanted him to come upstairs with her.

"No, thank you. I'll try to find you later. After I see about Markéta. If she's all right and Míša doesn't need me, I'd love to… just be with you. I don't want to go back to the barracks until I have to."

He nodded and said nothing.

Standing in the doorway of Oskar's room, Hannah saw him sitting on a crate, his back toward the door, shoulders rising and falling. His movement was subtle but jagged. When Hannah heard him muffle an anguished sound, she went inside. "Opa," Hannah said, now placing her hand gently on her grandfather's shoulder.

Oskar startled, pulling himself from another world. "*Mausi!*" he cried. His eyes were rimmed red, and he held his hands out, palms up. "They took everyone from my room. Everyone's gone but me. How do I sleep here tonight?"

Silence hung in the hot, thick air between them.

"Please don't hate me, *Mausi*," he pled.

"Hate you? How could I—"

Oskar interrupted, standing and lifting his hands again. "My lakeside cottage. Look at me, the big shot with my waterfront property."

"You were lied to. We all were," Hannah protested. She had once dreamt of the day Oskar admitted he was wrong, that he'd been fooled by the Nazis' promise of a Jewish settlement. Now it had come, but the concession brought no relief, only guilt that she ever wanted it.

"Opa, please, don't blame yourself. We all believed we would be safe in Theresienstadt."

"You didn't. You could have—" He wrapped his arms around his belly and sat again, letting his head drop. "You had a place to hide, *Mausi*, but I thought I knew better. Look at us now."

Hannah knelt in front of Oskar. "We don't know if I would have been safe at Paní Božiková's home. The SS might have found me, and that good woman would have been sent east with me. And…" She felt a lump form in her throat. "I couldn't leave you."

Oskar reached for Hannah's hands and offered a rueful grin. "You should have," he whispered.

She hadn't noticed how her grandfather's eyes had marbled with yellow over the years, a thin webbing of red showing the wear on his body. "Listen to me, Opa. You did the best thing for us given our choices. The war is almost over. You and I are going to do whatever it takes to stay off that transport list. Do you hear me?"

He nodded, his face a knot of tension.

Never letting go of Oskar's hands, Hannah pushed aside the discomfort of the floorboards pressing against her knees. "I am going to the Council of Elders tomorrow morning before work, and I'm getting myself transferred to the glimmer factory. Our work for the museum is nearly done, and that puts me at risk for transport."

"*Mausi*, you can't just ask the council for a new job."

"I'm not going to ask. I'm going to demand."

Oskar held Hannah's gaze for a moment, then lowered his head and sniffed. "You look just like her." He cleared his throat and raised his index fingers to his eyes and brushed away the tears that had escaped.

"I miss her."

"Me too, *Mausi*." Oskar remained silent, opening his mouth to speak several times before pressing his lips together and shaking his head.

"What is it, Opa?"

"When you talk to the council tomorrow, could you see about

getting Griselde transferred too? She's a good woman. I'll always love your oma, you know that, but Griselde… She is a great comfort to me."

Hannah's pulse hastened at the question that she had to ask next. "Do you love her?"

Oskar nodded, hesitant to admit this to Hannah, though he finally seemed to understand that Theresienstadt was no place for sparing her tender feelings.

"I'll do it under one condition," she said. "Marry her." She did not have to remind Oskar that the council tried to keep wedded couples together, so if Griselde was protected through her position at the glimmer factory, Oskar would be kept off the transport list too.

A snort of a laugh came from Oskar's nose. "I must admit, *Mausi*, that was not what I was expecting. But yes, you're right. I will ask her tonight."

"And the three of us will go to Palestine after the war."

———◇———

When Hannah reached the bottom of the stairwell at Magdeburg, she recognized Radek's form. His back was turned to her, but Hannah saw his curls sweeping against his neck, the awkward way he clasped his hands behind his back and strummed his fingers.

"Radek?"

He turned to Hannah. "Markéta's still here."

"Thank God," she sighed. "Does Míša know?"

"Yeah," he replied. "I just saw them and came back to tell you. How is Oskar?"

He had come back for her? In ordinary times, Hannah might not have registered such a small kindness. At Theresienstadt, it felt miraculous.

Soon the couple found themselves at the mouth of the tunnel they hadn't been to since their first kiss two years earlier. "Remember this place?" Radek asked with a tone that searched for her permission to recall happiness. Was it all right to visit fond memories while others were on trains bound east? Hannah didn't know either.

She grabbed his hand and led Radek toward the tunnel, and an image caught her eye in the upper left corner of the entry-way. Had the straight vertical line been carved into the outside brick by a person? Or had an animal or tree branch scratched it? "Radek," Hannah whispered. "Look there." She pointed and quickened her pace to get closer to the entrance, Radek by her side. Hannah squinted her eyes and saw that the line was topped by another one, this one horizontal. It was the letter T under the spotlight of the evening sun. In the shaded stone to the right, Hannah saw more letters: Picha. It was someone's name. Had this been there on their first night together, or was it new?

Hannah and Radek continued into the corridor together. Inside, there was more. Much more. Carved into the stone lining the tunnel was a Star of David with the initials UWT and the year 1944 beneath it. The word Žatec, the Czech village, was chiseled beside it. A set of initials with a heart surrounding it. Hannah's eyes moved right across the wall where more images were carved: names, transport numbers, dates. Stepping closer to the wall, Hannah lifted her hand and grazed a skillful relief, a caricature of the first camp commandant, Siegfried Seidl. There was another of the second, Anton Burger, and two of the current commandant, Karl Rahm. Dozens, maybe a hundred prisoners had come to this place to etch their marks on the ghetto. Hannah struggled to catch her breath, overwhelmed by emotion.

"All these people," Radek said but did not finish the thought. He just placed his fingertips on a carving of a flower. "These people," he whispered again, and Hannah understood. These people. They were here. It was important to them to be remembered.

Hannah closed her eyes, picturing the faces of those who had been transported east that day. The thousands of people who'd been sent away over the years.

———◇———

That night, Hannah looked around the third floor of the Dresden Barracks, the empty beds neatly made. She buried her face in her pillow and curled her body into a tight ball.

Beneath her, she heard a faint bleating, like an animal that had been injured. "Alice? Are you crying?"

Before Alice could respond, Hannah began to climb down the ladder. Her bare feet landed on the floor with a thud, and she knelt next to the bottom bunk. Hannah looked under the bed and pulled away the blanket covering the tiny space. There she saw two glazed brown eyes looking back at her. Just beneath them were two black coat buttons, the eyes of Adélka.

"Danuše?" Hannah cried.

The girl nodded. "Maminka said to hide."

"Oh my… What a brave girl you are. Your mama would be so proud."

Danuše pulled herself farther under the bed. "Where is she?"

"Come on out of there, *mufínek*," Hannah said, patting her lap. "It's safe now. Mama had to go to another…another village to work, and she asked me to look after you."

Hannah watched the little girl's face crumple and redden as she fought back more tears. "Come on out. Let me…" *Let me what?*

Silence.

"Danuše, please come out. I think Adélka is frightened, and I'd like to give her a hug."

"Maminka said to hide!" she cried.

"And you did it so well, *mamaleh*. But hiding time is over. Now it's time to do all the other things Mama wanted you to do. I can clean your teeth and read you a story if you come out."

Danuše emerged cautiously, turning her head from side to side as though she reserved the right to change her mind and retreat. When the child made her way out, Hannah pulled the girl into her arms and stroked the back of her head, hands trying to smooth the tangle of her hair. Hannah pulled away to face Danuše but held the little girl's shoulders. Her cheeks were marred by the dirt of the floor.

She searched for a clean rag and asked Alice to spare some of the witch hazel she'd traded for a piano lesson. "I used it all up," Alice replied, mouth twisted with regret before her eyes lit with an idea. She climbed down her ladder and made her way to another stall. Soon Alice returned, her tin cup filled with clear liquid.

Seeing Hannah's confusion, Alice explained. "Vodka."

Hannah nodded; no explanation was needed. Another

woman on the third floor had made a bargain with a worker at the *Schleuse*. Now, Alice owed the woman something.

"Thank you," Hannah said, turning her focus back to the little girl who needed her face cleaned.

Danuše's lips quivered, but what comfort could Hannah offer? She remembered the day of the hanging in the *Marktplatz*, how Olina had promised her daughter that they were safe. Hannah couldn't tell the child that now. Not that Hannah was unwilling to lie to offer solace. But Danuše was seven years old now, and she'd seen too much. The little girl would never believe Hannah.

"Climb up to my bed. You can sleep with me tonight. I'll be back in a minute. I need to speak with Míša."

The little girl didn't say a word. Danuše stood slowly and walked to the ladder near the foot of the bunk, Adélka tucked under her arm.

"Míša," Hannah said breathlessly when she saw her friend sitting on the lower bunk with Markéta, the two huddled together. At the crackle of Míša's cough, Markéta picked up Míša's tin cup and brought it to her daughter's mouth. Hannah crawled into the bunk and whispered, "Míša, we've got to… Do you think we can get a child out of the ghetto?" Not waiting for a response, Hannah lowered her voice until it was barely audible. "Danuše…she's still here. It's only a matter of time before… And food. How would we feed her here?" Hannah's thoughts swirled. Finally, she took a deep breath. "Míša, can we… We need to call a meeting at the glimmer factory. Tomorrow."

23

Hilde

Berlin
May 1944

HILDE PLACED THE TELEPHONE RECEIVER ONTO THE CRADLE so hard that the bell let out a short ring. Without looking at Susanna, she turned toward the office door and sped to exit, calling over her shoulder, "Cover for me, will you?" She didn't want to stop and chat with her workmate. No, Hilde had to make her way upstairs to share her good news with Martin.

If it weren't entirely unladylike, Hilde would have climbed two steps at a time. Instead, she hastened her clip, the cadence of her heels against the marble steps of the ministry reminding her of a ticking clock. She breezed by her fellow propagandists in the second-floor corridor, greeting them with cheerful *heils* to the führer. Her colleagues responded politely, though Hilde noticed that the crackle of excitement in the ministry had dimmed a bit after Germany withdrew troops from Stalingrad a year earlier. When twenty thousand people had been killed by the Allied attack on Hamburg ten months earlier, spirits plummeted. Reich employees would never voice the possibility of Germany losing the war, but Hilde could tell that faith was dwindling. Not hers, though. She knew something the others didn't. And she was ready to burst with the news.

"Martin!" Hilde opened the door to the graphic arts department without knocking. Four men at drafting tables all looked up. "Martin, guess where I'm going next week!" Before he could respond, Hilde blurted, "Theresienstadt and Auschwitz! The Red Cross is doing some sort of visit, and Herr Günther says if it goes well, we can finally shoot our documentary at Theresienstadt. For real this time. He says they've cleaned up the town, so it won't be a disaster like January."

Martin's face remained neutral, though Hilde watched his gaze sweep across the room to gauge his colleagues' reactions. Bodo rested his elbow on the table and cupped his chin in his hand, as though he were settling in to watch a good show. The new artist at the ministry, Karl, smirked. Yes, the men in the graphic arts department had their doubts about another attempt at a propaganda film set in Theresienstadt, but she'd prove them wrong.

"What the hell?" Hilde protested as Martin abruptly led her into the hallway.

"Don't make a fool of me like that!"

"A fool? Martin, I—"

Before Hilde could finish, Martin pulled away. "My wife comes marching into my office announcing that she's running off to the protectorate without even asking me? How do you think that makes me look?"

An officer passed them, sneering at the spectacle, so Martin threaded his arm through Hilde's and walked her toward a small alcove for privacy. A portrait of Reichsminister Joseph Goebbels peered down at Hilde as though he too were chastising her.

"Hilde, we've talked about this. The boys already give me a hard time about how…" He didn't finish the thought, and Hilde was grateful. Her entire life had been filled with criticism from her parents about how she was too loud, too forward. She wanted too much. She was too much.

"I thought you loved my dedication to the Reich."

"I do," he said, softening his tone. "It's definitely one of the reasons I married you." He touched Hilde's face tenderly with his palm. "But when you act like this, like you can just run off whenever you want, I look… It makes me look…weak."

"Martin, you knew when you married me that I wanted to be a filmmaker. You helped with my first film!"

"What about our visit to the Lebensborn home next week?"

Right. Hilde had forgotten about their appointment at the maternity home, but they hadn't agreed that they would adopt a baby that day. Even if they had, what was a few more months when Hilde's career was finally taking off?

She'd gotten lucky and never had to disclose her infertility to Martin.

Days before their *Rathaus* wedding, Martin came to Hilde on the verge of tears and told her that his mother had revealed an awful family secret. "Apparently she had another sister that the family never talked about," Martin confessed, squeezing his eyes tight in anguish. "Feeble-minded, dim-witted, whatever you want to call it. I never met her. I never even knew about her until now. She lived at a psychiatric hospital until…the policy, but that kind of defect, it's definitely in my bloodline." Martin said he would understand if Hilde wanted to call off the marriage, but she silently sighed with relief and told him she was happy to adopt babies from the Lebensborn Society. Hilde thought her magnanimity would serve as social currency in their marriage, but instead, Martin now seemed to mistake Hilde's reluctance to adopt as a rejection of his worth as a potential father. The man was so self-centered.

"Martin, the Lebensborn home will be there next month, and they'll have plenty of good babies for us. I've been waiting for this chance to make a film my entire life."

He pulled his mouth to the side, a sheepish look of concession. "Ask me next time."

That night, long after Martin had fallen asleep, Hilde lay beside him in their bed, unable to settle her mind. She was finally going to make a film for the Reich. And though she had no idea why, she was looking forward to seeing Hannah again. She'd tried to find Hannah when she and Herr Günther returned to Theresienstadt in January, but the commandant claimed he couldn't spare a laborer. Disappointed as she was, Hilde knew it was too risky to ask about Hannah twice. The men might wonder if Hilde couldn't do her job on her own. And who was this Jewess she was asking about?

Hannah wasn't a friend anymore, but she had been an important part of Hilde's childhood, a time when life was far less complicated. Hilde knew Jews were a danger to the *Volk*, but Hannah and her family had always been all right. Better than all right. They seemed to love her. And before she understood that they were *Untermenschen*, Hilde had loved them too.

———◦———

For the entire week of auditions for the *Grundschule* production of *Three Billy Goats Gruff*, Hilde had practiced her troll stance, back hunched from living under a bridge. She knew the drama teacher, Frau Lafferentz, always cast older students for starring roles in the school play, but she had to try. She was large for her seven years, but more importantly, she fully inhabited the role of the evil troll.

During the audition, Hilde jumped onto the small bridge and turned her head dramatically toward the seats in the auditorium and decided to improvise. She walked to the front of the stage and pointed at Frau Lafferentz. "I will pull this tree from the ground," she said, uprooting an imaginary oak, "and beat you all until you beg for mercy."

Frau Lafferentz told Hilde she was thoroughly convincing as the troll. "You're such a howl, Hilde," she cried, clasping her hands at her chest. Hilde left her audition beaming.

The following day when a group of students gathered around the bulletin board with the cast list, Hilde pushed her way to the front, only to find that she hadn't been cast as the troll. Instead, she was a flower. *A flower?* Emboldened by her outrage, seven-year-old Hilde marched to Frau Lafferentz's office and asked why she had been passed up for Klaus Biebow, a notorious playground bully. Frau Lafferentz insisted that Hilde should be grateful that she was cast at all. None of the other students in her grade would be in the play. "It's because you were so good that I let you in. But we don't need a flower if you don't want the part," she said, pointing toward the door.

Hilde stepped out of the office and made it four strides before collapsing onto the floor and sobbing. It was there that the quiet, little chubby girl from Hilde's class bent down to the ground and placed her hand on Hilde's heaving back.

"Will you ask Frau Lafferentz to change her mind?" Hilde asked, knowing the teacher would listen to Hannah, a student with a reputation for being smart and well behaved.

"Me? I don't…" Hannah's words tapered off.

"Tell her I am the best troll."

"Why don't you?"

"I already did," Hilde said, tucking her chin into her chest. When she looked up, Frau Lafferentz's silhouette appeared behind the mottled glass. She opened the door and stepped into the hallway.

"I thought I heard noise out here," she said, clutching a clipboard. "Hilde, stop the hysterics," she demanded. "You don't always get your way in life. You'll be a flower, or you'll sit in the audience like every other child your age."

"Frau Lafferentz," Hannah began tentatively. "I saw Hilde try out, and she was a really good troll."

Hilde's lips curled. Mein Gott, *she is lying for me?* Hannah was nowhere near the auditorium for tryouts.

"Agreed," Frau Lafferentz returned with a softer tone than she had used with Hilde. "I give the older students starring roles before they head to *Mittelschule* and are at the bottom of the heap."

"You're so nice," Hannah said. "Is there…um… Is there any rule that says there can only be one troll?"

"The story has one troll, Hannah. One troll. Three billy goats."

"What if the troll… What if he had a daughter troll, and he was teaching the baby troll how to…how to do troll stuff?"

Frau Lafferentz looked down at Hannah and Hilde, darting

her eyes between them. Hilde thought either they were both going to be in trouble, or Frau Lafferentz was considering it. "I'll think about it. No promises."

Miraculously, Frau Lafferentz announced the following day that she'd decided to add a new character, the baby troll, a sidekick who would offer comic relief during the scenes that might frighten the younger children. Hilde went on to play the baby troll and relished her role. Everyone agreed that Hilde upstaged Klaus, even though she had just one line. She scrunched her face and curled her fingers every time Klaus spoke. *Three Billy Goats Gruff* had been the beginning of Hilde's love of the stage and of Hannah Kaufman.

24

Hannah

B UT DANUŠE IS SO TINY!" HANNAH INSISTED AS SHE LOOKED at the faces of her friends gathered around the flashlight in the attic of the glimmer factory. "We cannot keep her safe here. She has no ration card. Someone will see her and report her to the SS."

"We'll hide her," Míša said. "The women in our stall can take turns."

"While we work?" Hannah shot back. "What if the Nazis do another head count? Look what happened to poor Jakob Edelstein."

Hannah's stomach soured every time she thought about how the council elder had been arrested and taken to the small fortress eight months earlier after the SS conducted a census of Theresienstadt. Guards had marched every prisoner out of the ghetto and into Bauschowitzer Kessel, a large hollow surrounded by low hills, because the Nazis suspected that Edelstein was inaccurately reporting population numbers in a plot to help prisoners escape. Rumor was that he had been sent east, and Hannah had no reason to doubt it.

"Look, Hannah, we've been lucky to get as many babies out as we have," Luděk said firmly.

Over the last two and a quarter years, they had managed to place four infants into the hands of the resistance. When Commandant Seidl was promoted to head the Bergen-Belsen concentration camp last July, he was replaced by Anton Burger, who began enforcing the mandatory abortion directive that Seidl had mostly overlooked. Soon, there was no need for their baby-smuggling operation. Even though Burger was replaced by Commandant Karl Rahm seven months later, there were no babies to smuggle from the ghetto anymore. The few pregnancies that took root ended either by miscarriage or abortion.

Luděk continued, "We'll never get Danuše out, and we'll likely get ourselves killed."

Placing a hand on Hannah's knee, Radek promised, "I will steal food. I will barter whatever I need to help Danuše. I'll take care of you both."

For a flicker of a moment, Hannah imagined hearing these words from Radek in the future, after the war was over and they were free. *I'll bet he'd be good at taking care of us.*

"If you want to help Danuše, make sure the Red Cross inspectors know what this place really is. When they ask questions, *pfft*, don't hold back."

Hannah knew what she wanted to tell the inspectors. In the time she had been a prisoner at Theresienstadt, she'd seen half the ghetto population shipped away. The ones left behind perished by the thousands from starvation and disease. Radek told her about one in five prisoners died, nearly all of them elders.

Could she really trust these Red Cross men, though? Were

they simply collaborators conducting a sham inspection? Would she even get to speak with the men privately? Perhaps she would be wise to keep her mouth shut and hang on for dear life until the war ended. Mouth radio whispered that Allied troops had landed in Europe, and the Soviets were moving west. Last year, Germany withdrew from Stalingrad, and Axis forces had been defeated in North Africa. And most gratifying, a ragtag band of Jews with homemade pipe bombs in the Warsaw ghetto rose up and fought the Nazis for four weeks.

Hannah closed her eyes for a moment to consider whether she was willing to take such a risk.

"All right, Míša, I'll do it, but I need everyone in this room to promise they will do whatever is needed to keep Danuše safe."

Radek wrapped his hand around Hannah's. "I promise."

"Me too," said Luděk.

"*Pfft*, I'm annoyed you'd even ask."

When the meeting ended, Hannah headed over to Oskar's new residence that he shared with Griselde, a one-room apartment near the secret synagogue, where Rabbi Baeck had performed their marriage ceremony. The couple had a small marital bed flanked by two wooden crates that served as both bedside tables and cubbies for clothing. They were given a chamber pot of their own, along with a pitcher so they could keep a private supply of water. The greatest luxury, though, was their very own door. Hannah was about to rap her knuckles against it when she heard a man's voice inside. "It sounds a little far-fetched, that's all."

Is that Rabbi Baeck?

Hannah lowered her fisted hand and looked down the hallway to see if anyone was about. There was no light spilling from cracks under neighboring doors, nor was there sound coming from the other residences. The coast was clear, so Hannah knelt to the floor and placed her cheek against it, moving her ear as close to the threshold as she could.

"Are you certain, Siegfried?" Oskar asked. "Did you see this with your own eyes."

Hannah startled at the sound of a bang from inside. Someone had smacked a hand against the wall. "Are you two insane?" A male voice shouted, then lowered his volume. "You think I escaped that hellhole and sneaked *into* Theresienstadt for you two to doubt me? Zyklon-B, that's what they're using at Auschwitz."

Zyklon-B?

"No, no, Siegfried," Oskar told the man. "They fumigated the barracks here with Zyklon-B last summer. It's for the bugs."

Hannah nearly gagged at the memory of sweeping away the tiny fleas, bubbles of lice, and armored cockroaches that littered the floor of the Dresden Barracks in August. But this man wasn't warning Oskar and the rabbi about exterminating vermin; it sounded as if they were gassing prisoners.

The Nazis couldn't afford to kill their labor force. There was no way this man—this Siegfried person—had it right. Plenty of people had lost their minds during the war, and he was clearly one of them.

"You two are fools!" Siegfried shouted. After a moment of silence, Hannah smelled burning tobacco and figured the visitor must have lit a cigarette. "I can't believe I wasted my time—" He paused to inhale, then let out a loud breath. "I'm telling you what I saw with my own eyes."

Rabbi Baeck spoke calmly. "This is all very shocking. We need to think through the wisest course of action. I will bring your news to the Council of Elders, and we will decide how to handle it. Even if what you're saying is right—"

"*If?* Gentlemen, I cannot speak more plainly. This is happening. Thousands every day. You must tell your people so they can decide what to do."

Rabbi Baeck sighed. "This isn't Warsaw. We have no weapons."

Oskar added, "What would be the point of telling our people? All this news would do is dampen their spirits."

Siegfried sighed with incredulous disgust. "Dampen their spirits?"

Just as Hannah was about to stand and knock on the door, she heard shoes quickly scratching against the wooden floor. Without thinking, she stood and ran around the hallway corner to hide, then listened to the footsteps storm down the staircase. Minutes later, Rabbi Baeck said good night to Oskar and left for his quarters.

"Opa?" Hannah said, knocking on his door. When there was no response, she knocked again. "Opa, it's me."

Nothing. Hannah turned the knob and pushed the door open a crack to find Oskar sitting on his kitchen bench staring at the floor with a vacant look.

"Opa, are you all right?"

"*Mausi*, what a treat!"

"Where's Griselde?"

"Grizzy's visiting a friend in the hospital. Come in. Sit, sit."

Hannah sat next to Oskar on the wooden bench. Curfew was in ten minutes, and Hannah didn't have time for pleasantries. "That man, the one who just left. What did he say about Auschwitz?"

Oskar simply shook his head.

"Opa, please. Klara and Friedl are there. What did the man tell you?"

Oskar placed his fingers on Hannah's chin and lifted her head so their eyes would meet. "Auschwitz is a big place, *Mausi*. There can be a lot of confusion about what goes on there. We have nothing to worry about."

Hannah swallowed hard, remembering Griselde telling her that Oskar had tried to discourage Pavel's father from smuggling letters from the ghetto. She would never know if it was her grandfather's loud voice that was responsible for tipping off the SS, and on some level, she was grateful that she would never know. But this was different. This was about events still to come, and it was information she had to share with Míša and the others. They still had a few days to discover which prisoners the commandant had selected to be interviewed by the Red Cross inspectors. Then they could determine who they trusted enough to pass along the warnings about Auschwitz.

25

Hilde

T RAILING THE FOUR RED CROSS INSPECTORS, SEVEN SS MEN, and Paul Eppstein, the new Jewish mayor of Theresienstadt, Hilde froze in her tracks when she first saw the transformation of the ghetto. She took in the scene in the town square. Gone were the workmen assembling crates. Now, residents spread about the grassy *Marktplatz*, sitting on picnic blankets with glass pitchers of milk and juice. As they listened to an accordion player pressing out an upbeat German folk tune, a set of parents unwrapped sausages from butcher paper and placed them before their three young children. A couple sat on the grass reading together, the woman's long brown hair spilling onto her lover's lap as the man sat upright, rapt in his text. The string quartet moved on to the next piece in its repertoire, a celebratory number that felt perfect for the summer afternoon in the park. The contingent was even given an eighteen-page catalog with skillful illustrations of life in the settlement. Commandant Rahm said it was a gift from one of their most talented artists, Joseph Spier.

The commandant and another officer wore their uniforms,

but the inspectors and SS were in civilian clothes. The new Jewish mayor Paul Eppstein led the tour. "I believe there's a soccer match this afternoon," he offered. "Shall we see if the game is still going?"

"Absolutely!" Red Cross inspector Maurice Rossel exclaimed. "Such good timing that we came on game day."

A short walk brought the contingent to the Dresden Barracks, where residents had transfigured the courtyard into a sports stadium. Crowded onto bleachers were Jewish men wearing ties and hats, neatly dressed women by their sides; children sat on the ledges of the building arcades, their legs dangling, and a few boys planted themselves on the roof.

At the sound of the cheering crowd, Hilde turned her attention back to the field where one team of players celebrated a goal scored, pumping fists and patting backs. A frustrated goalkeeper retrieved the soccer ball from the back of the net and tossed it to a referee in a black-and-white-striped jersey.

Commandant Rahm nodded with satisfaction. "Sporting events are held on Friday afternoons, but the real pride of the community is the culture. A resident can choose from a variety of concerts, poetry readings, plays. Herr Günther and Frau Bohle saw a children's opera during their first visit," he said, looking at Hilde expectantly.

"*Ja, ja,* I could…I could live here myself if I weren't so needed in Berlin."

The laughter of the men was its own music for Hilde, so she continued. "You know the Jews. They can always make themselves comfortable even during wartime."

Even Eppstein chuckled along, though Hilde saw the slightest flare in his nostrils as he turned away. "Shall we continue?"

Hilde glanced at Commandant Rahm's clipboard, which held a map of Theresienstadt with a thick red pencil line that marked their route.

To their right was a large field with women wearing apron dresses tending to their crops. Most knelt on the soil, some pulling carrots and radishes from the earth while others plucked berries growing on trellis cones. In the distance, a dozen men in coveralls swung sickle sheaths at their harvest. One stood to wipe the sweat from his brow and offered a smile and wave to the contingent of SS men and Red Cross inspectors. *They don't even have to salute. What a place to be a Jew!*

Hilde returned her focus to the path forward, and there she was. At the side of the road, Hannah and another woman held large wicker baskets piled high with produce: cherries and raspberries in Hannah's, chard and tomatoes in the other. At the sight of Hannah, Hilde felt a joy that had been all but lost to her since her youth. She understood that they were both twenty-three years old now, living in different worlds from each other, but her heart sped like a child seeing her best friend. Hilde longed for the simplicity and innocence of childhood.

"Oh. Hannah, you're funny," the woman said before the two looked over to Hilde and the cluster of men.

Hannah looked startled to see Hilde but recovered quickly and continued. "*Guten Tag*, Commandant Rahm. Ane and I are making your favorite jam this afternoon. We'll bring a jar to your office."

"You dear girls mustn't spoil me so," the commandant returned with a soft chuckle.

A boy with lanky legs and the first strands of a mustache

sped past them, holding several frocks on hangers above his head. "Don't eat too much of that jam, Hannah, or you won't be able to fit into any of these beauties Papa has just sewn. I'm taking them to the dress shop right now."

What a rude boy to say such a thing. Hannah had always struggled with her weight, but she looked downright slender now. She had always been too small and meek to snap back when classmates teased her, but Hilde could see her friend was upset by the barb. Sweet Hannah Kaufman was the same girl at the core, plastering a smile on her face to appear unbothered.

"Come, let's continue," the commandant said, holding out his arm and pointing toward a yellow building that housed the school. "The children have made a special art show for you today. Drawings and paintings of their life in the settlement. Wait until you see!"

One of the inspectors sounded a note of approval.

Wait…shouldn't we talk to Hannah about the gardens? Hilde held back the words, knowing that the commandant had a strict itinerary to follow. She had fought too hard to be part of this project to be cast aside now. She would find Hannah later to…to what? What did she want with a friend she had been estranged from for years? Hilde couldn't answer her own question, but there was something undeniably pulling her toward Hannah. Hilde sank her hand into her pocket and began to use her thumbnail as a razor against her skin.

The group continued walking toward a playground bustling with children, when Maurice Rossel stopped and lifted his camera. A ball rolled onto the path, and Commandant Rahm bent to pick it up, tossing it back to a small boy.

"Uncle Rahm," the little one said, "are we having sardines again?"

The commandant smiled and patted the child's head. "I'm afraid so," he replied.

A dozen little ones ran to Commandant Rahm and whined. "Not sardines again!" they cried in unison, then giggled.

Hilde heard the click of the shutter as the inspector aimed at two little girls with wedge haircuts and knobby knees. *Click.* A small boy rocking so feverishly on a toy horse that he looked as though he might break the spring on which it was mounted. *Click, click.* A woman the children called Teta Markéta held a silver tray with buttered bread slices and walked toward a row of young girls sunning on lounge chairs.

A man in oversize shoes and a curly red wig waddled onto the playground with a bucket and wand and asked who wanted to see him make giant bubbles. Hilde watched the children gather around the clown, who dipped a loop of rope attached to a stick into the soapy water and pulled out a translucent rainbow. He lifted it gently until a large bubble formed and floated through the air before popping.

"And here we are," the commandant announced, extending his arm toward a lemon-yellow schoolhouse. To the left of its red lacquered door was a mural in the style of a comic strip: girls balancing tall stacks of books, boys solving mathematics problems on the blackboard, a dog chasing his tail. Inside was equally colorful. Across the back wall was a clothesline with pencil drawings and paintings hanging alongside one another like laundered handkerchiefs drying in the sun. As Hilde followed the men inside the schoolhouse, her eye was drawn to a picture in the center, six people gathered in a cozy sitting room, where a little girl sat in a blue armchair listening to three men playing violin. A pink polka-dot couch matched the girl's dress and hair bow.

The Jews were building a community here, filled with music and art. They were surrounded by family and friends. The dozen pictures displayed on another clothesline depicted similarly homey environments, kitchens with pots and pans hanging from racks over cast iron stoves. A mother in an apron serving soup from a large vat. A grandfather smoking a pipe and reading a newspaper.

When Hilde turned her head to the left, she was struck by a wall of collages made from torn paper. Her favorite was a forest with a row of brown paper tree trunks cluttered with leaves in different shades of green. On another wall was a collection of collage butterflies made from scraps of orange paper and black chenille pipe-cleaning stems.

By day's end, the inspectors had been at Theresienstadt for eight hours, and Hilde could see that they were satisfied that the Jews were treated well. The commandant had made such improvements since the first time Hilde visited the settlement. Not only the condition of the grounds but the Jews seemed healthy and content here. The tour ended at the *Marktplatz*, where a jazz ensemble was playing in the outdoor pavilion. A saxophonist burst into an exuberant piece with an explosion of bold and brassy notes that made Hilde fight the urge to dance. She silently admitted that she missed this style of music that had been long since banned in the Reich. High notes of the piano flitted playfully, a perfect soundtrack to the scene outside: an old man teaching his grandson to fly a kite, girls chalking hopscotch boards on the sidewalk, sweethearts sharing wine and bread.

Commandant Rahm folded his arms across his chest. "You see, gentlemen, Theresienstadt is a paradise settlement for the Jews."

"Agreed," said Rossel.

Another added. "Your Jews are living better than anyone else in Europe right now."

Herr Günther curled his lips with satisfaction. "Are you certain you want to drive seven hours east to inspect Auschwitz? It seems an awfully long trip to see the same things as you witnessed here."

Hilde felt the breath leave her lungs, disappointed that Günther suggested canceling the most important part of their visit. Yes, it was a long drive to Poland, but Herr Günther was being shortsighted. They needed to prove to the Red Cross—and the world—that rumors of dangerous conditions at the camps were Jewish sensationalism.

Hilde watched Maurice Rossel exchange glances with his fellow inspectors. He cleared his throat while Hilde silently rooted for a continuation of their tour. *Go to Auschwitz. You need to see a larger camp. The higher-ups at the Red Cross will be angry if you skip it.*

"You gentlemen are right," Rossel said. "We have enough for our report. We won't need to visit Auschwitz."

26
Hannah

N OT A SINGLE QUESTION?" MÍŠA ASKED, STILL INCREDULOUS, although Hannah had already answered her twice. It wasn't that Red Cross inspectors hadn't spoken to prisoners. But they were only interested in hearing from new arrivals from Denmark, and SS officers were present during the interviews.

Sitting in the top bunk that Hannah now shared with Danuše, Míša slapped her forehead with her palm as she listened to Hannah recount what Radek had told her earlier: Alberte, the brave Dane who had agreed to tell the Red Cross about possible gas exterminations at Auschwitz, never got a moment alone with inspectors. During his interview, Alberte tried to signal the lead investigator by blinking an SOS in Morse code—three short blinks, followed by three long blinks, then a final trio that ended with wide eyes. The message did not seem to register.

The smell of hay from the mattress permeated the third floor of the Dresden Barracks, the heat holding it in the air like stale smoke. Hannah turned her attention to Danuše sitting beside her. "Open wide," she coaxed. Raising the spoon in her hand,

Hannah watched the child's eyes widen as she went through their mealtime ritual. "The airplane is coming in for a landing in baby Danuše's mouth. Open up," Hannah said. She had no idea how Danuše had the patience for this game; when Hannah was served food, she devoured it instantly. Danuše, however, now insisted on being fed like an infant, so Hannah mashed the boiled potato Radek had given her and fed Danuše with a wooden spoon. "That's a good baby," Hannah said as the little girl opened her mouth, now missing a front tooth.

Hannah continued. "I don't know why they only spoke with Danes. Ane and I did as we were told and walked right up to the group and told Commandant Rahm we were making jam for him, and they all just…just watched. They didn't say a word, not a hello or how are you. They just observed us like we were, I don't know, animals at the zoo."

"I seen a monkey at the zoo," Danuše offered with a full mouth.

"Monkeys are funny, aren't they?" Hannah replied, forcing herself to cross her eyes and stick out her tongue at her ward despite the pain radiating through her chest as she recalled the interaction with the Red Cross contingent. Should she have said something? Maybe one of the inspectors would have listened to Hannah if she'd gone off script and told them that nothing was as it appeared in Theresienstadt.

"Hilde Kramer was with them," Hannah continued bitterly. "She was with the same man who came with her two years ago. I don't know why she's involved in any of this. Do you think I should have said something to her?" The question pressed against her throat.

Míša's response was crushing. She looked down and scratched new bug bites on her wrists. Hannah didn't have to ask again. She knew what Míša was thinking: *I would have.*

"It was impossible, Míša. They would have told the inspectors I was from the insane asylum. They would have said they keep the crazy women busy here picking fruit and making jam. And then—"

"Adélka wants jam," Danuše said.

What?

The little girl picked up her doll and held her close to Hannah's face. "Adélka wants jam!"

"I don't have any jam," Hannah snapped, then immediately regretted her impatience. But she had to set the record straight with Míša. It was easy to imagine oneself as a fearless heroine when scenarios were hypothetical. It was a different story when a person stood face-to-face with the commandant of the ghetto where prisoners were regularly sent east and sometimes hanged for breaking rules. "I couldn't have said anything, Míša."

"*Pfft*, then why'd you ask?"

Why had she asked? The first answer was simple: she wanted Míša to assure her that she'd made the right choice. A second question niggled at Hannah, though. Why did she need Míša to tell her to trust her instincts, that she'd done what she needed to save her own life? "I shouldn't have asked," Hannah returned. "I should have told you that I did my best today so that I could live to do my best tomorrow."

Míša leaned forward and kissed her friend's forehead, pulling back before she coughed. "I'm proud of you, Hannah." She paused and looked at Danuše. "And of you too, brave little baby."

She leaned forward and whispered, "The only cowards today were the Red Cross inspectors. And the damn Nazis."

———o———

The glimmer factory did not have large glass windows like the museum workshop. Light came into the converted barn through cut-out rectangles with flap shutters held open with sticks. Women were cramped together at long tables with barely enough room to work their knives over the mica. A thick cloud of sparkling dust hovered over the tables. It was an unwelcoming setting to work in but also the safest.

Hannah had never seen the afternoon sky quite as sallow and stagnant, not a cloud floating in the distance nor a single bird flying above. Even the leaves on the treetops remained motionless in the still hour before sunset. She remembered her brother, Ben, catching fireflies in the summertime and trapping them under brown glass Knoll bottles. Hannah had always felt sorry for the lightning bugs as they flew frantically into the sides of the prison her brother had created. She wondered if the insects had any idea what was happening, why their world was suddenly shades darker, why it was so hard to breathe.

Returning her attention to the tedious work before her, Hannah steadied a small piece of mica with her left hand, cramped from holding the same position all day. Her right hand pushed a knife into the stone and trembled after hours of shaving chips from the block. Hannah found that the work shift grew more uncomfortable as the day went on, because as the mica stones diminished in size, she had to press harder to split off slender pieces. The cries of pain from the women at Hannah's workbench were more frequent at the end of the day when blades slipped and cut into fingers that never fully healed from their recent injuries.

Hannah looked across the table at Griselde sitting upright, dignified as a queen as she focused on her task. Míša had warned both Hannah and Griselde that their work at the glimmer factory would only give them protected status if they met their production quotas. Holding up an infected finger, she shrugged. "*Pfft*, you may cut yourself going fast, but at least you get to stay."

Griselde dabbed the perspiration from above her lip. "Any news…from Klara or Friedl?"

Hannah closed her eyes tight and rubbed her forehead. "Not since…" She couldn't finish. Griselde understood what Hannah meant: she hadn't received a word since the first postcard from Klara, a generic greeting about the beautiful settlement of Auschwitz, the lines of script plummeting down the paper.

When the work shift ended, Hannah and Míša walked toward the food line at the Engineer Barracks and saw a sheet of office paper tacked onto a signpost. ACTORS WANTED. Wordless, they drifted toward the announcement. Hannah's heart sped with hope that another humanitarian organization was demanding an inspection and that its men wouldn't be as easily deceived as the Red Cross. Sadly, the notice was an invitation for prisoners to participate in a film being shot in Theresienstadt the following month.

"That's why Hilde was here," Hannah whispered to Míša. "Hilde and her boss probably joined the Red Cross tour to gauge what resonated best with inspectors so they could use those scenes for their next attempt at a propaganda film."

"They never let up, do they?" Míša said, shaking her head.
"Neither will we."

According to the poster, this film would be directed by the
famous German-Jewish actor Kurt Gerron, a recent arrival in
the ghetto. He needed background players to dress in their finest
and listen to concerts and shows, children to sit in the audience
during *Brundibár*, and makeshift families to light Shabbat candles. The payment: cans of sardines, jarred fruit, pickled herring,
and extra ration tickets. Prisoners stood shoulder to shoulder,
crowding around the sign, deliberating whether they would participate in the Nazis' next charade.

"Let me do it while I still have meat on my bones."

"I'd rather die than be part of this."

"My parents are elderly. I must do anything."

"A sham!"

The lucky ones were those who faced a choice. The sickly
and wounded would not be considered for the film. And because
Nazis were oddly protective of the notion that Jews were dark-
haired, blonds and the half dozen redheads at Theresienstadt
were ineligible as well.

"Míša," Hannah said, pulling her friend away from the crowd.
"Let's meet tomorrow night with the others. There must be a way
to use this to our advantage."

———◇———

Hannah looked at the faces of her friends gathered around the
lantern in the attic of the glimmer factory. Luděk reminded her of
his cousin Pavel, with the same chin dimple and thick eyebrows,
but the young man had been stripped of the quiet confidence

they once shared. He turned to the others and asked, "Did the SS bring Gerron here just to direct the film?"

Hannah shrugged. "All I know is that this will be their third try, so it must be important for the Nazis to show the world we are thriving here. Hilde wanted to use me as her assistant the first time she came to Theresienstadt."

"But not the second time?" Radek asked.

"No. But I can try. She seems to have a soft spot for me."

"Who wouldn't?" he returned with a wink.

Míša added, "Why don't we get some of the actors to slip messages into the film, maybe not their dialogue but something that tells viewers that all is not as it seems. They'll want to show a scene in shul, won't they? Why don't we have the men daven and chant a prayer that will send a signal that we are in danger here."

Luděk hesitated. "It's not a terrible idea. Someone who knows Hebrew could see it. What if they show the film in America? What if they show it to the League of Nations? Someone there will understand."

An idea sparked. Hannah suggested, "What if they say something that makes no sense for the situation, like men lighting a *chanukiah* while reciting the Mourner's Kaddish?"

"That's good," Míša exclaimed. "Luděk, Radek, can you find men willing to do this?"

"It won't be easy," Radek conceded. "And what are the chances Gerron will cast our guys?"

Hannah closed her eyes and prayed for strength. "Whoever Gerron chooses, I'll tell Hilde they're no good. I'll offer to select trustworthy men."

"*Oy Gotenyu!* Don't get someone killed by saying he's

untrustworthy. Say the men are stupid or won't be able to stop looking into the camera or something innocuous."

Hannah couldn't help think about Pavel, Klara, and Iveta and how much they would have enjoyed hatching this plan. She felt a jolt at the idea of the new Nazi propaganda helping the prisoners instead of the SS.

"Pavel would be proud of us," Hannah said to Míša.

Míša smiled. "He always said there was a warrior inside our quiet little Hannah." Her eyes moistened as she disappeared into a memory.

27

Hilde

Theresienstadt
August 1944

THE SUN WAS BURIED UNDER SHEETS OF STEELY OVERCAST, and new leaves shivered on the branches outside. A crash of thunder shook the window of Commandant Rahm's office, cracking open the atramentous slate of sky for the downpour that had been threatening since early that morning. Hilde hoped the weather would relent before they began shooting the long-awaited Theresienstadt propaganda film later that week.

Sturmbannführer Günther pulled out a chair for Hilde and gestured for her to sit.

Rain tapped against the glass as Hilde watched a young woman in a gray housedress dust a bookcase. The lacquered walnut piece matched Commandant Rahm's desk with enamel inlay of flowers and leaves at the edges. The maid was no older than Hilde but carried herself like a crone, back bent and shoulders hunched. The contrast between the glossy furniture and the ragged woman was jarring. Hilde wished the woman had been assigned to an easy job like mica splitting before reminding herself that she was there to make a film, not question the commandant's camp management.

Noticing Hilde's gaze linger on the maid, Commandant Rahm must have assumed Hilde was concerned about their privacy. "Don't worry about Sarah," he assured her. "She is one of my most trusted workers." Directing his voice over his shoulder at the young woman, he asked, "Isn't that right?"

Sarah kept her head down, nodding once, then murmured, "*Ja, Kommandant.*"

Hilde tried not to cringe at the scratch of the woman's soft voice.

She pried her eyes away from Sarah and turned her attention to the commandant tapping the bottom of his papers on the desk to neaten the pile. He then handed the notes to Herr Günther.

"Here's the itinerary I used for the Red Cross inspection. They were satisfied with these scenes, so let's use the same ones."

A light flashed in the distant sky, a slender rod igniting the world for a moment. Hilde understood that men had steadier nerves than women but wondered how Sarah hadn't flinched at the boom of thunder that followed the light. She caught herself before gasping at the rumble of thunder. Hilde hoped Sarah would finish dusting and leave; her presence was distracting. The resonant voice of her supervisor returned Hilde's attention to the meeting.

"Commandant Rahm has a special assignment for you," Günther announced. "As you know, the first two film attempts were..."

Unsuccessful? Failures?

Günther groped for the right word, so Hilde jumped in. "Unfinished," she offered.

"Yes, unfinished," the commandant said with a sharp, defensive tone that told her that he hadn't needed her help. The men glanced at each other, and Hilde sensed that each blamed the other for the past breakdowns of the films. The commandant cleared his throat before continuing, "This time will be different. We have a beautified camp, *and* Kurt Gerron is a…resident here now." Turning to Hilde, he explained. "Kurt Gerron is a well-known—"

Hilde interrupted, unable to let these men assume she didn't know who Kurt Gerron was. "Actor and director, yes, I know. *The Threepenny Opera. The Blue Angel.*"

"Very good," the commandant said with a patronizing chuckle.

For a moment, Hilde wanted to shoot Sarah a look, to share an eye roll. *Men. They underestimate us so.*

"I had a Jewess assisting me when we first came to the ghetto. Hannah something or other," Hilde said, snapping her fingers as if she were trying to remember. "Reliable girl. Hard worker." It was unwise for Hilde to acknowledge that she remembered an *Untermensch*. The names and faces of Jews should barely register with her.

The commandant turned his attention to the itinerary Günther had slid across the table and shrugged. "If she's still here, but if not, we can make sure you have an assistant."

Inexplicably, Hilde felt a tightening in her chest. *Why wouldn't Hannah still be here?* She didn't want another assistant; she wanted Hannah by her side. "This one's a German," Hilde blurted.

The commandant narrowed his eyes. "You mean she speaks German."

Right, of course. "She's a German-speaking Jew. She speaks Czech too."

"Plenty of the residents speak both languages at Theresienstadt," the commandant said, eyes still focused on the papers before him.

Hilde feigned confidence. "Listen, this girl was helpful to me, and that's who I want." She was encouraged when neither of the men cared to argue.

———◦———

Hilde had just finished her list of suggested new scenes for the film—a wedding ceremony, sewing circle, girls calisthenics—when Hannah appeared in the doorway of her temporary office at SS headquarters in Theresienstadt, a police officer by her side.

"This the one?" he asked.

She tried not to show her shock at the sight of Hannah. Piercing the short sleeves of her canvas work dress, the tops of Hannah's arms were now as slender as her forearms; her elbows jutted out like the tips of spears. How had she thinned so much since the inspection in June, just two months earlier? Did her skin look gray, or did it just look lighter in the brown dress?

"It's good to see you," Hilde offered in an overly friendly tone that attempted to mask her discomfort. "Have a seat."

Rubbing her arms, Hilde watched Hannah settle into her chair across the desk. Hannah seemed to be negotiating with her body to find a position that didn't make her wince. It was more than the weight loss that made Hannah appear gutted, but still, Hilde reached into her rucksack and retrieved her afternoon snack, a sweet, poppy-filled *buchty* wrapped in a napkin. Placing it hastily on the desk, Hilde fumbled her words.

"I…um…I nearly forgot. I brought this for you. My host

in Kamýk is a marvelous baker. They're staying with family in Litoměřice while we shoot, but they bring treats for me every morning, and I…I remember how much you like sweets." Hilde felt conscious of her nervous rambling—who didn't like sweets? Who cared if her hosts were staying in Litoměřice?

Hesitating for a moment, Hannah looked at the pastry and bit her bottom lip as if the sight of it pained her. Then she grabbed the roll and placed it into her mouth and closed her eyes.

The film. You are here to do a job.

Hannah nodded. "Thank you, Frau Kramer," she managed after swallowing.

"Oh, Hannah, it's just me. Hilde. Anyway, it's Frau Bohle now, but when we're alone, you can just call me Hilde." Inside, she flinched, remembering how Otto had said the same thing to her during their first night together. "Anyway, I…I suppose you know why I'm back at Theresienstadt."

Hannah did not reply.

"We…the party, we're finally going to make the film about the settlement. So people can see…" Hilde decided not to finish the sentence. What would she say? So people could see how well the Jews were living? With a gaunt Hannah before her devouring a roll, the sentiment rang false. "I hear there's quite a cultural scene. The commandant says Rafael Schächter is conducting Verdi's Requiem."

Hannah grimaced. "I was hoping you still needed an assistant."

"*Mein Gott*, Hannah, you're a mind reader! That's why I called you here."

"Good. I very much appreciate the chance to assist you, Frau…Hilde."

"Yes, it will be a nice change of pace for you. Where do you work?"

"Do you have more food?" Hannah asked.

Hilde remembered that Martin had given her a bag of candied almonds for her train ride to Bauschowitz and reached into her jacket pocket, wishing she hadn't eaten so many. Hannah seemed grateful for the few that were left.

"Thank you. I work at the glimmer factory."

"The what?" Hilde asked.

"The mica-splitting workshop. We call it the glimmer factory."

"How creative," Hilde managed to say.

"It's supposed to be ironic."

"Right," she responded, allowing a huff of nervous laughter to escape. "How ironic." Hilde reached for a napkin and placed it on her lap to twist out of Hannah's sight.

"Do you have any cigarettes?" Hannah asked.

Hilde was a bit taken aback by the requests. Her friend had always been so shy and reserved.

"Um…sure," she said, reaching for her cigarette box and lighter. She placed one in her mouth, then extended her hand across the desk. "Would you like an extra one for later?"

Hannah eagerly plucked two smokes from the case, explaining, "I'm going to save both for later. If…if that's all right."

Hilde flicked her lighter and noticed her hand shaking, though she had no idea why. "Take them all," she said, emptying her case.

"Thanks," Hannah said, then nodded her chin toward the pad of paper on the desk. "Is that for the film?"

Another nervous huff escaped, though Hilde wasn't sure why the innocent question was unsettling. "*Ja*, my superiors want to stick with scenes that were on the Red Cross inspection, but I think we can do better. There's so much more to life in the settlement, and the world needs to see it." Hilde looked down at her hands and dug her thumbnail into her flesh. "I mean, I know it's not all concerts and shows here. I'm sure you work hard at this glimmer factory, and what you people have done with the settlement… It's so much nicer than the first time I visited."

Hilde saw Hannah's temples pulse before she offered a tight smile. Pointing to the paper on the desk, Hannah asked, "Can I take a look?"

Hilde obliged and watched her friend's eyes scan the paper.

"A wedding scene, that's good. Opa married a nice woman here in the ghetto. Maybe they could play your couple."

Hilde couldn't help gasp at the realization that if Oskar had married, Hannah's Oma Minna must have died. "When did… Oh, Hannah, she was a gem."

"Thank you," Hannah replied, shifting her weight in her chair.

Hilde initially thought younger people would be more appealing for a wedding scene, but then again, maybe they should cast Hannah's grandfather and his new bride to show the elderly thriving. Plus, it was a small thing she could do to please her old friend.

A memory of Hannah's family flashed in Hilde's mind. Oma Minna appeared bending at the waist over the gramophone and placing the needle onto the soundtrack record of stage musicals. Oskar let Hilde dance with the cane he never used and clapped uproariously when she tried to tap dance on their parquet floor and shuffle off to Buffalo.

Hannah squinted her eyes as she continued reading Hilde's notes. "No scenes of spiritual life? *Hmm*, that seems odd."

"Does it?"

"You know best, Hilde, but I'd think people would want to see that we are free to continue our religious practices," Hannah offered.

She was right. Why hadn't Hilde or Herr Günther considered this?

"Do you have a synagogue here?"

Hannah opened her mouth, then hesitated. "No, no synagogue. We just… We meet in cellars and attics, nothing special. But you've seen the beautiful church on the *Marktplatz*. It's locked up, but I'll bet you could convince the commandant to open it to film a Shabbat service. I know some young men. One is a Ghettowache officer and the other does manual labor. Nice strong men, that's who you want for your film."

Hilde felt the milk from her lunch begin to curdle in her stomach. Her childhood friend was still as kind and helpful as ever despite her current circumstances. Hilde wished Hannah's family had never left Germany and that she hadn't missed out on their friendship for nearly a decade. Yes, Hannah was a Jew, but she and her family were different from the rest of them.

"Listen, Hannah, we start shooting the film in three days. Is there anything I can… Do you need anything?"

Hannah looked up at Hilde and pressed her fingers into her temples. "Yes, my friend Klara Schneider was transported to Auschwitz three months ago. I got a postcard from her saying she arrived but…" Hannah trailed off. "I'm concerned about her. She's older, and I'm afraid she's ill or…worse." Hannah's eyes began to well with tears. "I'm just worried. Can you find out what's happened to her? There are others. Can I write down some names?"

Hilde felt a lump forming in her throat. "*Ja, ja*, of course, I will look into it right away. My husband is coming to visit on Saturday, but when he returns to Berlin, I'll have him check on Klara and the others. But you know Auschwitz isn't like this place. It's a real work camp, so people don't have a lot of time to write letters. I'm sure there's nothing to worry about. She's probably just very busy."

28

Hannah

HANNAH SHIFTED HER WEIGHT AS SHE STOOD BESIDE Hilde, whose eyes darted between the notes on her clipboard and the scene about to begin. Steps in front of them was Kurt Gerron, one eye squinting as the other pressed against the viewfinder of the Vinten sound camera, tripod planted in the grass of the *Marktplatz*.

Joining the director was a six-man crew from Aktualita, a Prague newsreel company the Nazis ordered to work on the film. Two men set their handheld cameras on their shoulders: one an Arriflex 35, the other a Bell & Howell Eyemo. Herr Günther used his hand to extend the visor of his hat while he focused on the set, a sidewalk on the periphery of the public square.

Necktie snaking down the front of his short-sleeved shirt, Gerron stepped back from the camera and patted his forehead with a handkerchief. Repositioning himself back at the helm, he called out, "*Und bitte!*" and a young man from the crew snapped a black clapboard.

"*Frische, Fische!*" shouted a fishmonger in a crisp white apron and paper skullcap as he stood in his stall. Shaded by a canvas tarp, the man gestured to the wooden boxes in front of him, overflowing and glimmering with the silver scales of carp. He continued shouting, this time in Czech: "*Ryby!*"

Hannah knew that the Nazis in charge of the film would set scenes to deceive viewers, but she hadn't fully grasped how unsettling the illusion would be. An outdoor food market spanned an entire block, with carts brimming with fresh cheeses, crusty *Brötchen*, and roasted nuts. The pungent aroma of Limburger layered with the yeasty scent of bread, and Hannah's head throbbed from the torturous tantalization. Sausages dangled from the wooden trusses of a canopy. At the corner, a produce vendor displayed overflowing baskets of fruits and vegetables on a large, wooden cart. Hannah's entire body shook, and she felt waves of nausea rolling through her belly. Or maybe it was hunger; the two felt similar these days.

Hannah inhaled deeply through her nose to calm herself, but her breath sputtered. She fidgeted with the strap of her messenger bag, then wrapped her arms around her stomach. There was no way to move that felt right. *Smile, even just a little*, she silently implored herself. Hannah could not afford to show her discomfort to Hilde, lest she be dismissed on her first day as helper to a Nazi production assistant.

"*Und danke!*" shouted Kurt Gerron. "Fishmonger, move to the left. Two steps!" he demanded in German, making a sweeping gesture with his hands, before turning to Hilde and explaining that the man's body obstructed part of the word KAFFEEHAUS on the glass window behind the stall. "Only the last four letters show. Let the audience see our nice coffeehouse in case we wind up cutting the scene inside it." Gerron looked at the fishmonger, who was now too far to the left, and sighed, exasperated. "Not so much," he called out, then instructed Hilde to run the ten meters to the fish stand and help the man find his mark.

"Hannah can do that," Hilde told Gerron with an edge that suggested the prisoner remember his place.

"Hannah, get over there," Hilde commanded.

"*Ja*, Frau Bohle," Hannah replied, smiling through her gritted teeth as she walked toward the Potemkin market. Moments later, Hannah stood in front of the fishmonger—really a new arrival from Copenhagen named Jens who had worked as an architect for his entire career—then turned back toward Hilde, waiting for instruction.

"A little to the right," Hilde called. "Good. Keep him there."

Before Hannah could tell Jens to remain in place, she heard a loud whistle from Hilde's supervisor, Herr Günther, who began shouting toward the produce stand at the corner. "*Achtung! Kinderschweine!* Get away! Not for you."

Hannah saw a trio of little boys scrambling near the apple cart at the corner. Two were dressed in coveralls with no shirts underneath, and the other boy wore a white shirt with a brown wool vest that matched his slacks. Hannah wondered which scenes they had been cast in and if she would see them later. The boys disappeared around the corner, and a green apple dropped and rolled onto the sidewalk. Hannah prayed the boys had full hands when they ran off. She curled a fist and tucked it under her arm out of sight and reminded herself that vindication awaited her at the end of the day. Just before sundown, the film crew would move their lights and cameras into the church for a scene featuring Radek,

Luděk, and eight of their most trustworthy friends, who would send flare signals through their words and actions. They would greet one another saying, "Shabbat shalom," then gather around a *chanukiah* and joyously recite the Mourner's Kaddish.

"*Frische, Fische!*" Jens shouted again.

"Get that girl out of the shot!" Gerron demanded, waving Hannah back to her post beside Hilde.

Four takes later, the scene was complete. Jens called out that he had fresh fish, and an old woman approached the stall. She pointed to a carp in the box, which the fishmonger then placed on a hanging metal scale. The two haggled animatedly, the woman leaning close to argue and pounding her fist on the counter; the man shook his head and pointed at the fish as if to say, *This is top quality*. After a minute of their theatrical bargaining, they nodded their heads in agreement at a price.

Hannah looked at Gerron, wondering how the man justified his participation in this sham, then silently chided herself for her harsh judgment. Their roles were different, but she was part of the production too. He wanted to save himself and his wife; she could understand that.

A man with a black handlebar mustache rounded the corner where the produce stand was, pulling a white cow by a halter. *What in God's name?* Gerron told one of his men to use a dolly to follow the movement of the man walking his cow to... Where were this man and his cow supposed to be going? The cameraman filmed it twice, then a third time, and then Gerron told Hilde he'd captured the shot he wanted—the man walking a cow through the *Marktplatz*.

Günther sat on a metal chair and crossed his foot onto his

opposite knee, then reached a hand toward Hilde and snapped in quick procession. "Hey, hey, hey," he beckoned. "What's Gerron filming next? The sick ward or the concert?"

Hilde flipped to the second page on her notes and cleared her throat. "The sick ward. Then lunch. Then we shoot the dance at the *Kaffeehaus* and end the day with the synagogue scene and Verdi's Requiem."

Soon, Hannah trailed behind Hilde, Gerron's collapsed tripod on her shoulder while a teen boy carried the camera and film canisters. The summer air was thick and still; Hannah thought a bug had flown under her shirt and wished she had a free hand to swat it away. A moment later, though, she felt the same irritating tickle and realized it was a bead of sweat running down her back.

"*Schnell, schnell,*" Hilde ordered her, then discreetly winked as though they shared a secret.

A cold rush of terror raced through Hannah's body. What if one of the men from the Aktualita film crew recognized the Mourner's Kaddish and realized something was amiss with the scene? Kurt Gerron would surely understand what was happening. What if he turned them in to protect himself?

As the crew made its way to the hospital, Günther walked alongside Hilde, giving her instructions for the next segment they would film. Hannah couldn't bear to hear it, remembering the sound of Míša's cough that morning. Her friend had not received medical attention in weeks while some of the healthiest bodies in the ghetto now lay in sick beds, flipping through magazines with empty porcelain teacups on their nightstands. The thought broiled inside Hannah.

"You!" Hilde barked at Hannah when they reached the second floor. Glancing at her supervisor ahead, she continued. "Come here. I need you to get some makeup on those girls." She pointed to a row of beds with young women propped up on pillows.

"Makeup?"

"Ja, Herr Günther says they look pale."

"Aren't they supposed to be ill?"

Hilde sighed loudly. "I don't have time to argue. Herr Günther wants them to look... I don't know...better. There's powder and rouge in your supply bag."

Hannah made her way into the ward, taking in the shelves in the background, clean glass jars that were newly stocked with cotton balls and swabs, amber bottles filled with pills and syrups. Two meters separated cots from one another as patients convalesced in luxury. Hannah sat on the bed beside a woman about her own age who she'd never met and wished there was a moment to exchange names. Hilde had made it clear, though, that Hannah needed to have the eight women in the sick ward made up and ready for the scene in the next five minutes.

Hannah reached into her bag, rifling through the rolls of electrical tape, a tin of tacks, and loose metal paper clips before she felt the slender silver handle of a makeup brush. She pulled it from her bag and fluffed the hoop of feathers, then placed it on her lap as she fished for the powder compact, rouge pot, and lipstick. Hannah wondered where the Nazis had found makeup when the führer frowned on its use for German women. *Strong and healthy genes are what makes the German woman beautiful, not face paints.* Silently, Hannah huffed bitterly. The Nazis got makeup the same way they acquired everything else, from art-work to food—they stole it.

Dusting the first woman's face, Hannah instructed her to close her eyes. She had to work quickly and accidentally patted too hard, and an apricot-colored cloud hovered above the wom-an's skin for a moment. "Sorry," Hannah whispered. "I wish I didn't have to rush."

"It's all right," the woman in the hospital bed assured Hannah.

Hannah knit her brow as she looked at the open sores on the woman's arms. "Are these from bedbugs? You really shouldn't scratch."

"I know, I know. Mama tells me the same thing. I can't help it."

Hannah eyed her compact, a slender ring of pressed powder that clung to the tin palette pan. She couldn't spare any makeup for this poor woman's arms; Hannah would be lucky if she could cover all the patients' faces. "I'm sorry I can't..." Hannah said again, then reached toward the woman's lace sleeve cuffs and pulled them down to her wrists.

The hospital scenes took more than four hours to shoot, nearly twice as long as they had scheduled, and Hannah began to fear that Günther might cut scenes, especially ones he hadn't come up with himself.

Only one mattered to Hannah—the synagogue scene at the church. Hannah searched her mind for reasons to skip the *Kaffeehaus* segment... *Do you really want the Ghetto Swingers playing at the coffeehouse, since Nazis believe jazz is degenerate music?* Hannah's shoulders slumped as she realized that this was precisely why the Germans wanted to feature *Entartete Musik*. She bit her bottom lip in concentration, trying to come up with reasons to shoot the prayer scene next. *Many of the men in the minyan do manual labor for the war effort. Let's shoot the scene now and keep them productive.* Balling her fists, Hannah understood this suggestion would be rejected as well—and in a potentially dangerous way. Nazis didn't care if their slave laborers had to work into the night to meet their quotas. And if they had concerns about how fatigue might affect production, Herr Günther would simply find other men for the prayer scene.

Hannah's only choice was to be patient—or at least hide her anxiety from Hilde.

After she returned from the midday food line, Hannah watched two dozen prisoners gather in the newly built *Kaffeehaus* on the *Marktplatz*. Round tables seating two and four people formed a horseshoe around a parquet dance floor, wooden tiles that would be removed when the film was completed. One of Radek's fellow Ghettowache officers, a man surely cast for his matinee idol good looks, stood behind a service counter next to a gleaming espresso machine. Only four of the Ghetto Swingers could fit on set, the men with the smallest instruments: two clarinet players, a saxophonist, and a trombonist.

Hannah felt a lump in her throat, a pang of nostalgia, as the band began playing Oma Minna's favorite tune: "Bei Mir Bist du Schön" or "To Me, You're Beautiful." The fast tempo was driven by the inventive melody. The catchy tune repeated as women dressed in modern panel or box-pleated skirts danced the Lindy Hop with men in smart fedoras and ties. Linking their right arms, men and women swiveled at the hips and bounced to the swing music. Hannah admired the moves of a young woman, a new arrival from Hungary, kicking up her leg, seeming to draw energy from memories of better times.

"*Und danke!*" Gerron called out once the music stopped. It was as though an electrical plug had been yanked from a wall socket. Bodies stopped abruptly, smiles melted from faces, and shoulders dropped as the actors found their way back to their seats. A woman about Markéta's age reached for the back of a chair to steady herself. It was exhausting just to watch the actors expend the energy to dance, not to mention forcing expressions of exuberant joy. If even one person failed to look as though they were having the time of their life, the entire sequence had to be shot again.

"You two," Günther shouted, pointing to a young man holding his dance partner's upper arm with one hand and clutching her elbow with the other. The woman's head was down, and her fingertips pressed against her eyelids in a gesture Hannah recognized. She was dizzy. "You two, this scene needs more *Funke*," he said, then turned to Gerron and told him he wanted the couple propped against a wall in the background kissing each other. "Make sure we get that profile," he said, and Hannah didn't have to ask why; the man had a hawkish nose that had clearly been broken and improperly reset.

Even the normally unflappable Gerron placed a hand on his chest, taken aback by the suggestion. "Sturmbannführer, it would be…unseemly…" The director drifted off, understanding that the distasteful image of Jewish people was precisely the point. "The two… They just met today."

Günther let out an incredulous snort and shrugged.

Gerron addressed Hilde. "Frau Bohle," he said softly, then

hesitated. "Never mind. I'll take care of it." His leaden body moved toward the couple.

———◇———

It wasn't until well after sunset—twelve hours into their workday—that the film crew arrived at the church, but Hannah was newly charged. This was the moment they had been waiting for, and she reminded herself that no one could hear the thumping in her chest. If she maintained the same manner she had all day, her actions would not tip anyone off.

The inside of the church matched the exterior in its modesty, though the walls were a duller shade of white than the freshly painted facade, and the dark wood pews were not polished like the entrance doors. Portraits of Christ were taken down and piled on a table near the church entrance. Jesus on the cross had been removed from above the altar, and Hannah could see his bloodied hand peeking under a curtain at the far end of the platform. The wall had been painted brown to cover the discoloration from the removal of the crucifix. The empty space in front of it was transformed into a makeshift bimah; at its center was a wooden crate covered with a tablecloth holding a Torah scroll with carved wooden crowns.

Gerron's crew began setting up lights, aiming them at the bimah. Hannah opened silver umbrellas and handed them to crew members, who angled them atop their bulbs. She peeked to the side where the minyan stood next to the hand of Jesus, waiting for their cue, Radek with the *chanukiah* in hand. As planned, they walked onto the stage and placed their tallitot and yarmulkes on the floor, hoping Gerron would film the men picking up the prayer shawls and skullcaps, readying themselves for worship. Even the most nonobservant Jew would recognize that allowing these sacred items to touch the floor was a serious breach of protocol, and it would signal that something was wrong.

Radek placed tall white candles in the *chanukiah* and lit them all at once.

Hannah glanced at Gerron behind the camera and saw the slightest smile escape. "*Gut!* Reminds me of my childhood synagogue in Berlin."

Hannah stood with her arms twisted in front, her stomach churning with anxiety. *Please God, let this work.*

The ten men huddled around the scroll at the center of a table on the bimah. The fringes of their tallitot brushed against their suit jackets, and Hannah couldn't help notice how handsome Radek looked dressed for shul. Then the men began to recite the Mourner's Kaddish, and Hannah watched Radek's eyes lift to check if anyone else understood what was happening. Gerron's expression remained impassive, and neither Hilde nor her superior or the Aktualita film crew seemed to suspect a thing.

In a split second, Hannah and Radek looked at each other, then quickly averted their gazes. She hoped he was imagining the same thing as she: the two standing together around a full dinner table, children of their own who were eager to pull a piece of challah from the loaf and sink their teeth into the sweet bread.

Hannah looked at the floor of the church because she could not contain her smile. The men's voices filled every part of the room and rang through Hannah's body. *Please God, we need this to work. We need a miracle.*

Ten minutes later, the scene was shot, and Hannah went to

the bimah to collect the tallitot and yarmulkes. She dared not say a word to the men, instead watching them file out the side door as the film crew headed toward the front entrance. Hannah could hardly wait to speak with Radek later that night, but her immediate need was making sure Hilde remained committed to keeping that scene in the final film. If Hilde believed it was critical to the success of the Reich documentary, she would pester her supervisor relentlessly.

Hannah knelt to the floor as she folded the prayer shawls. She thought she was alone until she felt a hand on her shoulder.

Bending her body, Hilde made her way close to Hannah and whispered, "I think I remember that prayer from Munich."

Hannah fought back a gasp. Hilde couldn't possibly have understood what the minyan had recited. Had Hilde ever attended a funeral or shiva with Hannah? She couldn't be certain.

Hannah stopped folding. The next words from her mouth could be the most important thing she would ever say. "Yes, Frau... Hilde, you are right. The Shabbat prayer. You have a good memory."

Hilde's face brightened. "I knew it! I *do* have a good memory."

Hannah couldn't afford to show her relief, so she offered a smile. "People will appreciate hearing the traditional Shabbat prayer, seeing that you allow us to practice our faith here. It was a smart suggestion you made."

"*Ja,*" Hilde said, looking toward the front door, still open after the last of the crew left. "They'll know it's a religious thing even if they can't hear the words."

Can't hear the words?

The floor liquefied beneath Hannah's knees, and she placed

her palm down to maintain her balance. "Why wouldn't... They'll hear the words."

Hilde shrugged. "No, the film is being narrated. We'll pipe in some music to set a mood, like flutes for the playground scenes and maybe some kind of violin music."

Hannah heaved as though she had been punched in the stomach, a solid shock to the gut followed by a dull pain that radiated through her back.

"Violin music? But...those men had such beautiful voices."

Hilde shrugged again. "We've got a lot of information to share about the settlement, so we'll use narration for most of the film."

Hannah clutched her stomach.

"*Mein Gott*, Hannah, are you all right? Do you need—"

Herr Günther returned to the church and stood at the doorway. He shouted, "Frau Bohle! Is the Jewess giving you trouble?"

"*Scheisse*," Hilde whispered, then called back. "No, she dropped her props." Hilde stood and snapped at Hannah, "Be careful next time!"

"*Gut*," Herr Günther said. "Bring my cigarette box. I left it in the pew in front."

Hilde obliged and hurried out, barking at Hannah that she'd better not be late to the next set. Turning back to Hannah, Hilde crumpled her face with apology for her harsh tone.

Hannah could not move until she realized that she had to. Minutes had gone by, and she needed to get to the musical hall. But this was a debilitating blow. Days of planning. Finding the right men. They had thought of everything except for the film being narrated.

Hannah was in a trance of despair as she caught up to and trailed behind the film crew from the church to Sokol Hall, where Verdi's Requiem would be performed. An inky blue sky was lit by a full moon that hovered over the ghetto, and a handful of crows swooped through the air, cawing. She continued walking, saddled by a supply bag and weighted by failure.

The music hall was filled with more than one hundred prisoners who had been cast as eager audience members for Verdi's Requiem, conducted by Rafael Schächter. Dressed impeccably, they sat at small round tables with potted flowers at the center. Hannah watched a woman dab her handkerchief at the corners of her eyes. The music had not yet begun, so she could not have been moved by it; Hannah wondered if she was remembering better days at the opera. The choir of sixty moved onto the stage, forming four rows of fifteen, with four soloists seated on chairs in the front.

Hannah noticed that Hilde planted herself next to Herr Günther at the back of the auditorium, so she moved closer in case Hilde had a task for her. She forced a smile, an expression that said, *Let me know if you need anything*.

Schächter stood before his choir, his posture erect, and held up his baton. He nodded toward Alice on the piano, then Hannah heard the opening notes of Verdi's Requiem, music like a lullaby before ethereal voices softly began to fill the concert hall. The piano and the lush, refined vocal harmony created a soothing effect. The voices of the soloists soared above the background harmony of the choir to chart their individual melody lines, pleading *Kyrie eleison*, Lord have mercy, starting with the tenor, who passed the plea on to the bass, then to the soprano and mezzo-soprano.

After the opening piece pacified the audience, Alice's hands struck five thunderous chords, the powerful beginning of "Dies Irae," the Day of Wrath. A wave of fury and a symphonic blast, a chilling cascade continued in the lowest register, then scaled powerfully down from the treble to bass, adding embellishments making rich and powerful harmony.

When Hannah initially expressed annoyance at Schächter's choice to perform a Catholic funeral mass, Oskar had explained that the conductor selected Verdi's Requiem so the prisoners could voice their warning that the Nazis would someday face the judgment of God. "We Jews can sing to the Nazis what we cannot say to them."

Oskar's earlier explanation of this had felt so hopeful at the time. Now, it only seemed naïve. Hannah understood that her mood had nothing to do with the music itself. She glanced at Hilde and gritted her teeth.

The furious tempo and the torrent of "Dies Irae" did not stop until the very end, when the sound calmed and the tempo slowed into a rich harmony.

—◇—

Míša pressed the heels of her palms into her eyes and shook her head. "Narration? *Pfft*, we should have known the damn Nazis wouldn't let us speak for ourselves."

Hannah extended her hand onto Míša's knee as she sat cross-legged on the wooden floor of the glimmer factory attic, exchanging a heavy glance with Radek and Luděk opposite her.

"Hannah," Míša said, clearing her throat a few times before speaking. "Your Nazi friend said *Brundibár* and the requiem won't be narrated. Do you think…" Míša drifted off, defeated, as she remembered that the requiem had already been filmed.

Hannah could see her friend's mind scramble for solutions, the same ones Hannah had considered earlier. Could they ask Honza Treichlinger, the teen boy who played Brundibár the organ-grinder, to sneak the Mourner's Kaddish into his lines by the next day? Maybe he could sing it while he played his accordion. The Nazis wouldn't feature the entire children's opera, though. Anyone who wanted to show a snippet of *Brundibár* would choose the finale, when all the children sing the victory march together. There was no way they could expect thirty children, some as young as four years old, to pull this off. To try would endanger their young lives.

"I hate to be the one…" Radek began, shifting his weight uncomfortably on the floor. "I'm afraid I have more bad news."

Hannah examined Radek's face to see if she could tell what was coming.

"There's going to be another transport after the film is complete."

"Where?" Luděk and Míša tripped over the same word.

"Auschwitz?" Hannah asked.

"No," Radek returned. "There's a work camp in Berlin that needs Jews."

"*Pfft*, you mean slaves. They need slaves."

"Yes, slaves," Radek said with a slow nod. "The council is making the list in the next few days, but it's…it's going to be a big one. Nearly half the ghetto."

29

Hilde

As Hilde and Martin crossed the Charles Bridge, she stopped herself from asking a stranger to take their photo, handing over her camera and giving instructions on how she wanted the image framed. Normally, she would love to capture a snapshot of herself looking her best in her blazer with the imperial eagle patch on her chest and a blue neckerchief adorned with Hakenkreuze. Today was different, though. It was Hilde's first time out of Germany since the war, save for her two earlier visits to Theresienstadt, and Prague civilians were not as welcoming as she had expected. Herr Günther told her the Czech people were grateful to be part of the Reich. Hilde had seen photographs of Czechs with their arms extended to salute the führer. But the people on the bridge seemed both afraid and irritated by Hilde and Martin's presence, their heads turning away when they caught the glint of their pins. A man pulled his lips to the side ever so slightly and huffed once their paths had crossed. A mother with a baby pram quickened her pace to try to pass them, but Martin insisted the woman stop so the couple could admire the infant.

She complied and stiffly accepted his praise of her good genes. "My wife and I will be parents ourselves very soon," he told the mother, who glanced at Hilde's flat stomach, then looked away.

Hilde and Martin continued toward Old Town to join the crowd gathered beneath the astronomical clock at the top of Staroměstská radnice. It was nearly seven, and Hilde wanted to watch the top of the hour Walk of the Apostles before the sky grew dark. When the couple arrived at the Old Town city hall, Hilde noticed that the cluster of Czechs dispersed, suddenly no longer interested in watching the spectacle. The bell rang, and twelve figures of the saints appeared one by one through two small doors just below the roofline. As if on a carousel, Saint Peter scrolled past with his large golden key, stopping and greeting the handful of onlookers below. Hilde hoped that once the war was over, the apostles would be replaced by the führer and his top men.

Hilde and Martin continued through the square, and Hilde noticed Czechs giving them a wide berth and quickening their pace, eyes cast down onto the gray cobblestones. A man with a thick beard sped past, holding a burlap sack, his left arm belting it to his shoulder. Four nuns glided through the Old Town square, heads high but eyes locked forward. Two older women wrapped the sleeves of their fraying blouses around their bellies as they passed Hilde and Martin, their words foreign but their tones frightened. Hilde wanted to shout at them, *What's wrong with you people? Can't you see how much better off you are as part of the Reich?* She stayed silent and tried to keep her focus elsewhere as she and Martin walked toward the Municipal House restaurant for supper. Hilde turned her head to the left and raised her eyes toward the twin spires of a Gothic church looming above.

"Should we…" Hilde couldn't bear the discomfort of being seen as the enemy any longer. "Should we go back to Kamýk and have supper at the house?"

Martin's head spun to meet Hilde's eyes. "No," he snapped, reaching across Hilde's back and resting his palm on her shoulder. "We are here to enjoy the city, and that is definitely what we are going to do. It's not like you to cower like this. Hold your head up, and remember who you are."

"Thank you, Martin," she said, appreciating the reminder.

After supper, Hilde looked at Martin behind the wheel of the ministry Mercedes and reminded herself to be grateful that she had such a good man by her side. Yes, the people in Prague seemed afraid of them, but it was better to be feared than fearful. On the open motorway, Hilde rolled down the passenger window and reached her arm out to feel the night air wash between her fingers. She tilted her head back and indulged in the sight of a skyful of stars unmuted by city light. Inhaling deeply, Hilde absorbed the earthy scent of the lush farmland of the growing Reich.

"Martin, I don't think I've ever been happier," she lied, trying to convince herself that saying something was the first step in making it true. Sliding across the front seat bench to close the space between them, Hilde rested her head on Martin's shoulder and imagined herself a film star in an epic love story.

"You deserve it, *Mein Liebchen*."

The couple spent the next hour in comfortable silence as the car rolled over the smooth new road. When they passed Klíčany, the terrain became rougher. Martin slowed the car, but the rubber tires against the pebbled dirt road still sounded like a frantic crackle of fireworks. Soon, Martin turned the car onto the wooded path to Kamýk, and the Mercedes was swallowed by the darkness, through a gauntlet of trees with trunk bottoms illuminated only by the lamplight of the automobile. Low, leafy branches dangled in the light of the bulbs, motionless in the stagnant summer air. At a turn in the road, Hilde spotted a white rabbit darting in front of them, red eyes glowing in the spotlight.

"Martin, watch it!"

"*Scheisse!*" he called out as Hilde felt the soft bump of its body under the wheel. Martin hit the brakes, and Hilde opened the door for herself, then ran back to search for the rabbit. Perhaps they had just injured it.

Hilde was on her knees beside the bloodied fur before Martin reached her. Lowering himself beside Hilde, his fingers pinched the bridge of his nose, and he shook his head with regret. "I hate it when that happens. I didn't see the little fellow. I feel awful."

"It's…it's fine, Martin. You didn't see it," she said, though the words felt hollow in her throat.

"Do you think we should take it back to the house?"

Hilde jarred at the suggestion. "Martin, there's no helping… It's dead."

"It's definitely dead, Hilde. I meant to cook it." He shrugged sheepishly. "I wish he hadn't run in front of the car, but…we could make a nice stew."

After a few moments passed, Hilde reminded herself that she had to respond to her husband. "Sure," she said, clearing her throat. "We'll make stew."

They drove for another few minutes in darkness and silence, the dead rabbit wrapped in Hilde's neckerchief on the seat beside her. Martin stopped the car and shifted the transmission stick into park, then pulled the brake lever.

The couple remained seated.

"Martin, I need a favor."

"You already know I would do anything for you and our future family."

She sighed internally. *Again with the future family.*

"Good. You remember that I mentioned my childhood schoolmate Hannah lives in Theresienstadt now."

Martin nodded.

"Some old *Hutzel* from the settlement was transferred to Auschwitz, and Hannah keeps haranguing me to check on her. Karla, Kamilka, something like that. If I get you her full name, would you check on her whereabouts once you're back in Berlin? There must be some sort of registry of camp residents. Hannah got a postcard from this woman and never heard from her again."

"Her *whereabouts?*"

"What part of the camp she's in, what her work assignment is, that sort of thing."

"Now, now, Hilde. The film cameras aren't rolling."

Hilde turned to him and raised her brows curiously.

Martin smiled. "You don't need to play dummkopf with me. I'm not a spy for the League of Nations."

"What the hell are you talking about? Why would I think you're a spy for the—"

"Hilde, come on. You know the old lady went up the chimney long ago."

"Up the… Martin, why would you say that? You think Hannah's friend died?"

He huffed, incredulous. "Do I think she *died?*"

"*Ja*, do you think she died and was cremated?"

"All right, Hilde, I get it. You're a wonderful actress, but we're alone now."

"What the hell, Martin? What do you mean *up the chimney?*"

He narrowed his eyes and bunched his face in confusion. "You said she was old. She was probably exterminated right after she wrote the postcard to your...to the Jewess."

Hilde sat on her hands to keep them from shaking and reminded herself to breathe. Her voice quivered. "*Exterminated?*"

"Yes, Hilde. Gassed, exterminated, whatever you want to call it," he replied, cocking his head in disbelief. "Why are you acting like you don't know this?"

"Martin, please," Hilde said, reaching for his hand. "Tell me you're joking."

He pulled away to examine Hilde's face. "What a terrible joke that would be. This is serious business, Hilde, very unpleasant work but necessary if we are going to create a better world for our children."

Hilde felt a wave of nausea move through her body, twisting her stomach.

"Martin, please... Why haven't you ever told me this?"

"I assumed you knew. It's definitely not something I was going to bring up at the dinner table, but Auschwitz has been using cyanide on the Jews for the last two years. Honestly, how could you *not* know?"

"Cyanide gas?"

"Shooting them was too hard on the soldiers. It's cleaner to use gas," he explained. "And cheaper."

Was this happening in the other camps? Was this happening at Theresienstadt, and she had somehow missed the signs? "Who else knows about this?"

Martin pinched his face with disgust. "Everyone who works for the Reich knows. Hilde, if you don't know about the Final Solution by now, it's because you don't want to."

"I didn't. I mean… When I worked at the Women's League, I saw reports of criminals being shot at Dachau, but only the dangerous ones."

He placed a comforting hand on her shoulder. "There you have it. We know Jews are dangerous to the *Volk*, so yes, only the dangerous ones," he said. "Can we go inside now?"

"Why didn't we deport them to Madagascar?" Her chin dropped so she could hide the tears collecting in her eyes.

"You know the Madagascar plan was never put into action. Herr Eichmann didn't call this the Final Solution because it was Germany's first idea for solving the Jewish problem. No one else wanted them." He reminded her that at the Évian Conference in 1938, thirty-two countries were more than happy to wag their fingers at Germany for its new laws and *Aktionen*, but only the Dominican Republic agreed to accept Jews fleeing Europe. Shanghai and the Philippines kept their doors open until both were seized by the Japanese. And Palestine took in as many European Jews as the British permitted. "You know the rest of the world wanted nothing to do with our *Untermenschen*," Martin said, growing more impassioned as he defended the German position. "We had no other choice."

Hilde remembered taking a lunchtime walk in Berlin with Lotte five years earlier, and her mentor shared the party's secret plan to weed out bad blood by euthanizing people with physical and mental disabilities. Lotte pointed to the villa at Tiergartenstrasse No. 4, where the program was to be launched. Hilde was initially uncomfortable with the idea, believing that sterilization was more humane, but she began to accept that Germany could not afford the economic drain of unproductive citizens. She had cringed at the term "useless eaters" when Lotte first used it, but the more Hilde heard it, the less shocking it became. Eventually, it sounded normal.

Otto had always scolded Hilde for asking too many questions. Now she realized she hadn't asked the right ones.

Sitting beside Martin in the car, Hilde's body was rigid, rocking slightly.

"There, there," Martin offered. "I thought you knew all this. It can be difficult to think about the big picture, especially since you were friendly with a Jewess before the war. Try to remember that Germany is doing something great, a hard job that Europe will thank us for someday."

Friendly. The word pierced Hilde's heart. They had been best friends.

Martin brushed away a tendril of Hilde's hair that had fallen loose during their drive. "I don't mean to sound cruel, but how could you possibly not know? Why do you think Herr Eichmann is making the Museum of Jewish Culture in Prague? It'll be filled with the relics of an extinct race, so our children can see them like the Neanderthals at the Museum für Naturkunde."

"Extinct? So every...*all* the Jews...they will all be..."

"Yes, Hilde, all of them," Martin said, seeming to lose patience. He pulled the key from the ignition and reached for his door handle. "That's why your film is so important. We need to use these actors while they're still around. When I told my superior I was coming here to visit you, he mentioned that a good-size transport will leave for Auschwitz after the project is complete."

"We finish filming in two days!" Hilde's stomach lunged, and she swallowed the bile that rose to her mouth. "Martin, I need you to do me a favor."

He smiled. "I already told you: anything."

An hour later, Hilde placed her pencil down next to the notes she'd scratched on four sheets of paper as the scent of broiling rabbit filled the kitchen. Martin had been silent as Hilde jotted her plan, so she looked at him expectantly at the kitchen table when she finished. "It's a perfect plan," she said with a satisfied grin.

Martin lowered his brows. "Definitely not perfect, Hilde."

She held back an exasperated sigh. It was important that her husband felt invested in Hilde's plan. "All right, Martin, what did I leave out?"

"Only the part where we commit treason by helping a Jew escape."

"Martin," she whined, reaching a hand to touch his arm. "I've already told you, Hannah's different. She was my best friend. Trust me, she's worth saving."

Martin did not reply, shaking his head with an expression of disbelief at Hilde's plea.

"No one will find out," Hilde pressed. "Once you get her new identification papers, that's who she'll be. I can get her out after the filming, we'll take her back to Berlin, and she can stay with us until everything is set."

Martin remained silent, his brows now knotted, and Hilde could see he was considering it.

"I'm *asking* you, Martin. As your wife, I'm asking your permission." Another idea sparked. "We can hire her as our maid so she doesn't have too much contact with the outside world. She'll live with us and help care for the baby."

"The baby?" Martin opened his mouth, looking incredulous, then shook his head. "*Our* baby?"

"*Ja*, the child we adopt. I'm ready, Martin. We can go to the Lebensborn Society as soon as the film is complete and adopt a baby…two babies if you want, and Hannah will help us raise them."

"Hannah? Hannah, the Jewess, will raise our children? And live in our home?"

"A separate area, of course, but it will be fine. You'll see. She's very clean. Please, Martin, I can't let Hannah die. She… Oh, Martin, she's special to me."

Martin stared ahead in silence for an agonizing few minutes, then turned to Hilde and touched her cheek, softening his posture. "I've heard of other Germans keeping a pet Jew, one they swear is not like the rest."

Hilde bristled at the characterization but did not let it show. Martin was moving in the direction she needed, and that was the most important thing.

"I suppose it would be all right if it makes you happy."

Hilde leapt into her husband's arms and rested her head on his shoulder, suddenly realizing she was crying. "Thank you, Martin," she sniffled. "I promise, you're going to love Hannah."

30

Hannah

H ANNAH KNELT BEFORE GRISELDE AS SHE STOOD ON THE
small platform in the tailor shop. She used a basting stitch
to take up the hem of Theresienstadt's shared wedding dress,
which a dressmaker had made two years earlier from an old duvet
cover the commandant had stained and discarded. Women from
the laundry scrubbed it as best they could before soaking the
gown in diluted ersatz coffee for an antiqued effect. Griselde had
worn the dress for the real wedding ceremony two years earlier,
but seventy more couples in the ghetto had married since then,
so the dress needed to be altered again. Griselde was shorter than
the last bride, so Hannah took up the length but used a wide
stitch so the next woman would be able to let it down easily.

"How do I look?" Griselde asked Míša, who was shortening
the sleeves of the wedding dress.

"Beautiful," Míša offered, and Hannah was grateful for the
lie. Griselde had fared better than most of the older women at
Theresienstadt, but her hair had thinned, and her face had grown
pale over the years. When Hannah saw Griselde's hands, fingers

slashed with fresh red cuts and raised scars from gashes that
hadn't been sutured, she tried to shake off the feelings of guilt
about the toll *Glimmerwerke* had taken on Griselde.

Griselde must have noticed Hannah's grimace, because she
patted Hannah's cheek and said, "They aren't pretty, but they are
why I'm alive."

Hannah looked away.

"Child, I know you think your opa and I have tomatoes on
our eyes, but we… Our generation saw a lot of men return from
the war shell-shocked. They were never their old selves again.
Plenty of them took their—" She dismissed the unpleasant
thought. "I know you find him frustrating, but your opa made
a choice to look at the good in the world no matter what, and I
find that admirable."

Hannah brushed away a tear. She'd forgotten—or maybe
never truly understood—that Oskar had an entire life indepen-
dent of Hannah. His sunny optimism had been a lifeline, and
Hannah hated herself for her harsh judgment of it. "You're…
Griselde, I'm happy he has you."

"Don't make me cry," Griselde said, sniffling. "Help me get
this veil on, will you?"

Hannah bit her lip as she felt the veil touch her fingertips,
remembering Friedl creating it from an old mosquito net the SS
had tossed, skillfully folding and fanning the mesh until it was fit
for the pages of *Čtení pro ženy*. That was Friedl's gift—she turned
rags into beauty. Hannah prayed Friedl and Klara were together
at Auschwitz, that Siegfried, the escaped prisoner she'd heard in
Oskar's room, had it wrong.

Theresienstadt was filled with both relief and anxiety—relief that this evening would be the film crew's last in the ghetto, anxiety about whose names would be on the transport list to a new work camp in Berlin that the council would post the following morning.

When they were alone last night, walking to their spot in the tunnel near the back gate, Radek had told Hannah that his Ghettowache status would no longer protect him from transport. Nor would Hannah's at the glimmer factory. Radek lifted his shoulders, feigning nonchalance, but the catch in his voice betrayed him. "At least we'll go to Berlin instead of the east," he said.

"We won't be on the list," Hannah assured him.

"We might. It's going to be a big one." Radek paused. "If your name is on the list tomorrow, I'm going to volunteer for the transport."

Hannah felt a punch of guilt as she realized she could not make the same promise. She had Danuše to look after. "Don't do that," she said. "The war will be over in a few months. It won't be too long before we can be together again. Besides, we won't be on this list. I'm certain of it."

Hannah wondered if Radek considered her a deluded fool, a charge she had lodged against Oskar so many times. A charge Oskar had leveled against himself in recent months.

"Should we...say goodbye? In case we don't get another chance."

"No. If I hear the words, it will be too... It will be like I'm surrendering to the inevitable. I have to hold on to hope." Hannah's heart plummeted, remembering Míša's warning when Hannah first arrived in the ghetto. Maybe she had been right and hope was the accomplice of the Nazis. Or perhaps it was a gift from God. Who knew in this upside-down world of evil and duplicity? Hannah sniffled and wiped her nose with her sleeve. "Do you know where you'll go after the war? Do you ever think about moving to Palestine?"

Radek looked down and shook his head. "If it was just me… I need to find my family and…" He bent down and leaned close to kiss Hannah. She ran her hands over his shoulders and arms, taking in the feel of his body. "Should we carve our names into the wall?" Radek asked.

Hannah considered it for a moment but told Radek that they would have plenty of time to etch their names into the sandstone later. "We won't be on the list," Hannah told him. "The Nazis need men to patrol the ghetto, and God knows why, but they seem to need their mica."

Radek looked down and swallowed hard. "I've never been to Berlin."

"And you're not going tomorrow," Hannah assured him.

Radek exhaled through his nose, a rueful laugh. "Sure thing," he said. "Listen, I just want to tell you that—I know we'll see each other again tomorrow because neither of us will be on the list, but…" He tapered off. "Our time together here, it's meant a lot to me. An elder in the barracks said the music was keeping him alive in the ghetto, and I think…I think what's been keeping me alive has been you. You're my music, Hannah."

The knock on the tailor shop door was as fast as a woodpecker and snapped Hannah back to the present. The heads of all three women turned toward the door, which opened before they could respond.

"Hilde, you're early," was all Hannah could muster.

On a mission, Hilde slipped through the door and closed it behind her. "I wanted to get here a little early and make sure the bride looks her best. And also…" She drifted off, looking about skittishly. "Hannah, can we talk outside?"

"Did you hear something about Klara?" Hannah's breath was trapped in her chest. "Is she…is Klara… How is she?"

"Hannah, I really can't…"

"*Pfft*, you go, Hannah. I'll tend to Griselde," Míša offered.

"Go on, child."

When they stepped outside, Hilde gestured toward a tall bush next to the tailor shop where they could speak in relative privacy.

"Is she all right?"

Hilde looked down at the dirt beneath her feet. "I don't know for certain, but she's older, and it is likely she…she died."

"You're not sure, though?"

Hilde looked away. "The older people… Hannah, I'm sorry, but your friend is dead."

Hannah let out a soft whimper, then held her hands over her face so Hilde couldn't see her cry. She had suspected that Klara wouldn't survive the harsh conditions at Auschwitz, but hearing Hilde confirm this tore Hannah open. Hannah wiped tears from her cheeks and fought the need to cry out. There was no way she would share any part of Klara with a Nazi—not even witnessing the mourning of her death. Finally, she grabbed the skirt of her work dress and wiped her face, reminding herself she could grieve later with people who knew and loved Klara, not entertain a Nazi with her sorrow. She sat up quickly and inhaled before she spoke.

"I don't know why I'm crying. I knew she was dead. She would have written to me if she were alive."

Hilde looked down and cupped her hands over her face, shaking her head. When she returned her gaze to Hannah, Hilde's eyes were red and glazed. "I'm sorry, Hannah, but there's more I need to tell you. It's bad. It's very bad, but I…I have a plan."

Hannah felt Hilde reach her arms onto her shoulders and, for a moment, almost allowed her old friend to comfort her. Quickly, she changed her mind and shook Hilde away. "What is your news?"

Hilde pressed. "The film finishes tonight, and there's a transport heading to Auschwitz in two days."

"No," Hannah said, shaking her head. "The transport is going to a labor camp in Berlin."

"Listen to me. There is no labor camp in Berlin. Half the ghetto is being transported to a death camp, and you're…"

"*Death* camp?" *That cannot be. The Nazis need workers in Berlin!*

"I'm sorry, Hannah, but I checked with the commandant, and you're on the transport list."

"No, that can't be right," Hannah protested, blinking as fireflies appeared before her eyes. "The council is still compiling the list." She placed a hand on her heart, hoping to slow its speed. Even when they were little girls, Hilde liked to pretend she knew more than she really did. It made her feel important to have the inside news or at least think she did. Hilde was still the same know-nothing windbag.

"Hannah, I can get you out of here tonight. My husband runs the graphic arts department at the ministry, and he's going to forge identity papers for you. You'll be a Christian woman from Hamburg who lives in Berlin now. We have it all worked out.

Meet me at SS headquarters just after curfew, and I will have a small uniform for you. We'll shorten the pant legs, cut your hair, put a cap on your head, and you'll walk out the gate with me."

Hannah focused on the silver pin attached to Hilde's lapel, the swastika on a white enamel oval. Maybe Hilde didn't want to see harm come to Hannah, but she was part of the organization that was responsible for the murders of Pavel and his father and the seven other men. The Kristallnacht riots. The Nuremberg Laws. She was the enemy.

Still, Hannah could not help herself from considering the offer. As a free woman, she could make her way to Geneva and tell the League of Nations what was really going on at Theresienstadt. "You don't think the gendarmes will notice?"

Hilde pulled Hannah closer and harshened her tone. "All they'll see is the uniform. Stand up straight, and walk proud like you're one of us."

Proud like one of them? The words were a smack in the face, a cold return to the reality that Hilde Kramer was a Nazi and could not be trusted.

Hannah stepped back, releasing herself from Hilde's grip. "Why would I believe you? How do I know this isn't some sort of trap?"

Hilde slapped her palms over her face with frustration. "I swear to you, you are heading to Auschwitz. And it's a death camp. *Mein Gott*, Hannah, you've got to trust me."

"Why would I?"

Hilde lowered her hands. "Because I'm your friend, Hannah. And I don't want you to die."

Hannah felt a strange current of hope and fear pulling her,

tempting her to take a chance at believing that there was some goodness at the core of Hilde. "What if I go with you? Your husband makes fake papers, and then what?"

Hilde placed a hand on top of Hannah's. "You'll live in Berlin and start a new life. You can pass as Aryan. I know it will be hard, but you'll go on."

I will go on? I will live among people who turned a blind eye to my persecution? Who took part in the smashing of windows, burning of synagogues, killing in the streets? She is asking me to pretend I am one of them?

Yet Hannah had Danuše to consider. Hands shaking and body coated with sweat, Hannah asked, "How many can you get out? I have a… There are children here."

Hilde's face knotted with question. "What do you mean? Hannah, I can get *you* out. That's all."

From the corner of her eye, Hannah saw a black mass moving toward them: the Aktualita film crew in their dark jackets and berets, followed by Kurt Gerron. "There are my assistants!" he bellowed in the direction of Hannah and Hilde. "Is our bride ready to go?"

Hilde shouted back. "Yes, all ready for the primping scene," then she lowered her head and whispered, "Meet me at SS headquarters at eleven tonight."

Hannah's heart sped at the thought of freedom, walking out the gate of Theresienstadt and finding her way to the League of Nations. A hot meal and a warm bath. But what about her family here at Theresienstadt? She couldn't just leave Oskar and Griselde. What would happen to Danuše and Alice? Or Míša and Markéta? Radek and Luděk?

The war couldn't go on much longer. Mouth radio buzzed about how Allied forces landed in Normandy three months earlier and began the liberation of France. One of Germany's last lines of defense in the Italian campaign had been breached. Paris, Rome, and Brussels had already been freed from Nazi occupation. The war was ending, and Hannah didn't need help from the likes of Hilde Kramer. Hilde Bohle. Whatever her name was now. Radek had never misled Hannah, and if he said the next transport was heading to Berlin, Hannah knew she could trust him. Maybe he would be on the transport list as well.

"Thank you, Hilde, but I'll stay here."

Hilde raised her eyebrows and stepped back farther. "You can't do that!"

The earnestness rattled Hannah. Could Hilde be right? No, the Council of Elders said the trains would head to Berlin. Radek said the same.

It was settled. "I'm not going," Hannah said and folded her arms across her chest.

"Hannah, are you completely turned through? I want to save you!"

"I don't need a savior, Hilde. I need friends, and you ceased to be one the day you joined the Nazi Party."

31

Hilde

Kamýk
September 1944

A s Hilde approached the farmhouse, driving the pickup truck her host family had left for her, she saw a Reich Mercedes parked close to the back door. Martin had returned early from his meeting with the Gestapo at Petschek Palace in Prague. Hilde felt a rush of gratitude that her husband always seemed to know when she needed him. Only he would understand her frustration with Hannah. They had gone through so much trouble to create this escape plan for her, and she refused it like a spoiled child. What was Hannah trying to prove to her grandfather and friends anyway? Her noble act of sacrifice would make no difference to any of them when they were dead.

Hilde spotted Martin squinting at the headlamps shining through the kitchen window. He turned quickly to his left, then right. Martin placed his hat on and rushed to the back door and stepped outside to greet her. "You're home early, Hilde!"

She had never been more relieved to see Martin. Running into his arms, she cried, "You got here early too, thank goodness," she said, resting her head on his chest. "You always seem to know when I need you. I've had a hard day, and I could use your advice."

Unlocking herself from Martin's embrace, Hilde rushed through the door and grabbed a glass. She turned on the faucet and gulped down her water, then sat at the kitchen table.

Martin followed her but remained standing, his fingers wrapping around the back of a wooden chair.

"I told Hannah about our plan, but she said no," Hilde explained in a flurry. "Can you imagine? I told her she's going to Auschwitz and just… She didn't believe me. And then we filmed her opa's new wife getting ready for her wedding." Hilde covered her face and began to sob, knowing Martin was the one person she could reveal her pain to. "I think she's gone mad at Theresienstadt. She walked away and there's nothing I can—" She stopped.

There was, in fact, something Hilde could do.

She stood and grabbed a napkin from a drawer of the kitchen hutch. "Hannah doesn't get to decide if she gets on the train," she thought aloud. "I can still have a Ghettowache officer bring her to me at SS headquarters for questioning tonight. If she makes a fuss about it, it will be even more convincing." Hilde paced the width of the kitchen, low heels clacking against the stone flooring. She flapped her hands, fanning herself from overheating with excitement. "*Ja, ja*, Hannah will be furious tonight, but she'll thank me for this one day."

Hilde turned to Martin, who stepped toward the arch that connected the kitchen to the living room, then glanced at the stairwell, jaw tensed.

"Martin, you haven't said a word," she huffed. "What do you

think of my—" She stopped at the sound of boots descending the steps. Turning, Hilde saw two men in uniform.

When the men reached the ground floor, they entered the kitchen, surprised to see Hilde. "Frau Bohle," said the Gestapo officer with a thin black line of a mustache. "You're back early." His counterpart turned his eyes down, looking as though he would rather be anywhere else. They couldn't have heard anything more than Hilde asking Martin what he thought of her plan.

Hilde extended her arm and hailed Hitler, but the officer declined to return the gesture. She turned her head toward Martin. *What the hell?*

"Let's skip the pretense, Frau Bohle," the first man said as he walked toward Hilde, checking the holster at his side. "We know you offered aid to a Jewess at Theresienstadt and tried to enlist Herr Bohle here in your plot."

He gripped her arm, and she felt each finger dig into her.

Hilde's throat tightened like a twisted cord. "No, no, I didn't. Tell them, Martin. I did no such thing."

Martin shrugged apologetically and stepped back. "I'm sorry, Hilde."

"You're sorry?" Her voice sounded thready with fear. "Sorry for what? Martin, please explain to them that—"

Martin interrupted her by holding up his hand and shaking his head. "I'm sorry things turned out this way, Hilde. I'm sorry for your misguided choices. You've definitely changed since coming here. The girl I fell in love with was loyal to the Reich."

She shook her head frantically, panting through her nose. "Hannah is...was an old friend. She manipulated me by constantly reminding me of memories we had together. They do that, you know they do, but I've come back to my senses." *Why is no one saying a word? Why is Martin looking out the kitchen window instead of at me?* "It was a lapse in judgment, a moment of weakness," she scrambled.

Martin turned back to her and offered a sympathetic smile.

"And I came back to my senses before any harm was done," Hilde went on. "Tell them, Martin. Explain how I told Hannah I wasn't going to help her after all. I refused, even after she begged."

Martin pressed his lips together. "Oh, Hilde."

Her heart raced with hope.

"You're not the girl I thought you were," he said, turning toward the men. "Did you find—"

The second man reached into his jacket and retrieved Hilde's notebook, holding it up for all to see. Hilde jolted with fear when she spotted uncrumpled papers peeking from behind the notebook cover. Her plan to save Hannah had been written with her own hand. "Martin?" was all she could say. Hilde tried to shake loose, but the Gestapo agent tightened his grip, slender fingers pressing deeper into her arm. "Where are you taking me? I demand to know where you are taking me!" Her eyes flitted about the kitchen, desperately hoping someone would answer her. On the countertop, Hilde noticed the paring knife she had left out that morning, and for a moment, she considered lunging for it and trying to fight her way out of the situation before realizing it would be futile. There were three men and only one of her. Where would she even go if she could manage to get away? No, Hilde understood that her only hope was to beg for mercy, to pray they would pity her. "Please. Tell me where we are going."

When the officer yanked Hilde's arm, she gasped from the pain that shot down the length of it. He pushed her toward the door. "Frau Bohle," the officer said, "understand that you are no longer in a position to make demands. You will know where we are taking you when we arrive. In the meantime, you would be wise to do as you are told without hysterics."

"Hold on a moment," Martin commanded. He took a step toward Hilde and softened his tone. "Hilde, you'll be given a trial."

"Will you…will you testify on my behalf? You know how devoted I am to the Reich."

"I'm sorry, Hilde. I've already given my statement."

Her heart plummeted. "Martin, please."

"As a citizen of the Reich, I must tell the truth, even when it comes at great personal cost to me."

The truth. Tears began to stream down Hilde's cheeks. Couldn't Martin understand that the truth could be different things? Yes, it was true that Hilde was loyal to the Reich, but it was also true that Hannah Kaufman was a friend, a person worth saving. Truth could take alternate forms and be no less true. Why couldn't Martin see that?

32

Hannah

Theresienstadt
September 1944

THE FIRST THING HANNAH HEARD WAS THE SOUND OF dozens of heavy boots stomping up the stairs, thundering louder as the Czech gendarmes reached the third story and disbursed themselves throughout the barracks. Then the forceful voices of men shouting for the prisoners to wake up, calling numbers without a pause between them. It didn't matter; everyone saw last night's list of who would be sent to the work camp in Berlin. No one needed the barking reminder.

A thousand women had padded these floors every day, but the heavy gait of the soldiers released dust that had settled into the grain and splits of wood over the years. Hannah blinked her eyes slowly, and the hazy figures of women rustling in their bunks sharpened in the dim barracks. The lucky ones hadn't yet been roused from sleep. Their breath was still steady, and Hannah envied their extra moments of peace but knew she had to hurry. Not only did she need to help Danuše hide, she had promised to meet Míša and Markéta by the back stairwell so they could search for Oskar and Griselde and remain together for the transport.

Wrapping her arm around Danuše beside her, Hannah gently jostled the little girl. *Time for you to go to your hiding spot, mamaleh.*

"I want to see Maminka," Danuše said groggily, stretching her legs and twisting her fists over her closed eyes. She sat upright, something even short Hannah couldn't manage. Instead, she hunched and turned to Danuše.

"I told you already. You'll stay back with Alice."

A gendarme struck his baton against the wooden beams of the bunks. "L-939, up now! Wake up! Move, move, move!" he shouted, the same command echoing across the third floor with different voices calling different numbers.

Thankfully, his eye had not traveled to the top level of the bunk and did not register little Danuše beside Hannah. She pushed the girl back and held a finger over her own lips. *Shh!* "No fussing," she whispered. They had discussed this the night before, and Danuše promised she would lie flat against the bed slats so that Hannah could cover her with the hay-filled mattress. After several refusals and sniffling tears, Danuše finally agreed. This was no time for her to go back on her promise.

Radek had been right. The sunrise transport to Berlin would be the largest ever; nearly half of the ghetto was on the list posted the day before. Radek and Alice had been spared transport and would remain at Theresienstadt, and they promised to look after Danuše. But Oskar and Griselde were on the list. So were Míša and Markéta. Luděk. Alena. Petra. And Hannah herself. She had touched her number on the list with fingers scarred from the glimmer factory, from the work that was meant to save her.

"No," the little girl's voice insisted. She reached for her doll and clutched it tight. "We're coming."

"Please, Danuše," Hannah whispered as she reached for her pouch filled with toiletries on the shelf beside her bunk. "You will be safer here with Alice."

Danuše lifted a sack she had used as a pillow and showed Hannah that she was already packed. She tightened her grip around its neck and bunched her lips. *I'm coming with you!*

Sighing impatiently, Hannah conceded. She had no energy to argue. "Fine." She hated when she lost patience with Danuše, but her nerves were frayed, and there were too many people for Hannah to keep track of already.

Hannah descended the ladder as Danuše followed, only one rung above. The little girl's foot accidentally kicked Hannah's forehead, scratching it with her jagged toenail. From the corner of her eye, Hannah watched other women roll from bottom bunks and work their way down from middle and top levels. Those staying behind murmured requests to look for loved ones.

"Try to find Mama."

"Stay strong. It won't be long."

"We will pray for you."

A handful pretended to sleep through the ordeal, though only the dead could possibly remain unconscious amid the men shouting and women weeping.

When Alice noticed Danuše making her way down the ladder, she jumped from her second-level bed. Once on the ground, her bare feet were grazed by the trim of her nightdress. She grabbed Hannah's hands. "She's staying with me, no?"

"She wants to come."

Alice knelt to meet the girl's gaze. "You'll have to work in Berlin," she said, her eyes volleying between Danuše and Hannah. "No music lessons, no art classes. Stay with Štěpán and me."

A man in a gendarme's green uniform appeared. "Move, move, move! You had the night to say goodbye." He looked at Hannah, pointing at Danuše. "Yours?"

"No, she's—"but before Hannah could explain that the child belonged with Alice, Danuše interrupted.

"Maminka!"

This child was too stubborn for her own good. The gendarme looked at Hannah with a smirk of disgust for denying her child. "You both need to be out in two minutes. At the tracks in ten."

Continuing his sweep, the gendarme left, and Alice grabbed Hannah's shoulders, pulling her in urgently for a hug. "God be with you," she whispered.

Gripping Danuše's palm with one hand and her suitcase with the other, Hannah made her way to the opposite end of the third floor, weaving through a stream of women walking toward her. Before she could see Míša, Hannah heard her friend's distinctive cough, a crumpling paper bag followed by a series of throat clears. As Hannah and Danuše continued across the floor, a woman with a leathery face bumped the little girl with her suitcase, then knelt to see if she was all right. A cluster of women behind the elder did not stop in time, and one nearly toppled the older woman. "Watch it," someone snapped.

"Keep moving!" a gendarme shouted over the din of terrified women, the metal smell of fear filling the barracks.

"We need to find Míša and Markéta," Hannah explained,

then saw her best friend with her mother speeding toward them, each holding a small valise.

"Good, you're here," Míša said. "Why is she... Danuše, you are staying back with Alice."

The girl bunched her face and said nothing, pretending not to hear.

"I tried."

"*Pfft.*" Míša shook her head. There was nothing more to say.

The moment the four stepped into the corridor of the third floor, they were engulfed in a stream of women's bodies flowing toward the staircase. *So many children*, Hannah noticed. It seemed odd to send little ones to a work camp, but perhaps there would be a place for children to put on plays and write poems as there was at Theresienstadt. The thought assuaged some of her guilt over taking Danuše. Younger women clasped elbows with elders, helping them maintain balance as their unsteady feet landed on each step.

Once on the ground floor, the women joined hundreds more on the narrow road that led to the *Stadtpark* before they turned left onto a main street toward the tracks.

There, gendarmes with their hands wrapped around their rifles formed two lines and instructed prisoners to stay between them. The crowd grew denser as they walked closer to the back gate, and Hannah began to see men emptying from the Magdeburg and Hamburg Barracks. Then married couples and families. Her eyes began a frantic search for Oskar and Griselde until she recognized Oskar's forest-green jacket.

"Opa!" Hannah called out. "Opa! Griselde!"

Griselde turned back, elbow nudging Oskar. She pointed at Hannah, then stepped off to the side to let her catch up.

"Move along," a gendarme warned, so Hannah hurried, jockeying her way past others to reach them, looking back to make sure Míša and Markéta were still within sight. She had never minded her short height until now, when she had to stand on her toes and even jump to see over the shoulders and heads that moved between her and her grandfather.

When Hannah and Danuše caught up, Oskar looked down at the child, a flicker of concern.

"Why is she—" he began, then waved a hand.

Hannah turned to check her other side to make sure Míša and Markéta hadn't been carried away in the current of humanity.

The voices of other prisoners rumbled through the crowd, though Hannah could not tell who was speaking.

"A munitions plant, I heard."

"You don't think… We're not going east, are we?"

"A rubber plant?"

"Auschwitz?"

Oskar stiffened at the word, and Hannah remembered overhearing the escaped Auschwitz prisoner's warning. "Opa, what do you know about Auschwitz?"

Hannah watched Oskar struggle to maintain a neutral expression, but his lips tightened, and she could hear the breath sputtering in his nostrils. "I know two things about Auschwitz. One, it's not where we're going. Two, I thank God for that."

He looked down at Danuše, who was telling her doll that they were going on a trip to a big city. He whispered, "It's where they send Jews when they have no more use for us."

"What are you saying?" Hannah asked. When Oskar did not reply, Hannah pressed. "Is it… Do they…"

Hannah saw the skin beneath Oskar's chin begin to shake. He nodded once. Hilde had been right? Klara and Friedl had been murdered? *With gas?* Hannah's throat burned with the thought. She looked down at Danuše holding on to Hannah with one hand and her pillowcase and doll with the other. The little girl would never see her mother again.

Oskar's voice pulled her from the thought. "We're going to Berlin. Berlin is where we're going," he insisted.

Trying to block out the cacophony of voices from prisoners pounding in her head, Hannah fought to remain standing. She gritted her teeth and whispered, "Why didn't you say anything? Those poor souls had a right to know where they were going!"

"For what, *Mausi*? So their final days would be filled with terror? Let them enjoy a novel or listen to some music. Let them make love."

Let them make love? Let them listen to music? "Have you lost your mind? It's not up to you to withhold the truth from people. You, you're no better than those filmmakers."

"Enough, Hannah!" Griselde snapped. "No one is in a position to judge."

Hannah pulled Danuše's hand back toward Míša and Markéta, training her eyes on Oskar and Griselde.

"I need to *pipi*," Danuše announced.

"Please try to hold it, *mamaleh*," was all Hannah could manage.

"I need to go," Danuše cried.

Oh God, no! Hannah thought, watching a trail of urine drizzle down Danuše's bare legs. "I'm sorry, *shayna punim*, but we need to keep moving. We'll get you dried off on the train."

Among the crush of prisoners, they remained silent until they arrived at the tracks, where links of cattle cars stretched across the rail, doors open. They looked different from the cattle cars that brought them to the ghetto nearly three years earlier. Instead of louvered metal windows, these compartments had two cutouts about thirty centimeters under the roof; two metal bars stretched across the width. Dozens of soldiers in Wehrmacht uniforms stood close to the trains, necks turning as they scanned the crowd.

"*Achtung!*" a soldier called, then blew his whistle. He checked a clipboard and shouted at a woman who had asked a question. "Quiet!"

"Don't let go of my hand," Hannah ordered Danuše as she turned to Oskar.

"So many," Griselde said, clucking her tongue.

Hannah thought this had to be a good sign. The Nazis wouldn't send thousands of prisoners off to be killed when they needed laborers for the war effort.

"Hannah?" she heard a familiar voice behind her.

"Luděk?" she called back. "Have you seen Radek?"

"Earlier," Luděk said. "He tried to find you, but…"

Hannah closed her eyes for a blink and tried to envision Radek running alongside the crowd, shouting her name. *I bet he looked handsome.*

Hannah saw streaks form in the dust on Danuše's legs and knelt to wipe them with her sleeve. "Stay with us, Luděk," she said, then motioned to Oskar and Griselde. "Stick together," she cried out. "Where's…" She turned to her right but did not see Míša and Markéta.

"Hannah!" she heard from the left, where the two had been pushed by the current of bodies.

Hannah called out to them. "Get back here!"

"We are trying!" Míša shouted back.

Hannah could see them drift farther, the force of prisoners too strong to fight.

She couldn't leave Oskar and Griselde, nor would Danuše make it through the crush of people. "Luděk," she cried. "Is there anything you can—"

"Keep moving!" a gendarme shouted.

Hannah held up her hand and tried to show Míša and Markéta where she was, because she had lost sight of them.

Moments later, she saw Míša at the top of a set of unfinished wooden steps that looked like the ones that had been built for the music pavilion. Hannah watched Míša's eyes searching for her as she was pushed toward the gaping mouths of cattle cars. "Míša! Míša, I'm over here!"

Míša and Markéta held hands as they stepped into the cattle car next to the one Hannah would be boarding.

"Míša!" Hannah shouted again, but her friend could not hear her over the noise, loved ones calling for each other, children crying.

Climbing the steps into the compartment with Oskar, Griselde, and Luděk, Hannah let go of Danuše's hand to hold her palm over her mouth and nose before she gagged from the stink of urine that had been absorbed by the wood. Inside, she reached down and clutched Danuše's hand again, lowering her head as she was further assaulted by body odor as the compartment filled.

Hannah's eyes were drawn to the rectangle of lavender light that appeared at the window above her head. Streaks of brightness from the outside world sliced through the narrow spaces between the slats that made the compartment walls.

It took less than five minutes to load about one hundred prisoners into the car, even with men like Oskar who limped and children with short strides. The cattle car darkened as a soldier outside strained to close the heavy door, rolling it on a metal track and slamming it shut. Then Hannah heard the iron bar being secured from the outside—a loud thump followed by a click. A hand outside knocked against the door twice to check. "All set," a man shouted, assuring someone that their *cargo* was secure.

Luděk pushed forward toward Hannah and reached up to the window, wrapping his fingers around the bottom. He climbed the side wall and pulled against the metal bar, shaking it frantically to see if it would budge.

"Push against the wall with your feet!" someone suggested as another man jostled his way toward the wall and began tapping planks with the toe of his boot. He placed his ear next to the slats and knocked to find places where termites or rot may have weakened the wood. They all watched hopefully, some doing the same.

A man whispered, "What are we listening for?"

The panic was contagious, and Danuše peed herself again.

The little girl looked at Hannah with quivering lips and teary eyes. Her gaze flitted to her doll, and she breathlessly told Hannah, "Adélka did it."

"There now, *mamaleh*, no one is angry with Adélka. We all have accidents."

The train jolted forward and stopped twice, but Hannah grabbed Danuše's collar before she toppled. Many of the elders lost their balance, but the arms of others buttressed them in place. Two collapsed and remained on the ground. Ten minutes later, several others joined them on the ground, folding their bodies into a fetal position and holding their arms in front of their faces. Hannah felt the train juddering beneath her feet and couldn't imagine how uncomfortable it must have been to sit.

Soon, prisoners found their place in the compartment, the lucky ones leaning against a wall. Danuše curled herself onto the floor beside the waste bucket and used Adélka as a pillow. Oskar stood beside Griselde, wrapping an arm around her as she rested her head on his shoulder.

Many hours passed, and Hannah kept her eyes on the light coming in through the window. She had prayed that Oskar was right, that they were heading to a labor camp in Berlin, but the sun told a different story.

"Opa," Hannah whispered, "this train isn't going north."

"Meh, the rails don't go in a straight line, *Mausi*. Sometimes we go a little to the west, a little to the south—"

"I've been looking out that window since we left. If we were heading to Berlin, the train would be going north, and the sun would have moved to the left by now. Look." She pointed. "Earlier, the sun rose slightly off to the right and has risen higher, but it hasn't moved to the left. This train is going east."

"It's not." Oskar widened his eyes with alarm. He tightened his grip on Griselde.

Luděk turned to Hannah and whispered, "You say we're headed east?"

Hannah nodded, and her skin flushed with cold sweat. "Yes, we're going east."

She kept her eyes on the windows, where the treetops sped by, an indistinguishable blur of leaves. Minutes later, though, the train slowed enough for Hannah to see it was oak and birch trees scrolling past them. The chug of the engine quieted. *Are we stopping?*

"Luděk, give me a boost," she asked over her shoulder.

Others crowded together even tighter, and within moments, Luděk was by Hannah's side, fingers weaved together and offering his palms as a stirrup. As Hannah stood on his hands and pulled the bottom bar, she felt the slightest give—not on the rod itself but from the left bolt that held the bar onto the wood.

She returned to the memory of Oskar and her first archaeological dig, how he taught her to lift the shovel from the ground using a tree branch. "Opa," Hannah said urgently, "give me your jacket."

He watched her eyes return to the window and seemed to understand. Hannah looped the green jacket around the two window bars and began twisting the fabric, knowing that in time, it would wear on the weakest point of connection, where the bolts met the wood. Once the bolts gave way, Hannah could pull down the bars and jump from the window the next time the train slowed down. What she would do from there, she had no idea.

The train sped up again, and one of the older men shouted for Hannah to stop, that they would never loosen the bolts. Even if they did, there was no guarantee that the train would slow again. "If the Nazis see you've damaged their train car, we'll all pay the price."

Arms trembling from the labor, Hannah looked down toward Luděk and told him she needed him to take over. "Sure," he replied, lowering Hannah down to the floor.

Remembering Oskar's words about how soaking fabric in liquid increased its tensile strength, Hannah knew what they had to do next. "I'm sorry, Luděk, but…we need to…" She didn't finish her sentence, instead removing Oskar's jacket from the window bars. "Danuše, push the bucket over here."

Hannah submerged the jacket into the urine and wrung it out before handing it back to Luděk, who quickly called for one of the men to boost him up to the window bars. He reached up and wrapped the jacket around the bars again and began twisting, streams of yellow trailing from his hands to his elbows, where the urine was absorbed by his rolled sleeves.

"Here!" Hannah called out, bending down to find her valise. Rifling through her belongings, she quickly found what she needed—the book Lenka had left behind. The biography of Katharina Paulus was hardbound, so if Hannah placed it at the center of the loop wrapped around the metal bars, Luděk could twist the fabric faster.

"Good thinking," he said, grabbing the tome.

An older man begged them to stop. "You're going to get us all killed."

A woman beside him on the bench told Hannah to keep twisting. "Let them try. If they have a chance… You just keep going before we get to Berlin."

Hannah froze with the woman's words. The others in the car still believed they were heading to Berlin.

"Berlin?" The word escaped from Hannah's lips.

Oskar cleared his throat. "This train is not heading to Berlin as we were told. We are heading east, likely to the Auschwitz camp, which may be a dangerous—"

May be dangerous? Hannah felt a rush of fury.

"No!" she shouted, turning her head only enough to direct her voice into the cattle car. "There's no *maybe* about it. We are going east, and when we arrive, most of us will be killed."

The car filled with rumbling voices of disbelief and terror. A man in the back corner dropped to the floor with a thud.

Hannah took a breath and continued. "This is the last choice some of us will ever be able to make, and I think we should try to escape if we can get—"

Luděk interrupted. "Hannah."

"What?"

"Listen," he said, nodding his chin toward the edge of the window as he continued to twist.

Crackle.

And then another. *Crackle.* There it was. The first break between the bolt and the wood.

"*Mein Gott!*" a woman whispered. The crowd grew silent, every prisoner straining to hear the faint crunch, the promise of freedom.

"Twist! Keep twisting!" the old man who had fallen cried out.

They'd been at it for what felt like a half hour, and the bolts from the bottom bar had loosened enough that the metal rod could be pulled away from the window. Hannah knew it would take even less time to remove the top bar now that they were using the book.

When the bolt loosened and the second bar could be pulled

down, it was time for the two most difficult jobs: waiting for the train to slow again and deciding who would be first to jump. Oskar suggested that when the train slowed—*It's not if, it's when!*—he would help the young people get to the window to jump. Danuše and Hannah would be first.

Hannah looked up at the bare window and knelt to give Danuše her instructions. "*Mamaleh*, after you land, I need you to run from the tracks." Hannah silently prayed that the train would stop beside a forest and not an open field. "Run as fast as you can for the count of fifty."

"I don't know that many numbers."

Hannah shook away her panic. "What's the highest number you can count to?"

"Twenty."

"All right, do that twice, then count to ten, and find a big tree or rock to hide behind."

Danuše nodded, seeming to understand the gravity.

"I will run back to where you are, and I will hoot like an owl. That's how you'll know it's me."

"What if there's a real owl?"

Hannah looked at the window again. "The owls are sleeping."

Prisoners came forward, offering their expertise. A man who looked older than Oskar instructed the young people to grab on to each side of the window and thrust themselves out to avoid the risk of dropping straight down and getting a pant leg—or worse—caught in the train wheel. "Tuck your head. Protect your head."

They nodded, and the train jolted. Were they slowing? Luděk pulled himself up from the bottom of the window opening and looked outside. "There's nothing but a pasture and cows out there."

The train continued forward slowly but only for seconds before speeding up again, and more farmland scrolled past. They were never going to escape. Hannah felt a lump rising in her throat. All that work for nothing but a few hours of false hope.

Hannah sat on the floor, knees bent and head down, not even smelling the urine anymore. The train squealed as the rhythm slowed. People in the car stood and woke those sleeping beside them. Had they arrived?

Luděk gripped the bottom of the window opening and pulled himself up until his eyes peered outside. He let his body drop and turned to Hannah with a smile. "There's a forest. Hurry!"

Oskar lowered his body onto all fours beneath the window, and Hannah dropped to the floor beside him to meet his eyes. "Opa, what are you doing? Your hip!"

"Step up on my back, Danuše. Luděk, help her from there."

Both did as they were instructed, and before Hannah could argue, the little girl's feet were perched on the bottom of the window opening, Adélka tucked under her armpit. She turned her head back to Hannah, raising her eyebrows with question.

"Go on," Hannah cried. "I'll be right behind you."

Danuše looked back at Hannah and then thrust herself out. "Opa, I…"

"Go. Let's not have a big scene." His eyes welled with tears.

"Now, Hannah!" Luděk called out.

Hannah planted her boot on Oskar's back as gently as she could, then placed her knee on Luděk's shoulder and let him boost her to the opening.

It was time to jump. The last thing Hannah heard was Oskar's voice beneath her. "Send my love to the family."

There was no time to turn back and respond. Feeling the unsteady tremble of the wooden windowsill beneath her as the train sped up, Hannah held her breath and jumped, replying to her grandfather silently, *I hope.*

Epilogue

Haifa, Israel
1988

HANNAH ENJOYED HER MORNING ROUTINE. AFTER HER HUS-
band, Pincus, left for his run, she had the apartment all to
herself and opened the window in the kitchen alcove to enjoy her
rye toast topped with sliced avocado. The noise from the busy
street below disturbed Pincus, but Hannah felt the voices filled
their home with life. From her third-floor window, she could hear
the high-pitched laughter of children making their way to school
floating atop the chatter of adults walking to the bus stop or
buying a newspaper from the stand. Today, the breeze delivered
the briny scent of Haifa Bay.

The phone rang, so Hannah stood to lower the radio in the
kitchen, embarrassed that anyone should discover that a woman
of sixty-seven years listened to Madonna carrying on about how
she felt like a virgin. Pincus often teased her about her love of
what he called teenybopper music, though she suspected he liked
it more than he let on. She often caught him tapping his foot to
the beat of pop hits on the radio. He sometimes amused Hannah
by singing her favorite songs with an exaggerated rasp of an *alte*

kaker. "That Billie Jean, she is not my lover," he would croon, leaning forward and snapping his fingers. "She's just a girl who says I am the one, but *oy*, that kid is not my son."

"*Allo*," Hannah sang into the receiver of her new push-button phone. "Yes, this is she," she replied, surprised when the caller asked for her by her maiden name. It had been so long since someone referred to her as Hannah Kaufman.

"It's Senitza now."

"Yes, I apologize. Mrs. Senitza." The young man's voice was deferential, one of the many things she loved about growing old. From Yad Vashem, he said.

Hannah sat down, the vinyl of the seat cushion hissing under her plump tuchus.

After confirming that Hannah was a survivor of the Theresienstadt ghetto, he explained that new fragments of the Kurt Gerron propaganda film had been found and the museum was enlisting the help of Theresienstadt survivors to identify people and provide deeper context for their researchers. "We understand it may be difficult, but your assistance would be invaluable. Can you attend a screening at the museum office on Friday morning?"

The spiral phone cord swept across the table and knocked her fork onto the floor. She felt the air pulling through her nose and filling her lungs, heard the ring of a bicycle bell on the street below. Her head turned to the orange clock on her kitchen counter as the minute panels flipped from eight twenty-nine to eight thirty.

"Mrs. Senitza?" the man repeated. "Mrs. Senitza, are you still there?"

"Yes," her voice fluttered. "Yes, I'm here. I just... I don't think... What did you say your name was, young man?"

"Elijah Weitz." After an awkward pause, he continued. "Eli."

"I have a grandson named Eli," she said.

The boy from Yad Vashem seemed like a nice young man, but Hannah could not allow herself to revisit painful memories. She looked out the window at the white, sun-bleached apartment buildings that stretched toward the beach where she had taught young Eli and his siblings Eitan and Idit how to swim. She could hear her next-door neighbor whistling absentmindedly as he leafed through his morning newspaper, the aroma of fried eggs and onions wafting into Hannah's window.

"Eli, I appreciate what you are doing there at Yad Vashem. I learned—" Her voice caught in her throat, and she was unable to finish the thought—that she'd learned the fates of her loved ones through the database the museum had compiled. As she feared, Klara and Friedl had been killed at Auschwitz. Oskar and Griselde and Míša were murdered in the gas chamber upon arrival. Luděk was killed days before the war ended, though his cause of death had not been determined. Her Radek had made it through a death march to Dresden in the final days of the war but died of pneumonia in a hospital at a displaced persons camp a month later. Olina had been killed after she used a stolen pen to stab an SS officer who had raped her repeatedly at the brothel at Auschwitz. Surviving witnesses said Olina defiantly grabbed the noose from her executioner and slipped it around her own neck. The others from the Dresden Barracks and glimmer factory all perished.

The only ones in Hannah's circle who survived were Markéta

and Alice. After losing her husband and daughter, Markéta moved to America after the war. Prague would never be Prague again without Míša and Šimon, she'd written in a letter. The two corresponded briefly, and Markéta told Hannah that she worked at a delicatessen on the Lower East Side of Manhattan. Alice and her son, Štěpán, moved to Palestine, where Alice was a music teacher for many years. Štěpán changed his name to Raphael and became a renowned cellist who toured the world as a musician and conductor. When he moved to London two years earlier, Alice followed. She and Hannah exchanged cards for Rosh Hashanah and met for lunch whenever Alice visited Israel.

Then there was Danuše. Hannah wiped away a tear whenever she remembered finding the little girl after she jumped from the train. Danuše managed to run into the woods but collapsed beside an ash tree. When Hannah finally spotted her, the girl was on her back, empty eyes staring at the sky, her left hand clutching her broken right wrist. Seven prisoners managed to jump from their cattle car, but only five made their way to safety.

Nearly a decade after Hannah moved to Israel, she decided to try to find out what happened to Hilde Kramer-Bohle. She was not listed with Yad Vashem because she was not a righteous gentile. Hilde had been an active part of the Nazi machinery, and Hannah despised what had become of the fun-loving girl she'd once known. After enlisting the help of a researcher in Berlin, Hannah discovered that Hilde was found guilty of treason and executed just days after their last interaction.

Since the day Hannah had met Hilde in *Grundschule*, the poor girl had been scratching and clawing for love, for the warmth of the spotlight she craved so desperately. For a brief moment, her humanity glimmered through, and she tried to help Hannah. But Hilde's offer was never truly an act of compassion or atonement. She hadn't renounced the party or its actions; she just wanted to keep her friend alive for reasons Hannah would never understand. *May she finally know peace*, Hannah prayed silently.

"Eli, I want to help Yad Vashem, but this… It's too much."

"We wouldn't ask unless we had found something so few people witnessed firsthand. Do you remember anything about the filming?"

I remember everything. The smell of the leather camera cases. The word VINTEN in capital letters stamped on both cylindrical film canisters of the sound camera. The feeling of her heart plummeting as Hilde told her that the prayer scene they'd just filmed would be narrated.

"I was…I was an assistant to the crew."

"You were? My goodness, I… How did you—" he said, breathless.

Hannah's voice shook as she spoke, "I had a friend…" She cleared her throat. "A childhood friend was on the film crew."

"That's incredible," he said. "I don't want to pressure you, but your input would be invaluable. You could give so much insight into the images we unearthed."

Unearthed.

In some ways, Hannah had fulfilled her dream of being an archaeologist, though it certainly wasn't what she had in mind when she and Oskar had searched for relics of lost civilizations in Hofgarten years ago in Munich. After relocating to Palestine after the war, Hannah went to school and earned her master's degree in psychology and began helping Holocaust survivors mine through their trauma. There were plenty living in Haifa; she had no shortage of patients. And wasn't she always encouraging them to confront their painful memories, to try to process them and claim their own narratives?

"All right, Eli," she said. "I'll come to the screening. Have you called Danuše? Danuše Mizrahi, my daughter?"

She was next on his list.

Ten minutes later, when Hannah heard the knock on the door, she did not need to ask who it was. "Come in, *mamaleh*," she called out. As she expected, it was Danuše, wearing dungaree coveralls and a kerchief over her long brown hair, now salted with strands of silver.

"Are you going?"

"I am and so are you," Hannah replied, knowing that Danuše would be hesitant to revisit her childhood. She had little memory of Theresienstadt, her escape from the cattle car, or the eight months the kind Polish family kept them hidden in their root cellar.

"I don't know, Mama. I—"

"*Mamaleh*, it will be good for you. Good for both of us."

"I don't think so. The children are coming for Shabbat, and Idit is bringing home a new boyfriend."

"*Mamaleh*, the screening is at ten in the morning. You think Yad Vashem is open late on Fridays?" Hannah knew Danuše was making excuses. The two had been preparing Friday night dinners together for forty years, the last five on their own after Hannah's mother, Ingrid, passed away after a short battle with breast cancer. "We're cooking for a small group tonight," Hannah said, reminding Danuše that Ben and his wife, Maia, were traveling for the month, celebrating their retirement as high school teachers. Ben and Maia had four children, but Hannah and Pincus decided Danuše would be their one and only. All Hannah's nieces and nephews would bring their children to Shabbat that week—eighteen guests in all, including Hannah's ninety-two-year-old father, Rolf.

When Hannah saw Eli in the lobby of Yad Vashem, she thought he looked all of twelve years old with lustrous brown curls reaching past his ears. He laughed and assured Hannah he was nearly thirty. Addressing Hannah and Danuše by their married names, Eli extended his hand. "Mrs. Senitza, Mrs. Mizrahi, it's an honor to meet you both."

She noticed a quick wink of light, a small diamond in his right ear, which her granddaughter, Idit, said meant that he liked boys. How wonderful it was that they lived in a time and place where a young man could choose to decorate himself with jewels instead of being forced to wear a pink triangle on his prison uniform like in the camps in the east.

"Follow me," Eli said, leading the women through the lobby and down a corridor of gray marble lit from the floor and ceiling. "Mrs. Stein-Weissberger and Mrs. Herz-Sommer will be joining you this morning. They are already in the screening room."

Hannah had already telephoned Alice, who told her that she was flying from London for the screening. "I wouldn't miss it for the world," she'd said, and Hannah felt guilty for ever hesitating.

"Stein-Weissberger?" Hannah asked.

Seeing Hannah's knit brow, Eli quickly clarified: "I'm sorry, Mrs. Senitza. Ela Steinová. You may remember her as the cat in *Brundibár*."

As they entered the screening room, Hannah couldn't help herself. Opening her arms wide, she cried out, "There's my favorite kitty cat!"

Ela may have been a fifty-eight-year-old woman with a lined face, wearing a mint-green pantsuit and silver wristwatch, but Hannah could still see the little girl with cat whiskers and bare feet. Ela rose and made her way to Hannah to hug her.

Alice was eighty-five years old with a short silver wave of hair brushed back neatly. Her eyes were bright with joy, and she had a large brown mole above her left cheek. She still sat with perfectly erect posture as though she were on the piano bench, ready to perform a concert. She was still playing and said she would never stop as long as she lived.

The four women sat together in the back row of the room, Alice reaching her hands out to Ela and Hannah beside her. Hannah wove her fingers with Danuše's to her left.

They sat linked when Eli asked if they were ready to watch the surviving fragments of the propaganda films the Nazis shot at Theresienstadt forty-four years earlier. "With the new footage, we have twenty minutes of film," he explained. "And we can take as many breaks as you need. We are just so grateful for your courage."

Hannah inhaled deeply and heard Ela struggle. *Mm-hmm.* Alice squeezed Hannah's hand, and Danuše turned back to Eli at the film projector on the stand behind them. "We're ready," she said.

———◦———

Four fashionable young brunettes huddled around a wooden table in an immaculate dormitory playing bridge, chatting affably as a maid appeared with a porcelain pot and refilled their dainty coffee cups.

The film narrator's resonant voice told viewers, "While the Jews sit in the Theresienstadt settlement with coffee and cake, German soldiers bear all the burdens of a terrible war, want and deprivation, to defend the homeland."

Hannah's pulse sped. She knew the Nazis had planned to use their film to convince the world that the Jews were living comfortably in Theresienstadt. Still, hearing the guttural sound of her native tongue spewing these lies was a searing pain.

To Eli at the projector, Hannah snapped, "Believe me, there were no coffee klatches in the ghetto."

"You okay, Mama?" Danuše whispered. "If this is too difficult, we can leave."

Hannah heard Ela mutter, "Are those… Are the maids serving *cookies*?"

On the screen, another image appeared. A mother balanced a girl of about six or seven years old on her lap as the two shared a rocking chair and flipped through a storybook. The mother's T-strap high heels tapped the floor planks as a gramophone spun a record beside her.

The scene was quick and devoid of narration, and the film jumped abruptly to the library, where a line of young men sat at tables reading books. Then nearly a minute of the Ghetto Swingers playing at the *Kaffeehaus*, where prisoners danced the

Lindy Hop before the cameras stopped and they collapsed from exhaustion.

"Such talent," Alice whispered.

Hannah couldn't help but smile at Alice's pure love of music.

Not everything the Nazis filmed at Theresienstadt was fiction. Prisoners really did create a vibrant cultural life for themselves at Theresienstadt. There were plays and concerts performed, drawings and paintings created, and lectures and lessons given by some of the most brilliant minds in Europe. For participating in the film, prisoners were paid with increased rations, but they weren't fattened up beforehand. Some had been able to steal, barter, or earn just enough food to stave off starvation. Hannah was often reluctant to share this with people, lest they think Theresienstadt wasn't *that bad*. It was hell. And if the filmmakers had pulled back their cameras and allowed viewers to see beyond the frame of their lens, they would have revealed the true suffering, the walking skeletons of the *Muselmänner*, the bugs swirling around corpses in the street.

At the next image on-screen, Hannah felt as though she inhaled all the air in the room. Her gasp panicked Danuše, and she turned to address Eli. "Can we get some water for my mother, please?"

"No," Hannah insisted. "Don't stop." She hadn't seen the faces of her friend Luděk and her beloved Radek in forty-four years, and she was not about to wait another moment. Hannah's entire body prickled, and her eyes began to fill with tears as she saw Luděk and Radek joined by the eight other brave men who had agreed to recite the Mourner's Kaddish at the ghetto church. Hannah wondered if she was imagining the look of hope on their faces as their mouths moved on-screen. *My God, they were young.*

Hannah shivered at the memory of standing beside Hilde, just meters behind Kurt Gerron at the camera when this scene was filmed. She squeezed the hands of Alice and Danuše, anchoring herself to the present, reminding herself that she could not stand up and walk into the past on-screen. But how she would have loved to step back in time, into that black-and-white image for just a moment and say thank you to the people who had risked their lives to try to send the world a message: *All is not what it seems.*

The ticking of the film rolling in the projector led to a flash of white on-screen, then continued to a scene Hannah remembered well, the glimmer factory. Not the attic where the resistance group met but the workshop where Hannah had hunched over tables splitting mica into thin slivers. The Nazis hadn't wanted to shoot a scene in the glimmer factory until Günther passed by the workshop and peeked his head inside to observe. "*Schnell, schnell!*" he called out to a cameraman, waving a hand. "Go inside. Get a close-up of all that mica. *Mein Gott*, the sparkling is almost magical, like a snow globe."

"We worked there," Hannah said to Eli. "Hundreds of us over the years."

Ten years earlier, Hannah stunned a radiologist who performed her chest X-ray when he suspected pneumonia. "Your…" He paused, incredulous. "Your lungs are glittering."

"Eli?" Hannah turned to ask. "What did they do with the mica anyway? We never knew why the Nazis wanted all those glimmer flakes."

Eli stopped the film to explain. "Mica was used as an electrical insulator in vacuum tubes and other electronic components in Luftwaffe aircraft to keep them from shorting out."

"Shorting out?" Ela asked.

"Yeah, shorting out could've caused a fire and might make the radio or other components fail."

Hannah stood too quickly, then sat before she lost her balance in the dark room. "You're saying we slaved away at the glimmer factory to save the lives of Nazi pilots?"

"No," he replied kindly. "You did it to survive. And to save your daughter's life."

"Mama, are you all right?" Danuše asked. "Maybe this is too much."

"I'm all right," Hannah assured them both. "It's just… It's so unimaginably evil. Not just Theresienstadt." She inhaled deeply. Six million Jews and five million other people murdered because Hitler deemed them unworthy of life. She swallowed hard, unable to fathom what would drive people to do this to one another. "But it happened. And we must make sure it never happens again. Let's continue to watch and tell the world what we saw. Eli, please, turn the film back on. Let us go on."

Author's Note

The sun is setting on the *Marktplatz* in Terezín, where I have spent the last five days. In this tiny Czech village, the Nazis created Theresienstadt, their "model ghetto," used for propaganda films and Red Cross inspections.

When I began my research for this novel, I knew I had to visit the site of the former ghetto and spend unhurried time exploring the artwork, architecture, and natural environment of the three-and-a-half-square-mile town of Terezín. I booked my flight from my home in San Diego and found a hotel that once housed the *Kaffeehaus* where Red Cross inspectors were shown happy residents dancing to the Ghetto Swingers jazz band. This was one of the many scenes staged and rehearsed for the visitors from the Red Cross.

In its three and a half years, Theresienstadt served as a Jewish ghetto and way station to death camps in the east. Prisoners performed slave labor for the Nazi war effort, received starvation rations, and lived in crowded barracks. At the same time, many prisoners at Theresienstadt were world-renowned artists, musicians, and intellectuals, so a vibrant cultural scene sprang to life. More than five thousand pieces of art were created by prisoners, everything from children's drawings to paintings by some of Europe's most gifted artists. Over one thousand musical works were performed at Theresienstadt, some of which were composed in the ghetto. Five hundred prisoners gave twenty-four hundred lectures on literature, medicine, and philosophy, among other topics.

Památník Terezín Muzeum Ghetta has done a remarkable job recreating prisoner lodging, mostly barracks rooms complete with triple-decker bunk beds with original linens and articles of clothing with yellow stars hanging from hooks. Museum curators have lined shelves with prisoner hairbrushes, diaries, and half-finished books. They have also included original leather suitcases stacked in corners, marked in white paint with the names and hometowns of Theresienstadt prisoners.

While I had read about the railroad extension project that connected the two miles between the Bauschowitz train station and Theresienstadt, seeing the tracks was deeply moving. Tracks that carried cattle cars filled with prisoners into the ghetto—and also to death camps in the east—still line the ground in Terezín, grass and flowers now growing between the rails.

———◦———

My visit to Terezín was filled with unexpected surprises. First, Andrea Kubiková allowed me to stay with her family at the Memorial Hotel on the *Marktplatz* even though the facility was closed for renovations. After a meeting with a Terezín historian, Dr. Tomáš Fedorovič, I showed up for my group tour, and guide Rosa Machácová told me I was her only guest that day. I explained that I was working on a novel and had specific places I wanted to see, and she smiled and told me to get into her car.

She provided a four-hour tour tailored to my research needs. We became fast friends, and Rosa took me to dinner the following night in neighboring Litoměřice, where she lives. Zuzana Ouhrabková, a historian of twentieth-century European history, spent another day with me in Terezín and the deportation site in Prague. She introduced me to David Wagner, who took me inside the shuttered ghetto hospital, which he was redeveloping.

On my final day in Terezín, I was at the cemetery when my friend and fellow author Kathi Diamant sent a message saying that her colleague Judita Matyášová, who lives in Prague, might be able to connect me with local contacts. Judita called her friend, František Tichý, who is the founder and director of the Natural School in Prague, who was in Terezín that day with students as part of a long-term research project on the history of the village. He invited me to a student meeting in the *Stadtpark* but said one of his teachers and her students were making a documentary film on the other side of Terezín, and I could join them if I'd like.

I hurried from the memorial site to a bridge behind the church to meet Natural School teacher Tereza Rejíková and her students. They were shooting a documentary film on the discovery of a photo album depicting real life in the ghetto rather than staged propaganda taken by Nazis and their collaborators. I learned a great deal from these amazing high school students: Jáchym, Tomáš, Josef, Adam, Tobiáš, and Anna.

After observing their film shoot, I met František and a dozen students under a leafy tree in the *Stadtpark* and listened to their progress reports on their work. There were three student projects: the documentary film, attic and basement excavations, and tunnel etchings. That afternoon, I joined students Johan, Matous, and

Šimon for the latter. They led me through a hole in a chain-link fence to see prisoner etchings in the many tunnels of Terezín. The young men explained that they authenticated these by matching names with prisoner records at the Theresienstadt archive. This experience was the inspiration for the scene where the characters Hannah and Radek see hundreds of names and transport numbers carved into brick and sandstone.

Because music was an important part of life in Theresienstadt, my earbuds provided an almost-constant soundtrack while I explored Terezín. I listened to Czech classical music and jazz of the era, along with the soundtracks of the many musicals and operas performed at Theresienstadt. Kol Nidrei, the Hebrew chant that ushers in the Yom Kippur Day of Atonement, felt appropriate as I walked the grounds. The children's opera *Brundibár*, which was performed fifty-five times at Theresienstadt, kept me company as I examined items made by and for young prisoners: cloth dolls, artwork, poetry, and underground magazines created by teens.

And tonight, on my final evening in Terezín, I am doing what I have every night here: listening to Verdi's Requiem as I sit on a bench in the *Marktplatz*, watching the sky darken to its palette of ambers, pinks, and blues. When performed at Theresienstadt, Verdi's Requiem was called the Defiant Requiem because choir leader Rafael Schächter told the prisoners to sing to the Nazis what they could not say: "Someday you will incur the wrath of God."

———◇———

According to the Yad Vashem World Holocaust Remembrance Center, 155,000 prisoners were sent to Theresienstadt. Among them, 88,000 were deported east, and 35,440 died of starvation and disease. The remainder survived either Theresienstadt or the Nazi death camps where they were transported.

Theresienstadt was testament to the resilience of the human spirit and the healing power of the arts. I read and viewed testimony from survivors compiled by the USC Shoah Foundation, Yad Vashem, the Leo Baeck Institute, and Památník Terezín Muzeum Ghetta. I also read published and unpublished prisoner diaries and academic papers. Each prisoner experienced Theresienstadt differently, but many said that the thousands of concerts, readings, lectures, and shows offered at the ghetto gave them comfort. Several referred to their time onstage or in the audience as "hours of freedom."

When I wrote my debut historical novel, *Cradles of the Reich*, I was amazed at how many cultural and linguistic details an author needs to research. Once again, I relied on author Bernhard Schlink for a manuscript review to ensure German customs and expressions were authentic. Marcia Tatz Wollner, director of the Western Region March of the Living, combed through my pages to make sure I used the appropriate prayers and traditions for Reform Jews in Europe in the 1940s. My dear friend Markéta Hancová also read the manuscript for Czech language and culture accuracy, or what we called the "Czech check." She is a music instructor who explained the backstories of many of the performances mentioned in this novel.

Many books about Theresienstadt were helpful in my research, but none more than *The Last Ghetto: An Everyday*

History of Theresienstadt by Dr. Anna Hájková, a historian of the Holocaust. Dr. Hájková was kind enough to answer my multitude of questions about cultural details about life in the ghetto. Drs. Karel Margry, World War II historian, was enormously generous in helping me understand the complex history of the fate of the Nazi propaganda films. Robert Ehrenreich, director of national academic programs at the United States Holocaust Museum and Memorial, was a wealth of information about the mica-splitting operation the prisoners called the glimmer factory. He also kindly allowed me to borrow his father's story of learning the language of his new country. His father learned English by riding the Tube after arriving in London via the Kindertransport. His story gave me the idea to have Míša teach Hannah the Czech language on the public trolley.

I consulted with food historian Ursula Heinzelmann for information on civilian access to food during wartime Germany. Historian of Nazi propaganda Dr. Randall Bytwerk and architectural historian Charles Belfoure were kind enough to answer my questions so I could ensure readers a historically accurate landscape. I also had the privilege of consulting with Theresienstadt researcher Pavel Batel, whose patience for my questions seemed limitless.

That said, any errors are my own.

———◇———

As often as I can, I like to include expressions I heard from Holocaust survivors or read in their written testimony or diaries. Throughout this novel, I used some real situations and their actual language to include their voices in my story. Author and Holocaust survivor Tova Friedman wrote in her memoir *Daughter of Auschwitz* that hope was the accomplice of the Nazis, an idea that I wanted to include in this novel. When I met Tova at the Tucson Book Festival, she gave me her blessing to use this idea in *The Girls of the Glimmer Factory*. The characterization of a large group of people wearing yellow Stars of David as a "Milky Way" comes from Petr Ginz, a teen who edited the arts magazine *Vedem*. Jiří Lauscher really was a carpenter from Prague who saved his family by making a toy dog the Nazis decided to mass produce for German children.

Sharing a barracks stall with Hannah are two names that may sound familiar to those who have read about Theresienstadt. Alice Herz-Sommer was a renowned pianist who offered lessons to the children of the ghetto, and Friedl Dicker-Brandeis taught art, using it as an outlet for creative expression. Herz-Sommer had a son named Raphael, often called Rafi. I refer to him as Štěpán in this novel because he did not change his name to Rafael until well after the war. Herz-Sommer survived Theresienstadt and lived to age 110. She is the subject of the Academy Award–winning short documentary *The Lady in Number Six*, which was based on Caroline Stoessinger's interviews of Herz-Sommer for her book *A Century of Wisdom*. Sadly, Dicker-Brandeis perished after she was transported to Auschwitz in 1944.

If you are interested in more of the real heroes who are mentioned in this novel, I invite you to read about Marie Schmolka, the Czech social worker who aided many Jews in Prague; Jakob Edelstein, the first leader of the Theresienstadt Council of Elders who was transported to Auschwitz after a long stay at the small fortress at Theresienstadt where he had been sent when the commandant suspected that Edelstein had adjusted the ghetto head count to aid prisoner escapes; Leopold Hecht and Arnold Zadikow, the men who stole linden wood from the SS and created the *chanukiah*, a Chanukah menorah, used in the candle-lighting scene in the book; Siegfried Lederer, who escaped from Auschwitz and went to Theresienstadt to report the atrocities he witnessed; Jozef Gabčík and Jan Kubiš, the Czech resistance fighters who assassinated Reinhard Heydrich; Rafael Schächter, the composer who formed the choir that performed Verdi's Requiem; Ela Steinová, Štěpán Herz-Sommer, and Hana Pollaková, who played the cat, the bird, and the dog in *Brundibár*; and teen Honza Treichlinger, who was beloved in the ghetto for his titular role in *Brundibár*. The three names that the character of Hannah hears people calling during the transport scene—Ida Fleishmann, Edith Laufer, and Georg Kafka—were all prisoners that were sent east in the transport before the June 1944 Red Cross inspection. (The transport of 7,503 prisoners took place over the course of several days, not one as I have written.) The famous actor and director Kurt Gerron, who was brought to Theresienstadt so he could direct the third attempt at a propaganda film, was promised that he and his wife would be spared transport east. When the film was completed, they were sent to Auschwitz, where they were sent to the gas chamber shortly after their arrival.

I also like to use the names of real Nazis as often as possible, especially the small players who most people don't know, like schoolteacher Frau Borsig, who tossed a bouquet of flowers in the trash that her student, Jewish schoolgirl Elsbeth Emmerich—not the fictional Hannah Kaufman—presented to her. Borsig then insisted the girl salute Hitler. High-ranking Nazi officials named in this novel are real except for the supervisor of the book's character Hilde, Otto Mazuw.

———◇———

With all works of historical fiction, it is important to get the details right. When writing a novel about the dangers of propaganda, it is especially critical to provide readers with a fact-based story. However, there were several instances where I compressed events or used creative license for the sake of the narrative.

The question I asked myself in making these decisions was whether changing a detail would make a substantive difference in telling a truthful story.

For example, on January 10, 1942, nine men were hanged for attempting to smuggle out letters prior to the ghetto's first transport, which was to Riga. However, if I remained entirely historically accurate, it would have meant having the men hanged at 10:00 a.m. in the courtyard of Ústí barracks on the perimeter of the ghetto instead of earlier in the central *Marktplatz*. I felt it was more important for the characters of Hannah and Míša to witness this chilling event than to report history to the letter.

Further disclosures are as follows:

The mica-splitting workshop known as the glimmer factory was not established until 1943 and was initially housed outside the ghetto itself, and never in a converted barn in the ghetto. Like many prisoners, the women of the glimmer factory were transported or marched to off-site workshops.

I was intrigued by Adolf Eichmann's preservation of Judaica, which he planned to later use in a museum for an extinct race. This project took place in Prague and did not have an outpost at Theresienstadt, though. Transcription of Jewish holy texts was done by rabbis and Talmudic scholars, not laywomen like Hannah and Klara. Similarly, there was no baby-smuggling operation at Theresienstadt, though many Kindertransport efforts throughout Europe saved the lives of countless Jewish children prior to the war. In Prague, Nicholas Winton managed to get 669 Czech Jewish children to safety.

Assassinated Nazi leader Obergruppenführer Reinhard Heydrich died eight days after being attacked in Prague by Czech resistance members Jozef Gabčík and Jan Kubiš on May 27, 194, but he was pronounced dead at 4:30 a.m., not at night as I have written.

Rabbi Leo Baeck was a prisoner at Theresienstadt, but he arrived in January 1943, not December 1941. I also bring Alice Herz-Sommer and Friedl Dicker-Brandeis to Theresienstadt on the December 16, 1941, transport with Hannah. In fact, Herz-Sommers did not arrive until July 1943, and Dicker-Brandeis did not arrive until December 1942. I give each an early arrival for one reason: they were important figures in the cultural life at Theresienstadt, and I wanted to include them in early scenes.

I included other facts about life in Theresienstadt earlier than they occurred. Food rationing by age and labor assignment did not happen until 1942. People with only one Jewish parent like the characters Iveta and Danuše, so-called *Mischlinge*, were not included in early transports to Theresienstadt. I also shortened the length of Hannah and Oskar's intake into the ghetto from several days to just hours. I began the extension of the railroad tracks months before it really began as well. Additionally, the crematorium was not built until 1943.

The Theresienstadt arts scene also did not spring to life quite as quickly as it does in this novel. Performances were initially prohibited until the Council of Elders appealed to the SS, which agreed to allow these events only if they operated under the supervision of a leisure time committee, a group of Jewish prisoners who were closely monitored by the Nazis. *Brundibár* premiered in September 1943, not June 1942 as I write. The final performance of the Defiant Requiem took place at the Red Cross inspection in June 1944 and was not filmed for the Gerron-directed documentary months later. I also took creative liberty with the dates of the performances of *Tevye the Milkman*, *The Magic Flute*, and *The Bartered Bride*.

The *chanukiah* made by Leopold Hecht and Arnold Zadikow from stolen wood is an exquisite piece on display at the Jewish Museum in New York but was made in 1942, not 1941. Additionally, Chanukah in 1941 fell two days prior to the second transport to Theresienstadt, so Hannah would not have arrived yet.

Escaped Auschwitz prisoner Siegfried Lederer snuck into the Theresienstadt ghetto to warn the Council of Elders about the mass extermination of Jews and others in the east, but this occurred in April 1944, not June 1944, as I have written.

Three British Royal Air Force planes flew above Berlin during a speech by Reichsmarschall Hermann Göring, head of the Nazi Luftwaffe, causing the radio station to broadcast an hour of classical music to a confused German public. That incident happened on January 30, 1943, a National Day of Celebration in Germany, marking the tenth anniversary of Hitler's rise to power, not in May 1942.

I tried to stay true to the layout of the ghetto but took creative license in the placement of the gate reading ARBEIT MACHT FREI, which is at the entrance of the ghetto prison, the small fortress, not the main gate where prisoners arrived.

Along a similar vein, I took some license with how and where prisoners were housed. The barracks were originally referred to by letters and numbers according to their location. I refer to them by the names they were given later throughout the novel rather than change them midnovel. I wanted to give Hannah connections with pianist Alice Herz-Sommer and artist Friedl Dicker-Brandeis, though neither lived in the Dresden Barracks. Prisoners were often grouped with others of the same age and nationality, so Hannah would not likely be housed with elderly prisoners like Klara or Austrians like Friedl. There are some accounts that the SS often forced prisoners to move bunks frequently so they would not establish bonds and attachments.

There is a scene in which Hannah hears a prisoner playing Kol Nidrei on his violin for the commandant. This story is a homage to prisoner Srebrenik, who entertained camp officers at Auschwitz with the music that accompanies the chant to usher in Yom Kippur. The Nazis loved the sound of the music and had no idea the meaning of what they were listening to.

Although more than four hundred weddings took place in Theresienstadt, there is no evidence of a shared wedding dress made from bed linens or a veil made from mosquito netting. These two items, however, did exists in the Ferramonti internment camp in Italy.

I fictionalized the interior of Café Kranzler in Berlin after months of fruitless searching for archive photos. Also, the

National Socialist Women's League, the Frauenschaft, did not have an office on Tiergartenstrasse in Berlin.

———◇———

After the June 23, 1944, inspection led by the International Committee of the Red Cross, it is rumored that one of the officials said they no longer needed to visit Auschwitz after seeing how well the prisoners at Theresienstadt were treated. Two Theresienstadt survivors reported they heard this secondhand. As for the role of the inspectors, after reviewing the Red Cross report and interviews with lead inspector Maurice Rossel, I was appalled by the inspection that was conducted by men who were, at best, incompetent and, at worst, complicit. During a recorded interview at the end of his life, Rossel seemed to blame prisoners for not making more of an effort to signal their distress to him.

Every scene I describe in the inspection and film really happened except four. There was no clown entertaining the children by making bubbles. The scene featuring men praying is entirely fictional. There was no wedding-preparation scene, nor were there any shots of women splitting mica at the glimmer factory.

All but one of the films mentioned in this novel are real, including the early attempt at a propaganda film made by prisoner Irena Dodalová, who had been a film studio executive in Prague. The Nazis made a *Titanic* film that blamed American arrogance and British incompetence for the sinking of the ship. The only fictional movie is Hilde's failed children's short, *Hitlerstadt*.

The Theresienstadt documentary is often referred to as *Hitler Gives a Gift to the Jews* or *Hitler Gives a Village to the Jews*, but the actual title was *Terezín: A Documentary Film of the Jewish*

Resettlement. In this novel, there is a scene where Hilde suggests shooting footage of rich Jews indifferent to the suffering of the poor Jews in the ghetto. This false narrative was used in a different Nazi propaganda film about life in the Warsaw ghetto.

—◦—

The heroic escape from the cattle car en route to Auschwitz was inspired by the story of Leo Bretholz, who managed to remove the bars of a small window in his train car with the help of a urine-soaked sweater. He survived the war and lived to be ninety-three years old. At least 764 Jews managed to escape the Holocaust by jumping out of moving trains on their way to death camps. However, this escape was only possible for Bretholz because he was transported from the Drancy transit camp in France, where the Nazis used cattle cars with window bars bolted to the interior of the compartments. Trains from Theresienstadt had bars bolted to the outside or a different design altogether, usually louvered metal shades.

And finally, the reference to a doctor seeing sparkles in a former prisoner's chest X-ray was shared by survivor and mica splitter Ria Dora Segalow in her USC Shoah Foundation Visual History Archive testimony.

Writing *The Girls of the Glimmer Factory* was a true labor of love because it allowed me to explore what I fear and cherish most. Propaganda has the power to divide us, make enemies of our neighbors, and even physically harm one another. Dictators propagating false narratives are nothing new but always dangerous. On the other hand, human connection—women's friendships in particular—has the power to help us discover who were really are and find our strength when we need it most.

READ ON FOR A LOOK AT ANOTHER
NOVEL BY JENNIFER COBURN

AVAILABLE NOW FROM
SOURCEBOOKS LANDMARK

I

Gundi

I F GUNDI SCHILLER THOUGHT SHE HAD FELT SICK THIS MORN-
ing, it was nothing compared to the wave of nausea that hit
her as she walked into Dr. Vogel's office for the results of her
pregnancy test and found her mother perched on a chair, knitting
needles clacking against each other.

Elsbeth looked up and smiled at her daughter, never dropping
a stitch, the thick brown wool in her lap growing into a blanket.
Though her mother's presence in the waiting room was an unwel-
come intrusion, at the same time, there was nothing that made
Gundi feel more safe than having her mother by her side. Since she
began university two years ago, Gundi found that she had a tangle
of conflicting feelings about her mother.

"Mutti, are you not well?" Gundi asked, hoping that this was
all just an odd coincidence. Perhaps Elsbeth was here to see Dr.
Vogel about her stiff shoulder. He was the family physician after
all. Maybe Dr. Vogel had asked to see Gundi in person rather
than reporting the test results over the phone because he wanted
to discourage her from having premarital sex. He might want to

wag his finger and warn her that next time, she might not be so lucky. *Please God, let this be the case.*

"I'm feeling wonderful, *Liebchen*," Gundi's mother said, her knitting needles finally stopping. Elsbeth's smile reminded Gundi of a buttered roll, sweet and filling. It didn't hurt that her mother's body was short and round. Elsbeth lifted her eyebrows. "The more important question is how are *you* feeling?"

She knows. Gundi's heart sped, and she felt prickles of cold sweat forming around the soft blond wisps of hair that fringed her forehead. *How did she find out?*

Gundi clung to the fraying possibility that maybe it was an innocent question. "I think my lunch disagreed with me. That's all," she returned with a thin smile.

A nurse with a slick bun resting on the nape of her neck opened the door leading to the exam rooms. "Gundi Schiller," she announced with a melodic voice that belied her severe appearance. When the nurse's gaze found Gundi, she gave her a look the girl had grown used to: instant approval. People seemed to know all they needed to when they took in Gundi's angelic face. Even her one imperfection, the sliver of a gap between her two front teeth, seemed disarmingly appealing. Gundi had enjoyed the attention when she first started to blossom into a woman, but now, by the age of twenty, she was starting to realize that her beauty didn't give her any actual power but rather the illusion of it. Fewer and fewer people seemed interested in what she had to say these days; they smiled and nodded as she spoke while creating their own version of who they wanted this beautiful girl to be.

Gundi silently begged God to confirm that she was not, in

fact, pregnant. But she was almost certainly carrying the child of a man she hadn't seen in two months. Gundi knew that Leo would have never left Germany without her, though. And yet where was he?

She closed her eyes for a moment, recalling his voice urging her to run off to Paris with him. They would never have to see another Nazi again. Their resistance work could be even more effective from a safe distance, Leo promised.

She should have listened. No one in the Edelweiss Pirates was anywhere to be found anymore. The only people she could rely on for information were likely in hiding or, worse, had been arrested.

"Fräulein Schiller, the doctor will see you now," said the nurse with some impatience.

Elsbeth rose from her chair and placed her hands on both of Gundi's cheeks, offering a gentle smile. "Dr. Vogel called me this morning. We have a plan."

Gundi's eyes welled with tears. These were the exact words she needed to hear, just not from her mother.

As they walked down the corridor, Elsbeth took two steps for each of Gundi's long strides. Mother and daughter entered Dr. Vogel's office, where there was a second white-coated man.

"Gundi, Frau Schiller, it is good to see you both," Dr. Vogel said, gesturing for Gundi to sit on the exam table and Elsbeth to take the stool in the corner. "I've asked Dr. Gregor Ebner to join us today."

Dr. Ebner was no larger than Dr. Vogel, but somehow he occupied more space. His round, owlish eyeglasses rested on the apples of his cheeks. As he jutted his chin, Dr. Ebner moved about the exam room, circling Gundi with icy appraisal, hands clasped behind his back.

Gundi recognized the black swastika pin on Dr. Ebner's lapel. The gold rim meant he was one of the early members of the National Socialist Party, a true believer. Many Germans jumped aboard Hitler's bandwagon after he became führer, but the men who had pledged their loyalty to a fringe National Socialist Party were a different breed.

Gundi turned her head from Dr. Ebner and focused instead on the wall clock over the door. It was twenty minutes after four. Sitting on the padded exam table, she imagined herself instead in a wooden chair at the front of the lecture hall at Humboldt University, where Professor Hirsch would be finishing his economics lecture and beginning to field questions from students. How she wished she were there, less than a kilometer away but a universe apart.

Dr. Vogel hadn't changed the décor of his office in the fifteen years Gundi had been in his care. The room was sparse—a full-size skeleton next to an eye chart on the white wall and a scale planted on the floor. Beside the exam table was a metal rolling cart holding cotton swabs, glass vials, and something that looked like the drawing compass she had used for geometry class in *Gymnasium*. Gundi rubbed her bare arms, feeling a chill.

She looked through the window and noticed that the *Kirschbaum* on the street outside was already blooming. Its tiny pink flowers were half-open, as if they were waking from a deep sleep.

"Well, I see you weren't exaggerating. What a beauty." Dr. Ebner gave a short laugh, patting Dr. Vogel on the back. Finally, he turned to Elsbeth. "Dr. Vogel tells me you are a widow," he said, tilting his chin down in a manner that seemed rehearsed. Elsbeth nodded solemnly as Dr. Ebner continued. "It takes a strong woman to raise a child alone. I'm sorry you had to bear the burden by yourself."

Gundi saw her mother's tight smile and sensed her bristling internally. People often presumed that raising a child alone was a burden, but Gundi's mother always said life was simpler as the sole parent. Without Walter, there was less money, but there was also peace.

Dr. Vogel's voice brought Gundi back to the present. "Your test results came in this morning, and congratulations are in order, though the circumstances are not ideal, of course," he said, nodding as if to coax her agreement.

Gundi's fear landed with a thud in her heart. She was going to be a mother. Her missed periods, swollen breasts, and nausea had told her as much. The timing couldn't be worse. Germany was becoming more dangerous every day, and her child's father was missing. Yet Gundi couldn't help also feeling the slightest flicker of joy. She was going to have Leo's baby. In another world, at another time, Gundi would have run straight from the doctor's office into Leo's arms. The two would rush to marry and playfully bicker over names. She would tell him she knew it was a boy; Leo would insist they were having a girl. Gundi knew he would want to name his daughter Nadja, after his grandmother who had recently died. Gundi would agree easily because she was certain they would be naming the child after her grandfather Josef anyway.

Before Gundi could fully absorb the news, Dr. Ebner slipped

a small envelope from his pocket. He opened it and slid out cards in various shades of flesh tones, from porcelain white to a rich vanilla cream. He glanced up at Gundi and laid out on a rolling cart three skin shades that most closely resembled hers. Placing the color swatches beside Gundi's cheek one by one, Dr. Ebner was silent until he offered a light huff of approval, signaling that he had found the perfect match for her pale skin.

"*Hellhäutig*. Number three," he snapped at Dr. Vogel beside him, signaling that his colleague should mark Gundi's chart accordingly. Gundi had first seen this kind of racial screening tool five years earlier, when Jewish students were still permitted to attend public schools, before the Nazis had deemed classrooms too crowded for children no longer considered German citizens. The Nazis were as obsessed with skin, hair, and eye coloring as they were the size and positioning of facial features.

Even before Jews were banned from public schools, some of Gundi's teachers had shown students how to quickly detect physical characteristics of the inferior *Untermenschen*. When Gundi was in *Mittelschule*, her teacher, Herr Richter, humiliated her classmate Samuel Braus by calling him to the front of the room for inspection. The teacher held a fistful of Sammy's thick brown curls and turned his head to the side so hard that his eyeglasses fell to the ground. Offering the other students a profile view of their Jewish classmate, Herr Richter pointed out that Sammy's nose looked like the number six. That was just one way to spot a Jew. As the teacher was pacing, he stepped on Sammy's spectacles. Everyone in the class heard the crunch. Herr Richter was no kinder to Gundi's friend Rose, whom he addressed only as "the Jewess in the back row." Gundi was often required to line up beside the object of her teacher's ridicule to serve as a counterpoint, an example of pure German beauty. As she stood at the front of the classroom, her cheeks reddened, but Herr Richter called it a healthy glow. Herr Richter also favored Gundi's best friend, Erich Meyer, a boy whose chiseled features and butterscotch hair made him look as if he'd been plucked straight off a Nazi propaganda poster.

Much like Gundi's schoolteacher, Dr. Ebner now peppered his inspection with praise. "The freckles are sweet. You love the sunshine, Gundi?" he asked, reaching into his white coat pocket for a card with a row of tiny blue, green, and hazel buttons fastened to the oak tag. Each color had a corresponding number. "I think Gundi's eye color is a five," he said to Dr. Vogel with professorial authority. Holding the iris color samples next to Gundi's right eye, Dr. Ebner squinted to double-check the match. "And I am correct," he said, lips curling with pride. "Such pretty blue eyes." Dr. Ebner was ebullient once again when he found a hair sample that exactly matched Gundi's sandy-blond locks.

Gundi turned to her mother, furrowing her brows to silently communicate her confusion and concern. But Elsbeth seemed relieved, letting out a sigh and nodding with Dr. Ebner's praise. Gundi perched herself at the edge of the exam table and looked around the room. *What is going on here?* She took a deep breath and regarded the skeleton in the corner. *Why is Dr. Vogel saying nothing? Why does Mutti seem so agreeable?*

Dr. Ebner lifted Gundi's chin and opened a pair of calipers to measure her skull, nose, and forehead, issuing grunts of approval after each measurement.

Turning to Elsbeth, Dr. Ebner asked if she had remembered

to bring documentation of her family lineage. She reached into her bag for a thick folder and held it out for him with a hopeful smile.

Dr. Ebner set it down next to Gundi, who watched him leaf through not only her baptism papers, birth certificate, and medical records but similar documents for her parents and grandparents. She knit her brows when she saw the old-fashioned daguerreotype wedding portrait of her paternal grandparents. She hadn't seen them since her father's funeral. What did they have to do with her baby?

Looking up from Gundi's file, Dr. Ebner turned to Elsbeth planted in the corner. "Frau Schiller, I will need to examine the girl further. Please wait outside."

"Of course, Doctor," Elsbeth said, too quickly for Gundi's comfort.

When the door closed, Dr. Ebner turned to Gundi, raising his eyebrows as he scanned her from head to toe. "What are you waiting for? This is not a dental exam."

"I don't understand," she responded, her voice catching. How many times had she practiced sounding calm in the face of danger? *Apparently, not enough.* Gundi focused on the sound of the clock, inhaling deeply, trying to let her heart slow to the cadence of its steady ticking.

But Dr. Ebner's throaty laughter broke her concentration. "University girls," he scoffed with a shrug toward Dr. Vogel. "They know how to lie back and spread their legs like whores, but when a doctor needs to examine them, they suddenly don't understand."

Gundi's eyes darted toward Dr. Vogel, sure that he would

CRADLES OF THE REICH 447

object to such a crass characterization of her. But he only laughed awkwardly and looked down at the speckled oilcloth flooring. Dr. Vogel had known Gundi since she was a child, always encouraging her curious nature and answering her endless questions about why there were buds on her tongue and wax in her ears. Now this trusted family doctor slinked to the back of his own office, suddenly fascinated with a shelf lined with glass jars of cotton balls and swabs. Gundi clenched her teeth. How vile she found his weakness.

Could she just run? If she refused to be examined, would Dr. Ebner look more closely into her private life? How long would it take for him to discover that her boyfriend was Jewish? When would he find out about the anti-Nazi flyers Gundi and her friends had distributed or the resistance meetings they'd attended? Gundi couldn't afford to be impulsive, so she began unlacing the black shoes she'd bought when she first started university. The girl she had been then seemed like a different person than Gundi now, though not even two years had passed since Mutti had taken her shopping for smart outfits to wear to class. The two had been giddy with hope that day. Gundi had needed a fall jacket, but she certainly didn't need one with red lapels shaped like two halves of a heart. It wasn't the most sensible choice, but Elsbeth had said, "Everyone at university will know you as the girl with the beautiful heart."

Gundi's mother had not gone to university and had worked as a file clerk at the Reich Chancellery over the last decade, so the start of Gundi's university career was something they had both anticipated with equal excitement.

Now, as Dr. Ebner stood waiting, Gundi unbuttoned her

linen skirt, and it fell to the floor. She knelt down to pick it up, embarrassed by her shaky hands, and folded it on the stool where her mother had been seated. The skirt was a favorite of hers: buttercup with peach pleats peeking out. As she unfastened her white short-sleeved blouse, Dr. Ebner watched her, leaning back against the wall, arms crossed. When she was down to her undergarments, Gundi mustered the courage to ask for a gown to cover up.

"That will not be necessary," Dr. Ebner said. "Come now. Off with the rest of it."

"I don't think—" Gundi began.

"No, you don't." Dr. Ebner chuckled. "Which is exactly how you got yourself into this situation."

Gundi felt the urge to stride across the room in her underwear and kick Dr. Ebner in the groin. Instead, she fell mute, the shame of her predicament beginning to sink in. She always thought of herself as smart, but clearly she hadn't been smart enough to avoid being an unmarried, pregnant woman locked in an office with a Nazi measuring her head. Exhaling deeply, Gundi resigned herself to endure the humiliation of the exam and leave as soon as possible.

Moments later, she stood naked before Dr. Ebner while he regarded her as if she were a sculpture in a museum, slowly examining her from many angles, scanning up and down. When he stopped in front of her, he met her eyes. She noted they were the same height, and he seemed to understand that too, straightening his spine and removing a comb from the top of Gundi's head in order to unwrap her braids. Dr. Ebner then used his fingers to loosen the plaits and sweep Gundi's hair behind her shoulders.

"You, my dear, are perfection," he said. "I have been waiting for a girl with your features since we started the program four years ago."

"Program?" Gundi asked, projecting her voice in hopes that Dr. Vogel would turn his attention back to her. She boiled with rage, betrayed by the doctor she had trusted since she was five years old. *Help me, you pathetic* Feigling!

When Dr. Vogel finally turned around, Gundi thought he resembled a frightened animal, his eyes wide, his body tucked into a corner of the room, trying, it seemed, to disappear. He mumbled, "There is no need to be shy, Gundi. Dr. Ebner needs to make sure your baby is healthy." Gundi tried to catch his eye before Dr. Vogel turned his back to her again and recommenced moving instruments from one side of the shelf to the other.

Dr. Ebner pressed the front of himself against Gundi's naked backside, reaching his hands around to grasp her breasts. Her body tightened with revulsion as a volcano of acid began to rise from her stomach. Dr. Ebner squeezed her, speaking softly into Gundi's ear. "These will be good for the baby," he whispered as his erection pressed against her. Then, in a normal volume, he added, "Gundi, everything looks beautiful. You're a strong and healthy expectant mother." He patted the exam table. "Now, let's see how your baby is growing."

Reading Group Guide

1. Hannah's family is forced into a situation where they would be leaving the grandparents behind, perhaps without the chance of seeing them again. What would you do on the last day before leaving someone? What would you try to remember?

2. Hilde is unable to have children biologically and feels shamed by this. Is there still a stigma around people who cannot have biological children? Why is that the case?

3. Whether it is a fascist regime or a high school clique, there are always people who want to conform to their society and their society's standards. What makes people want to "fit in"? What makes someone want to be proud of the group of which they're a part?

4. Is hope helpful or hurtful? Can it cause inaction when action is necessary? Or does it lend itself toward survival rather than risk?

5. Is Hannah's grandfather Oskar optimistic, naïve, just trying to manage, or something completely different? Do you

think he ever believed in his dream of the lakeside cottage in Theresienstadt?

6. Imagine you are back in a time when photographs aren't your constant companion on your phone and computer. How would you treat a photograph you have only one copy of in the world? Which photographs would you treasure the most?

7. Hilde's ambition leads her to isolating herself from any potential friends. How do you think this impacts her state of mind when she meets Hannah again?

8. How would history have been written had the Nazis been the victors of the war? Is history always written by the victors? Consider also the histories that are written but not commonly taught in schools.

9. Compare the sexual situations of Hannah versus Hilde. How are both women being used? How are they being used differently?

10. How has Hannah changed as a person from the beginning of the novel to the end?

11. In one of Hannah's memories, we hear Hilde as a child parroting her father's antisemitic views in front of Oma. How much of prejudice is learned from our parents? How much is ingrained in the society in which we grew up? How can we try to avoid such prejudices?

12. Why is the work Elijah is doing in the epilogue so important? Why must we remember the evils perpetrated in the past?

13. How did the Nazis in this book try to use propaganda to their advantage? How does cleverly (or maliciously) executed propaganda influence how we see the world and other people?

A Conversation
with the Author

What made you want to write about Theresienstadt?

While researching my debut historical novel, *Cradles of the Reich*, I was amazed at just how far and deep the tentacles of the Nazi propaganda machine spread. I learned that there was a ghetto in Czechoslovakia created specifically for propaganda and had to find out more. Once I began reading about Theresienstadt, I could not stop thinking about the propagandic strategies and tactics the Nazis used to advance their evil agenda. Equally chilling were the parallels to what we are seeing now—how dictators around the world today deny facts and replace them with their own self-serving narratives.

How was writing from Hilde's perspective different from writing from Hannah's perspective?

In writing both *Cradles of the Reich* and *The Girls of the Glimmer Factory*, several people asked why I included the point of view of Hilde, a devoted Nazi. (My mother, in particular, asked why I would give oxygen to her voice.) I wanted to write Hilde as a pathetic character who operated from a position of desperation because it is too easy to have a character who's simply a bad person doing bad things. I didn't want to write a character that readers simply ask: *What is wrong with her?* But rather: *What happened to her?* As a Jewish woman, it was difficult for me to try to step into Hilde's shoes and see the world from her point of view, but when I did, I felt deep sadness, rejection, and loneliness. I never want to justify or excuse the actions of perpetrators or bystanders, but I do want to examine them as a way of understanding how we can combat antisemitism, racism, and hate in the world.

Hannah was a pleasure to spend time with. I enjoyed being with her as she discovered her strength during her time at Theresienstadt. I completely understood her survival instinct but really loved writing the scenes where she joined the resistance.

Was Hilde's fate planned from the beginning?

While Hannah needed to find her courage, Hilde had to find her humanity. And yet, having her completely transform felt inauthentic for someone who attached so much of her identity to the Reich. Hilde grew but never enough to sacrifice her own desires. I wanted the message of Hilde's journey to be: one cannot be part of such an evil movement without great personal cost in the end.

Why is it important to keep telling stories set in this time period?

When I was younger, I read Holocaust-era novels to learn about how those awful people—over there, long ago—behaved so despicably. Now, I read novels set in this period to better understand how *any* culture—at any time and in any place—can descend into a cult of madness. I am particularly interested in the similarities between Nazi Germany and earlier (and current) regimes. Oppressors are the least creative people in the world. They constantly borrow one another's ideas, and if we learn the early warning signs, we are better equipped to defeat them.

What do you want readers to take away from this book?

I hope to leave readers with the sense that our friendships can carry us through even the most harrowing times.

Acknowledgments

It truly took a shtetl to bring *The Girls of the Glimmer Factory* into the world, and I am grateful to have so many gifted and generous people in my life.

My daughter, Katie O'Nell, is a busy PhD candidate but always makes time to read my manuscripts and provide insightful notes. Literary agent extraordinaire Marly Rusoff has been a tireless advocate for my historical fiction and has also become so much more than a business partner to me over the years. Kathie Bennett at Magic Time Literary Publicity is a fierce champion who I am lucky to have manage my book tours. When my life flashes before my eyes, one of my favorite memories will be celebrating her birthday with Marly, Mihai, and a handful of wonderful women at Cassandra Conroy's home in South Carolina.

Alexandra Shelley is a brilliant developmental editor I've had the privilege of working with. I appreciate her incisive comments, advice, and friendship. I am thrilled to work with Sourcebooks and their incredible editorial and marketing teams once again. It is such a joy to collaborate with Shana Drehs, who made the decision to bring this story to light and helped shape it with her keen observations. I am grateful that the Sourcebooks marketing team includes Molly Waxman, Cristina Arreola, and Anna

Venckus, who are so bright and creative in their approach to connecting readers and novels. The sales team at Sourcebooks has made sure indie booksellers are excited about my novels and find opportunities to promote them. Thank you to production editor, Jessica Thelander; art director, Sarah Brody; cover production lead, Stephanie Rocha; manufacturing lead, Erin LaPointe; internal page layout designer, Laura Boren; and copy editor, Sabrina Baskey. Of course, I appreciate Sourcebooks publisher Dominique Raccah for believing the story of the women of the glimmer factory needed to be told.

I had an incredible amount of support in researching this novel, starting with my husband, William O'Nell, who joined me in the Czech Republic for part of my research. On the ground in Europe, I relied on the following historians: Zuzana Ouhrabková, Dr. Tomáš Fedorovič, Rosa Machácová, Judita Matyášová, and David Wagner. I also had the pleasure of spending the day with František Tichý, founder and director of the Natural School in Prague, teacher Tereza Rejíková, and their students working on a Terezín research project.

Prior to my arrival in the Czech Republic, I received research support from Dr. Robert Ehrenreich, director of national academic programs at the United States Holocaust Memorial and Museum; Drs. Karel Margry, World War II historian; Dr. Anna Hájková, historian of the Holocaust and author of *The Last Ghetto: An Everyday History of Theresienstadt*; Dr. Karen L. Uslin, director of research at the Defiant Requiem Foundation; Torsten Jugl, photo archivist at the Wiener Holocaust Library; Dr. Kai Uwe Bormann, lieutenant colonel at the Center for Military History and Social Sciences of the Bundeswehr; Sandra

Scheller, founder of the Remember Us The Holocaust (RUTH) Project; the Leo Baeck Institute for Jewish Studies, the USC Shoah Foundation, and Yad Vashem.

I am indebted to the four subject matter experts who reviewed my manuscript for authenticity and redirected me when I went astray on language, culture, traditions, or the laws of nature. German author Bernhard Schlink was kind enough to offer his cultural and linguistic support, as he did with *Cradles of the Reich.* My dear friend and music professor, the real Markéta Hančová, not only guided me through the complexities of Czech traditions and expressions but helped me understand music terminology. Jewish educator Marcia Tatz Wollner, director of the Western Region March of the Living, made sure I used the appropriate prayers and practices for Reform Jews in Europe in the 1940s. And my cousin Bill Monahan, program specialist at the Nassau Board of Cooperative Educational Services, helped make sure I had my facts straight about the natural world.

Many friends and colleagues generously offered guidance, unfailingly answering emails and phone calls about details in their areas of specialty. Professor Randall Bytwerk once again assisted me with his knowledge of Nazi propaganda. Food historian Ursula Heinzelmann helped me set the table with authentic German foods, and Charles Belfoure guided me through creating German and Czech cityscapes.

Filmmaker Jonathan Hammond was a wealth of information on movie-making technology, techniques, and history. Musician Ira Rosenblum helped me better understand the context of Jewish music and chants. Artist Steve Florman became as fascinated with the linden wood chanukiah as I did and taught me about the materials needed and process used to create it. One of my oldest friends, Lieutenant Colonel Donald Kennedy, took me through the military weaponry and functionality of the era as well as how sound travels based on where weapons are launched or dropped. My dear friend and newly minted library scientist, Jonathan Dale, made me a chart of all bombs dropped on Germany during the war so I could accurately reflect varying levels of civilian caution, casualties, and damage at different periods of the war. Jeff Schindler, whose father survived Theresienstadt, and his wife, Rachel, were both extremely helpful and supportive, opening many doors that might have been otherwise closed to me.

I also receive quite a bit of love and support from my friends and family. Rachel Biermann and Eilene Zimmerman are both terrific writers and offered so many ideas to make this novel better. Edit Zelkind was always there for the intense crises of confidence, which often came in the middle of the night. My friends from the University of Michigan and Camp St. Regis came out in full force to events. And my mother, Carol Krickett Coburn, knows how to pack an event with her friends, especially her longtime bestie, Sandy Geis.

I had the privilege of traveling to eighteen states to discuss *Cradles of the Reich*. I loved connecting with readers, librarians, book clubs, influencers, and booksellers. A real highlight was getting to travel through the South with Cousin Debbie Breen, the northeast with Cousin Kathy Krickett, and the Beltway with Cousin Robin Verity. My college roommate, Evelyn Berrios Adams, and I drove many miles together on the Florida leg. There, my sister-in-law, Maureen O'Nell, brought her entire office to an event, which was par for the course for the O'Nell family, who showed up to support me in Indiana and Kentucky. Thank you Terry O'Nell, Susan O'Nell, Ruth O'Nell, Jim and Rosemary Ballard, and Stephanie McDaniels. Erika O'Nell-Catalán was kind enough to bring her book club to a bookstore in upstate New York, even though she was due to give birth that week. My New York City family—Richard and Tom Ellenson, Cameron and Melanie Breen—was always there to support and assist at events, and Lora and Taite Ellenson were there in spirit. Behind the wheel on the Midwest leg of the tour was William O'Nell, who was nothing short of heroic driving in harsh weather and handled more than a few logistical snafus with his usual grace and kindness.

I cherish my writer friends, who always lift one another up in this tough business. I am so grateful for the support of Writing Women of San Diego and to Kathi Diamant, who invited me to the group seventeen years ago. It is also an honor to know writers like Denise Davidson, Liz Fenton, Marni Freedman, Michelle Gable, Shilpi Gowda, Martha Hall Kelly, Jill Hall, Sarah McCoy, Susan Meissner, Kate Quinn, Lisa Steinke, and Kitty Zeldis.

Susan McBeth, the founder of Adventures by the Book, is the best friend an author could have. Her events and book club network are truly top notch, and I'm thrilled to work with this consummate professional and excellent lunch buddy. I adored working with library event planners like Robin Hoklotubbe, Liz Hamilton, Ron Block, Ashleigh Hvinden, Shaun Briley, Lynn Barnhill, Trina Rushing, Sarah McGowan, Kristy Lorenz, Jennifer Neruda, Amy Mclanahan, Maribeth Pelly, Amy Williams, Angelina DiMasco, Frank Collerius, Scott Erig, and David Ege. Thank you to everyone who invited me to their homes, book festivals, bookstores, and events. Meeting readers was the best part of this incredible experience.

Thank you to the friends, reviewers, and Bookstagrammers who spread the word about *Cradles of the Reich*. Without you, I could not do this work. I am deeply grateful for the opportunity to research and write about historical events that shaped our current affairs. I hope this novel can add to the discussion about how understanding the past can help us create a kinder, more just world.

About the Author

Jennifer Coburn is the author of *Cradles of the Reich*, a historical novel about three very different women living at a Nazi Lebensborn breeding home at the start of World War II. She has also published a mother-daughter travel memoir, *We'll Always Have Paris*, as well as six contemporary women's novels. Additionally, Jennifer has contributed to five literary anthologies, including *A Paris All Your Own*.

Jennifer lives in San Diego with her husband, William. Their daughter, Katie, is currently in graduate school. When Jennifer is not going down historical research rabbit holes, she volunteers with So Say We All, a live storytelling organization, where she is a performer, producer, and performance coach. She is also an active volunteer with Reality Changers, a nonprofit that supports low-income high school students in becoming the first in their families to attend college.

CRADLES OF THE REICH

Three women and a nation on the brink of disaster...

At the Heim Hochland maternity home in Bavaria, three women's lives converge as they find themselves there under very different circumstances. Gundi is a pregnant university student from Berlin. An Aryan beauty, she's secretly a member of a resistance group. Hilde, only eighteen, is a true believer in the cause and is thrilled to carry a Nazi official's child. And Irma, a forty-four-year-old nurse, is desperate to build a new life for herself after personal devastation. Despite their opposing beliefs, all three have everything to lose as they begin to realize they are trapped within Hitler's terrifying scheme to build a Nazi-Aryan nation.

A cautionary tale for modern times told in stunning detail, *Cradles of the Reich* uncovers a little-known Nazi atrocity but also carries an uplifting reminder of the power of women to set aside differences and work together in solidarity in the face of oppression.

"Every historical fiction novel should strive to be this compelling."
—*Associated Press*

For more Jennifer Coburn, visit:
sourcebooks.com